KATARINA'S DARK JOURNEY

KATARINA'S DARK JOURNEY

UKRAINE: LABOR PAINS — 1918

RUSSIAN MENNONITE CHRONICLES
BOOK 2

MJ KRAUSE-CHIVERS

BLUE SUNFLOWERS

COPYRIGHT

Blue Sunflowers: c/o Miranda J. Chivers, P.O. Box 55, St. David's, Ontario, Canada, L0S 1P0. For more information: Email the author at miranda@mirandajchivers.com

ISBN: Print: 978-1775-1895-9-6
E-book: Amazon Kindle B0C6W8BXFN

Cover Design: White Rabbit Arts
Editor: Nicole Lamont

TRIGGER WARNING: This story contains graphic descriptions of wartime violence, ethnic and sexual discrimination, violence against women, conservative religious views, and related subject matters that may be upsetting to some readers.

DEDICATION

To my mother, whose interest in genealogy and curiosity about lost relatives encouraged me to research my family's history.

INSPIRED BY TRUE STORIES AND ACTUAL EVENTS

MAPS

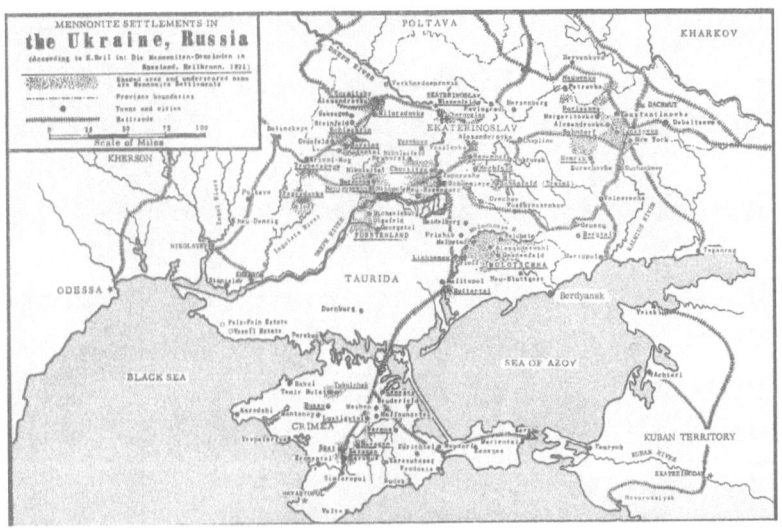

ME4 764 MAPS Attribute Source: https://gameo.org/index.php?title=File: ME4_764.jpg

Figure 1. The southern Ukraine region in 1921. Mennonites Settlements in European Russia.

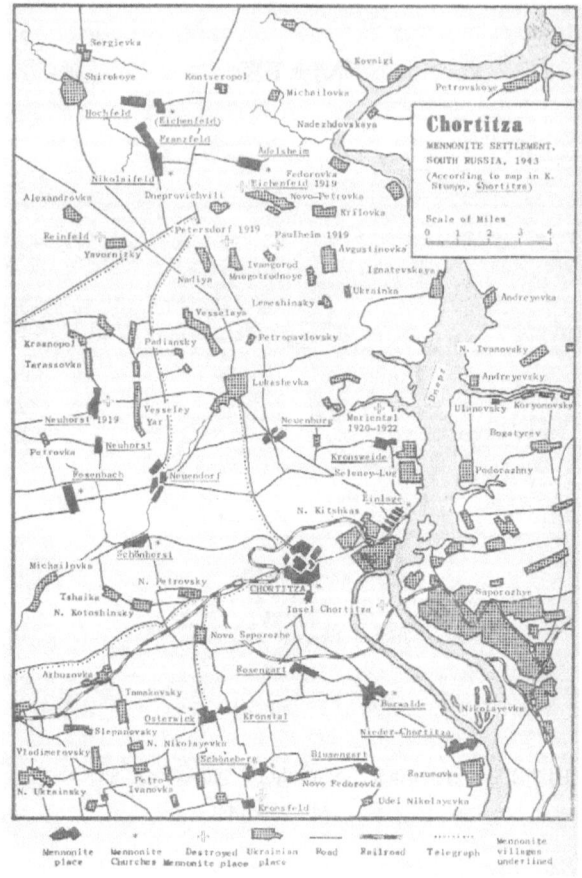

Figure 2. In 1943, Ukraine was part of the Soviet system. White crosses show razed Mennonite settlements. Much ethnic cleansing of the German and Mennonite peoples had taken place by this point, and some villages had reverted to Russian names.

AUTHOR'S NOTE

Dear Reader:

This fictional story contains some heritage elements related to the author's family background. Although this book was inspired by the Mennonite story in Ukraine, it is not an accurate retelling of that horror. For more information, please refer to the detailed historical section at the back of this book.

Please note the inset maps: Figure 1, dated 1921, refers to the region as The Ukraine, Russia, whereas Figure 2, dated 1943, claims the area as South Russia. Few historical maps of this area exist in the English-speaking world.

This fictional epic saga takes place during those few years when Ukraine legally held independence between 1917-1922. The 1921 map is the only one I found pertaining to this period.

∿

My grandparents called themselves "Russian Mennonites" because the land of their birth was then known as *South Russia* or *Little Russia*. More recently, some say "Mennonites from Ukraine." When I published *Katarina's Dark Shadow* in 2021 (before Russia's attack on Ukraine in 2022), the earlier wording was still in common use.

Prior to 1917, Ukraine was a political territory governed by Russia. In late 1917, Ukraine formed a provisional government. On January 22, 1918, it declared independence. However, in 1922, it succumbed to Soviet Socialist rule. It didn't regain independence until 1991. During those earlier years, Lenin's Bolshevik army and counter-revolutionary forces rocked the country with violence.

As a dominant power, Russia has repeatedly attempted to erase the indigenous Ukrainians and claim their land. This recent war proves that Russia's tactics haven't changed. It continues to destroy distinctiveness with the goal of assimilating all under one cultural flag. The German Mennonite story in Ukraine is another example of Russia's determination to destroy differing ethnicities.

Ethnic cleansing began with lawlessness during the Russian Civil War era, expanded with Makhno, and continued under Stalin. Many survivors sent to places such as Kazakhstan and Siberia eventually acculturated into the Russian populace, as Stalin intended.

In 2019/2020, a land development project on Khortytsia Island in southern Ukraine discovered broken and buried gravestones that were later identified as Mennonite markers razed during the communist era. Local historians familiar with the stories of the German Mennonite populace began the painstaking job of identifying, repairing, and notifying the North American Mennonite communities.

After the public release of the names of the deceased, I checked the Mennonite genealogical database for matches with my family lineage. There were several. I soberly reflected on my ancestors' heartbreak as they witnessed the devastation of their villages and culture. More research led to gruesome details that were almost too awful to read. I imagined the horror as they watched their loved ones murdered; and then endured further suffering through starvation, unlawful imprisonment, and other tortures. Sadly, this persecution was largely due to their ethnic roots and odd religion.

I recalled my own grade school bullying incident when I was spat upon and called a "Nazi" because of my German-speaking culture. My parents answered as best they could. How does one explain cultural hatred to a child? At the age of eight, I became ashamed of my rich roots.

Although this abuse was minor compared to my family's experience in southern Ukraine, we must recognize that there was ethnic discrimination in North America, too. Feeling unwanted is a terrible thing.

Growing up, prejudice left me feeling lost within my country and confused about my national identity. Although Canada welcomes cultural diversity today, this wasn't always the case. During the census years of the twentieth century, we were often asked to identify our heritage. At home, we spoke English and German, so I checked the German box. But in fact, we weren't German since my grandparents had come from the Ukraine region of Soviet Russia. But they spoke German. To make matters more confusing, my family claimed Dutch and Polish roots, too.

My parents explained the Russian Mennonites were a unique people — a peace-loving sect originally from northern Europe who fled the religious persecution directed towards Anabaptist followers. Originally anti-political in nature, the religion held to the notion that we were citizens of a higher calling and therefore we should not identify with any statehood.

As a young woman, I found this belief illogical. I needed to belong somewhere. A governmental umbrella offers both legal and emotional acceptance to every settler and conveys the message 'You belong here.' When I received my first passport at the age of sixteen, I embraced my Canadian identity. But I still wondered about my family's history.

While studying both the European Mennonite struggle birthed by Menno Simons and the violence my ancestors suffered in Russia, I finally understood my grandparents' distrust of governments and borders.

During those years before the civil war, the Russian Mennonites believed the Czar would always support and protect them. They never dreamt that the Crown would disappear. Or that Germany wouldn't have their backs if things went badly. To make matters worse, the combination of faith and the confused German-Russian self-identification complicated emigration prospects. Canada outrightly denied access to these faithful followers from 1918 to 1921.

After everything they went through, how could they trust any government again?

One hundred years later — in 2021 — after the discovery and repair of those newly found headstones, the Ukraine people established a memorial to the Mennonites on Khortytsia Island.

Sadly, today, war has once again decimated this region. As of this writing, many of the former Mennonite lands are now occupied by the Russian military. Further archeological recovery will probably not resume in the foreseeable future. After the Soviet Union fell in 1991, more historical data about the Mennonite and German populace in Ukraine emerged; and interest in this era continues to grow. Consequently, we've discovered more ancestors, more relatives, and more stories about our past — all enriching our lives and helping us to further understand our identity and our faith.

On behalf of the descendants, I say thank you to the translators, genealogists, archeologists, and historians who've dedicated their lives to retrieving and translating these vital records so we can learn more about our history.

Russian Mennonite Chronicles honors the memories of those unknown heroes of the faith while exploring this challenging history through the medium of fiction. A portion of the proceeds from the sale of this book series benefits the charity organization: Friends of Mennonites in Ukraine, and The Chortitza Headstone Project.
The danger of losing this important history increases daily. Please help us keep it alive by donating to these important charities. Links are provided in the references section of this book.

Thanks for purchasing this novel and joining me on this dark journey.

—Miranda

REFLECTION

"For they speak not peace: but they devise deceitful matters against them that are quiet in the land." Psalms 35:20 KJV

1

PETER AND MAX

1951 OCTOBER. MUNICH, POST-WAR GERMANY.

GRIEF CRASHED LIKE A ROGUE OCEAN WAVE, TOSSING PETER against the meat counter, and ripping the air from his lungs. His knees buckled and he gripped the edge of the chrome table for support.

Somewhere, over the past sixteen years, he'd buried the guilt surrounding his father's fatal fishing accident in an unmarked grave, together with other painful memories. But Max's blunt and sudden mention of Peter Senior's passing sixteen years ago pushed both tears and nerves to the surface. It was as if the original news was still fresh. And his own sudden overreaction shocked him. He was usually more controlled than this.

Peter turned his face, wiped his cheeks with his fist, and swallowed the tears trailing down his throat. He took a deep breath and steadied himself before answering. "I ... I don't know what to say, Max." He blinked rapidly and pasted a fake grin on his face before accepting the memorial gift from the aging butcher. "Thanks."

"Your Papa was my best friend, Peetar," Max continued. "We were gonna announce our business deal at a party that Saturday night. But ... it didn't happen. I hoped you'd take his place here at the shop, and then we'd crack the bottle together. But you'd other plans. I was gonna give it to your *Mutter*. But when Katarina never came back from the war ... Anyway, I've hung onto it long enough. Take the whisky home and celebrate your Papa's life with it."

Peter sniffled and shook his head. "Thanks, Max. But ... Heidi's pregnant." He blurted the news as if it was an afterthought — even though he'd specifically walked the three kilometers to the butchershop to deliver the announcement. But Max had blindsided him before he'd had a chance.

After his father's funeral, everyone said he shouldn't feel guilty. But he did. His mother, Katarina, had blamed him — screaming that her husband might still be alive if he'd gone fishing with him. Peter knew it was grief talking, but the remark stuck in his soul, and he couldn't erase it.

Despite the passage of time, every visit to the meat shop triggered the old memory. He avoided going as much as possible, but Max had been like an uncle to him. Not seeing him was just bad manners. Besides, Max's continued use of Peter Senior's secret recipe made Peter Junior feel like he owned a small piece of the place. The addictive flavor of the long, thin pork sausages with their mild coriander, caraway, and garlic seasoning drew him back to the store time and time again. Each aromatic bite reminded him of his father's boisterous laugh and somehow assuaged his guilt, if only temporarily.

The good memory didn't diminish the sting of Katarina's accusation. Much later, she'd apologized, but the damage had been done and repair impossible. Their relationship was forever scarred.

Despite Peter's repeated visits, Max never mentioned the

tragic death. Until today. The conversation combined with the anniversary gift shook him to the core.

"Congratulations, *mein Sohn*. Well done. Your Papa would be proud," Max said, referring to Heidi's pregnancy. He wrapped one burly arm around Peter's shoulders while handing him the bottle with the other. "Listen, dis was an expensive label before the war. I can't imagine what it's worth now. If you need extra money, you can auction it off to pay for expenses."

Peter chuckled. "*Ja.* I might have to. Heidi's quitting her good job at the *Telekom*. And the university doesn't pay well." As soon as the words spilled from his mouth, another rogue wave washed over him. *Heidi.* This time the dam broke. Tears cascaded down his cheeks and his shoulders shook. He set the bottle down beside the package of Thüringen Rost Bratwurst sausages.

"Is everything all right, *Söhnchen?*" Max's bushy gray eyebrows furrowed with concern. In characteristic stoic fashion, Max pulled away to give Peter time to compose himself and focused on the ties of his clean white apron — untying, then tightening and re-tying them around his portly middle.

Peter noticed Max's discomfort and waved his palm in the air before drying his face with the back of his hand. "I'm fine. I'm a little off today." He pointed to the bottle. "I wasn't expecting this." Except he wasn't fine. The arguments with Heidi were getting worse, not better. And the whisky wouldn't help. If he opened it at home, she'd make a big deal out of it and accuse him of running away from his problems again. The evil English children's poem taunted. *Peter, Peter, pumpkin-eater, had a wife and couldn't keep her.* He pulled a handkerchief out of his pocket and blew his nose.

"Is you still transcribing Katarina's diaries? Is that making you sad?" Max's gray-blue eyes flickered. He put a hand on Peter's shoulder. "Reading those books must toy with your head. It would, for me. Seeing the war through a young girl's eyes. She wasn't even twenty yet. And learning about your birth parents when they was still alive."

Peter shook his head. He picked up the bottle and the package of sausages, then set them back down again. "No. It's not that. I just started a new job, and it's taking me some time to learn. Between Heidi's pregnancy and work, I've been too busy." *And Heidi doesn't want me translating the diaries anymore.*

Max nodded. "Ah. You have a new job and a child on the way. Big stresses. But the country's booming now. You can have your pick of jobs. If money's tight, come work for me for a few days. I need help. I can't keep up anymore." He removed his white hat and scratched his bald spot. "I should retire. But I can't afford to yet. I have too many expenses." He slapped Peter on his arm. "But youse a smart man. You'll be fine. Your whole life's ahead of you. The war's over. Forget about the past. It's time to move on."

"But everything has changed, Max. The world is spinning so fast, I can't keep up. And I feel lost. Like an orphan. And I don't know who I am anymore."

"Ah. Ja. The war ripped families apart. Nobody trusts anybody anymore. But don't be ashamed. *Deutschland* has apologized to the world. You did what you thought was right. And now you's an orphan. But you's not alone. Just no parents." Max paused and his mouth twitched to the side. "Say, how's *deine Schwester in Kanada*? Do you two send letters?"

Peter nodded. "Ja. Sometimes. But I don't really feel connected to my sister or our other relatives over there. They didn't go through the war like I did. It's probably embarrassing for them to admit they have family in Germany."

"Nonsense. Some of them went through the war in *Russ-*

land. They know exactly how you feel. You can tell them what happened here. *Die Welt* already knows. Nobody blames you."

"Max, I barely know them. They emigrated before I started school. I wouldn't recognize them if I saw them on the street. Marta left in '37. And we never had much of a relationship, anyway. She was only thirteen then."

"Listen, Peetar, get your nose back into Katarina's *Russlander* books. Then, you'll understand more. You must learn about your parents and their history. It will help you feel settled. And share it with your Schwester. She deserves to know her parents' story."

"I doubt she cares. She has a busy life. I'll probably never see her again."

Max snorted. "Never say never. Maybe one day you'll visit Canada."

Peter almost choked on Max's comment. "Not while there are babies to take care of."

"Babies. So, you're thinking of more than one?" Max joked as he stepped behind the meat counter and pulled a paper bag from the lower shelf.

"If Heidi has her way."

Max put the bottle inside the bag and thrust it at Peter. "Here. We best hide this. I don't want you getting robbed."

The silver bells over the shop entrance jingled. Peter picked up his purchases and the bottle, stretched a stiff smile across his face, and extended his hand. Max took it and pumped vigorously.

"Listen, Peetar. There's no need to feel lonely. I know we're not related, but to me — you's family. If you ever need anything, call me." Max jerked his chin at the customer eyeing the meat. "Enjoy the sausage. Give my best to your wife. Tell her congratulations for me. And don't waste the whisky. It's expensive."

2

REINHART

1951 OCTOBER. MUNICH.

REINHART HUNG UP THE TELEPHONE AND ENTERED THE client's scheduled date in his logbook. He flicked back to the previous month to add a checkmark to confirm the follow-up as done; then paged through the preceding months, ignoring those who'd never booked a subsequent appointment and examining those with colored checkmarks but without dates, which meant pending. A rare star noted the few who'd published.

Most writers checked in at least once a month. But others quit when the slogging got too murky or the financial burden of authoring their life story became too heavy. Reinhart believed almost anyone could succeed if they tried hard enough. However, he understood that writing was a thankless and lonely endeavor, hard on relationships and on the pocketbook. Many tried, but few survived. The rich ones hired him to ghostwrite. The rest paid when they could.

His eyes stopped on a familiar name circled with no follow-up date. Peter K. Six months! Reinhart frowned.

Considering the client's enthusiasm for translating his adopted mother's Cyrillic and Gothic diaries, his absence was odd.

Reinhart recalled the story. After Katarina disappeared in Ukraine in 1942, Peter clung to an unsubstantiated hunch that his adoptive mother was still alive but had disappeared in the post-war chaos while searching for her long-lost son, Jacob. Secondly, the scant information about Peter's biological parents and their demise during the Russian civil war inflamed his quest.

However, since no proof of life for either Katarina or Jacob had surfaced, Reinhart felt Peter was searching for a needle in the proverbial haystack. But he'd encouraged him to comb through the diaries, hoping the clues to Katarina's past would help Peter find closure.

Despite Peter's gloomy demeanor, restless disposition, and the dark tone of their analytical and pedantic chats, Reinhart enjoyed the visits. He found the historical and political details intriguing, and the Mennonite culture curious. Since the Iron Curtain limited fact-finding, and survivors from the civil war rarely spoke about their experiences to outsiders, Katarina's diaries offered an undisputed insider's view.

Reinhart tapped the pencil on the side of the desk. He'd felt their relationship had grown beyond professional. Maybe he was wrong.

Granted, his cousin, Gerhard — a professor at the university where Peter worked, whom Reinhart depended on for business leads, and with whom Peter had worked — mentioned that Peter was distracted easily and often needed firm and clear direction to stay on track. "The man's clearly intelligent," Gerhard said, "but struggles with focus. And I'm not interested in babysitting."

A meow at his feet pulled Reinhart from his musings. He reached into his lunch pail and tossed Willie a *Nuernberger*

Rost Bratwurst. The tiny sausage had become both his and the senior feline's daily treat over the past year and likely contributed to both of their obese states. But Reinhart made the twice weekly trip to the butcher shop anyways, if for no other reason than to give the cat some pleasure in his last days.

The gray mouser gobbled up the meat and promptly whined again. "One more, that's it," he said, before nudging the cat away with his foot. Willie snarled and slunk under the desk.

"Now, where was I?" Reinhart scratched his bald scalp, then picked up his pencil and opened the journal. "Oh, yes. Peter. I should call him." He scribbled a note, then retrieved the index card with Peter's phone number. But the new novel lying there caught his eye and he picked it up. After reading the first two pages, he rolled back in his new executive chair and put his feet on the oaken desk.

AN HOUR LATER, the triple knock jerked Reinhart from his fictional world. He groaned and scowled at the door. There were no further appointments today, and no urgent matters to attend to. Maybe he should ignore it. Probably another salesman, he thought. The knocks repeated. "Ja. Coming," he yelled. He inserted the bookmarker, set the novel on a stack of manuscripts, then slowly removed and folded his reading glasses, and placed them on top of the book.

He rolled the chair back, lifting his feet in boyish fun — enjoying the smooth glide of the steel wheels against the hardwood floor. The expensive leather purchase — with its sleek lines, plush seating, and padded chocolate arms — was a welcome change from the old, curved hardback.

Sauntering to the door, he stumbled over the cat stretched

out lengthwise on the narrow path between the desk and the overflowing bookcases. "Willie, move your butt. Good grief, do you really need to park yourself in my walking space?"

The cat yowled and his sharp canines hooked the hem of Reinhart's trousers. As he released the cat from his pant leg, the triple knock repeated. "I'm coming," he barked. Once freed, the animal promptly bolted under the desk.

The brass doorknob on the heavy oak panel rattled and shifted as he yanked on it. "Drat. I forgot to bring the screwdriver again," he mumbled as the door swung aside. "Sorry about the delay. I was on the phone," he lied before recognizing the lanky man with light chestnut hair and deep-set blue eyes. "Peter? Well, this is a pleasant surprise. I was just thinking about you. It's been months. How've you been?"

Peter grinned and handed him a brown paper bag wrinkled snugly around the top. "Fine. I was in the neighborhood and thought I'd stop in. I hope it's not a bad time."

"Not at all. Great timing, actually. Please come in." Reinhart opened the bag and pulled out the bottle. *Macallan Scotch. Bottled in 1935. Aged thirty-six years.* He looked up, aghast. "Where did you find this? Did you win the lottery? What are we celebrating?" He scanned over Peter's well-dressed frame as he breezed past him into the room. "Let me guess. New tweed jacket, nicely pressed pants, new shoes. You got a new job."

"I did. Research assistant to Professor Braun, Cultural Anthropology department. It's official today with an increase in pay."

"Judging by this label, this new job must be quite the status change." Reinhart pointed to the old wooden chair — now relocated beside the Tiffany floor lamp. "Please have a seat. You realize that if I crack this seal, we'll have to finish it before it goes bad. So, before I do, please explain why I'm the receiver of this rare item."

"Let's just say I came by it honestly. I wanted to share it with someone who appreciates old notes." Peter plopped down and pulled the chain on the light. "I thought of you."

"I'm honored. Although this is truly unnecessary." *And excessive.* Reinhart proceeded to the antique liquor cabinet behind his desk and removed two square crystal tumblers, then decanted the liquor and poured a double shot into each. As he turned, he spotted Willie sitting on his haunches, his eyes narrowed, suspiciously scrutinizing the visitor. *No. Willie. Don't jump.* Peter stared back, his hands gripped around the chair's arms, the knuckles white.

"Willie." Reinhart snapped. The cat turned and slunk back under the desk. "Don't mind him, Peter. He's old and harmless," he said as he handed Peter the glass.

"I'm not afraid of him," Peter said, releasing his grip on the chair as he accepted the drink. "As long as he doesn't jump. I overreact badly to cats jumping on me. It's an old war wound, I suppose." He flicked his hand in the air. "No worries. I'd miss the gray tub if he wasn't here."

"Right." *Cats and cadavers.*

"Thankfully, the nightmares don't wake me as much as they used to."

Reinhart wiggled back into his soft seat. "I have bad dreams, too, sometimes. My time as a soldier in Poland wasn't pretty. The Warsaw ghetto ..." He pulled a linen handkerchief from his pocket and blew his nose. "But let's not talk about that." He sipped the whisky. "Speaking of old memories and wartime, how are you making out with translating your mother's diaries?"

Peter tugged at the hem of his jacket. "Uh. Well. I've been busy. The new job. And ... Heidi's pregnant."

Reinhart held up the glass in a toast. "So, double congratulations are in order. Although, to be honest, I heard you were leaving the history department. From my cousin."

Peter rubbed his chin. "Ja. We agreed to part ways amicably. 'No dark feelings,' he said. I concurred."

"There's nothing worse than an unhappy relationship. Your wife must be relieved."

Peter's eyes circled the room. "Ja. Sort of. Heidi and I've been sparring lately. About money, mostly. We're fixing up the apartment and she plans to quit work in a few months. To be honest, I don't know how we're going to manage."

Financial problems. That's why he hasn't been by. Reinhart nodded sympathetically.

Peter waved the glass under his nose and inhaled deeply before drawing the amber liquid between his lips. He chewed and rolled the alcohol around in his mouth before swallowing. Upon leaning back, he stretched out his long legs, crossed his ankles, and smiled. "This *is* powerful stuff."

Reinhart pretended to ignore Peter's pretentiousness. "Yes. She's a dignified old lady with strong legs." He wanted to probe further about the rare bottle but suspected Peter knew little about fine scotch. And he surmised the gift wasn't Peter's main reason for the visit. "Did I ever tell you about my two daughters? They're nine and eleven now. But I still remember the scary feeling of becoming a parent."

"Thanks for the sympathy, Reinhart. It doesn't feel real yet, but when it does, I'll be knocking on your door." Peter tapped the glass with his fingernail. "Listen. I want to apologize for being out of touch for so long. I've barely touched the diaries lately. Between Heidi, this baby stuff, and my job, I've been preoccupied. Translating is arduous work. I need quiet time to concentrate. I haven't had that lately."

"No need to feel guilty, Peter. Life happens. As I've explained before, writing is like taking baby steps. You can't run until you've learned how to walk. But eventually, you'll get to the finish line. Now, if I remember correctly, the last time we talked, you'd gotten to the end of 1917. Are you ready to go forward?"

Peter held up his glass to show he wanted a refill. "Yes and no. Every time I pick up the books, I'm afraid I might learn something I'd rather not know. And I'm reminded of when Mutter left for the war. And the argument we had. We never got the chance to make peace."

"Ah, the pang of regret. But — the joy of discovering skeletons in the family closet. Warning: danger and drama ahead." Reinhart chuckled and pushed the bottle across the desk. "Peter, tell me — why are you transcribing the journals? To learn about the family history, or to get closure on Katarina's death?"

"Closure?" Peter set his glass on the side table. "What's that? Putting the lid on the casket? If so, maybe. I haven't even seen my birth parents' graves. At times, I wonder if they even existed. I dunno what I'm after, Reinhart. I have too many questions and too few answers." He reached inside the chest pocket of his jacket and pulled out a sepia photo, then slipped it across the desk. "It's my only picture of my first Papa. I hoped working through the diaries would give me a sense of him."

Reinhart studied the photograph. "Nice-looking guy. But broad shoulders and burly. Not a bean pole like you."

"Thanks. Apparently, I take after my mothers' side." Peter patted his gut. "Except now I'm getting a bit paunchy with Heidi's cooking."

Reinhart grinned. "You're too young to worry about weight." He returned the picture. "So, when you say you want to know where to search—"

"—I want clues. Names, dates, that sort of thing. Listen, Reinhart, the old neighborhood is gone. Munich isn't the same. I've lost touch with so many since the war. I want to find someone who knew my family back then." Peter waved his hand in the air. "Ach. Maybe you're right. I'm on an impossible quest. I should just keep drinking. At least it makes the pain stop for a short while."

Reinhart studied Peter as he rambled on while helping himself to another drink. The man stared at the liquor bottle as if it was a majestic piece of art. And his twirling of the glass — tilting the crystal just enough to make the amber liquid swirl in a particular pattern, reminded Reinhart of other troubled war survivors he'd met. He'd never known Peter to be attracted to alcohol. And it made him wonder if the man had developed a drinking problem.

3

TOO MUCH THINKING

ALTHOUGH REINHART HADN'T SEEN THIS SIDE OF PETER before, he wasn't entirely surprised. Alcohol abuse was a common way to cope with the haunting memories of war. Sleeplessness, depression, angry outbursts, and other erratic behavior affected sociability, work performance, and self-esteem. Challenged survivors felt mentally inferior. Guilt and shame led to more drinking, which only increased the problems further.

While families bore the brunt of this dysfunction, employers used words such as incompetent and lazy. Doctors had few answers and no cures. No one knew how to get back to *normal*. Whatever *normal* meant. Reinhart knew that staying occupied and working hard were the healthiest solutions. Although this strategy wasn't foolproof, it helped him manage his own demons.

He'd thought Peter managed better than most. But perhaps Peter's dysthymic personality confused the truth of his injuries. Besides war trauma, Peter carried the grief and sadness of being orphaned. Twice. If he'd been raised with Katarina's son, Jacob, then his life would've been different.

But the child disappeared during the civil war. Finding him now was unlikely. The records were either gone or hidden in Stalin's Russia. Even if they weren't, the Mennonite customs of marrying cousins and naming children after favorite relatives created such confusion in the genealogical charts that any search for the missing and dead was almost impossible.

Genealogy! Family history! Estrangement! Reinhart was startled at his own realization. Peter obviously felt lost, as if his identity had disappeared. That's why he needed to find the truth about his family. A wave of compassion washed over Reinhart, and he zeroed in on his hunch. "Have you found any more clues about Katarina's death?" He casually picked up a pencil and twirled it between his fingers.

Peter caressed the glass with his thumb and shook his head. "The diaries aren't helping yet. And I haven't found another source. There's a missing link somewhere. If I could go back to Ukraine, I'd find it."

"Surely, you're not thinking of crossing the Iron Curtain and putting your life on the line, are you? I hope you're only speaking metaphorically."

"No, of course not. I'm no fool. Stalin would kill me. But when Stalin dies, Russia will be free again. Then I'll go ... Sometimes I wonder if Mutter is sitting in a camp in Siberia. If she stayed in Ukraine after Germany retreated, anything could've happened. They would've arrested her."

"Don't torture yourself, Peter. Accept what the government told you — she died in '42 — after the battle for Kyiv. Look, millions of Ukrainians died during the war. More dead than all the losses of Europe and North America combined. Stalin sacrificed the people like lambs. Ukraine was cannon fodder between Russia and Germany. Now, think about this. If any of your family were alive then, chances are pretty good they're not now. And if Katarina survived the bloodbath, she would have written, at least. If for no other reason than to let you know she was alive."

"Unless she didn't want to be discovered. Especially if she hadn't yet found Jacob or my father, David."

"Peter, stop this wishful thinking. Focus your energies on your new job. Your mother's been gone for over ten years with no word. Don't let the past control the present."

Peter nodded. "You're right. My search is irrational. But I want to seal this part of my life. Position a tombstone on a plot. Take my child there and say, 'Look. Here lies your grandmother. She saved my life in the Great War. Because of her, you are alive.' Except I can't live with unanswered questions. The kind a child asks."

Reinhart rubbed his chin and glanced at the bookshelf. "I'm sorry. I know this is hard. Have you ever asked your sister about it?"

"My sister?" Peter's thick brown eyebrows shot up at the question. "Good grief, no. I wrote to her when I received the official notice. But after a few letters, we never talked about it again. I don't want to upset her happy life."

"Didn't she want details about her mother's death?" Reinhart thumbed the side of the glass. "Most women want to know all the facts."

"Reinhart, you must remember, she was thirteen when she left Germany in '37. She was so young. We barely knew each other. When she went for a summer vacation in Canada, Mutter forwarded guardianship papers to Aunt Justina and Uncle Heinrich so she could go to school and live there. Mum sensed life was about to get ugly in Germany and she didn't want Marta exposed to any of it. She wanted me to go too, but I refused. I wanted to fly for the Luftwaffe. All levels of the military were hiring en masse. It sounded so exciting."

"But things didn't turn out the way you expected, did they?"

Peter shook his head. "After I was swarmed by hobos that summer, my chances of flying went up in smoke. Between the broken ribs and my kidney problems, I couldn't pass the medical exams. What a wimp! Man, talk about feeling humiliated."

"It wasn't your fault."

"I know. Maybe it was better that way." Peter shrugged. "At least I survived. Maybe I was only pushing papers and delivering parts, but at least I got to hang out with the airplanes and aviators."

"Right. You escaped the worst." Images of bloodied cadavers and the rat-a-tat of machine guns flashed through Reinhart's mind. He squeezed his eyes to black them out.

Peter's gaze fixed on him — as if he'd also seen the ugly past display on the mental movie screen. "Reinhart? Are you alright?"

"Huh?" He shook his head and jerked his thoughts back to the present. "Sorry, I was lost in my thoughts for a second." His heart raced. Why couldn't he control the ugly memories? After all these years, he should be able to. No wonder his peers drank to excess! Thankfully, *he* had more self-discipline. "Umm. When did you last see her?"

"Mum — Katarina?" Peter's face brightened. "In Marien-burg. I arrived with an injured Junker. We left Danzig that morning to deliver supplies to another airbase. But en route, we hit debris from an exploding aircraft, and the next thing we knew, we had an engine fire. We made it, but barely. I expected a couple or three days of R&R after that. After lunch, I wandered to the supply depot but stopped to watch a landing. The airplane was marked SS, so it piqued my interest. I was surprised to see Mutter deplaning. But since she was a translator for them, I wasn't exactly shocked. Surprised, though. What're the chances of us being at the same place at the same time?"

Reinhart leaned forward. "What happened next? What was she doing there?"

"Well, interrogating the prisoners, of course."

"What do you mean?"

"Look, the Luftwaffe was short of workers. So they grabbed all the help they could get. The POWs were free labor and sometimes experienced, too. This airbase used slaves for everything from mechanics to drivers to kitchen help. Of course, as you can imagine, this setup didn't last long. It didn't take a rocket scientist to explain the lunacy of it. Sabotage was bound to happen, eventually.

"Anyway, on this night, the SS set up their interrogation stations. I passed by and stuck my head in the door and got her attention. We had an affectionate exchange, but her position limited fraternizing, so we played it cool. We agreed to meet after supper for a chat."

"What did you talk about?"

"Well, we didn't, really."

Reinhart perked up. "What do you mean?"

"I went to the agreed upon spot and she was there all right — talking in Russian to a red-haired POW. She seemed agitated. They both noticed me, and he immediately turned on his heels and left. I asked her 'What was that all about.' She shook her head. 'I can't talk about it,' she said. But she looked like she was near tears. Then she said, 'Katya. Katya knows the truth.' I asked her what she meant. Instead, she put her hand on my shoulder and said, I need to tell you something, but not here. Let's meet in the morning before work. At zero five hundred. Sure, I said. But then, at zero three-thirty, I left on an unscheduled run to Danzig. I didn't get to see her again. A few days later, we were back at the same base, but she was gone."

"What do you think she wanted to tell you?"

Peter shrugged.

"Do you think it had something to do with the red-haired man?"

"Maybe. But I didn't know who he was, so I couldn't track him down either."

"Hmm." Reinhart bit the corner of his bottom lip. "That's unfortunate. But what's the connection to the diaries?"

"I dunno. But there is one. I'm sure of it. Except the wider I open Pandora's Box, the scarier it is."

"I respect that. Dark journeys are lonely. The paths are filled with muddy ruts and things that go bump in the night. You can't unsee or un-know something."

"Exactly." Peter sighed and set the glass on the end table. "In the diaries, Mum often prefaces the bad parts as if explaining things to herself. I can usually gauge by the tone whether it's something I want to read further. I skip a lot of the girly stuff. But learning about my birth father drives me. Sadly, I haven't read too much about him so far. But I've barely scratched the surface on 1918."

"1918. The infamous treaty at Brest-Litovsk. Russia was losing the war and Germany was itching to take control of Ukraine and the Baltics to expand the Reich. In political terms, the treaty was severe, with serious consequences for Russia."

Peter shifted in his seat. "A great thing for the German colonists. At least in the beginning. I heard they rejoiced when their German saviors arrived. They expected peace and prosperity to return to Ukraine."

Reinhart nodded. "Good times. Some soldiers probably returned home. Did your father?"

"Ja. He was there when I was born. And Katarina turned eighteen then. We always celebrated our birthdays together after that."

"This should be a cheerful story, then. What are you waiting for?"

Peter's lips tightened. "Now you're pushing. I must get settled into the new job first."

"You're procrastinating, Peter. Fear is controlling you. You're tormented by the monsters in the closet! Like I told my daughters — they're always gone by morning. They evaporate in daylight." Reinhart made a ball in the air with his hands. "Poof. Face your fears, Peter."

"I hope you're right. I'll let you know in a few weeks." Peter got up and buttoned his jacket. "I'll call ahead. I promise. When things calm down at work, I'll have more time."

"Good luck with the new job. I'm sure you'll do fine." Reinhart stood up and led Peter to the door. "Give my love to Heidi. Let's get together for dinner sometime. Before your baby arrives and life gets too busy. Helga loves to cook for visitors." Reinhart held out his hand.

Peter reciprocated and said, "That's an offer I can't refuse. Send an invitation anytime."

After Peter left, Reinhart examined the expensive bottle again and grimaced. Helga would tan his hide if he ever spent that much on such a simple luxury. If Peter had invited him to the pub for a drink, they could have enjoyed a few hours for much less money. He was certain the man could not afford this gift. Why give it to him? It wasn't as if they were close friends. At least not from his perspective. More like acquaintances, really. Reinhart shook his head. He was probably making too much of it. *Let it go.*

He blew out a long deep exhalation, then secured the cork and placed the bottle in the antique liquor chest behind the desk. Then he grabbed his raincoat and set out for the butcher shop to buy sausage treats for Willie.

4

OPPORTUNITY

1951 DECEMBER. MUNICH.

PETER ROUGHLY GRABBED HIS WIFE'S SHOULDERS AND pulled her into him, returning her light peck on his cheek with a firm kiss on the lips. Before she could push him away again, he released her and stepped back. His eyes fell on the large suitcase on the floor beside her.

"It's only three nights, Peter. There's food in the refrigerator. You won't go hungry. Besides, you have tons of work to do." Heidi wiggled a finger at the stack of papers on the floor beside the couch. "And you need some time alone without my constant interruptions."

"Fine, but I don't understand why you need to shop in Nuremberg when we have everything here. And why do you need such a big suitcase?" He brushed a stray blond hair off Heidi's shoulder, hoping the affectionate gesture on his part would spark a more loving tone from her.

Heidi rolled her round baby-blue eyes. "I need the space, silly. I'm looking for toys and other baby things at the Christmas market. This is my last chance to go crazy before I become a mum. I won't be able to go next year. Besides, Elsa and I need to catch up. We haven't seen each other in ages."

"Please don't spend too much. Or we won't have enough to buy the crib."

"Don't worry. I'm more frugal than you." Heidi picked up the suitcase and moved to the doorway.

"Fine. I'll work. You go play," Peter grumbled.

"Don't be grumpy, or I won't buy you a present." Heidi opened the door and stepped into the hallway. "I'll see you Monday."

Peter waved. "You owe me a tasty dinner to make up for this. Go. Have a good time. I'll suffer here. Alone."

Heidi grinned and rolled her eyes. *"Auf wiedersehen mein Schatz,"* she said as the door clicked closed behind her.

"Goodbye my love to you, too," Peter muttered the German farewell as the doorknob clicked. He stood glaring at the door for a minute, hoping his wife would return — if only to provide extra reassurance. A more loving kiss would help him feel better. When it didn't happen, he turned and went to the refrigerator, grabbed a beer, and cracked it open, then plopped on the couch. He sucked on his bottom lip and scanned the pile of pending papers to be sorted and marked. Three whole days to do what he wanted. And collating papers wasn't one of them.

He stood up and went to the closet, removed the carved walnut box from the top shelf, and carried it to the couch. The brass catch snapped open with light finger pressure. He lifted the lid. The worn books lay in the same order as he'd left them; but this time, he chose the second one with the dusty rose cover deeply marred by a young woman's doodling of roses and nonsensical Gothic and Cyrillic lettering.

As he lifted it from the chest, his hand brushed against a small, soft pouch squashed into the corner. He set the journal aside and pulled out the lambskin square before examining it.

He fiddled with the knotted ties for a few minutes before giving up and shuffling to the kitchen to retrieve the scissors. After cutting the leather strings, he shook out the contents. A familiar heart-shaped gold locket with a heavy gold chain dropped into his hands. The professionally engraved back with the letters *KJ* identified the owner as Katarina's maternal grandmother. He snapped it open and studied the two sepia photos of his great-grandparents. Katarina had been so afraid of losing the locket that she'd only worn it on special occasions.

"Well, if I have a daughter, she now has a special souvenir from her ancestors," Peter murmured aloud. He put it back in the pouch and then into the chest. After a long swig of beer, he put his feet on the coffee table and cracked the diary open.

5

THEN CAME THE FIRES

1918 FEBRUARY (JULIAN CALENDAR). HALBSTADT, MOLOTSCHNA COLONY, UKRAINE.

THE WINDOW RATTLED. KATARINA BOLTED UPRIGHT IN BED. In a split second, she'd gone from a dead sleep to wide awake. Her heart thumped wildly, her forearms tingled, and her ears hurt as if the air had just been sucked out of the room. She was certain the bed had moved. But that was impossible. It must have been a nightmare.

Across the room, a thin band of morning light peeked between the gap of the navy floral curtains. It was almost time to get up. But since her heart was still racing, she snuggled back under the weighted wool comforter and buried her face in the pillow.

A sharp crack on the roof preceded the rolling sound of a sheet of ice cascading down the side of the house. It crashed past Katarina's second-story window and shattered on the ground below. She groaned and pulled the duvet over her head.

Seconds later, a loud boom blasted in the distance, and a

series of cracking and popping sounds followed. Katarina flung back the blankets and sat up, snarling, "Blasted hunters! Shooting up the sky and waking up the world! What are they doing? Blowing up bridges?"

Scratching the sand from her blue eyes, she slipped out of bed, wiggled into her sheepskin slippers, and retrieved her white velvet robe from its scrunched spot between the mattress and the hand-carved oaken footboard. Then she schlepped to the window and yanked open the heavy curtains, hoping to spot the offenders of the obtrusive wake-up call. But all she could see were the smoky-white puffs dotting the pink horizon and clear blue skies hanging over the snow-covered sunflower fields. Yet Katarina sensed something was wrong.

She tore apart her ash-blond braid and went to the Delft basin to wash up and brush her hair. While finishing her ablutions and re-braiding her waist-length locks, another explosion shook the house and a slow tremor vibrated across the floor.

"This isn't good." Muttering to herself, she returned to the window to appraise the goings-on with a more critical eye. A hay wagon sat in its place under the sleeping apple tree with the hand plow on its back — both buried in snow. The hedge of stately spruce trees lining the long circular driveway sparkled majestically with the fresh white coating on their branches. Despite constraining the effects of the wintery winds, they obscured the northern skyline over the neighboring fields.

"Aargh. I can't see a thing," she groaned.

She picked up her toothbrush and cup from the washstand and headed down the hall to the newly constructed toileting room, but immediately bumped into Kiva, the scullery maid — her arms laden with stuffed pillowcases. Katarina startled at the brazen red kerchief covering the servant's puffy brown hair. She was about to confront the servant on her inappropriate dress and ask about the pillowcase contents when Kiva said, "Best hurry. Anna's waiting," and breezed by without stopping or clarifying.

Katarina stared open-mouthed as the maid disappeared down the hall and around the corner. *She didn't even say good morning! How rude! Where is she going in such a hurry?* Mumbling to herself, Katarina stomped down the hallway to the commode. She'd discuss the disrespect with her sister, Anna, at breakfast.

While in the middle of brushing her teeth, a fervent knocking accompanied Anna's impatient tone. "Katarina."

Katarina groaned and spit into the cup. Lately, her sister's urgent bathroom trips were a nuisance. As far as she was concerned, the baby couldn't arrive soon enough.

"One second." She straightened her robe and took a deep breath. Today's rough start could not ruin her day. Despite the angst of war hanging in the air and the rumors of soldiers pushing into the territory, she still had to maintain a cheerful decorum in the classroom. Only yesterday, she'd reminded her students that the grim situation wasn't in their control. But keeping them focused on their studies was challenging. Everyone was worried.

War. Guns. The noise. A chill passed through her. The hair on the back of her neck bristled and her toothbrush dropped to the floor. *It can't be. Not here.*

"Katarina, we need to leave now." Anna's knock repeated.

"Good grief. One second, I said." Katarina picked up her toiletries and opened the door to a frazzled-looking Anna, fully dressed in winter garb and holding a large traveling bag. Her neatly trimmed blond eyebrows furrowed together in a worried frown, her thin lips stretched tight in a straight line, and her pale face whiter than usual.

"What do you mean, leave now? Is the clock broken?

According to the chimes, I still have an hour before school. Are you heading into town, too?" Katarina scanned her sister's bulky outfit. The center large button clasping the old-fashioned sheepskin coat over Anna's swollen belly strained to tear away from the leather. "You should really fix that button before you go anywhere. It's about to pop." Katarina pointed at the straining thread. "Why aren't you wearing your wool coat? It fits so much better."

"This is the warmest thing I own. And why aren't you dressed yet?" Anna snapped.

Katarina bit her lip to keep from joking about the odd outfit. It puffed out in two "v" shapes above and below the feeble fastening. The black skirts ballooned below the coat, draping the wooden floor like a dust mop; and the oversized white wool scarf wrapped around her neck and shoulders dwarfed Anna's pixie face. Only a few strands of her honey-blond hair poked out from beneath the white and red flowered kerchief tied under her chin. On top of the babushka, Anna wore her favorite black felt hat — with the family's emblem of three white roses stitched on the wide brim — untied, with the strings hanging over her ears. Although the clownish costume was completely out of character for her sister's usual fashion sense, Anna's serious expression explained it as intentional. Katarina held her tongue and only said, "You shouldn't wear white against your face, Anna. It makes you look ill."

Anna's eyes flickered with annoyance and the muscles in her jaw flexed. "Katarina, stop playing around. We must leave now."

"Why? What's the problem? And what's that noise?" Katarina asked as another boom blasted in the distance.

"We're being bombed. Now hurry. Get dressed and pack your bags. We must leave now." Anna grabbed her by the arm. "Come."

Bombs? The children spoke of soldiers heading this way. Katarina shivered. *No. It can't be true.* She dried her hands on her robe as Anna dragged her down the hall. "What do you mean? Bombed? By whom?"

"Bolshevik soldiers in the village. Didn't the servants wake you?" Anna scowled.

"No-o-o." Katarina frowned. "I saw Kiva in the hallway, but she said nothing. And no one woke me up."

"Tsk, tsk," Anna clucked as she shoved Katarina into her bedroom. "I can't believe this. I specifically told Kiva to wake you up. What is wrong with the servants these days? No one listens to me anymore. Listen, there's no time to explain. Layer up your warmest clothes. Olek is getting the sleigh ready. Get dressed and packed. Hurry."

"I'm confused. Why do we have to leave? Is the estate in trouble? We have armed guards all around the perimeter." Katarina tucked a stray strand into place. "We're supposed to be well protected from invaders."

"No. I told you." Anna snapped her fingers in the air. "*Schnell. Schnell.* Hop to it. Meet us in the sleigh. And throw a few extra clothes in a bag. And take all your valuables, especially your jewelry. We could be gone for a few days. Or weeks even." Anna waddled to the hall, then turned around and said firmly, "This is not a game Katarina. War has arrived. This is life and death. We must leave now."

Katarina stood with her mouth agape as Anna disappeared down the stairs. Had war really arrived at their doorstep? But that was ridiculous! The peace talks were ongoing at Brest-Litovsk. The war was almost over. Why would the Red Army want to destroy the Mennonite villages now? They weren't anyone's enemies! Everyone knew the peaceful community didn't have the firepower to fight back, and that they wouldn't even if they did.

Yet Katarina knew that war had no logic. Power-hungry

31

forces trapped ordinary people in their violent clashes. Those who didn't choose a side were assigned one. Amid the battle, neutral innocents became guilty opponents and were sentenced to death. And today, she and Anna were two unremarkable women in such life-threatening circumstances. This was the real world. Not a clipping from their cousin Regier's weekly newspaper.

As the gravity of the situation dawned on Katarina, her eyes widened. "This is war. They've come to kill us." Saying it out loud gave her the impetus she needed. She flew into action, ripped off her nightclothes, yanked the dresser drawers from the chest, and dumped the entire contents onto the floor. She quickly sorted through the pile for two sets of heavy woolen undergarments and threw them on the bed.

Another rumble shook the house. She froze and waited for it to pass, then shivered when it did. The hair on the back of her neck bristled and goosebumps rose on her arms.

"Get dressed. Hurry." She snorted in ragged beats, urging herself on while tugging on the undergarments. Then she scratched her head while deciding on her traveling wardrobe. The frigid temperatures on the open steppes demanded heavy, woolen layers. She spun between the closet and the bed — then grabbed yesterday's skirt from the chair and another from the hangar. While slipping them on, her shaking hands refused to cooperate with tying and buttoning. She took a deep breath, screamed a loud "Grr," and tried to refocus.

Her head pounded and the blood whooshed loudly in her ears. A prickly sensation spread across her upper back and the fingers of her gimpy arm tingled. She argued with the pain and rubbed her hands. "Focus, Katarina."

Anna yelled from the bottom of the stairs, urging her to expedite. Katarina pulled a floral garment bag out of the closet and tossed it on the bed. Next, she grabbed a skirt, two winter tops, a sweater from the closet shelves, and the heavy black wool shawl off the hook on the wall and crammed everything pell-mell into the bag. She tapped her fingers on her hips, analyzing the contents and justifying the disorder. Then, she retrieved an extra set of undergarments — just in case.

"Katarina, it's time. Now." Anna's urgent shouts repeated.

She picked up the bag, then remembered Anna's emphasis on jewelry and valuables, and returned to the dresser to retrieve the small wooden jewelry box. She opened the lid and toyed with the contents. A cameo broach, her maternal grandmother's gold locket, a pearl necklace from her aunt Maria, and a few other items of lesser worth. Thieves would likely steal everything, regardless of value. So, she dumped the entire contents directly into the garment bag and shook it to scatter the items to the bottom. She'd reorganize it later.

Anna hollered again. Clutching her bag, Katarina ran down the hall and flew down the stairs.

"Good grief, Katarina. What took you so long? We are running for our lives." Anna pulled her towards the back door. "Now, pull on your boots and grab your coat. Olek and Alyona are already in the sleigh."

"Why is Olek taking us? Who's going to oversee the guards and the servants while we're gone?"

"We need his expertise with the troika. It's the fastest thing we have, and he's the only one properly trained to drive the team," Anna snapped.

"We'll never outrun the army with a sleigh," Katarina scoffed. "If David had bought one of those fancy automobiles before he left for the war, maybe we'd have a better chance."

Anna pivoted on her heel and narrowed her eyes. "How dare you insult my husband! And now, of all days. Now, get your hambones into the sleigh before I have this baby and we all die." Anna turned and waddled out the door.

Stunned by her sister's verbal slap, Katarina fell silent and retrieved her sheepskin coat and leather boots from the mudroom. A twinge of guilt flickered over the death of Anna and David's infant daughter Margaretha last year. Although she'd doted on the baby for those brief three months, she hadn't been home when the child died. Their mother, Lena, blamed Katarina for being too wrapped up in her work to help Anna in her time of need. It wasn't true, of course. Margaretha's sickness was no one's fault. But Katarina vowed to never abandon her sister or her sister's children again.

Suddenly remembering her diary, she quickly retrieved it from the shelf beside the kitchen table and tossed it into the garment bag. Upon tying her winter boots, she applauded herself for replacing the leather soles and woolen liners in a timely fashion before the weather became unbearably cold.

She dashed outside, climbed up the sleigh, and threw her bag on the deck; then yelled at the middle-aged servant holding the reins. "I'm ready, let's go."

"Wait," Anna scolded, "Katarina, I'm not settled yet. You mustn't yell go while someone is still moving about."

"I thought you were ready. You said everyone was waiting for me." Katarina unfolded the horsehair blanket and wrapped it around her legs.

"I decide when we leave. I'm the lady of the house, not you." Anna whispered sternly as she tucked her own blanket around her hips. She nodded at the Russian servant. "Now we can go."

Olek nodded to the eight-year-old stable-boy standing on the snowbank, holding the center horse's harness. When the child waved and stepped back, Olek snapped the reins. The three horses strained, and the harness pulled tight. The sleigh jerked several times, then slithered on the icy base. With another snap, the horses trotted forward, and the vehicle floated smoothly behind them.

Katarina pulled down the ear flaps of her fur hat and

raised her collar. "If we're in such a hurry, why are we using this cumbersome sleigh? The smaller one is faster."

Anna's mouth twitched. She turned sideways and glared at Katarina. "I don't question Olek's decisions. David said to trust him and that's what I do. He said we need extra supplies. Like hay for the horses and food for us. And we don't know where we'll spend the night. Besides, if this baby arrives early and there are no conveniences, I must be prepared. Anyway, you were still buried in your mattress while we were deciding."

"Oba, nay. Please don't tell me we might sleep in the box. It's February. We could freeze to death."

"God only knows. Speaking of which, we should say a prayer for our safety."

"Ja." Katarina wrapped a second heavy quilt around her upper body. She noticed Anna and her elderly servant, Alyona, had covered their knees with lighter wool blankets. Anna's coat barely covered her large belly. "Are you two warm enough? I've got the best blankets. I don't mind trading."

"We're good," Anna said without checking her maid's status. Her chin flexed, and she chewed on her bottom lip nervously.

"Dear God," Katarina prayed silently. "Please protect us. This is not a good time for a baby to arrive."

At that moment, she realized they'd both grown up. They weren't running through the meadows like two carefree young girls. They were fleeing for their lives — she, her sister, and an unborn child together with two trusted servants. Anything could happen. She reached into the storage box behind the seat and pulled out a spare quilt. "You best keep the baby warm."

Anna looked surprised. "Thanks. But I said I'm fine."

"Your tummy looks cold. Besides, you're carrying my niece or nephew. I don't want anything happening to him or her."

Anna smiled and patted Katarina's leg. "I love you too, sis."

Katarina blinked back the welling tears. What was wrong with her this morning? She wasn't normally this sentimental. Was it the flash of baby Margaretha lying cold in the white coffin that triggered her so? Katarina shivered. They shouldn't be traveling now. Anna's time was much too close. But when Anna's husband, David, left for the war front, she promised him that she'd take care of his wife. And she meant to keep that pledge. Whatever it took.

6

RED, BLACK, AND WHITE

A DENSE, SMOKY HAZE FILTERED THE MORNING SUN AND enveloped the estate's tree plantation in a milky cloud. The stench of charred wood and sulfur permeated the air and seared Katarina's sensitive lungs. She coughed and cleared her throat several times, to no avail. Frustrated, she rearranged the long scarf to filter her mouth and nose, while keeping it tied over her head and around her neck. After tucking the ends behind her collar, she yanked her fur hat over the scarf and pulled the earflaps down, leaving only her eyes exposed. But the heavy smoke irritated them, too.

The silly get-up made her feel self-conscious and she scanned Anna's to compare it with her own. Her sister usually dressed in the latest fashions, but today she resembled a mummified Madonna. Katarina suspected she did, too. She feared becoming the talk of the town if anyone important spotted them.

A thundering rat-a-tat-tat in the village behind them clashed with the rhythmic clip, clop of the horses' hooves, and the melodic swishing of the sleigh over the snow-covered field. Then, after a moment of absolute stillness, there was a loud rumble and a screeching explosion.

All three women simultaneously turned and stared. Orange flames lit up the early morning sky and white smoke billowed high. A long series of popping sounds followed.

"Good grief. It's like fireworks on New Year's. What blew up?" Katarina mused out loud. She didn't expect an answer and was surprised when Anna did.

"My guess is the ammunition depot."

"What? The town has an ammunition depot?"

"Where do you think the men get the bullets for the guns?"

"I assumed they went to Tokmak or another Russian town. That's where Papa always went."

"Not since they started collecting materials for the *Selbstschutz*[1] that they're trying to organize."

"A *Selbstschutz* — a self-defense unit with guns? Here? That's impossible. Surely, we don't have so many guns or ammunition."

Anna chuckled. "More than you think."

"But the government confiscated our weapons. We've only a few hunting rifles. And not every home has one."

"You've had your head in too many books, Katarina. Believe me, some homes have many guns, and not just hunting rifles, either."

"Oba. Nay." Katarina thought for a minute. "But where did we get them from? Germany?" She looked at Anna incredulously.

"At our last sewing circle, we discussed the buildup of arms. You know — the one you missed. *Again*." Anna said. "This is exactly what the wives predicted. When the guns began arriving, we said it was only a matter of time until the Bolsheviks learned of them. And I'll bet that Makhno and his cohorts found out, and reported us."

Katarina shrugged off Anna's snide remark about her lack of attendance at the weekly women's group. "We're doomed. They'll kill us all. What were the men thinking? They should never have accepted those shipments."

"You're preaching to the choir, Katarina."

"But our faith is about peace. We're taught to use our words to fight, not weapons. Surely, the church doesn't condone this. Was there no resistance by the leadership?"

"The brotherhood's had many discussions. But the pastor is only one voice. Trust me, Kat, the world is not as black and white as the church says it is."

Katarina crossed her arms and scowled while doing a mental walk-through of the town's main street. "Where is this ammunition depot?"

"Under the brewery. You passed it every day when you went to work."

"Oba. Nay. How did I miss it?"

"Sometimes things are better hidden in plain sight."

Another bombing rocked the air. The horses startled and Olek deftly maneuvered the reins to keep them on track.

"I hope the newspaper office survives. All those records ... and the school." It was all Katarina could think about as they exited the rear of the estate and crossed the wooden bridge over the frozen Molochnaya River. Along the riverbank, the deciduous grove shrouded the hazy sky with an icy hue, and the feathery gray fingers of the frosted underbrush draped into the snowy blanket beneath them. A fetid dampness hovered in the air. Katarina shivered and pulled her hat over her brow.

Anna patted Katarina's leg. "I'm sorry. You put a lot of work into those books."

"I hope Regier locked everything up well. It'll be a disaster for the town if we lose all those records." Katarina's heart sank to her stomach.

"Doesn't the office have a cellar?"

"Ja. We store copies of every newspaper published there. And the church records, too. The stone foundation provides the perfect dry storage."

"Then they'll be fine. The soldiers won't be going into dark cellars to light books on fire," Anna reassured. "Regardless, our men will repair the buildings later."

"I hope so." Katarina grimaced. "But that's not all I'm worried about. My personal journals are down there, too."

"What?" Anna cocked her head with a disapproving frown. "Why are you keeping them there?"

"Because I didn't want anyone to read them. When I started working at the newspaper office, the cellar seemed like the perfect place to write without being interrupted. Plus, it felt like the safest place to store my books so they wouldn't get lost. But I never dreamt war would come to us."

"Well, let's hope they're not destroyed," Anna said. "Did Regier permit you to play with your writing when you were working?"

"He thought I was sorting through the genealogical records."

"What? You were stealing time from your employer?" Anna looked aghast.

"File sorting is tedious work," Katarina explained. Not that she needed to justify herself. Her sister had never held a job in her life. Anna didn't know how things worked in the real world. "I need occasional breaks. Anyway, I came clean. Regier said he could see my point but asked me to pay back the time. So, I keep track of my breaks now and subtract them from my hours. Regier's fine with it. Really, he is. Besides, I have a key to the office. I'm not always working late, you know."

"And here I worried about you working your fingers to the bone. You brat." Anna shook her head. "You and your writing.

Honestly, Kat. When are you going to put aside such childish nonsense?"

"Nonsense? What's more interesting than books? Creating books."

Anna snorted, "No one reads books by women writers. Maybe children's books, but nothing more serious."

"Oh, I disagree. I'm sure I can prove it, too."

"I'm not sure I want to read such nonsense anyway. It seems scandalous to me. Anyway, I'm sure your books will be safe. The Bolsheviks won't care about a woman's literature. This little battle of theirs will be over in a day or two."

---

1 THE SELBSTSCHUTZ were self-defense units that the Mennonites attempted to organize in response to the rebel attacks. During the German occupation of Ukraine in 1918, the German army provided weapons to the villages and trained the units. The Selbstschutz were not yet fully functional in the winter of 1917-1918. The faithful disagreed strongly about the Biblical justification for self-defense. See this article for more information: https://gameo.org/index.php?title=Selbstschutz

7

WHERE IS SAFETY?

As Olek snapped the reins and spurred the horses across the snow-covered rutted fields, Katarina held fast to the padded wooden bench and prayed the trusted servant would find a safe hideout quickly.

Until today, she'd scarcely appreciated the educated Russian's sharp eyes and quick wit. In fact, when Anna bragged about Olek being a former bodyguard to the Duke, Katarina scoffed, retorting that the Penners considered themselves much too lofty. But when Anna's husband, David, and his brothers left to aid the Czar's military campaign, he'd put the middle-aged servant in charge of the estate's farming and security matters — even though a Bolshevik assault on the property seemed improbable. Now Katarina was grateful to be under Olek's watchful eye.

"Where are we headed?" She asked after they'd exited the safe confines of the estate.

Anna jutted her chin forward and her nose to the sky while calling out to the servant, "Olek, where are we going?"

The Russian servant answered in his stiff, but fluent

German, "My idea is Aleksandrovsk. Maybe we can disappear in the big city. But where is safety?" He pulled on the earflaps of his fur *ushanka* hat and shrugged. "We wait. Maybe we meet others."

"I agree. Olek, you're so wise. I appreciate your concern for our well-being." Anna turned to Katarina and grinned. "There you see. He has it all figured out."

Katarina rolled her eyes and cringed at her sister's condescending attitude. One day, she'd put Anna in her place. But not today. She sucked on her teeth. "If we're going in that direction anyway, should we cross the Dnieper? Maybe go to Chortitza and see our parents? Surely the soldiers won't be on both sides of the river ... will they?"

"Nonsense. We won't be gone that long. By tomorrow, the Bolsheviks will have moved on toward Moscow."

"I hope you're right. I don't relish the idea of sleeping on the sleigh."

"Nor I." Anna cupped her belly and shouted, "Olek, where will we spend the night? We don't want to travel all day."

The servant turned his head. "First, we find safety. Then we decide."

Anna grimaced. "I feel so vulnerable racing across the wide open. We're sitting ducks out here. I can't believe that we're not permitted to take the trains. Our family name alone should allow us passage."

"Did you ask him?"

"Yes, earlier. Olek said something about the soldiers using them. Not all the tracks are operational. Whatever that means. Anyway, I suppose we must trust what he says."

"Ja. Protecting us *is* his job."

Anna sighed and patted her belly. "Nonetheless, I'd like some idea where we're heading. We can't just sled across the wide-open steppes with no direction. I fear we'll end up going in circles."

"I'm sure Olek knows how to get to the city. But I dread being stranded amongst strangers, even if it's only for a few days."

"I do as well. But our parents' farm is a three-day trip. Besides, getting there is one thing. We also need valid permits to cross jurisdictions and women aren't allowed to purchase them."

Katarina gave her sister a cock-eyed frown. "What do you mean? I have my identification papers. Isn't that enough?"

"Have you ever tried to travel alone? Without a man? Trust me, it's not easy."

"But we have Olek."

"Yes, but there are rules. He's only a servant. Not family."

"Oh." Now that Anna mentioned it, Katarina remembered it had always been their father, an uncle, or Anna's husband David who'd purchased tickets and filled out the paperwork. Other than proof of residency, she wasn't aware of the travel regulations. However, she'd heard how war-time ordinances complicated civilian movement and left women and children stranded at checkpoints until a male family member could retrieve them.

Anna twisted her mouth from side to side and tapped her belly as if she, too, was thinking about the dilemma. Then she burst out, screeching in crude Russian, "Olek? How can we get papers for the river crossing?"

Katarina cringed. The man wasn't deaf. There was no need for Anna to yell. And since Olek was fluent in German, Anna's attempt to practice her Russian on him seemed both unnecessary and silly.

"*Da. V Aleksandrovske.*" He replied calmly in Russian.

"Good, that's settled then. Olek will figure it out when we get to the city." Anna straightened her shoulders and pulled the blanket over her belly.

Katarina's mind drifted back to the firefight. She

wondered about their friends and loved ones. "Are any of David's family left in town? Or are they all in Yalta for the winter with your mother-in-law?"

"I can't keep track of thirteen siblings. If they're not traveling for work, they're vacationing. The farms and factories operate whether they're here or not. If we'd driven through the estate to check on them, we'd have gone straight into the line of fire. We can only pray everyone got out in time." Anna sighed and tapped her belly. "We're on our own now. God help us."

Behind them, another explosion rocked the air. The trio of horses whinnied, and the dappled gray jerked right. Katarina sucked in her breath and tightened her mittened grip on the bench. Anna's face paled. Alyona hugged the wall with both hands.

"Good grief. How long will this continue?" Katarina muttered under her breath while she quickly eyeballed Anna. The responsibility of keeping her sister safe weighed heavily. Baby Margaretha had arrived prematurely and before the midwife arrived. What if this child was born early — in the middle of nowhere? Even though the due date was two weeks away, babies had their own timelines.

Worse yet — what if there was an accident and Anna got hurt? *No!* She couldn't think like that. Besides, Alyona had proved her competence during Margaretha's birth. She'd be equally adept this time. Everything would work out fine. If they trusted in the Almighty, he would protect and guide them through this dark journey. Silently, she recited Psalm ninety-one.

He that dwelleth in the secret place of the most High shall abide under the shadow of the Almighty. I will say of the Lord, He is my refuge and my fortress: my God; in him will I trust. Surely, he shall deliver thee from the snare of the fowler, and from the noisome pestilence. He shall cover thee with his feathers, and under his wings shalt thou trust: His truth shall be thy shield and buckler.

8

THE ANXIETY OF NOT KNOWING

AFTER AN HOUR OF TRAVEL, THEY'D RUN OUT OF THINGS TO talk about. As the haze and the putrid stench from the fires slowly dissipated, Katarina loosened her scarf and pulled it away from her mouth. She crossed and uncrossed her legs, while vexing about both the war and Anna's pregnancy, and fuming about the lousy timing of both.

Anna put a pillow behind her back and rolled her hands over her belly repeatedly. Katarina could see her sister was uncomfortable and worried. She wished to reassure her and promise a happy ending to this confusing nightmare. But there were no guarantees, no easy answers. Nothing in this war made sense.

She took a deep breath and exhaled with a long stream through her mouth while watching her breath spiral upwards in the frosty air. "What do the Bolsheviks want with us, Anna? Don't they have bigger bones to pick? We're a self-governing colony. We don't need or want government interference."

"My dear, when you figure that out, please let me know. This Communist manifesto is nonsensical. Lenin wishes to

49

divide and collectivize our lands. *Our lands!* And I heard that Makhno and his separatist hordes agree with Lenin on this point. Everyone wants to destroy our estates. And Russia demands all our grain, too. Our hard work is going to nothingness. It's all so confusing."

"So, they want both the land AND the bread? What are we to live on? Do we not have any legal rights? The Imperial Crown gave us this land. We purchased the rest. It sounds like Lenin wants to reverse two hundred years of progress!?" Katarina tapped her fingers on her lap. "22 January 1918. Only last month, Ukraine declared independence. [1] We're supposed to be a separate country now with a new government. Ukraine should run its own affairs without Russian interference. We must protest to the new Rada, not the Soviets. Unless ... did something not get ratified?"

"You tell me, sister. You're the journalist's assistant, the local schoolteacher, and the family historian. Don't you know the details?"

"Honestly, I don't think anyone knows exactly what's going on. For the last four years, the Russian government's been flexing its muscles with the world, but it's lost control of itself. Ukraine's a political waste bucket that no one wants to deal with and yet we're the rope in a game of tug of war. Independence is the only way Ukraine can ever be free."

Anna turned to the elderly house servant. "I'm hungry, Alyona. Let's eat."

Katarina chuckled. "Food! Yes. That's the answer to everything!"

"It helps me think," Anna said. "And it makes me feel better."

"But it won't solve our problems today. Unfortunately."

Alyona pulled out a box from under the bench, removed two zwieback rolls and a sausage ring, and gave them to her mistress. Anna broke the meat in half and offered Katarina the other half. Katarina hesitated, then shook her head. "No thanks. I'm not that hungry."

"But you didn't have breakfast yet." Anna cocked her head at her sister. "You must be ravenous. I am."

"Well, of course, you are. You're eating for two. Don't worry about me. I'll wait until we get to the next town."

"Are you sure?" Anna said biting into the sausage.

"I'm fine. Really, I am," Katarina lied. Her stomach was growling, but their discussion about Russia's confiscation of grain and land bothered her more. Surely Russia wouldn't take *all* the harvest. Granted, the soldiers needed to eat, but so did everyone else. Lenin couldn't possibly be so inhumane as to take it all. Even money couldn't buy food when none existed.

It was because of the war, Katarina rationalized. This economic crisis would end once the war was over. It had to. But the reminder of the national food shortage made her wonder if they'd packed enough for this trip. Anna was eating for two and she couldn't do without. But she, Katarina, could easily control her appetite for a few days, or at least until they knew their destination.

She focused on the rhythmic bobbing of the horses' heads as they trekked over the snow-covered steppe. Their jingling bells clashed with the strange yellow sky, pretending cheeriness when there was none to be had.

So much had changed in the past three years.

It all started on Anna's wedding day, with a frightening encounter with a Cossack rider on a black stallion. He'd burst into the barn, knocked her down, and sent her sailing across the concrete floor. The accident tore the muscles in her shoulder and broke her arm. Neither had healed properly. According to the best medical advice available, the limb would never work the same again. After the event, she'd developed an allergy to horses. The doctors couldn't explain this, except to say it was an emotional reaction to the stress and would likely go away in time.

But following the accident, the nightmares persisted. When she couldn't overcome them, her parents encouraged her to move to Molotschna, attend teachers' college, and live with Anna and David. That was before her brother-in-law left to serve as a paramedic in the war.

Then, last year, the Czar resigned, and political upheaval escalated at a dizzying speed. Overnight, civil disobedience spread like wildfire on a wheat field. While the imperial army struggled to regain control, the Bolsheviks took charge. Now the Reds were blazing across the countryside, killing the loyalists of the old guard.

When Ukraine sought to defend itself from the chaos and declared independence, Russia ignored the new political realm, determined to impose its sovereignty on the fledging country. And while freedom fighters fought both Bolsheviks and Imperialists, they too eliminated all those who disagreed with them. And thus, more blood spilled on the land. Even law-abiding sleepy rural communities were trampled, and simple farms razed.

Even more worrisome was the active and growing threat along the southern steppes. Determined to control the political direction of the region, a man who'd grown up near the Mennonite villages formed a militia and now turned against the German-speaking peoples. It was this local anarchist, Nestor Makhno, and his growing Black army that concerned Katarina the most. But then, she'd never imagined the Reds would travel this far south and attack them, too.

It was all too bizarre. How did their peaceful people suddenly become the enemy of the nations? They had built homes, farms, businesses, and factories — providing jobs and industry to the steppes. Hadn't they proved to be honorable citizens deserving of Russian admiration? Why attack them?

That final thought caused the stallion from her night-mares to appear. Katarina squeezed her eyes tight, but the image wouldn't stop. Her heart raced, her breathing quickened, and sweat poured between her breasts. Her mind replayed the breath-stopping smack on the concrete floor. She held her hand over her mouth to keep from screaming out loud. A sourness crept up her throat.

Embarrassed by her imagination, she turned and stared at the red clouds of war behind them. But her mother's scalding voice shouted through the dark recesses of her mind, "Katarina, don't be so thin-skinned. You best toughen up girl, or you'll never get through life. No man wants a whiner for a wife."

She swallowed the vomit and rubbed her aching arm. Blood pounded in her ears. She stretched her neck on each side and dug her fingers into the angry, eternal knot behind her left shoulder.

They couldn't go home to where her nightmares began. They just couldn't. She considered other acceptable and equally safe options. Their sister, Maria, and her husband George owned a large dairy farm on the Dnieper lowlands, near the village of Einlage. They could stay there and still be close enough to visit their parents for a day or two.

Katarina turned to Anna, "When's the last time we heard from Maria?"

"Um. A few weeks ago. Maybe a month." Anna chomped on her zwieback and licked the jam from her fingers.

"Isn't that odd?"

"Perhaps. But she and the boys must run the farm while George is away at war. Plus, she's got the little ones. She probably doesn't have time to write letters to everyone. Besides, our parents aren't that far away. I'm sure they check on her from time to time."

"I suppose. Does she still have servants? So many are leaving the farms these days."

"Kat, you read the letters, too. Why are you asking me?"

"I was just thinking. Between the migrants drifting in from the war-front and the river pirates, the riverbanks aren't safe. Their farm is in such a vulnerable location. They're bound to be harassed. Or worse."

"Kat. Let's concern ourselves with our own problems. Getting to Maria's is just as complicated as going to Chortitza. We'd still have to cross the river. I'm more concerned about where we're spending the night tonight."

"Do you think the war is on both sides of the river?"

Anna looked at Katarina incredulously. "Whatever do you mean?"

"Where were the Reds coming from before they hit Halbstadt? What other villages did they hit?"

"Well, the Czar's army isn't anywhere near here. The nearest troops are south of Kherson."

"And Makhno's militants? Where is he hiding? Along the riverbanks? His army is growing. They're just as merciless as the Bolsheviks. What if we drive straight into them?"

"Katarina, stop it. You're making things worse. Let's just deal with today, shall we?"

An icy finger traced its way down Katarina's spine and goosebumps rose on the back of her arms. She'd always wanted to spread her wings and see the world. Traveling was supposed to be a romantic and carefree adventure. Not unpredictable, dark, and filled with anxiety. War wasn't in her plans.

God help us. Katarina clasped her hands, closed her eyes, and prayed for safety.

---

1 Ukraine Declaration of Independence: https://soviethistory.msu.edu/1954-2/the-gift-of-crimea/the-gift-of-crimea-texts/ukrainian-declaration-of-independence/

9

PETER'S WARNING

KATARINA MARVELED AS OLEK DEFTLY MANIPULATED THE four sets of reins on the troika, skillfully switching the leads between the shaft and the two trace horses. "What incredible horsemanship!" She whispered. "And the animals are so well-trained, too. I knew he was an expert. But this takes horse mastery to another level."

"Olek's been training the team for years, but there are few opportunities to use them like this. We don't get as much snowfall here as Petrograd and Moscow." Anna pointed to the triad and then to the connecting harness and hand-painted wooden bow. "Did you know that training a troika takes ten years? And there aren't many such contraptions left in the world. Few can afford such luxury." [1]

"Huh. How did you come by it?"

"David's great-grandparents brought it with them from Prussia. After the original horses died, the *Duga* —" Anna pointed to the center-shaft bow "— and harness gathered dust until Olek came along. Buying the right horses is one thing, finding a qualified trainer is not so easy."

The sleigh jerked as they went over another bump. Katarina slammed her heels into the floor and gripped the seat with both hands. "I love the gorgeous hand-painted ivy and roses. It makes me feel like I'm going to a wedding instead of fleeing a war zone."

"That it does. But beauty aside, a troika is also faster than anything else. And because of how they're hitched, the horses don't tire as easily. I only wish this vehicle wasn't so uncomfortable. It's hard for me in my condition to handle all this bouncing and swishing about."

"Perhaps you can rest on the hay in the back when we get further along."

"I shall."

"I often wondered why Olek spends all his time in the stable and the paddock instead of overseeing the fields." Katarina repositioned her feet on the brick-lined foot warmer. It was still nice and hot, but the coals would need refreshing in a few hours. She hoped they'd find safety before then.

"Yes. But the field managers know where to find him if they need him. David said his father expanded the stables and renovated both the offices and overseer's quarters before Olek was hired. I suspect that was just to impress Olek — being that he'd worked for the duke. David gave me the impression that whatever Olek wanted, he got."

"He's certainly much more than a stable manager."

"That he is. We're in excellent hands."

The center horse adjusted its speed to allow the left pacer to control the icy turn as they entered the main road. "We must find another vehicle before we reach Alexandrovsk," Olek yelled as the sleigh sailed over another bump. "The sleigh needs ice or snow. The roads in the city may be too muddy." He pointed at the runners and made a grinding noise.

"Must we go that far?" Anna asked. "That's another day's drive!"

"If we end up in Alexandrovsk, we can cross over at the Kichkas." Katarina mused out loud.

"Kichkas bridge is too dry," Olek said. "Too much strain for the troika."

"Plus, we need permits, remember?" Anna said, grimacing. "Olek, is there another way to cross the river?"

"Nyet. Seventy versts of rapids on the Dnieper, and much ice flow. No safe crossing in winter. No ferries."

"Good grief. No permits, no male relatives to buy our tickets, and now we have the wrong vehicle to cross the river. Did we bring enough money for hotel rooms?"

Anna patted Katarina's leg. "One thing at a time. We'll cross that bridge when we come to it."

"I'm beginning to think we won't." Katarina pushed Anna's hand away. Her sister's tendency to mother her was annoying. "I hope this battle blows over quickly. I want to go home." She twisted in her seat to face Anna directly. "How did we know the estate was in harm's way before we left? The place is guarded like a military fortress. Why didn't we wait and see?"

Anna's long lashes blinked twice. Surprise mixed with horror showed in her cornflower blue eyes. "You would take such a chance with our lives? The Bolsheviks are burning fields and houses, and probably murdering people in the streets. You think you could have a conversation with such devils?"

"No, I suppose not. I just find this too hard to believe. The world's been at war for almost four years, yet we've never been disturbed. Then suddenly, the government of Russia changes, Ukraine rebels, and the German colonies become trapped. Misery plagues us. Whom can we trust?"

"I agree. It's a bit overwhelming. I wish David was here to explain it to us."

"Where is he, now? Have you received a letter lately?"

"His notes are a bit cryptic. He tells me to share the letters with Regier. The newspaperman will clarify, he says. I'm protesting. Letters between husbands and wives are private. I want my husband to speak clearly to me. Honestly. Am I not worth the time and the cost of an extra piece of paper? If David has messages for Regier, he should address him directly. I don't want to be a cog in his wheel."

Katarina bit her lips and snapped her head away to keep from laughing. Anna's complaint seemed highly exaggerated and hilarious. "Did you ask Regier about it?"

"No, I refuse."

"Maybe he only wants to help you understand. Or ..." Katarina considered the possibility of conspiracy. "David wants to send a message to Regier, and he doesn't want it to be intercepted. Regier has a lot of connections."

Anna's eyebrows raised. "Oh. I never thought of that."

"If you wish, I can take the letters to him."

"My letters with my husband? Now my sister wants to read my love letters with my husband and share them with the local newspaperman, too? Is there no privacy left? Next, you'll want to publish them in a column and the entire world will analyze my marriage." Anna stared back at Katarina. "I've lost control. You've all lost your minds."

"I didn't mean all the letters, Anna. Just the ones where he asks you to talk to Regier. Maybe Regier knows something."

"Fine. I'll consider it when we get back home. *If* we get back home." Anna pointed toward a lone rider leading a trail of riderless horses heading towards them. "Look up, detective. Twelve o'clock. We've got company."

The red star on the *budenovka* — a felt cap with a pointed tip on the crown — identified the uniform. "It's a Bolshevik soldier." Katarina's heart raced. What could he want with them?

"Is he one of ours?" Anna asked.

"Ours?" Katarina wrinkled her brow. "Since when do our people fight for the Reds? We support the Czar."

"At gunpoint, even our men change sides."

Katarina groaned. "Good grief. What has the world come to? Does no one have scruples anymore?"

Olek turned around. "He's seeing us. I must stop if he asks." He muttered softly in Russian. "I'll try to convince him not to shoot us. It's best you say nothing."

Anna grabbed Katarina's arm. Their eyes met. "God be with us," Anna whispered. As the soldier approached, she straightened her shoulders and yanked at the gap of her sheepskin coat.

Katarina took a deep breath and blew it out slowly. She hoped this would be their one and only encounter with the enemy.

"Halt," the rider yelled as he approached. He raised his gun in the air but didn't fire.

Olek brought the horses to a stop. He spoke softly over his shoulder, "He's not shooting. We won't die today."

The soldier rode up and removed his cap.

Katarina gasped. "Peter! What are you doing here? Why are you wearing that uniform?"

Their distant cousin and son of the famed veterinarian returned a sheepish grin. "I'm sorry that you should see me like this, Katarina. And Anna. The Reds have hired us to refresh their horses while they are in the area. I must wear the uniform. It's not by choice, I assure you."

As the horse crept alongside the vehicle, Katarina sneezed three times. Peter stopped and pulled the animal back. "Ah, my apologies. I forgot about your allergies."

Katarina grimaced and silently cursed her sinuses. She pulled a handkerchief from her sleeve and blew her nose. "I'm fine if you stay further back. Don't come so close."

Anna patted Katarina on the leg. Embarrassed by the

reprimand, Katarina clenched her fists and pushed Anna's hand away. Her sister was shushing her as if she were a little child. Just like their mother often did. She wanted to slap her.

"Are your parents well?" Anna asked.

"My family is under great strain, but we are all alive. Thank God."

"Yes. Thank the Lord," Anna replied. "Why are you traveling so far east? This is days from your farm."

"I'm refreshing horses. I'm headed towards Halbstadt. Are you leaving the zone?"

"Ja, they ..." Katarina's eyes narrowed. "*Your* army is burning down our village and threatening our lives. Can you do something? We'd like to go home." Katarina stared at the chestnut-haired, lanky soldier with deep-set sapphire eyes. The man was unbearably good-looking. But the Red uniform was disconcerting.

"You're fortunate you ran into me. Others would take your horses and your money and leave you stranded." The deep blue eyes stared back, unblinking, his expression serious.

"I suppose we should thank you, then," Katarina snorted. Anna elbowed her in the ribs.

Peter seemed to ignore Katarina's acerbic remark and shifted his gaze to Olek. "Where are you going?"

Olek jerked his head. "Aleksandrovsk. Or further — if we can cross the river. But wherever we can find safety."

"Do you have transit papers?"

Olek shook his head. "We'll buy at the bridge. At the government office."

Peter shook his head. "You'll have problems, Olek. A male family member must accompany all female travelers. Only they can purchase the passes to cross the territory. The authorities at the Kichkas bridge inspect all identification closely. It's the only accessible exit from the region."

"What are we supposed to do?" Anna's eyes widened.

"Stay in some hovel until we can get tickets? I'm with child. I need safe accommodation."

Peter gave a sympathetic smile. "I understand. But the Reds are swarming Aleksandrovsk. They're like ants on an anthill there — picking off the fleeing colonists as they show up at the perimeter. And they're not the only problem. Makhno's men have control of the West Bank. And they're working with the Reds now."

"What?" Katarina exclaimed in disbelief. "Makhno aligned with the Reds? That's impossible. The man doesn't believe in government."

Peter sucked on his bottom lip before answering. "Some believe he's had a change of heart. But be that as it may — even with proper transit papers, you'll face trouble. On top of that, the government office may be closed, too. Their hours aren't predictable. And the army has taken all the hotel rooms."

"So, what do you suggest?" Anna's eyebrows knit together in one long, blond line.

"Can we get to Schoenwiese?" Olek asked.

"You can try, but the factories have suffered uprisings and strikes. It's not a safe area. And it's close to the city. By the time you see the troops, it'll be too late. You'll be doing some fast talking."

Olek chuckled, "I'm an artist. I find ways. I can talk my way through anything."

"That may save your bacon through general inquiries, but if they start on the women —"

"I speak good Russian," Katarina interrupted. "They don't have to know who we are."

"I'm sorry Katarina, but you're too well dressed to pass as a local. And your accent gives you away," Peter said.

"I have an accent?" Katarina said, surprised. No one had ever commented on her tongue before.

"Is there another way out of here?" Anna asked. "We can't be too careful."

Peter shook his head. "I'm sorry, Anna. You're in a tough way. Personally, I'd stay south of the city and head due west across the steppe. Then I'd take the barge across the Dnieper to Nikopol. But if you decide to go that way, keep an eye out for Makhno's rebels."

"What are the better odds? The Reds or Makhno?"

"I pray you don't face either."

Olek shook his head. "I know good Russians in Schoenwiese. They can hide us. They help with transit papers."

Peter cleared his throat and pulled down his cap. "Olek, be careful what you say to me. As unfair as things may be, I must fulfill my duties as an honest soldier. I don't want to take you into custody or see you face a firing squad. I suggest you say no more."

A chill traveled down Katarina's spine. Peter had changed. He'd become a cruel military man. She gave Anna a despairing look and slowly shook her head from side to side.

"I must go." Peter broke the awkward silence and backed his horse away. "I'll try to steer the Reds away from the estate. But I can't guarantee anything. I'm just a horse trader to them."

"Thank you for your help," Katarina and Anna said in unison.

"God protect you. Ladies." Peter touched his cap and pulled on the reins. He checked the trail of horses behind him before nudging the lead with this boot.

"God protect us all," Anna said as Peter trotted off.

1 About the troika: https://www.macalester.edu/russian/about/resources/miscellany/troikasleigh/

10

WOMEN'S WORK

KATARINA WAITED UNTIL PETER WAS OUT OF EARSHOT. "Now what are we supposed to do?" A cold lump settled in the pit of her stomach. The news left her feeling trapped in the middle of the open steppes.

"Thank God we met up with *him* and not a real soldier. Surely God sent him to warn us and steer us away from trouble." Anna exhaled loudly. Then her face lit up with a huge grin. "I noticed you two couldn't keep your eyes off each other."

Katarina shrugged and glanced back at the trailing pack. "He looks nice. But he's a traitor."

"Nice? He looks nice. That's the best you can say? Are you embarrassed to say handsome, or mouth-watering gorgeous?" Anna raised her eyebrows. "I'm a married woman, and I think he's exceptional husband material. If I were single, I'd be sure to let him know I was interested."

"I only said I like his looks. That's all."

"Oh, Katarina. I waste my time trying to teach you about men."

"Teach me about men? Why do I need to learn about men? I don't plan to marry soon."

"Katarina, you'll be eighteen in a few weeks. You need to find a husband. Peter is a great catch."

"And now he's a Bolshevik fighting in a war. I don't want a Bolshevik husband."

"He's only wearing the uniform, Kat. It doesn't mean he's embraced the politics."

"I know that. But I need more than a candy wrapper. I want to know what's inside before I take a bite. Looks aren't everything and wrappers fade. Besides, I'm allergic to horses."

"Oh, your allergy won't kill you." Anna waved her hand in the air in a dismissive gesture. "I'm sure you'd figure out something if you had to. Are you going to throw away a perfectly good man because of your sensitivities? He's smart, educated, and comes from an excellent family. They own land. What more do you need to know?"

"I want to know him. His soul and his heart. But most of all, his mind. I want a man that can carry on an intelligent conversation with me. I want to grow old with someone who is also my friend."

"You're overthinking this, Kat. Men have their interests. Women have theirs. They rarely match up. Men work and take care of things. Women cook, look after the house, and take care of the children. They don't need to be friends."

"And what happens when the children grow up and leave home? Then it's just the two of them. Look at Mutter and Papa. She's either complaining or spreading gossip from the sewing circle. Papa escapes to the woodpile or the barn. That gives her more to complain about. She spent her whole life cooking, sewing, and raising kids. If they'd been friends, they wouldn't be so bored and lonely now." Katarina tightened the blanket around her legs.

"How do you know? You haven't been home in more than

a year. Things could have changed between them." Anna repositioned the pillow behind her back.

"I suppose that's possible." Katarina shrugged. "Anyway, I want some promise of a happy life. I don't want to get married for convenience or convention."

"Well, if you wait too long, Peter will marry someone else. I'm sure many girls have their eyes on him. You don't want to lose out."

"Well, if he's that desperate to get married, then he's not right for me. Besides, if God has chosen him for me, then he'll wait." Katarina crossed her arms over her chest.

"God doesn't intervene in man's affairs. We make our own choices in life." Anna repositioned her blanket. "Wisdom is available to all who ask. God helps us walk through the fire, but he doesn't light the match."

"Is that so? I've heard preachers debate such theories."

"And I suppose you've studied the Bible enough to under-stand the debates."

Katarina clucked her tongue. "I've heard enough. I enjoy such discussions."

"Ugh. They're ridiculous. Some of those preachers are so heavenly-minded, they're no earthly good. I fall asleep at those meetings."

"That's not surprising. You're not attracted to intelligence," Katarina sassed.

Olek shifted in his seat and pointed to a grove of poplar trees. "We stop for a break now. The horses need rest."

∾

OLEK GATHERED TWIGS, built a small campfire, and set a bucket of snow on top of the fire to melt. Alyona opened the basket of food and prepared the samovar for tea.

"The water's still hot from the morning coals," the elderly

maidservant said. "With the melted snow, we'll have enough to last the day."

"The horses need water, too," Olek said as he added more snow to the pail. "They can eat the snow, but water is better for them."

Anna nudged Katarina and pointed at the trees. "Come with me. I must stretch my legs."

As they ambled through the crusty drift, Katarina pulled up the mink collar on her sheepskin coat and tightened the wool scarf under her chin. "This would be a fun winter picnic if it weren't so cold."

"Or if we weren't running for our lives." Anna squatted behind a leafless bush. "My bladder is giving me problems. I feel bad asking Olek to stop so often. It's embarrassing." She stood up and straightened her skirt.

"Don't be ashamed. You have a good excuse," Katarina said sympathetically.

When they returned to the sleigh, Alyona had spread a wide selection of food on the fold-down bench. "Sausage, zwieback, honey, beet kvass, cheese, pickles, onions, apples. Alyona, you've thought of everything!" Katarina picked up a jar and chuckled, "And sauerkraut, too! Are you planning to make sour cabbage soup on the open fire?"

A rare smile passed over the maid's sallow face as she handed out cups of tea. "Sauerkraut and onions keep the stomach healthy."

Katarina groaned. "Alyona's always thinking of our health."

"And I'm glad she does." Anna grabbed a bun, crimped a piece of sausage from the ring, and passed it to Katarina. "I need her wisdom these days."

"Ja. I understand that." Katarina tucked the sausage into the bun's center and shook out her legs while she chewed. "It feels good to stretch and get the cramps out of my calves.

How long have we been traveling? It feels like forever and the sun's barely past noon."

"I'm tired, too. Olek, how much further will we drive today?" Anna paced around the fire.

"A long way yet. The sleigh is heavy. I don't wish to push the horses."

"The troika may be fast, but this big sleigh isn't the most practical or comfortable vehicle," Anna said in a matter-of-fact tone. "But under the circumstances —"

"In Schoenwiese, we trade. This harness will give good value," Olek said abruptly, between sips. "I have friends there."

Katarina stared at Olek, wide-eyed and then at Anna. Did she hear right? Was the servant planning to trade or sell this prized family heirloom? But Anna wasn't disagreeing. Katarina blinked several times. Had Anna and Olek previously discussed this?

"Peter suggested we stay away from the cities. We should respect his advice," Anna said softly. "Olek, please explain to me again about the problem with the trains. Can we change direction and go to Melitopol? Maybe those trains are working. I'd like to go to the sea. It's warmer there. How long will it take?"

The servant chuckled and shook his head. "A train, in your condition? Nyet. Too many soldiers. No seats for women."

"I agree. The sea sounds lovely," Katarina murmured. "I suspect Regier went there. Or to Crimea. He has family there. I hope he got away safely before the firestorm. When the Thiessens were murdered last year, he suggested we pack our bags immediately and head south. Behind the lines of the Imperial Army. Where it would be safer. I told him we couldn't go now because of the baby." Katarina tapped her fingernails on the cup. "Anna, considering the current circumstances, will David's family stay in Yalta until after the muddy season?"

Anna nodded. "Quite likely. I doubt we can depend on their help anytime soon."

"But if this siege continues, we may not go home for weeks. And what if the house is damaged? Repairs could take months. If we turned south now, we could meet up with them and stay there until the summer."

Anna's eyes brimmed with tears. "We don't have time to travel south. This baby could come any day. We need a safe place now." Anna covered her face with her hands and sobbed. "Katarina, I'm so afraid. I'm going to have a baby in the middle of the war. In some stranger's bed. With guns all around. If only David was here. He'd know what to do. Dear God, I can't lose another child."

Katarina went to her sister and wrapped an arm around Anna's shoulders. "Then we must pray for an answer. Thank God we have Olek and Alyona to help us."

Anna looked up with reddened eyes, her cheeks flushed. "I want to go home, Katarina. To Chortitza. I miss Mutter's borsch and her *pluma moos.*"

Katarina burst out laughing. "I'm glad I'm not pregnant. Plum soup does not pair well with beets and cabbage in my stomach."

Anna sniffled as a tear slipped down her cheek. "I miss our folks. Besides, if there's one haven left in the Land of the Mennonites, it must be Chortitza."

"What? Do you really think Chortitza is safe? Have you forgotten what happened to me there, Anna? The rebels burned down the mill and attacked the farm in the middle of your wedding! I still have nightmares about it. And my crooked arm gives me painful reminders every day."

"That was three years ago. There have been no troubles lately. Besides, Papa won't let anything happen to that farm.

It's his pride and joy." Anna squeezed Katarina's arm. "I'm worried about our parents, though. And I'll venture they're fearful for us, too. They know the Penners are away for the winter." Anna stared up at the hazy sky, then inhaled sharply and twirled around. "Oh, dear! I hope Papa isn't traveling to Halbstadt to check on us. That would put him in harm's way."

"Good grief, Anna. I never considered that. You're right. If Papa leaves to search for us and Makhno's gangs show up there, what will happen to Mutter?"

"That's a terrifying thought. Although they have Katya and Dimitri ..." Anna shook her head. "Oh, I forgot. He's not there anymore. But there are other day laborers. Mutter managed on her own before. And they have good neighbors."

Katarina sighed. "Fretting about them is not helping us here. If Papa sends out a search party to find us ... We should send a note."

"There should be a wire service at the next town."

"Ja. Hopefully. We need a warm place to spend the night, too. I don't relish sleeping on a bed of hay in the freezing cold."

Anna nodded. "I agree on that point. So. Are we in agreement about heading for Chortitza?"

"I suppose so." Katarina nodded.

Anna walked over to Olek. He was buckling the gear on the horses after feeding and brushing them. "Olek, please find us a good place to sleep. Then tomorrow, we head to Chortitza."

The servant frowned. "Your friend said it's not safe. And we can't cross the bridge without papers."

"You said you had friends that can help."

"*Da.* In Schoenwiese. But it will cost rubles."

Anna pointed to her chest. "I have Kerenka."

Olek grimaced. "Maybe. We can try. I'll work on a plan."

11

GRUSHKA AND PYLYP

As the day waned, Olek pointed at the twinkling lights on the dusky amber horizon. "Look — a village. We take the main road now and find a friendly house."

Katarina checked on Anna, resting on a bed of hay in the sleigh's storage box. Her face looked unusually pale. Katarina turned to Alyona. "We've stopped so many times for her toileting. Is this normal for so late in her condition?"

Alyona wiped a gray strand from her face and smiled sympathetically. "She needs to drink more. And to stay warm. Otherwise, she gets a fever. Don't fear. We protect Frau Anna."

Katarina chewed on her bottom lip. Anna couldn't get sick now. They were in the middle of a lawless wilderness and inside a war zone. It was likely impossible to find a doctor. *God, please help. Don't let Anna get sick. And please don't let her have the baby before we get to Mutter and Papa's.*

As the troika engaged with the main road, a firm clip-clopping on the hard stony surface replaced the soft crunching of hooves against snow. The heavy sleigh's runners squeaked and scraped as Olek pushed the horses to increase their pace. But the animals strained and tired quickly. Katarina despaired. This heavy vehicle was designed for function, not speed. Evading detection would be difficult.

At the edge of town, smoke wafted from the chimney of a tiny wood and stucco house. The faded business sign in the blue paint-chipped window said *Tobacco and Tea*. Olek stopped the troika beside the ramshackle barn attached to the rear of the house. He motioned to Alyona. "Hold the reins. I'll be right back."

Alyona climbed up to the driver's seat, but her eyes darted around the property. She tightened her kerchief and yanked the sheepskin coat around her knees. Katarina sensed the maid's anxiety and glanced back at her sister, who was still sound asleep.

Olek stopped outside the door and crossed himself before knocking. The door opened, and he stepped inside. A few minutes later, he came out and strode briskly to the sleigh. "They're separatists," he said. "Everyone in this village is. We stay at our own risk."

"It's late. We don't have another choice. It's too cold to sleep outside. And Anna ..."

At the mention of her name, Anna opened her eyes. "Are we stopped? Where are we?"

"We're in a rebel town, Anna. There's nowhere else to go. How well can you pretend?"

Anna rolled onto her side and groaned. She slowly pushed herself up and dusted the loose hay out of her hair. "What do you mean, pretend?"

"We must let Olek do the talking and act as if we agree with their political jargon. We need a warm place to sleep."

"Well, provided I don't have to tell a lie, I suppose." Anna made a sour face. "I need to pass my water. Do they have an indoor pot?"

Katarina scowled. "Does it matter? I don't think you have a choice."

"Come." Olek opened the panel door and offered his hand.

"Where will you sleep tonight, Olek?" Katarina asked as she stepped down.

He pointed to the box where Anna had been sleeping. "I keep watch on the horses — to guard against horse thieves."

"And Alyona?"

"She stays with you. Her Ukraine dialect is local. For tonight, you must behave as friends, not servants and masters." He helped Anna off the back of the box sleigh and switched to German. "Please be safe. Do not speak in your native tongue. This causes trouble. And ..." his voice trailed.

Katarina guessed by the look on Olek's face that Anna's accent would give her away. Plus, her Ukrainian was poor, and her Russian wasn't much better. "Are you suggesting we don't speak at all?"

Olek nodded. "That would be best."

Anna gasped. Her eyes widened. "Do you mean to tell me that we are sleeping with enemies tonight? They could kill us in our sleep."

Katarina shivered as a chill passed through her. "Dear God, keep us safe," she breathed. A Bible passage came to her as she exited the sleigh. "Anna, Psalm twenty-three. King David talked about setting a table in the presence of his enemies."

Anna stared up at the open sky and blinked several times. "That's it, Kat. Food. Food is always the answer." She turned to the maid. "Alyona, bring some sausages and a jar of Kvass and some pickles. These locals won't kill us after we pamper their stomachs."

GRUSHKA AND PYLYP POLYSCHCHUK beamed at their tired guests as they trudged into the two-room house with their traveling bags. The tiny, wiry woman tied a black kerchief with embroidered red roses over her gray bun while directing Anna towards the master bed in the only separate room.

"You sleep until supper is ready," Grushka ordered.

"Toilet?" Anna asked while rubbing her baby bump. The wrinkled old woman gave a yellow-toothed smile and pointed outside. Anna groaned and grabbed Katarina's arm. "Come with me."

"We'll be in the barn." The corners of the little man's beady black eyes crinkled as he directed them around the corner to the outhouse and beckoned the others to follow him.

"They seem friendly enough," Anna whispered as she entered the dilapidated wooden shack. Upon seeing the hole in the muddy ground marked by a simple wooden frame, she groaned. "What I wouldn't give for my toilet box right now."

"Surely, they have a chamber pot inside. This is disgusting." Katarina peeked in, then stepped back to give Anna privacy. "Olek said they're separatists. Does that mean they're following Makhno?" She shivered and rubbed her arms.

"That's a scary thought." The thin door slapped behind Anna. "Hold your nose when you go in." She cleaned her hands on her coat.

Katarina shrugged. "It is what it is, I suppose. I only hope we don't get robbed. Or worse. If they find out that we're Mennonites, they'll assume we're friends of the Czar. We won't stand a chance." She squatted over the hole, carefully sidestepping the questionable muddy perimeter. "You're right. This toilet — if we can call it that — is beyond disgusting. We should use a tree next time."

"A tree? In the middle of the open steppes! Now, that would be nice! I'll pray for one for tomorrow. Maybe it will magically appear," Anna scoffed, then became more serious. "Speaking of prayer, Kat, listen. We must pray for protection tonight. I realize I'm rather useless in my condition. And I need to sleep. So, I'm putting you in charge. Do whatever you must do to keep us safe."

"I'll do my best." While Anna waddled back to the house, Katarina strode to the small, attached barn.

Olek, Alyona, and the elderly couple were selecting straw bales to use as furniture and beds. Olek gave a firm kick to each side of one. "There they go," he chuckled, as several mice scurried out.

Katarina laughed out loud at the tiny mammals zipping across the dirt floor, but then quickly palmed her mouth to keep herself from speaking.

"God has chosen our entertainment for tonight," Alyona guffawed.

"Ni," Grushka exclaimed. "I don't want them inside. They'll eat the vegetables."

"Don't you have cats?" Alyona asked, looking around the barn.

Grushka jerked her chin to the loft. "Tak. But he doesn't like them in the house."

Later, as the bales warmed near the cookstove, two more mice wriggled out of the bales and ran across the floor. Pylyp grumbled, "Grushka, you get your wish for tomorrow. One cat, but only one."

Awakened by the chatter but oblivious to the goings-on, Anna stumbled out of the master bedroom, still half asleep. She nonchalantly picked up a glass from the kitchen table and went to the water barrel and filled it. Then, she shuffled over to an empty straw bale, sat down on the edge, and took a sip from her glass. At that moment, a mouse dropped from her skirt and streaked across the floor. Anna let out an ear-splitting squeal and jumped to her feet — sending the glass sailing across the room. It shattered against the coal-fired cookstove.

At seeing the mouse, Katarina also jumped up and shrieked. The animal disappeared inside another bale. She froze and stared wide-eyed at the floor, unsure of how to move or where to go to. Laughter broke out around the room.

Pylyp slapped his thin legs and stomped his feet, his wrinkled face lighting up with a wide, brown tooth grin revealing several broken teeth. "Haven't you seen a mouse before? You must be prissy city girls!" He roared and pointed a crooked finger at them. "Tomorrow, I go to the *pab* and tell my friends."

Anna's face flushed, and she slowly sank back on the bale. But on touching it, she immediately stood up again. She stayed standing there, looking back and forth between the straw and the floor while pleading to Katarina with her eyes.

Poor Anna. She'll never live this down. As she recovered from her fright, Katarina covered her mouth with her hands and giggled. If the circumstances were different, she'd join in the teasing. But they weren't supposed to attract attention now, and she didn't want to embarrass her sister further.

As Anna's color returned to normal, she shook out her coat, spread it out on the straw bale and slowly eased down. She sat in a ladylike pose, prim and proper, with her back straight, her skirts perfectly spread, and her ankles crossed. Katarina held her breath. Between her sister's mannerisms and the embroidered clothing and bags, their status as *kulaks* was far too obvious.[1] If the elderly couple hadn't figured out their social status yet, they would soon. Katarina glanced at the old man to see if he'd noticed.

A leering grin floated across Pylyp's face while he sucked on his pipe and blew smoke rings in the air. A chill traveled down Katarina's spine. *I hope he doesn't say anything to his friends before we're gone. God forbid rebels or soldiers hunt us down.* Katarina took a deep breath and exhaled while biting her bottom lip. *Dear God, please don't let this salty-mouthed man expose us.*

Katarina tried to catch Alyona's eye, hoping the maid would jump to their defense, but she'd begun helping their hostess in the kitchen.

While Alyona mixed the bread dough on the little blue wooden table, Grushka prepared soup from potatoes, carrots, onions, and Anna's gift of sausage and pickles. She examined the meat with a critical eye and sniffed it. "From the Mennonites?" she whispered to Alyona. "This is so hard to find. And it's expensive." She scrutinized her guests. "Where are you from?"

"I grew up on the other side of the river, near the island."

"You don't say! Once when I was a child, I saw the famous old oak tree. Is it still there?"

"Tak. Tall and proud. As stately as ever. My family loved to picnic there."

"The land of the fighting Cossacks." Pylyp bellowed from his rocking chair. He sucked on his pipe, blew out a smoke circle then stabbed at it with the stem. "Our ancestors. We had this land first before Russia and the Mennonites stole it from us."

"Tak." Grushka added water to the soup pot. "But one day soon, the steppes will be ours again and we will decide who comes in and goes out." She leaned towards Alyona and whispered, "Can you believe it? We may live long enough to see it happen. Ukraine is a country now."

"Maybe so. But violence on the steppes continues. I want peace to come. When I was a child ..." Alyona changed the subject to her childhood memories. From that point on, she skillfully controlled the conversation, weaving animated details of her personal family life around Grushka and Pylyp's vain attempts to talk politics.

Katarina had never seen this talkative side of the elderly

maid before, nor had she heard Alyona speak about her personal life. She caught Anna's eye, and they both raised their eyebrows at the same time. The tales were obviously new to her sister, too.

During Alyona's colorful storytelling, Grushka poured the beet *kvass*[2] into a dented tin pot and set it on the coal-fired cookstove to warm. When steam rose from the pot, Katarina became alarmed. Everyone knew fermented juice shouldn't be boiled. But the women seemed to be ignoring it. She wondered whether she should interrupt them or take the pot off the heat herself. Would they see her as rude if she did? Or privileged if she didn't? Then, just as she raised a finger in the air to say something, Alyona leaped into action with one fell swoop. She ripped the crocheted potholders from the wall hook and deftly nabbed the pot from the heat. Katarina exhaled.

The maid set the handle-less pot on the small table under the window, retrieved four cups from the three open kitchen shelves beside the stove, and poured the beverage into an unmatched assortment of cups and glasses. Then she frowned and returned to the shelving to retrieve another. But there weren't any more.

Katarina noticed the problem and was about to offer to share a cup with her sister, but then remembered the threat to their safety. She clamped her lips between her teeth, sat on her hands, and curled her fists around the straw.

Alyona solved the dilemma with a small yellow ceramic bowl with ears. She filled it with juice and brought it to Pylyp. He grunted, removed the pipe from his mouth, tapped it on the arm of the chair, and stuck it in his vest pocket before accepting the drink. Alyona stood in front of him, waiting until he'd taken the first sip. He slurped noisily, then winked at her. Alyona nodded and returned to the kitchen.

Katarina's heart sank. First, Anna's prissiness was too

obvious to overlook, and now Alyona had slipped into a servant role. *We can't hide much longer. They'll throw us out on the streets if they find out that we're wealthy Mennonites. I must do something.*

She jumped up and scurried to the table, grabbed the two smaller cups, and served her sister before plunking down beside Anna. She put her feet on the straw bale and drew her knees to her chest in tom-boy style. The position exposed her long undergarments, but she didn't care. Her legs were well covered. There was nothing for the old man to gawk at.

But Anna cocked her head disapprovingly and flashed her eyes at Katarina's legs. Katarina grimaced and shifted into a crossed-leg position and yanked her dress over her ankles. She checked Grushka and Pylyp's faces for a reaction, but their attention was on Alyona's storytelling. Katarina relaxed, sipped on the warm juice, and listened to the chummy bantering.

Alyona's friendliness with the couple concerned her. The maid was giving too much personal information to these strangers and siding with their politics. Katarina recalled Regier saying that even the most loyal of servants would turn-coat at the last minute to save their own skin. Anna had insisted her servants were loyal to the death. Katarina wasn't convinced. If the evening turned sour and Makhno's bandits suddenly burst in, would Alyona protect them, scatter, or side with the enemy? It was impossible to predict. She'd have to keep a close eye on the maid. If they had to flee quickly, they'd do so with or without Alyona. Preferably with.

Katarina slid back on the straw bale to lean her head against the wall and stretched out her legs. Anna sat on the bale beside her, with her head back, her eyes closed, and her hands cupping her baby bump. Katarina watched her sister's stomach rise and fall with each labored breath. Who was she kidding? They couldn't run anywhere by themselves. Whether the servants could be trusted or not, they were both needed for every step of this dangerous journey.

Her eyes drifted to their garment bags. Everything precious was in those few bags, including their grandmother's gold locket with the diamond inset. But the item's sentimental value was worth more. If it vanished, the entire family would blame her for not protecting it. Katarina decided that, after everyone was asleep, she'd slip it on underneath her blouse and keep it there until they were safe.

Grushka interrupted her musings. "And what about you ladies? Did you grow up on the river, too?"

"Tak." Katarina nodded.

"Our mothers knew each other from the annual harvest festival." Alyona jumped in before Katarina said more. "We've been family for as long as I can remember. I can tell stories about their young lives, too."

Katarina cringed and stared at the floor so they wouldn't see her eyes widen. The maid's white lies were more than just a little. Alyona had been a servant with David's family for decades. But she hadn't known *their* family, the Rempels. And she doubted Alyona knew her mother at all.

"And did both your families work for the Mennonites?" Grushka asked a second time.

Katarina slowly nodded, but her stomach tightened. The old woman was probing, looking for family connections, guessing at their identities.

Once again, Alyona answered, scoffing, "Doesn't everyone? They own all the big factories and half the land."

Then Katarina realized Alyona was deliberately interrupting, telling stories, and lying to protect the sisters and keep them from speaking. She'd taken Olek's warning of danger seriously. And Katarina's heart towards the servant softened.

But Grushka glared at Katarina with one eyebrow raised and her lips twisted sideways. The woman sensed something was off. Katarina returned Grushka's suspicious look with a stiff smile. But her conscience niggled. She'd been taught that not correcting someone when they were wrong was agreeing with a lie. And that was wrong. Katarina gritted her teeth and prayed for forgiveness.

1 Kulaks were a wealthy peasant class. Collectivization involved elimination of these farms and their owners. See http://www.encyclopediaofukraine.com/display.asp?linkpath=pages%5CK%5CU%5CKulak.htm

2 Beet kvass: A fermented beverage made from beetroots.

12

POLITICS

THE OUTSIDE DOOR OPENED, AND A BLAST OF ICY AIR followed Olek as he stomped in and shook the snow off his boots. He greeted the group while removing his winter outerwear and rubber galoshes, keeping the *valenki* on. The boots' felt liners doubled as warm slippers on the chilly plank flooring. He shuffled to the cast iron stove and warmed his hands before accepting the bowl of soup and two chunks of bread from Grushka. Standing with his back to the sisters, he ate and conversed casually with the others.

Katarina felt insulted that both servants were deliberately ignoring them. But the elderly couple interrogated Olek, just as they had Alyona. Katarina sensed a conspiracy afoot. The back of her arms tingled. It was only a matter of time before they were discovered.

"Where did you grow up?" Pylyp asked Olek.

"Moskov. Near the factories. Then, I went east to the coal mines until I made enough money to go to university here in Aleksandrovsk. I worked in the factories in Schoenwiese while I studied."

Katarina noticed Olek guarding the truth and twisting the facts just enough to make them acceptable to the separatists.

"So, you're a Russian," Pylyp declared. "And an intelligentsia at that." He spat on the floor. "Are you supporting the imperialists or the Bolsheviks?"

Olek laughed. "Everyone comes from somewhere, Pylyp. I've lived in many regions. I have two sides, or maybe three or even four."

Tension built in Katarina's chest. The conversation was going downhill fast. If they started arguing about politics, anything could happen.

Pylyp grunted and pointed to the floor. "This is Ukraine. The land belongs to those born here. Not to some bureaucrats in Petrograd or Moskov."

"Then what should I do?" Olek answered. "Do I leave and move back to a country I no longer know? This is my home now. I've been here for twenty years."

Pylyp jerked his index finger in the air. "Then you must join the fight to push Russia out of our country. They have no right to this land anymore. As of 22 January 1918, Ukraine is independent. Russia must leave."

"Tak. But a mother bear doesn't leave her cubs."

"The cub has grown up. Mother Russia must back away and let Ukraine fend for itself."

Grushka summoned Katarina and Anna to eat. But there were only two chairs in the room. Olek and Alyona refused to sit and offered the chairs to the sisters. "Let the mother-to-be take the chair," Olek said. But Anna scrutinized the eating utensils before sipping the soup in proper fashion from the edge of her spoon. Grushka's eyes narrowed. The hair on the back of Katarina's neck rose. But the woman said nothing.

Olek and Pylyp bantered peacefully while the evening progressed with Olek deftly sidestepping the politics. His savvy answers amazed Katarina — especially since he'd earlier cautioned them not to engage in such discussions. "War is a deadly endgame," he said. "Blood is being spilled for no other reason than differences in opinion." The rowdy debate between the two men made it impossible for anyone else to interject or even speak. For the first time that evening, Katarina was thankful to be ignored.

"I'll get your beds ready," Alyona whispered to Katarina during a momentary lull in the discourse. "Go with Anna to the outhouse." She jerked her chin at Anna who was pulling on her coat.

Olek escorted them outside. "Everything is going well," he assured them both. "Get some rest and I'll see you at daybreak."

"I'm going crazy listening to all that nonsense," Anna said from behind the wooden barrier. "And we can't even leave or send them to another room. How can people live like this — in such a tiny space? And I can't understand half of what they're saying. Their dialect is too difficult for me."

"Personally, I find it very hard to stay silent," Katarina said as she took her turn over the muddy hole. "I find the subject fascinating."

"But we can't speak," Anna insisted. "It could get us in trouble."

"This will all be over in a few hours," Katarina reassured her. "We can get through this."

When they returned, the elder women had moved the bales closer to the stove, untied the twine, and made sleeping piles from the straw. Grushka shooed away another two mice and smiled a tobacco-stained grin at Anna. "Here," she said in Ukrainian, "good enough to have a baby."

Katarina thanked Grushka with a nod and a smile. Their accommodations were simple, but under the circumstances, there were no other options.

Anna sighed loudly. Then she frowned and shook her head

slowly. Katarina smiled sympathetically, understanding the problem. There was no bedding. The servants hadn't retrieved the quilts because Olek was sleeping in the freezing cold sleigh tonight. He'd need the extra layers. Evidently, the couple didn't have any to spare.

"We can use our coats as blankets," Katarina whispered in Anna's ear. "At least we're inside where it's warm."

Alyona cleared her throat as Grushka pulled out a metal pail from behind the stove and set it beside their straw beds. "Here," the woman said. "Your toilet for tonight."

Anna blanched and whispered into Katarina's ear. "Is there no decent chamber pot? The outhouse was bad enough. The rags weren't even clean."

Katarina returned a dirty stare and bit her lips between her teeth before answering. Then she palmed her mouth and whispered, "I hope you didn't use those. You can't risk an infection."

"I couldn't use my hands. There's no soap to wash. And the water in the basin outside is frozen." Anna spoke out loudly in Low German. "And I have to go again."

The old man in the rocking chair startled at Anna's outburst, raised his fist in the air and pointed at them. "I knew it. I knew something was off from the minute you walked in the door. You are Jews. Grushka, we have Jews in our house."

Anna paled, realizing her mistake. She burst into tears, plunked down in the straw bed, and buried her face in her hands.

"Nepravda, nepravda," Alyona argued. "Not true, not true." She looked sympathetically at Anna and shook her head from side to side.

The room went dead silent as three sets of eyes turned to stare at the sisters. Katarina blanched. She had to save the situation and beg for mercy. *Tell the truth.* She burst out in fluent Ukrainian. "We are Mennonites from Halbstadt. The Bolsheviks are burning our town. We are peacemakers, not warmongers." She cringed as the last sentence left her mouth. She hadn't meant to imply that others were seeking violence, only that the Mennonites didn't do so.

Surprise and distrust registered on the couple's faces. Pylyp's eyes narrowed, and his mouth twitched. He took the pipe out of his shirt pocket and sucked on it while studying them.

"Olek and I are helping the sisters," Alyona said quickly. "The pregnant one isn't well."

Please don't throw us out in this cold, stormy weather. We'll freeze to death. Katarina squeezed her eyes shut and prayed for wisdom.

Anna threw on her coat, pulled on her boots, and walked out of the house. Katarina assumed she was heading for the toilet. She'd likely speak to Olek on the way.

What was it that David had said before he left for the war? "Everyone has a price." What was this couple's price? Katarina considered the jewelry in her bag. Should she offer something? No, it was too soon. She flexed her fists and scratched her fingernails with her thumbs, waiting for the proverbial shoe to drop.

"Let me guess," Pylyp continued. "You're married to rich men. This is your ledi-in-waiting," he pointed to Alyona.

"Ni," Alyona exclaimed loudly. "They're not that fancy. Don't be imagining things that aren't so."

"Who else would hire an educated coachman?" Pylyp argued. "Only the guilty rich run and hide." He paused and tapped his fingers on the armchair. "Who are you? Tell me now. If I find out you're related to the Czar ..." Pylyp sneered at them. "You're worth a lot of money. Dead or alive."

Katarina felt the blood drain from her face and her hands went ice cold. "Nay. We have no royal connections. We're

Mennonites, I tell you the truth. Simple farmers. We have no interest in trouble."

The door opened and a frigid draft announced Anna's return from the outhouse. She wiped her boots on the rag rug and staggered to the straw bed without removing them.

Grushka pointed at Anna. "Pylyp. Enough already. Can't you see there's a sick woman here? Let them spend the night as planned."

"Grushka. If we're caught harboring enemies, we're dead." Pylyp stood up and wiggled his finger at the door. "Makhno will kill us all. It's not safe. They should leave now."

Grushka waved her hand at her husband. "It's late. Let them sleep a few hours. They can leave at dawn." She plopped down on the wooden chair. "Besides, Makhno's not in town tonight."

"Does it matter? His recruits live down the road. They see everything. For certain, they'll ask questions in the morning. This won't go unnoticed." Pylyp nervously ran his fingers through his thinning salt and pepper hair.

Anna took off her coat and patted the straw bed, checking for mice. She lay down, covered herself with her coat, and wrapped her arms around her swollen belly. Perspiration beaded on her forehead.

"Is all well?" Katarina swept her hand over Anna's face. "There's no fever, thank God. Anna, your frequent toileting has me worried. We should find a doctor or an herbalist. I think you need help."

"I know I do," Anna whimpered. "But we're in a bad place now. I'll pray for tomorrow."

Grushka and Alyona hovered nearby, their faces etched with concern. The maid turned to their host. "She needs herbs. Do you have any to sell?"

The older woman nodded, held out her hand, and wiggled her fingers. Alyona went to Anna and whispered in her ear.

Anna pulled a note from her moneybelt and gave it to the maid, who immediately passed it to Grushka. After examining the cash, the woman tucked it into her skirt. Grushka crawled under the table and pushed aside the rag rug covering the trapdoor to the dirt cellar and pulled it open. She climbed down, re-emerging a minute later with a box of jars filled with varying hues of green and gray leafy powders.

With a loud grunt, Grushka heaved the box onto the wooden chair, then pulled herself upright. Holding each jar up to the dim light of the coal oil lamp, she scrutinized the labels and set aside three from the group. She grabbed a spoon from the table and scooped two spoonfuls of dried herbs from each container into a small empty jar. After stirring the mixture together, she sealed the glass and handed it to Katarina. "For your sister. To help with passing her water. Five times a day."

"Are you an herbalist?" Katarina asked, surprised.

Grushka snorted. "Old women and pregnant ones have the same problems. The remedy is the same." Then she retrieved the pot of simmering water from the stove and prepared some herbal tea.

Katarina pondered the miracle of quiet coincidences. She thanked Grushka profusely and went to pack the jar in her duffel. But as she did so, Pylyp barked from his chair in the corner. "Not so fast, young ledi. There's a price for that. Nothing's for free. Not even your life."

Katarina froze and sucked in her breath. Of course, nothing could be this simple. But Anna had already paid. What else did he want? Her heart dropped into her stomach. She straightened up, hugged the jar to her chest, and pivoted on her heel to meet Pylyp's sneering grin. "Of course, sir. We expect nothing for free. But my sister already paid your wife."

"With Kerenkas — Russian money. Not the type of cash we want to see around here." He jerked his chin at Grushka. "Now we know you are German scum. Friends of the enemies. You risk our lives by your very presence. The usual price doesn't apply."

Katarina swallowed and tightened her grip on the jar. Her heart thumped wildly in her chest. "We appreciate the hospitality and the compassion that you've shown us this cold night, Pylyp Polyschchuk. You've kept us from freezing to death on the open road. And we're grateful for these herbs that will make my sister comfortable until we reach our destination. Although she's not dying — these wouldn't save her life if she was. So, she can live without them. We can do without this generous help. However, you ..." *Be careful what you say, Katarina.* She straightened her shoulders and glared at the man straight on, unblinking. *Whatever I give you won't spare your life if Makhno shows up.* "You are a kind and honorable man who does not wish to see a woman and her unborn child suffer. If Anna was your daughter, I'm sure you'd do everything to ease her pain."

"I have no daughter." Pylyp averted his gaze to the coal oil lamp. Grushka slid onto the chair and stared down at the table — a sad expression on her face.

Intuitively, Katarina sensed she touched on a sore spot in the couple's lives. She wondered if they'd once had one or were disappointed because they didn't.

Pylyp broke the awkward silence and looked back at Katarina. "I want more sausage and kvass. Enough to last the winter."

Sausage. He's settling for sausage. But Kvass? Katarina stared at him, dumbfounded by the comment. Kvass was easy to come by. Beets were a staple in every Russian household. They wintered well in the dark root cellars, and the drink was easily prepared in a few days. However, the demand for sausage was understandable. The meat was a specialty item available only from the Mennonite farms and village butchers.

Every year, at the regional harvest festivals, farmers

competed for the best sausage. Unique smoking methods and secret blends of herbs and spices made for stiff competition and plenty of gossip. The Rempels had won the blue ribbon three years in a row. As far as Katarina was concerned, their family's sausage was the very best. Although David and Anna's family recipe was almost as good.

Since they'd only brought a few rings with them on this trip, Pylyp's arrogant request was practically thievery as far as she was concerned. Her blood ran cold, and she gritted her teeth. This situation was eerily reminiscent of her accident with the black stallion during Anna and David's wedding. After lighting the flour mill, the raiders looted all the hams and sausages from their parents' smokehouse.

Sausage meat had been scarce that year until the slaughtering time arrived in the autumn. Her family had been shame-faced — accepting charity from the neighbors and buying meat from the local butcher — like common city folk. But it never tasted the same as her parents' sausage.

But today was not about something that happened three years ago. This was about Anna's comfort and safety. So, Katarina looked at Alyona and jerked her chin at the door. "Alyona, please talk to Olek. Pylyp wants sausage for the winter. Did we bring enough to feed him? I'd hate to see these people starve to death after all the kindness they've shown us."

"Tak." Alyona retrieved her felt valenki from beside the stove and pulled them on. Skirting past Anna, she slipped out into the dark night.

Grushka poured a cup of herbal tea and handed it to Katarina. "Here. Wake up your sister. She needs to drink this."

Katarina jostled her sister's shoulder. "Anna. Here. You need to drink."

"No. I want to sleep. No drinking. I don't want to pee anymore."

Katarina poked her again and shoved the tea under her sister's nose. "Anna, please. You'll get sicker if you don't. This is medicine. It will help."

Anna groaned, opened her eyes, and sat up. "What makes you so sure? The old woman's probably trying to kill us."

"Just drink it. It's the only medicine we have. Grushka gave us enough for the rest of the trip. It will help until we get to Mutter and Papa's."

Anna sighed and obediently gulped the tea. Then she lay down and went back to sleep.

"It won't work right away," Grushka said sympathetically. "She'll be uncomfortable for a few more days. But it will help."

Katarina prayed the concoction would work quickly. Anna's time was much too close for comfort.

Alyona returned with a jar and a package wrapped in a towel. Olek trailed behind her. "I'm so sorry, Pylyp." Olek apologized as he removed his sheepskin mittens and rubbed his hands. "We neglected to plan for our friends. We didn't expect to be gone for more than a day or two and we've barely enough to feed ourselves. But I want to give you a special gift so you can remember us. In case we meet again."

Katarina rolled her eyes. *God forbid we meet again.*

A broken tooth flashed behind Pylyp's yellow-stained grin. He eagerly accepted the package and ripped it open; then closed his eyes and sniffed the smoky meat. "Olek, my dear friend. How generous of you. Of course, I'll help you. Your friends are welcome to spend the night here by my warm stove. And you, too, if you wish."

Olek nodded, "I'm grateful for your generosity, Pylyp Polyschchuk, my dear friend. And your lovely wife, Grushka.

May her beauty never leave. It's my honor to be here. I wish I could do more to repay you."

While the fake niceties continued, Katarina spread her coat on the straw bale beside Anna and curled up. As her eyes closed, sleep washed over her and the voices in the room blurred into a distant hum.

13

HEIDI

1952 DECEMBER. MUNICH.

HEIDI STARED AT THE SIX EMPTY BEER BOTTLES ON THE floor beside her husband who was slouching on the couch. "Peter, I thought you were working on exam papers today. Have you finished?"

Clink, clink, clink. Peter tapped a metal object against the beer stein.

Heidi inhaled deeply, crossed her arms over her chest, and clicked her heel on the floor. "Peter, please don't be rude to me."

He untangled the strand wrapped around his palm and held it up. An antique heart-shaped locket on a gold chain dropped and dangled in the air.

Heidi softened her stance and walked up to the couch to study the pendant with the tiny sparkling diamond inset. "It's gorgeous. But it looks expensive. How could you afford this?" She stretched out her palm.

Peter chuckled and pulled the locket away in a deliberate

tease. "Don't worry. I didn't buy it. This was Mutter's neck-lace. It was inside the box of diaries."

"You've never mentioned it before." Heidi put her hands on her hips, enviously eyeing the item. "Why are you playing with it? You're supposed to be working."

"I'd forgotten about it. I found it when you were away at the Christmas market." Peter re-wrapped the chain around his hand. "And now I'm just thinking."

Heidi pursed her lips and pointed to the mess on the floor. "Drinking and thinking, by the looks of it. That's not a good combination. You told me you were busy this weekend marking exams for the professor. That's why we couldn't accept my sister's invitation to dinner."

"I got side-tracked." Peter rubbed the locket with his thumb.

"I'll say. When will you get the work done? Doesn't the professor need the results by Monday?"

"I'll get to it. I still have tomorrow." He raised the glass in a salute.

"Please don't be obnoxious." Heidi jutted her chin at the ceiling and exhaled loudly through her mouth. "Listen, Peter. If you don't get this done today, then you'll be cramming tomorrow. It will take you all day and night and you'll be in a miserable mood. That will make both of us unhappy."

Heidi sat down in the pink wing chair beside the couch and angled herself to face her husband more directly. "I don't know what's going on with you lately. You've been a jerk for weeks. You're treating me like I'm a sack of garbage and you're drinking constantly. Talk to me, please. We can't go on like this."

Peter set the stein on the doily-covered end table. He glanced sideways at his wife, then glared at the box of files at his feet and grimaced. "I know. You're right. I should be working."

"What's put you down in the dumps again?" Heidi crossed her legs and clasped her hands in her lap. Tick, tick, tick. She watched the second hand sweep around the face of the wall clock. Peter was taking much too long to answer. Then, she scrubbed at her cuticles, contemplating her next words, and wondering how best to motivate him. "Listen, my love. In a few months, we'll be parents. But if you're not interested in being a papa, tell me now. I'll go move in with my sister before I'm too big to do so."

Her threat produced an immediate reaction. Peter jolted upright, and he looked directly at her. Shock registered on his face. "No. No. It's not you, Heidi. It's not the baby. I'm just under a lot of pressure at work right now. Can't I take a day to drink and free my thoughts?"

"Drinking solves nothing. If you keep this up, you'll have more problems. Talking is a much better solution. So, speak, please. I'm begging you. I'll sit here and listen all day if you need me to." Heidi massaged her palms. She didn't really want to listen to him all day, but if it helped, she would.

Peter unwrapped the necklace again and twirled the heart-shaped locket in the air. "Something's nagging at me about the day I found this and the diaries. They were just lying there on a rock in plain sight. I'm missing something. My memories seem confused."

"Peter, stop making so much out of this. After the war, everyone in Munich worked together to clean up the rubble. When we found important stuff, we set it aside to be marked and collected. It just happened that *you found* your mother's things." Heidi sat back and frowned. "Peter, don't do this to yourself."

"Do what?"

"Over-analyze things. It will only depress you more."

"No, Heidi. Listen to me. Just for a minute. I'd forgotten about the locket. When you were away at the Christmas market, I opened the box, and there it was. I tried to remember the last time I saw Mutter wearing it. I couldn't. She mentioned it in this diary. It was her grandmother's." Peter passed a hand through his light chestnut hair.

"Uh-huh. I thought we agreed you'd put those stories away. Concentrate on more important matters. Like work."

Peter waved his hand. "I know. I know. But Heidi, the box wasn't there one minute and the next it was."

"You're reading too much into this, my love. Obviously, a volunteer found the box. Peter, you *were* searching for your belongings. What did you expect to find? Nothing? Be thankful you weren't home when the bombs landed. You're lucky to be alive." Heidi tugged at the waist of her floral dress and sighed. Her clothes were getting too tight, but the new maternity outfit she'd bought at the Christmas market was still too loose. Should she add more elastic to the oversized skirt, or buy another one?

"Kaboom!" Peter bellowed and made an explosive gesture with his hands.

The sudden outburst threw Heidi back in her seat. Her heart raced. "Peter! Don't scare me like that!"

"Sorry, I was just making a point."

"Then make it. I don't have all day." Heidi screwed up her face. "Stop being such a child."

"I'm no child. I protected the Fatherland and helped fight Hitler's enemies. That was naïve of me, but not childish. If I'd gone to Russia with Mum, maybe she'd still be alive."

"You had your job, Peter. She had hers. Stop with the what ifs. You can't change history." She blew out a long, loud sigh. "This melodrama of yours is becoming tiresome."

"But think about this, Heidi. Katarina left with the army in '42. But if she went AWOL and melted into the background when Germany left Ukraine in '43, maybe the boxes and the locket are a sign that she's alive but can't show herself.

She could be walking around in plain sight right now, watching us." He pointed to the window.

"Oh, for crying out loud, Peter!" Heidi's jaw dropped and she stared at her husband in disbelief. "Are we seriously back to this? Wondering if Katarina is still alive? Like she's some spy in hiding? And you're wishing you were back in Russia? Stupid fantasies, Peter. *Stupid.* If your mother was alive, she'd have let you know. And if you try to go back to Russia, Stalin will throw you in the camps. Don't be ridiculous."

"No, Heidi. Don't worry." Peter waved his hand in the air. "I have no intention of risking my life. But I'm positive she went back to Ukraine to search for Jacob. I want to know what happened there. There must be a way to find out. I'm reading the diaries for clues. Names, dates, places, that kind of thing." Peter cocked his head and gazed at her with an earnest and innocent expression.

Heidi tried to ignore the little-boy look that made her want to wrap her arms around him and soothe his troubled soul. At the same time, she wanted to slap his face. "You're driving yourself crazy with these what-ifs, my love. Look, the government says she died in the war. You're one of the lucky ones to have documented proof. Many don't. It's supposed to help you find closure. So accept it and move on."

"I suppose. But my mother was a survivor. Every time something bad happened, she made it through. The revolution, the civil war, the Great War ... why wouldn't she make it through this one, too? She could get through anything." Peter flicked the gold locket back and forth in his hand, tracing the monogram on the back with his fingers.

"So, you want to know how she died? Why torture yourself with that information? What if her commanding officer shot her in the back? Would you want to know that? Or if she did something terrible under the war crimes act? That would be an even worse detail. Let it go, Peter. You're

driving yourself insane. It's best not to know those things."
Heidi gritted her teeth. Peter's brooding was making her
crazy.

Peter rubbed the gold heart between his fingers and
clicked on the catch. It opened to reveal two sepia photos. He
stared at them for a minute, then stood up and walked over to
Heidi, and gave her the locket. "Pictures of my great-grandparents, I believe."

Heidi accepted the necklace and examined the photos.
"You think? You don't know? Then, how do you know for
certain it was Katarina's necklace?"

Peter pointed at the pictures. "Oh, it's hers alright. I
remember her wearing it. And her initials are on the back.
Well, not hers, exactly. The grandmother she was named after.
That's how they did it then. They named everyone after
someone else in the family. And every family had a Katharina
or a variation of that name."

"Why?" She turned the locket over and examined the
exquisite engraving. It would make a great family heirloom.
And the stories about old family jewelry made for entertaining conversations. She itched to know this tale.

"Katharina die Grosse — Catherine the Great — was so
highly revered for giving the land to the Mennonites, that —
from that point on — most families named a daughter after
her."

Heidi bit her bottom lip and gave her husband a flirtatious
smile. "So, if we have a girl, is that what you want to name
her?"

Peter's face flickered with a dampened smile, acknowl-
edging her flirt. "No ... I don't know. But I'd like to carry on
some type of tradition. Name her or him after someone in
our family. And I don't want some weird modern version. I
want the old-fashioned kind."

"Well, that's fine with me. Do you have something in

mind?" She leaned back and brushed back the blond strands from her eyes.

"Not yet. It's still too early. I want to think about it for a while." He picked up the stein and took another sip. "And don't worry. I won't allow this to become a habit."

"Well, it had better not. It's an expensive vice. And we'll need to be frugal when I quit working." Heidi unpinned her hair and finger-combed the golden locks before twirling them in her hand and re-pinning them into a bun. "I want to be a good mum and raise my children properly."

Peter sighed as he drained the stein. "Ja. Children. More than one. We need more money. More pressure."

Heidi handed the locket back to him. "Do you want to sell the necklace?"

He looked up, horrified. "Good grief, no. I could never do that. It's a family heirloom. I want you to have it. Change the pictures if you like. One day, you can give it to our daughter. Or in-law. Whichever you choose."

Heidi blinked. "Whatever I choose? Don't you want to be part of that discussion?"

"If you want me to." Peter shrugged again and scratched his chin.

"Of course, I want you to." Heidi hated it when Peter was so noncommittal. Why couldn't he just say yes or no? Or be more affectionate?

Peter got up from the couch and walked over. He put the locket in her hand and kissed her forehead. "It's yours. Do what you want with it. Consider it an early Christmas present."

"Thank you, my love. I'll wear it proudly." Heidi grinned and opened the clasp, then fastened the chain around her neck and patted the heart against her chest. "It's beautiful. I'll take good care of it."

"It looks nice on you. It's a lovely piece of history. Mutter would want you to have it. You're right. It's time I let go of a few things." His face lit up with an approving smile.

Heidi toyed with the locket and suddenly thought about Peter's sister. It felt wrong accepting an expensive piece of jewelry that rightfully belonged to someone else. "Are you sure it shouldn't go to Marta? She's the rightful heir."

"I doubt she'll mind. If it makes you feel better, I'll write her and ask. But I think she'll appreciate the diaries more. After I've transcribed them, and when I've saved up enough money to travel to Canada, then I'll bring them to her." His face brightened with a sad smile. "But by then, we'll probably both be old. With grandchildren." He picked up a file, opened it, then closed it and returned it to the pile.

"Let's hope not. I'd love to meet her before I'm too old." Heidi rose from the chair. "I'm putting the kettle on. Would you like a cup of tea?"

"No, thanks." Peter appraised the empty beer bottles on the floor, then got up and strode to the storage closet to retrieve a cardboard box. After cramming the bottles into it, he rearranged them several times until they fit, then carried the container to the door. "I need to discard these." He said while combing through the closet. "Where are my shoes?"

"You can't leave now. You have work to do." Heidi put her hands on her hips. "Stop procrastinating."

"Since when are you my mother?" Peter re-entered the room and glared at her. "If I don't clean this up now, you'll be nagging about it later."

Heidi pointed to the couch. "Back to work, now! If I must act like your mother to get you to finish your work, I'll do it. You'll thank me tomorrow."

Peter threw his hands in the air. "Fine. You win. Anything to get some peace around here." He strode back to the couch and picked up a file. "I'm working now. Are you happy?"

Heidi studied her husband from across the room. He

flicked through the files, grumbling to himself while making red marks on the pages.

She dropped two tea bags in the teapot and stood beside the stove, waiting for the kettle to boil. When it did, she added water to the pot and stirred the tea until it had steeped to a light caramel color, then poured a cup and carried it to the wing chair. "Peter, what else is bothering you? You're not being very open. I feel like I'm pulling words out of your mouth today. I know it's not just the necklace. And it's not just Katarina's diaries. What are you not telling me? Please. I'm an adult. You don't have to protect me. Talk to me."

Peter stared at a blank space on the far wall and sucked on his lower lip. "I don't like my job. There, I said it."

Heidi's mouth dropped open. "What? You don't like your job! You've been there less than a year. Three jobs in five years. Peter! When are you going to find some ground under your feet?"

He shrugged. "I'm bored."

Heidi's heart thumped wildly. *He can't do this to us. Not now.* She took a deep breath and blew it out slowly. "Peter, you can't keep doing this to us. You've studied in half a dozen departments and worked in three of them. You've taken more courses than most professors and have only one degree to show for it. You know the underbelly of that university better than the administration. It's time you stopped bouncing around, set some goals for your life, and stick to them." She swallowed her anger and refocused. "Listen, Peter, I'm sorry I got mad. I love you. But I can't live with this uncertainty. I need stability in my life. And so does our child."

Peter fidgeted with the file in his hand. "You're right. But don't worry about me. I'll figure it out."

"Well, you best figure it out soon. Either you stick with this job and grow with it until it pays better, or move on to one that will. You can't be a research assistant forever. If I'm to stay home and raise our family, we need a predictable and good income. I've already told *The Telekom* that I'll be leaving in the spring." Heidi set the teacup on the end table.

Fear registered on Peter's face. "Family. One income. Some little thing calling me Papa. Do you have any idea how scary this is?"

Heidi slapped the arms of the chair. "For crying out loud, Peter. Don't you think I'm scared? We can't turn the clock back here. We're supposed to be working as a team — you and me. You can't opt out at this stage."

"I know that. You want me to be honest. I'm being honest. I'm afraid that my wages won't be enough." Peter grimaced and his mouth twisted to one side.

Heidi seethed with impatience. "Then do something about it. You're a man, but you're acting like a boy. Buckle up and get to work. Look, I wish you were happy at this job, but you can't take the risk of getting fired. Not now. Look at the prices of things. We can't afford for you to be without work. We must be smart here."

Peter palmed his face and groaned, "I know you're right, Heidi. But I also want to get back into my mother's diary and do more transcribing. I've had little time recently."

"That won't pay the bills." Heidi sat rigid with her eyes wide and her knuckles white as she gripped the arms of the wing chair. Didn't he understand the financial crunch they were facing?

"I know." He shrugged again and avoided her gaze.

Heidi took a deep breath and tried again. "Please, my love. Set that hobby aside. It puts you in a melancholy mood. You dwell too much on things that make you sad. Think more about happy things. Go out for a social evening with your friends."

"Friends? I don't have time for them these days. Except for Reinhart. By the way, he's inviting us over for supper sometime. Would you like to go?" A forced grin spread across his face.

"You've been talking to him about the diaries again, haven't you?" Heidi deliberately evaded his question and fingered the locket around her neck. Even if there was something to Peter's suspicion about Katarina's death, his relationship with the editor was an excuse to wander down never-ending rabbit trails and avoid his more practical responsibilities.

Peter nodded sheepishly. "Well, sort of."

"After you promised that you'd put them away and distance yourself from the past." Heidi set her teacup on the coffee table and turned to face him more directly. "These diaries are ghosts that haunt our relationship. I can't live like this, Peter. We need our own life. When are you going to focus on our happiness?"

"Happiness. Ja. I'm trying to find that elusive pot at the end of the rainbow. There isn't one, though, is there? You know, when I was a boy, I worked at the butcher shop with my Papa. That was a fun time, even though it was hard work. After he died, all I wanted to do was join the Luftwaffe. I thought I could avoid the horrors of war by flying above the clouds. But my injury got in the way. In the end, I saw way too much ugliness. Now, I realize I've been on the losing side of life the whole time and I'm feeling lost." Peter slouched back on the couch.

Heidi sighed. "You're not lost, Peter. Just temporarily confused. You must embrace your responsibilities as a husband and father. The happiness will come later. After the hard work is done. It won't come from a new job or even finding the secrets in your mother's diaries. It certainly won't come from drunkenness." Heidi stood up and tapped the back of the chair. "One finds joy in the little things in life. Like scrubbing my burnt pots or finishing the task ahead of you, like that box of files at your feet. So then, after that, you can get further satisfaction by scrubbing my burnt pots again." She gave Peter a sympathetic smile.

Peter chuckled and pointed to the kitchen. "One of these days, you'll learn to cook a roast properly."

"Ah, and then I'll be happy." Heidi chuckled.

"But only for a while." He wrinkled his nose and gave her the eye.

"There's always sausage." Heidi returned the flirt by running her tongue over her lips.

"Ja. That was Mutter's favorite food."

14

ACROSS THE STEPPES

1918 FEBRUARY (JULIAN CALENDAR). ON THE OPEN STEPPE BETWEEN HALBSTADT AND THE LEFT BANK OF THE DNIEPER RIVER, UKRAINE

A GENTLE TUG ON HER FEET WOKE KATARINA FROM A restless sleep. She opened her eyes to the glare of a flickering oil lamp.

The light framed Alyona in a ghostly silhouette. "It's time to go."

Anna — on the straw bed beside Katarina — stretched her arms and groaned. "What? Are we leaving already?"

Alyona held a cup of herbal tea in front of Anna. "How did you sleep?"

"Surprisingly well. But now I must pass my water." Anna took a couple of sips, then ran over to the night pot.

"What time is it?" Katarina looked at the window across the room. "It's still pitch black."

"We leave before the rebels come. Olek's getting the horses ready. Do your business and then march to the sleigh. Don't waste time." Alyona dusted the straw from Anna's coat.

"Did you make tea for me, too?"

"The samovar's heating on the sleigh. We can have a quick cup while Olek packs up. He's filled the foot-warmers with hot bricks and coals. There was another storm last night. Lots of fresh snow. If it stays cold, we make good time today."

Pylyp's snoring from the tiny bedroom almost drowned out Grushka's whispers as she emerged from behind a second oil lamp. She handed Alyona a loaf of bread and a tiny package of salt. "Here. Sustenance for the journey. May you find safety today."

Alyona gave Grushka an affectionate hug and a kiss on both cheeks. "Thank you for everything."

After they said goodbye to their hostess, the three women walked out into the freezing cold.

IN THE ALMOST WINDLESS pre-dawn dark, the full moon peeked through the clouds and lit up the snow-covered stubbled fields and rutted roads. Charcoal curls drifted from the chimneys above the straw-thatched roofs in the Ukrainian village. The scenery plus the jingle of the *Duga's* bells created a surreal dissonance with the group's reality.

"If not for the danger, it could be Christmas," Katarina mused as she soaked in the pristine view. For a moment, the grim threats seemed fantastical. How was it possible for evil to prevail when surrounded by such beauty? If it was true what the church said — that 'all things work together for good' — and that light always overcomes the darkness, then goodness should also overcome badness and peace should overcome war. But how would it come about? And where was God on this journey? Her esoteric questions hung in the quiet darkness, unanswered.

After they'd passed the village, she asked, "Olek, how far will we travel today?"

"Today, we go to Schoenwiese," he said. "We must check the political situation before crossing the Dnieper. Pylyp said there are military maneuvers on both sides of the river. But my friends in Schoenwiese know more. They'll help us."

"But Peter warned us not to go that way. It's too close to the city."

"Peter doesn't know my people. They'll keep us safe. I trust them."

Your people? Katarina wondered what was so special about Olek's friends. Perhaps they were his old university pals. But that possibility was equally worrisome. Many intelligentsia supported the Bolshevik party and encouraged revolution.

Katarina nudged Anna with her elbow. "Anna, are you sure Olek knows what he's doing? I'm worried."

Anna grabbed Katarina's hand and squeezed. "He's kept us safe so far. We've traveled a long way and we've had no real trouble yet. Besides, David said we could trust him completely. And we have no other choice."

"If you mean Grushka and Pylyp, that's as close to trouble as I hope to get on this trip." Katarina chewed on her bottom lip. She hoped Anna was right. If only she could trust so blindly.

BY THE TIME the sun burst across the morning horizon, the women were fast asleep on each other's shoulders. Katarina woke long enough to ask Olek about their whereabouts before nodding back to sleep. By mid-morning, she was more bored than tired. But the ominous quiet was too much so, and she continually searched the skyline for potential danger.

Thankfully, Anna's toileting breaks had become less frequent — which Katarina credited to Grushka's herbal medicine.

As they neared a small grove of poplars, Katarina spotted a murky yellowish cloud in the distance.

Olek drove up to the trees, stopped the sleigh, and pointed to the light. "Schoenwiese."

"Is that where the riots happened? At the factories?" Katarina had heard about the protests in the industrial town near the port of Aleksandrovsk — the city at the bottom of a long stretch of treacherous river rapids — but she couldn't remember ever visiting it.

"We don't go there," Olek said in Russian as he jumped off the sleigh. "My friend's house is close." He opened the panel and helped the women step down, then grunted to Alyona, "Tea."

Alyona removed the lid from the silver samovar nestled between the two foot-warmers and checked the water level. Next, she dropped two pinecones on the smoldering grate and waited until a trace of smoke emerged before replacing the chimney. She looked up at Olek. "We need more water soon."

"Next stop," he answered in Ukrainian.

Katarina shivered from the cold. She stamped her feet and squinted at the sky. "Why is the air such a funny color?"

Olek switched back to Russian. "Too much industry from coal. Less snow there. The sleigh won't do well in that mud. Without snow and ice, we must drive on the grass. But ... let's eat first. Worry later." He reached into the storage bench and pulled out a pail.

Katarina took the pail from him and opened the lid. She looked inside and gasped. "I thought we gave Pylyp all the sausage."

Olek and Alyona chuckled simultaneously. "We came prepared to barter," Olek said.

Anna stared in amazement. "What would we do without you two?"

Alyona handed Anna a cup of the special herbal tea. "Drink it up, then go use the trees." She gestured towards the poplars.

The sisters relieved themselves behind the trees and came back to find a rustic meal spread out on the bench seat. They drank tea and nibbled while Olek fed the horses, cleaned their hooves, and removed the ice build-up around the sleigh's runners.

Katarina studied the open field and skyline. "Olek," she asked nervously, "are you sure this area is safe for us? Is there a chance of more labor revolts happening while we're here?"

He laughed and answered her in German, "Katarina, don't worry. I went to school here — I know these parts well. We'll steer clear of trouble."

Since Anna tended to ignore conversations in other languages, Olek often switched to German to include her. Katarina was amazed at how smoothly he moved between Russian, German, and Ukrainian. Few servants were so devoted to learning new languages. Even Alyona, despite her local upbringing and years of work experience with the Mennonites, barely managed the two German dialects.

Katarina had never asked Olek if he spoke any other foreign tongues, but she'd heard that he'd studied linguistics and literature at the university before working with the Grand Duke's security staff. Proficiency in multiple languages was an essential requirement for that kind of job — making him a highly sought-after servant.

Intelligence and language skills aside, David claimed Olek's previous work experience made him trustworthy, and therefore he was an invaluable asset. And yet, despite Olek's lofty history, the servant was humble enough to serve as coachman. This further endeared the man to the family.

But considering all the radical upheaval in the country, Katarina worried. Would Olek risk his life for them if they got into difficulty? What were his true political beliefs? Perhaps the man was more skilled with a weapon than any local policeman, but he'd worked for the Imperial government. If they encountered rebels, would his background be an asset or a liability?

Her eyes drifted to Anna's swollen stomach, the pregnancy clearly obvious even under the thick layers of clothing. Dark rumors circulated between the villages — about how amoral subversives terrorized such vulnerable women. The rebel-held territory was filled with vagrants of all sorts — mercenaries, draft dodgers, military deserters, and displaced persons from the war fronts. They camped on the riverbanks and roamed these black, loamy flatlands searching for food, money, and warm clothing. The possibility of meeting up with such despicable characters terrified her.

Katarina shivered, then took a deep breath and blew it out in a long stream through her mouth. "God knows the end from the beginning," she whispered to herself. "There is nothing to fear." She gave her empty cup to Alyona and climbed into the sleigh.

As Olek's expert hand guided the horses across the snow-covered grassy plane, Katarina kept her eyes peeled for signs of trouble.

Anna jostled her elbow. "You look worried, Kat. What are you thinking about?"

Katarina bit the inside of her cheek, wondering how much she could say without upsetting her sister. "I'm wondering where the derelicts hang out in this cold weather. In the summer, there were tent cities all along the riverbanks. I'm a bit worried, to be honest."

Anna nodded. "This is the calm area of the lower Dnieper. All the boats stop and unload here because of the rapids upriver. The shipyards and factories attract both hard workers and ruffians — the disgruntled sinners who look for easy pickings."

"Papa called them good-for-nothings who don't deserve charity," Katarina said.

"Never mind Papa when he says such things, Kat. He'd give any starving man the shirt off his back if he felt they were deserving. And even the worst deserve to eat. Papa gets frustrated with the lazy. But some workers can't manage the physical demands of farm labor well. I think that's all he meant."

"Still, I remember at your wedding, Mr. Lentz said the locals don't take their jobs seriously. They protest the wages and working conditions. I don't understand. If the drifters need work and the locals don't appreciate theirs, why don't the factories just fire the delinquents and hire those who are more responsible?"

Anna shrugged. "I asked David the same question. He said they've formed unions to prevent that from happening."

"I'm not clear how a union operates. How can a group of malcontents dictate to a company how to run it? The owner has his life invested in that place."

"The workers allege mistreatment."

"Then they should quit and go elsewhere. What's so complicated about that?" Katarina rubbed her nose. "It stinks here. Can you imagine living with this stench? How do they manage?"

Anna laughed, "Some say the same about barnyards. I think one gets used to it when they smell it every day."

"I suppose." Katarina drummed her fingers on the seat. "Have our servants ever complained of maltreatment from us?"

"Not that I'm aware of. But Katarina, didn't we discuss this once before?"

"Ja, when I found the threatening sign by our dead dog at the river. Last October." The fetid scene still sent shivers down her back and made her stomach turn.

Anna grimaced. "Please don't remind me. I'm on pins and needles right now, worrying about the estate. I have nightmares picturing Kiva and the others waving a white rag at the soldiers and buying them off with the Delft and the silver, and our family heirlooms. I pray the Bolsheviks don't burn the house down, too."

Katarina's eyes widened. "Do you expect our servants to guard our belongings at the cost of their lives?"

"Well, no. And I pray the violence won't come to that. Olek left a contingent of trained men to protect the perimeter. And all who stayed behind are being paid to remain in place. They're not to leave the house vacant. That would guarantee disaster."

"Sometimes I think we're expecting too much of them. It's almost as if we're saying that our lives are more important than theirs."

"Oh, Katarina. Don't be absurd. We're not saying that. The rebels and Bolsheviks don't care about the servants' political alignments. They're threatening us, not them. But some workers have switched sides and joined the insurgents. That's a growing concern."

"Ja. Our cousin Regier said the same. It's hard to know who to trust anymore. Speaking of him ... I hope he escaped the fires."

"Don't worry. Our people are all protected by God. Nothing will happen to him," Anna said.

Olek brought the sleigh to a stop and pointed to a wood and stone building with a thatched roof barely visible on the side of a small hill. A thin column of smoke rose from the chimney. "There's the house. Now we must walk."

Katarina squinted at the building. "That's a house? Are you sure? It looks like a run-down abandoned shack."

"Da. This is the right place." He looked back at Anna. "Can you make it? Or shall I find a buggy?"

Anna shifted her bulk from the seat. "It's not that far, Olek. And the exercise will do me good."

"There's one thing I should tell you about my friend," he said as he helped them off the sleigh.

It was the low tone of Olek's voice that caused the hair to rise on the back of Katarina's arms. It reminded her of when he'd warned her to be cautious around a stray dog. "What?"

"There are no rules here."

"What does that mean?" Katarina asked.

"Sergei believes in freedom for all."

"I don't understand," Anna said as she stepped down.

"You will." Olek unhitched the horses and tethered them to the trees before escorting the women down the steep, rocky driveway.

15

SERGEI

It didn't take long for Katarina to figure out what Olek meant by 'no rules.'

"I wasn't expecting guests today," exclaimed the wild-looking man with unruly copper hair as they entered the archaic dacha. "But any friend of Olek's is a friend of mine." Before they'd removed their coats, Sergei embraced Olek and kissed him on both cheeks.

The party stood in a confused circle, with their boots dripping melting snow on the rough plank flooring, while the unrefined man brazenly greeted each person in the same friendly fashion. Katarina froze when he grabbed her shoulders — unsure of whether to slap him or respond likewise. So, she did neither. In her community, they reserved such greetings for family and same-sex friends, which Sergei was not. A handshake or a polite head nod would've been more appropriate. But she noticed she wasn't alone in her response to the physical contact. Anna's puffy cheeks flushed to a deep pink while Alyona's brown eyebrows shot straight up as she inhaled sharply.

As Olek made introductions, Sergei Lebedev finger-combed his messy shoulder-length locks and tied them into a ponytail with a piece of yellow twine he pulled from the rough corded belt holding up his grimy black pants. Katarina decided that since the man hadn't been expecting guests and didn't know who they were, she'd forgive him for his improprieties.

But when the irregularities continued, she looked at Olek sideways and wondered about his friendship with the coarse character.

"We must celebrate, old friend," Sergei said to Olek after he'd taken everyone's coats and hung them on the wall hook behind the door. He strode to the small wooden kitchen table, took two tumblers from the slat shelving above it, filled them with vodka from a large bottle sitting on the table, and offered one to Olek. After the men clinked their glasses and downed the shot, Sergei took a chipped Chinese teapot from the shelf and added three scoops of peppermint leaves, then went to the coal cookstove and filled the pot with hot water from a battered metal Samovar simmering there.

"Tea for the ladies, vodka for the men," Sergei joked, as he poured a second round of drinks for himself and Olek.

The women stood politely in the middle of the room, staring at the two men as they clapped each other on the back and gulped vodka. How ignorant, Katarina thought as she tapped her fingers on her hips. Couldn't the man see that Anna was with child?

Anna's jaw flexed with annoyance, and she rubbed her lower back with both hands.

Alyona finally broke the awkward moment and muttered softly in Russian, "The ladies wish to sit."

"Da. Sit." Sergei pointed at the two rod-back wooden side chairs beside the table as he poured the tea. "Make yourselves at home."

Katarina snorted as she followed Anna to the little table. In her opinion, there weren't enough furnishings here to make a home with.

Sergei poured the tea, serving the first cup to Alyona, who immediately passed it to Anna and whispered an apology in her ear for her countryman's bad manners. Anna looked at Katarina and rolled her eyes — which Katarina took to mean she considered the man incorrigible.

Although catering to men before women was socially appropriate, Sergei was wrong to indulge a servant first. Katarina concluded their host was a solitary man who lacked proper breeding. A wife would have trained him differently, but there was no sign that a woman lived here.

What an odd man, Katarina thought. He was different from Grushka and Pylyp, yet still ungodly. She stood up and offered Alyona her chair, then picked up her teacup and meandered in circles around the room, clicking her fingernails against the glass and wondering about the varying social differences in the group.

She recalled a Sunday sermon about the importance of maintaining a virtuous life. Since the world was full of vile persons, faithful believers must separate themselves from unbelievers, the preacher had said. In the past, she'd often questioned the wisdom of being so focused on the dangers of being led astray while avoiding the very sinners who needed the gospel. "That is the brotherhood's job," she was told bluntly when she asked. But the church's fear of unbelievers seemed illogical. How could a little worldly education — like what she was experiencing on this journey — tarnish her? Surely, she could learn about the local ways without staining her reputation or dismantling her faith.

And then the truth dawned. The religious belief of remaining separate was designed to protect the faith and its adherents. It made life easier for everyone. However, educating herself about other ways wouldn't send her to hell. The foundational model for future missionaries was written in the book of Acts where the Apostle Paul challenged the Greeks' idol worship in Athens. One had to understand other cultures before teaching them. It was almost like learning a new language.

With that revelation, Katarina took a deep breath. Instead of being frightened by these strange customs and odd persons, she'd embrace this journey as her first missionary adventure. She'd pretend that the people were like monkeys in a circus with each character trapped within their own circle of beliefs, yet all connected to their Heavenly Father by an invisible spider web. She would learn their ways and then teach them hers. With that realization, she took a deep breath and relaxed her shoulders.

Sergei left the room and went down a short hallway, returning a few seconds later with two large and well-worn straw-filled pillows that he tossed on the hewn plank floor in front of Olek. Olek kicked one to the wall and plopped down, using the square timbered beam as a backrest.

"Please bring your tea and sit down," Sergei beckoned to Katarina with a long bony finger and jerked his head towards the pillow.

"Thank you. But I've been sitting for two days. I wish to walk about, if you don't mind."

Sergei shrugged, went back to the table and picked up the bottle of vodka. He refilled the men's tumblers before plopping down beside Olek on the second pillow. The two promptly engaged in a rowdy conversation about old friends and former adventures while updating each other about recent political events.

Katarina circled the room and warmed her hands on the teacup. The nakedness of the place reeked of an unsavory atmosphere. Whether the man was living here or just squatting, she couldn't tell. Besides the table, chairs, and the samovar on the stove, the five shelves beside the kitchen prep table under a cracked window held an unmatched assortment of basic cookware and dishes. There seemed little else in the simple hut.

Since the vulgar character had few possessions and no obvious wealth, Katarina wondered why Olek held Sergei in such high esteem. In her opinion, there was nothing special about this scrawny and disheveled looking Russian with a hook-shaped nose that seemed too big for his narrow face. Even his clothes stank of poverty. His elbows poked through the ratty oversized gray sweater covering the dingy and wrinkled peasant shirt. But instead of wearing the thigh-length tunic on the outside, as was the custom, he'd tucked it in — under the filthy, coarse woolen pants. She assumed that it probably served as a nightshirt. Despite his slovenly appearance, the tied-back hair gave him a more respectable appearance than when they'd arrived.

Sergei vaguely reminded her of the curious-looking Hungarian gypsies she'd seen once as a small child. Her mother had quickly shuffled them away from the door when they'd come peddling their wares. "Dangerous people," her mother, Lena, had said. "Thieves and malcontents." She'd given them bread and sent them on their way. The memory warned her to be wary today.

Katarina wandered to the cracked window and stood on her tiptoes to peer outside. The door was closed on the small, abutting barn. No creatures wandered the fenceless yard. If the man had a horse or other farm animals, at least he was kind enough to protect them from the elements. He wasn't a total outlaw.

But the murky and moving shadows gave the dimly lit

place a criminal ambiance. Between the kerosene lamp on the table and the dappled light seeping through the wavy panes of two dirty and undressed windows, there was barely enough light for reading.

Katarina swallowed the last of her tea and considered asking for more when she spotted a tall bookcase on the back of a door in the short hallway. It was built in such a way as to disguise the door. Had it not been ajar, the adjoining room would have been hidden.

She wandered up to it and examined both the bookcase and its contents. The frame was handmade and properly finished with a dark patina, but the shelves were of rough lumber, sanded but not painted. The wall unit was obviously an afterthought — built in several stages and never completed.

Katarina brushed her hand over the worn volumes and studied the titles. While there were a few familiar names, most were foreign to her. She leaned in and inhaled deeply of the comforting scent of aging leather and decaying paper. Evidently, the man spent all his money on books instead of a lifestyle or furnishings. Perhaps he wasn't so uncultured after all. As she touched the cover of Chernyshevsky's *What is to be Done*, she leaned forward to inhale again. Her toe kicked the door. It gave way, and she leaped back to maintain her balance.

Through the space, she spotted a wood and metal contraption partially hidden under a tarp. The unmistakable and pungent smell of fresh ink hit her nose. She pushed gently on the door. It opened to a cluttered room filled with boxes of paper, books, and newsprint. The room was the size of a small bedroom, barely big enough to contain what she guessed was something like a small printing press, a typewriter, and an artist's drawing table with a flat wooden stool positioned beneath it.

"Find what you're looking for?" Sergei whispered over her shoulder.

Katarina jumped. The empty teacup in her hand clattered against the shelf and she scrambled to hold on to it before it could fall or shatter. After steadying herself, she spun around to come eye to eye with the man, his face only inches from hers. A teasing twinkle shone in the steely eyes. He stepped back and leaned a bony arm on the inside of the doorframe.

A twinge of guilt provoked her cheeks to flush and an unfamiliar, warm sensation spread through her groin. "I saw the books. I'm sorry. I didn't mean to snoop."

"Ah. You like books? Me, too. Which one is your favorite?"

"This one. I think. I don't know. There are so many." She nervously pointed to *Chernyshevsky*, then peeked over her shoulder and down the hallway. The others were engaged in conversation and not noticing her inappropriate situation. In her world, it was bad manners for a man to approach a woman so intimately. Her pulse quickened.

"Ah." His hand skirted her waist as he reached behind her to pull a book off the shelf. "*What is to be Done?*"

The distinct odor of alcohol wafted from the man's breath. Katarina's legs trembled and her heart pounded in her ears. She'd never been in such a situation before. What should she do? She didn't want to behave rudely by marching away. The man would feel insulted and then Olek would be upset. Anna would blame her for ruining the evening. So, Katarina pushed her knees together, stiffened her spine, and stared blankly at Sergei. "What?"

"The tale of a young woman seeking freedom from her confining life. But her mother is insistent on marrying her off to their wealthy landlord. So, she frees herself by running away and marrying someone she doesn't love. But at least she's made her own choice."

"Is that the story?" Her voice scraped her throat.

"You haven't read it then?" The gray eyes met hers, then flicked downward — gawking at her full bodice before returning to her face.

Katarina shook her head. "No. I haven't had the luxury. At home, we read the Bible and children's books." She cleared her throat. Heat rose from her abdomen and sweat pooled between her breasts. Somewhere here, there was a murky line that she should not cross. She could feel it, but it was undefinable.

He held the book in front of her. "Here. Be my guest."

"Oh, I couldn't." She rubbed her damp palms on her skirt and stepped back.

"Books are to be read. And borrowed. I have an extra lantern if you wish to read all night." A smile played at the corners of his lips and the skin around his gray eyes crinkled.

Katarina sucked on her cheeks and swallowed the tightness in her throat, then nodded and accepted the volume before pointing to the small room. "Is that an Underwood?"

"Tak. My pride and joy and my constant companion."

"Do you write?"

"A little. Do you?"

"I try. Sort of. I'm not good at it. It's just a hobby, really." She half-smiled, her lips trembling.

"No one is good at it in the beginning." He said with a soft, deep, intoxicating chuckle. "Not even after many years of practice."

Katarina straightened her shoulders, took a deep breath, and stepped back. Sergei immediately stepped closer. Katarina wanted to command the butterflies in her stomach to stop and her racing heart to calm. If the man dared touch her, Katarina knew Olek and Alyona would immediately come to her defense, but her body defied logic. The nearer he came, the more her knees quaked and her hands shook. She cleared her throat and jerked her chin toward the room. "Is that a printing press under that canvas?" She asked with utmost curiosity — her voice warbling with nervousness.

"Tak. Of a sort."

"What do you print?"

"Whatever I'm paid to do. Anything and everything." The steely eyes burrowed into hers.

She wet her lips and rubbed them together. "Politics?"

He shrugged. "Sometimes."

"Are you a Bolshevik?"

"Nyet. I have no personal leanings." Sergei snorted. "Politics create stress. People need freedom, not rules and pandering. I believe everyone has the same needs. Food, shelter, clothing. And love. I embrace the simple things in life. Forget everything else. Life should be simple, not complicated." He moved closer, almost touching her now. Drops of sweat beaded on his forehead and his pale skin shone with a yellowish cast.

He's sick.

Sergei placed his hand on the shelf behind her and whispered, "I ran away from the war. I share no interest in killing. I'm a lover, not a fighter."

Katarina couldn't tell if he was speaking the truth or using his lack of military involvement as an excuse to cover up his illness. Pretending to be a conscientious objector carried notes of defiance and righteousness. It was better to die a hero for one's values than to be forgotten after suffering a long, debilitating death.

"Aren't you afraid the army will find you? You'll be shot for treason."

"Nyet. No one knows where I am."

"Olek did."

"He has connections. And we have history together."

"From the university?"

"You could say that. But our education goes beyond schoolbooks."

Katarina was afraid to ask any more. Goosebumps traveled up her arms. They were close, too close for comfort, their breaths mingling in the same space. She could almost taste the alcohol. The stench wafted over her, and her stomach revolted. She fought the urge to vomit.

Every muscle in her body wanted to run. Her eyes darted past his shoulder to the print room, and she stepped back, hitting her heel against the bookcase. The teacup flew into the air and shattered on the floor, and the book dropped to her feet. Her knees weakened, and she grabbed onto a shelf for support.

"I'm so sorry. I lost my balance." Katarina spouted as the tears welled in her eyes. "I'll clean it up." She suddenly felt foolish. What was she thinking — that this old man was attracted to a young woman like herself?

Sergei bent down to pick up the book, and they bumped heads. When he stood up, his copper hair released from the twine and fell forward. He brushed it away from his face with a long bony hand. Scolding her with a shake of his index finger and a "tsk, tsk" he handed the book back to her. "The cup can be replaced. But books like these are very expensive."

She blinked and nodded.

"You'll find the broom beside the front door. But first, do you want to see the press?" He walked into the cluttered room without waiting for an answer, pulled off the tarp, and set the ink box to the side. "Do you have something for me to copy?"

"Copy?"

He held out his hand and flicked his fingers. "Your papers, Fräulein. Give me your identification and transit papers."

"Oh." Still feeling flustered, Katarina fingered her waist belt. She opened the flap to the secret pouch, removed her identification papers, and handed them to Sergei. Their hands brushed and a strange tingling passed through her. She stood there for a second, unmoving, reveling in the flush. What was this strange carnal attraction she felt for this educated, but crude bohemian?

Disgusted with herself, she shook the thoughts from her head and blinked her eyes several times to regain her composure and her thoughts. Why did he want her papers? She was about to ask him when Olek tapped her on the shoulder.

"Excuse me. I need to get by you. The mattresses are in here."

"What? Ah, watch the glass." Katarina spun around with her finger in the air, prepared to point out the mess, but someone had already kicked the shards to the side. Olek squeezed past her and opened a sliding panel. It revealed a bedroom with a stack of straw-filled mattresses. He removed two and dragged them out. Katarina frowned. Anna's servant seemed incredibly familiar with the house. He'd obviously been here before.

Olek jerked his chin at the main room. "I'm getting the beds ready. Frau Penner wants to sleep. And Alyona is cooking noodles. And you? Are you getting familiar with Sergei's work?"

She nodded, but wondered if she should explain herself. She glanced back at Sergei. He was already seated at the drafting table heavily engaged in examining her papers.

"Good." Olek patted her on the shoulder as she moved aside to let him pass. "It's best to let him work in peace. Otherwise, he'll be up all night. Did he give you a book to read?"

"Ja." She looked down at the volume in her hand. Should she tell Anna what just transpired? The eccentric man had done nothing to her. Maybe she was imagining things. He obviously had work to do. She'd been in his way, and he'd wanted her to move. The whole thing was her fault. She needed to clean up the broken glass and return to the main room.

From her vantage point, she could hear Anna giving orders and see Alyona rearranging things. The house was small enough for everyone to see everything. And yet no one had noticed her dilemma. If Sergei had done something criminal to her, they would've been too busy to notice. *Nonsense*, she argued with the voice in her head. Olek's friend had to be harmless. Their trusted servant wouldn't deliberately put them in danger.

Olek dragged the thin mattresses to the room and laid them side by side along the wall. He helped Anna to one, whispering to her as she lowered herself to the floor. She nodded and pulled several bills and her identification papers from her pouch and handed them to Olek. He thanked her and stuffed the money in his pants pocket.

Katarina watched the secret exchange, then caught Olek's eye as he turned around. She raised her brows questioningly. He smiled and winked at her, then strolled into Sergei's office. After a few muffled words and brief laughter, Sergei said a loud thank you and good night. The door clicked closed.

Olek returned a few minutes later with two more mattresses that he laid perpendicular on the floor along the wall. "Your bed, Fräulein Katarina. And I'll get a lamp so you can read. But first, we must eat. Sergei wants to taste some of your family's fine sausage. I'll be back with the meat after I've checked on the horses."

He grabbed his coat from the hook. "Rest until supper is ready, Fräulein. You look tired. Alyona can clean up the glass."

Katarina plunked down on her mattress and gazed at Anna, now fast asleep. Her pumpkin-size stomach rose and fell with every breath. Her sister was running out of time. Already, the trip had been dangerous and fear filled. Chortitza was so close, yet still so far away. In a few days, they'd be safe at their parents' home. But would they make it before the baby came? Katarina buried her face in her hands and prayed.

16

FORGERIES

"Shall I wake her?" Alyona jutted her chin at Anna. She dabbed at a grimy spot on the table with a frayed yellow kitchen towel before setting down the steaming bowl of fragrant noodles for her mistress.

Katarina shook her head and replied with her mouth full. "Nay. Let her rest as long as she wants. She can eat when she wakes up."

"But her supper will be cold. There're no decent pots to keep it warm."

"It doesn't matter," Katarina said between mouthfuls. "Noodles and sausage are good cold, too. Besides, after three days of sausage, she must be tired of eating the same thing. I know I am."

When Alyona's brown eyes flickered, Katarina realized she'd offended the maid. "I didn't mean I don't like it. It's just that I'm ready for a change, that's all. Some borsch would be nice."

The maid jerked her chin towards the back room. "This one doesn't have much food. One half-full pail of flour in the house. A dozen onions, some garlic, a box of carrots, and a half barrel of cabbage in the cold cellar outside. A few jars of dried beef. No pickles. No beets. I took only two onions." She moved the bowl to the side. "I leave it for Anna. For when she wakes up."

Katarina nodded. "He lives alone. Maybe he doesn't cook much. Did you see inside the barn?"

"Tak." Alyona nodded. "Six chickens, a rooster, and a goat. I took eggs and milk to make noodles."

"No horse or cows?"

Alyona shook her head.

Katarina twirled her fork around the noodles. "Well, then. He's either destitute or he doesn't live here very much."

"Unless ... soldiers. No horse, no buggy."

"Good grief. How does he get into town?"

"He's a strange one. He hides from the world."

Sergei sauntered into the room with an unsteady gait, slurring his words, his eyes bloodshot. "I smell home cooking." He wrinkled his nose and sniffed. "Did you leave some for me?"

"Tak, I'll get it now." Alyona scurried past him to the kitchen.

"What's wrong with this bowl?" Sergei plopped down across from Katarina and gawked at the bowl of noodles. An alcoholic stench wafted across the table. Katarina backed her chair against the wall.

"That's for my sister."

He looked over at Anna. "She's sleeping. Let her eat the next one."

Alyona waltzed over and slapped his hand as he picked up the fork. "Nyet. This one has special herbs for the pregnant woman."

Sergei chuckled and raised his hands. "Oh. Then take it away, comrade. Bring me something hot." His eyes followed Alyona as she walked away with the special dish. Then, he turned to Katarina. "I finished my artwork. Do you want to see it?"

"Later." She palmed her face to cover her nose. "You should eat first."

"Da. I haven't eaten all day. Only vodka. And too much, I admit. Now I'm hungry." He leaned across the table and patted her on the forearm. Katarina jerked her arm away. Sergei blinked and straightened up. "Sorry. You're not used to this." He pointed to himself. "I'm a Russian man. Lots of passion. But we drink too much and make lousy husbands."

Katarina forced herself to keep a straight face. "Are you married?"

"Nyet. Not anymore. My wife, she threw me out. Many years ago. She says I drink too much. Can you believe that?" He chuckled. "Ah. And now, I have no money. She lives in Moskov. I live here. It's all good."

"Do you have children?"

Sergei looked at the ceiling and sighed. "A daughter. I saw her once. As a baby." He drew a feminine form in the air with both hands. "Now, she's a young woman. Maybe like you. But younger. My wife — she's right. I'm no good."

"You could change that."

"Me change? Nyet." He laughed. "Then I lose my freedom. I enjoy doing what I want when I want. I get to meet nice people. Lovely ladies like you. A wife is nice, but too much work." He glanced at the open book lying on the mattress. "How are you enjoying *Chernyshevsky*? Good book, no?"

"Fascinating. Thank you."

"We discuss the plot later. After supper. I eat first."

Alyona returned with a bowl of noodles and sausage for Sergei, but her eyes darted back and forth between the two. She met Katarina's eye. A worried look passed over her stern face and the wrinkles around her mouth tightened into straight lines. Katarina shook her head to indicate she was fine. The maid stood behind their host, twisting the dirty kitchen towel between her fists. "How is the food, Sergei Lebedev?"

Sergei put his face over the bowl, closed his eyes, and inhaled. "Ah. Sausage! And Mennonite sausage, too. I can't remember the last time I ate such good food." He grinned and tapped the side of the bowl with his fork. "You know what they say. Once you have Mennonite sausage, you will never eat another."

Katarina stretched a tight smile across her face. "So, they say." She picked up her bowl, intending to finish her meal on the mattress. But Sergei's hand flew to stop her. "Don't leave me sitting here all alone. You haven't finished eating yet. There's still food in your bowl."

"I don't eat with strange men."

Surprise flashed across Sergei's face. "We're not strangers. Not anymore."

Katarina stammered for an explanation. "You're not family. And our women don't eat with men who are not family."

"Who made up that silly rule? Come on. It's a small house. Stay." He waved at her until she sat back down. "Finish your meal. I insist."

"I'm not hungry anymore." She really wasn't. The man's breath was foul. The stench was enough to destroy any remaining appetite.

"Don't insult me. Eat." Sergei held the bowl with one hand and shoveled the food into his mouth with the other, the fork meeting his lips before he'd finished chewing the last bite.

Katarina's eyes widened. The man gobbled as if he hadn't eaten in days. Both pity and disgust washed over her. She pushed her bowl over to him. "I really am done. You're welcome to the rest of mine."

Sergei looked up at her in the middle of slurping three long noodles. He sucked them up and swallowed. "In that case, I don't mind if I do." He tipped her dish into his and hunched over and attacked the food. "It's the best meal I've had in weeks." He put his elbow on the table while he ate and talked with his mouth full. "I'm too lazy to cook. I make eggs and soup. Every day, it's the same. Until summer. Then I walk to town, visit with the ladies. And they invite me for a meal. And I go home with bags of bread and pastries. But now, in winter, the women stay inside. They don't see me. So, I get no invitations."

A freeloader. And a womanizer, too. He's despicable. Katarina turned her head and rolled her eyes at the wall.

Sergei carried on between mouthfuls. "But I get by. Now, your sister gives me money. Tomorrow, I go to town and buy meat and potatoes. I get food for a few more weeks. Life is good. Things always work out for the best, da?"

"Da." Katarina sucked on her cheeks. She wanted to vomit. How much longer did she have to suffer so? And where was Olek when she needed him?

Sergei polished off the rest of the meal, then pushed his dish away and wiped his mouth on his sleeve. "Ah. Now I feel better. Where is my friend, Olek?" He scanned the room and stopped at Anna snoring softly in the corner. "Shh." He raised his index finger over his mouth. "We must be quiet. We don't want to wake the blossoming mother." He scraped back his chair slowly. "I'll go check on our friend. Maybe he's sleeping, too."

After Sergei left the room, Katarina exhaled a loud stream through her mouth. A rare grin slipped out the corners of Alyona's mouth. She clamped her lips between her teeth and her shoulders shook with controlled laughter. Katarina palmed her mouth and giggled. "He's such a character. I've never met anyone like this before. He's so brash."

"That he is. You be careful." Alyona shook an index finger in front of her chest. "This type is trouble."

Katarina shrugged. "Thank the Lord that I have you and Olek here to protect me. Although, I doubt he'll try anything stupid."

"I hope not. But Katarina, tonight I wish to put my mattress next to you."

"I suppose that would be wise." She grimaced and leaned her head against the wall. "I hear voices. Olek must be awake."

"I'll get his supper ready."

Olek strode into the room rubbing his face and finger-combing the thin, stringy hair on the back of his balding head. He tucked his wrinkled shirt into his rumpled pants as he walked, stopping only to readjust his suspenders. He headed to the kitchen washbasin and poured water into the tub from the blue enamel pitcher and scrubbed his face; then ran his fingers around the washstand searching for the soap. Finding none, he rinsed his hands a second time and dried both his face and hands on the grungy brown towel hanging on the hook beside it. He turned and grunted at Alyona who stood at the tiny cook-stove, warming his food. She pointed to the table. He moved towards it, but when he saw Katarina seated there, he stopped.

"Please, Olek." Katarina stood up. "Sit down. I'm finished eating."

"Thank you, Fräulein Katarina. This is not like home, is it?" He strode over and pulled back the chair.

"Do you think it's safe to go home, yet?" she asked, anxiously hoping for a different answer.

Olek shook his head. "Nyet. We must carry on with our plans. If all goes well, we'll be at your parents' tomorrow night."

One more day. She was about to ask if he'd learned any

more about the status of the soldiers policing the bridge when Alyona placed a bowl of noodles and sausage in front of him. It was best to let the man eat in peace.

Katarina itched to examine Sergei's library again, but she didn't wish to risk another encounter with him or feel him breathing down her neck. Since the door to the print room was ajar, she assumed he'd returned to his work. She left the table, sank down on the mattress, and picked up the book.

Isn't that always the way it is: if a person's inclined to look for something, he finds it wherever he looks. Even if there's no trace of it at all, he still finds clear evidence. Even if there's not even a shadow, still he sees not only a shadow of what he's looking for but everything he's looking for. He sees it in the most unmistakable terms, and these terms become clearer with each new glance and every new thought. [1]

Katarina felt a twinge of guilt reading such secular works which would never be approved by the church. She looked toward the bookcase. Did the man even own a Bible? She couldn't recall seeing one.

OLEK PUSHED the bowl aside and scraped his chair from the table. He wiped his mouth on the back of his hands, then stood up and snapped his suspenders, before cleaning his hands on his pants. "Come." He said to Katarina. "Let's go see what Sergei has done."

She followed him to the print room but stopped by the bookshelves. The bottom three rows were filled with cardboard-covered volumes crudely held together with twine. Her eyes widened, and she leaned in for a closer look.

"You want to read my work?" The putrid breath sang from beside her elbow.

"You really are a writer!" She gasped as she twirled to face him.

"I try. But no one buys my work. Maybe one day."

"But you have a printing press. You can publish it yourself."

Sergei chuckled. "You're a funny woman. Even then. Who would sell it? This is a factory town. There are no educated people here. No bookstores."

"Go to the city. The universities will buy."

"And where do I live then, huh? Some slum apartments with screaming children, overflowing toilets, and men beating their women. What kind of life is that? No. Here I write in peace. With the birds and the bees. And a few chickens and a goat. And my vodka. I am content."

Katarina stared into the steely gray eyes. So, this was what a proper writer looked like! Unkempt, unwashed, and with no family or true friends. The loneliness was almost palpable. But also, oddly attractive. She felt both pity and envy for the man.

"So." He straightened his shoulders and tapped the wall with a long, bony finger. "Are you ready to see my work?"

Katarina looked over at Olek who was watching her from the doorway and shrugged, confused by Sergei's question. Olek stepped back and jerked his head, indicating she should step inside.

Sergei patted a stack of roughly built wooden crates filled with books. "Sit. We discuss."

Discuss what? Katarina chose a knee-high makeshift stool composed of a stack of two boxes and wiped the dusty top with her hands before sitting down. A draft from the tiny window in front of the typewriter played with a cobweb in the corner. The filmy light highlighted grayish wisps and tiny white dots floating in the air. Katarina felt a sneeze rise and quickly squeezed her nose to stop it.

Sergei pulled a sheaf of documents from the drawing table and handed two pages to her. "Tell me what you think."

His tone had changed, she noted — the voice now steadier and absent of the earlier drunkenness, his demeanor almost business-like.

She studied the parchment. One was her identification paper, but something had changed. Olek's name was listed as next of kin. She looked at the other. A transit pass to cross the bridge, stamped paid in full, and valid for thirty days. Her jaw dropped as she studied the documents. She looked up. "How in the world?"

"Compare to the others." Sergei handed her two more pages.

It was obvious these were the original. The transit pass was an old, expired one with Anna's name on it, signed by David. Katarina compared the first to the second. Except for the content which she knew to be false and the unmistakable fresh ink, everything in the forgery — including the government stamp — looked authentic.

"By tomorrow the ink will be well set. No one can tell which is which. I do good work, da?"

She held the copies up and tried to give them back to Sergei, but he crossed his arms and refused them. "Surely, these are not legal. These are forgeries."

Olek and Sergei simultaneously burst out laughing.

"There is no 'legal' in this part of the country anymore. No law and order. We do what we can and then ... we bribe," Sergei scoffed.

"It's true, Fräulein," Olek added. "The police make up the law as they go along. And the soldiers can't be trusted. The papers look real, and we'll have a better chance crossing with them."

"But it still seems wrong. I don't like this." The pages trembled in her hands.

"It's the only way. Your sister agreed. She paid to have this done."

Katarina shook her head. "No, Olek. I don't believe you. Anna would never pay for a crime. If we're caught —"

"— They'll never notice," Sergei interrupted, laughing. "One quick glance and they'll wave you through. I've done it dozens of times. You'll be fine."

"Fräulein, the police look away. There's no real crime here."

Olek's vague reassurances left Katarina feeling uncertain, and her conscience pricked. "But it's still wrong. I can't believe Anna agreed to this. She wouldn't."

"Fräulein Katarina," Olek pleaded. "Listen to me. You are not understanding the problem. The Bolsheviks police the bridge. One must have proper papers to cross."

"Proper, ja. Legal, ja. Which these are not. So, then we cross somewhere else." She slumped against the wall. The tension coursed through the old sore shoulder and spread up her neck. Her head throbbed. Surely there was another way. What had Olek gotten them into?

"Where do you suggest?" Olek continued. "If we go south, the area is overrun with Makhno's men and criminals along the riverfronts. We'll be robbed for sure. We'll never make it over to Nikopol alive. And how can we get there? There's little snow that far south and we don't have the right vehicle."

"We have three horses. Surely, we can ride."

"Frau Penner cannot ride a horse. She's heavy with child. And every extra day away from home threatens both her life and the life of the little one. This is the fastest way to get to the other side of the river. And there is no other way." Olek raised his bushy gray eyebrows and looked over at Sergei. The latter glared at her and twitched his mouth from side to side.

"Unless you want to stay here until the baby is born," Olek said.

Katarina swallowed hard. There was no way she was staying in this hovel with this horrid alcoholic. Anna would never agree either. Was there another way? She mulled over the possibilities. Could they rent a room in the city until the baby was born? It would be safer than this. Although, Sergei's description of the city didn't sound pleasant, either. And they would need money for rent. How much money did Anna have with her? How much would her jewelry fetch? She sparked another idea.

"They need teachers in Schoenwiese and Aleksandrovsk. I can teach." As soon as she said it, Katarina realized her mistake.

Olek and Sergei burst out laughing. "So now you want to live here and find a job?" Olek scratched his head. "And what about your sister? Do you want her to have the baby here?"

"Until my parents can come and get us." Katarina's cheeks warmed with embarrassment.

Olek shook his head. "It takes time to find a place. Furnished apartments are expensive. Or filled with rats and lice. In rooming houses, many people live squeezed together. It's no place for two high-class Mennonite ladies."

"Are there no inns? Surely in the big city, there are hotels."

Sergei, who'd been listening with his hands linked behind his head, repositioned himself and leaned forward. "The army takes the best rooms for themselves. There's nothing left for tourists."

Her stomach sank. Maybe Olek was right. "I need to think. I know you mean well. But I need to discuss this with Anna."

"Will you wake her? Now?"

Katarina shook her head. "Nyet. I'll wait until she wakes up. She hasn't eaten yet. She'll be hungry soon."

Olek passed his hand over the bare patch on his head. "Da. We can wait. It won't change anything."

Katarina stood to exit the room but turned when another idea popped into her mind. "What's north of the city? Can't we go around it and cross there?"

Sergei leaned his elbows on the drawing table and cocked his head at Olek.

"Only ice and rapids." Both sarcasm and frustration resonated in the servant's tone. "Fräulein Katarina, surely you know about the deadly white water between Ekaterinoslav and Aleksandrovsk. The turbulence will cause your sister great discomfort. Just take the papers. It's the easiest way."

Do what's right, not what's easy. Lena's voice echoed in her head. Then Peter's followed — *How will you get over the river, Olek? You can't pretend to be a Mennonite. No one will buy the accent. You'll get these women killed.* The sapphire eyes pierced her soul. Peter had defied his faith and put on a Bolshevik uniform to save his life. Was this a similar sin? But it wasn't the same situation, she argued with herself. Peter had not committed a crime. This was a legal violation — even if Olek and Sergei said otherwise. Regardless of the political situation in the country, there was still a difference between truth and lies. The Bible said that truth was written on one's heart. And this felt like lying. And lying was always sin ... wasn't it?

Katarina rubbed her face. "I can't decide right now, Olek. I commend you on your excellent work, Sergei. And I appreciate what you've both done for us. But my faith forbids me to tell a lie."

"You don't have to tell lies, Fräulein Katarina," Olek said softly. "I will."

"And then, if they catch you, we're all at risk. And it's my responsibility because I put your life in danger. If you die because of us, my soul bears the cost."

"But your sister can't wait much longer. Her life is in great peril."

Katarina looked up at the rafters and blew a long stream through her mouth. "Grr. I don't have peace." She spun on her heels and left the room. Sinking to her mattress on the floor, she prayed, "God, please help us through this. We're in an impossible spot and I don't know what to do."

1 Nikolai Chernyshevsky, *What is to be Done*. 1863.

17

THE PLIGHT OF NIGHT

"Forgery?" Anna's blue eyes widened as she studied the papers. "Are you sure? Is that what he meant when he said his friend could arrange our pass?" She looked sheepishly at Katarina. "But I didn't know. Honest. I trusted Olek. David said we should."

"But what do you think now?" Katarina wrapped the quilt around her legs and stared at the flickering coal oil lamp. The flame rose and fell in a mesmerizing beat, matching the pulsing of the frigid draft blowing through the cracks in the poorly chinked stone walls and timbered slats. Outside, the wind howled steadily, and ice pellets clinked against the windowpane. Katarina shivered. "I mean, what do you think we should do?"

Anna pushed away the half-eaten bowl of noodles and left the table. She returned to her mattress and leaned against the wall and slowly slid down until her bottom touched the floor. "Well, if there's no other choice ... I'll keep my eyes to the ground and hope no one notices."

"But it's not right, Anna. Olek will have to lie for us."

"Katarina, I know it's a sin. But what other choice do we

have? We can't go home. Both the Bolsheviks and Makhno's army are swarming the countryside. We're in harm's way. God forbid they show up here — before the night is done." Anna wriggled her legs and stretched her arms, trying to reach her ankles. She sighed and slapped her hands on the mattress. "I give up. Kat, help me with these socks, please. I'm too heavy with child to dress myself."

Katarina removed Anna's soiled socks from her feet, turned them inside out, and slipped them back on. "They're not that dirty. One more day. Alyona's washing the spares. They'll be dry by morning."

"Uggh. I can't fault her. She's doing the best she can. We're all going through this together." Anna leaned her head against the wall.

"I'm so sorry you're suffering so. But don't worry. God is guiding us."

"Don't worry, she says," Anna mocked. "In my condition, how can I do anything but?"

Katarina sucked on her cheek. *God, this baby can't come yet. But Anna can't go on like this either.* "Listen, I have another idea. We can go north — past the city. Do you remember? There used to be an old ferry between the last two sets of rapids."

Anna rolled her eyes. "Are you suggesting the ferry that goes to Einlage? Near Maria and George's house? That's almost scarier than the bridge. I'd be surprised if it's still in operation. Everyone uses the bridge these days."

"We should at least check it out. It's only one extra day, Anna. Can you make it?"

"Can I, what?" Anna's eyes nearly popped out of her head. "Katarina, do you honestly think I have any control over when this baby comes?"

"Nay. I know you don't." Katarina scrubbed at her fingernails. "I'm just asking if you think it's a feasible solution."

"Katarina, it's not possible. The rapids are wicked. And we could be hit by floating icebergs."

"If we don't take the ferry, then we must lie to go across the bridge." Katarina crossed her arms over her chest and cocked her head at her sister.

Anna sighed. "This war will be the death of us yet. What has this world come to when one must give up their integrity to save their life? Is there no church nearby where we can get advice?"

"Schoenwiese is a Mennonite town. Do you want to find a church and speak to an Elder?"

Anna slapped the floor. "Thank you, Katarina. Yes, I do. Please wake up Olek. I must speak with him."

Katarina cast the quilt aside, picked up the oil lamp, and side-stepped around Alyona who'd fallen asleep on the mattress beside them. She tiptoed down the hallway towards the duet of snoring coming from the rear bedroom and tapped lightly on the door. There was no response. "Olek." She called out in a hoarse whisper. Still nothing. She tried again, this time with a sharper tone. "Olek." There was a sharp snort and the clearing of a throat.

"Da. Da." Blankets rustled, and the rope bed squeaked as it rubbed against the wood supports. An object scraped across the hewn flooring and a second later the door opened. "Is there a problem?"

"Anna wants to talk to you."

Olek stood in the dim light and rubbed his unshaven chin, then tucked his crumpled shirt into his wrinkled pants. "Da." He motioned for Katarina to lead the way. They padded back to the main room where Anna sat on the mattress with her back against the wall and the quilt draped over her knees. "What is it, Frau Penner? How can I help?"

"Olek, we need spiritual advice on this transportation problem. Can you bring me to a church in town?"

"Now?"

"No. Not now. At first light."

The servant sighed. "That's a problem."

"Why?" Anna's eyebrows furrowed.

Olek spoke slowly in German for Anna's sake, halting between sentences as if he was thinking out loud. "Because we have only a sleigh. This storm has much ice. The snow melts in the city. No place for a sleigh to drive. The horses will get stolen. We need wheels. Sergei borrowed out his buggy. We have three driving horses and no saddles. It's not safe."

"I see. Yes, you're right. This is a problem." Anna tapped her chin. "Doesn't Sergei have a saddle you can use?"

Katarina interrupted, thinking out loud. "Why would he lend out his only vehicle? Who borrows such and doesn't return it?"

"You're not helping, Katarina," Anna said firmly.

"Sorry." Katarina covered her mouth with her hands.

Olek shrugged. "My friend gives freely to his friends. But no one gives to him." He turned to Katarina and reverted to Russian. "Sergei is generous to the point of poverty."

"How far is it to town?" Anna asked.

"Maybe ten versts."

"Can you walk it? Or take one of the horses? You could use a blanket for a saddle." Anna crossed her arms and tapped her fingers impatiently on her forearm.

"Da. Two hours in fit weather. But now we have ice." He emphasized the road conditions again. "I go to the church. I wait for your preacher. Then come back." His gaze drifted to the ceiling. He held a fist in front of his chest and his fingers snapped out one at a time, as if counting. "You stay alone with Sergei. Maybe five hours. Maybe longer."

"Oh." Anna waved a hand in the air, dismissing his concerns. "I'm sure we can manage the little man."

Katarina slapped the mattress. "No, Anna. I forbid it. You can't expect Olek to run such an errand in the middle of an ice storm. He'll break his neck out there. He's putting his life at risk as it is. Look, we have only two choices here. Either we lie to get across the bridge, or we go north and take the old ferry. Getting spiritual advice for this won't change the facts."

Anna inhaled deeply and blew it out in a long stream. "Oh. I suppose you're right, Katarina. Although, speaking to an elder would assuage my conscience."

"Not only yours, but mine too." Katarina unpinned her hair and pulled apart the long, single braid, and finger-combed it. "But we are also responsible for others. We should not put them in such a position."

"I realize that." Anna snapped and tapped her chin with her index finger.

Olek cleared his throat.

"What is it?" Anna's eyes flashed with irritation.

"There is another problem."

"Which is?" Fatigue registered in Anna's voice, her tone dry and gravelly.

"If there's no ice and snow in Aleksandrovsk, then we have a problem with the sleigh. We need wheels for the bridge. We wait for Sergei's friend to bring the buggy. Or we take the train. Sergei wrote tickets."

"But they're forgeries, Olek. We can't use them." Katarina scowled. She yanked at the quilt and tucked it under her legs.

Olek shrugged. "Up to you."

"Didn't you say the soldiers are controlling the trains? Has something changed?" Anna's eyebrows knit together.

"Travel to Crimea is not possible. But to cross the Kichkas bridge is different. Sergei says the Reds permit citizens on the train — sometimes — when there's space. We go. We wait for permission."

Anna thumped the floor in exasperation. "Sometimes?

How long must we wait to cross? Hours or days? Good grief, Olek. Again, I say. We don't want to use forged papers. Oh, for goodness sake. We have no choice." She threw her hands in the air.

"I don't understand." Olek scratched his unshaven chin.

"I don't either," Katarina said.

"Well, it's obvious. Now we must go north. To the Einlage crossing."

A look of alarm passed over Olek's face. "Frau Penner, the route is dangerous. Only a small channel between the rapids. The current is very fast. And ice on the river."

"I understand the risk, Olek." Anna looked at him sternly. "Our sister and her husband live outside the village. We've been there many times. We practically grew up on the Dnieper. I'm well aware of the ice and the rapids. God will protect us."

"If this is your wish. We leave before dawn when the ground is more frozen. Then travel around the city and soldiers. It will be slow. Many hours. Maybe a day or longer. The horses will not do well with the ice." Olek sighed and rubbed his chin.

"I'm going to pray for more snow. If the soldiers are cold, they'll be trying to stay warm. Then they won't bother us." Katarina sighed with relief as the weight lifted from her shoulders.

"Oh Katarina, don't start," Anna snapped. "The last thing we want is more cold and snow."

"It's a good thing God controls the weather and not you. We need the snow on this trip. What's wrong with praying for it?" Katarina said sarcastically.

"I pray for summer, but it doesn't come any faster." Anna's eyes flashed. "The weather is the weather."

"It worked for Israel." Katarina knew that this wasn't the

time for an argument, but she couldn't drop it. But neither could Anna.

"That was then. God doesn't work that way anymore."

"God doesn't change."

Olek cleared his throat and interrupted. "Everyone is awake now. Shall I get horses ready?"

"Oh. Yes, Olek that would be a good idea. We'll take a quick nap, and you can wake us when it's time to leave." Anna gave Katarina a stern look and pulled the quilt up around her belly.

Katarina caught the smirk on Olek's face before he scratched his chin. He turned and tucked his baggy shirt into his pants and padded back to the bedroom.

"What's that funny look on your face?" Anna asked with a critical tone.

"Nothing." Katarina shook her head. "It's just that you expect too much of the servants at times."

"I don't think that's true." Anna yanked on the quilt.

"It is true. But never mind. Let's get some sleep. Olek will wake us up before we know it." Katarina yawned and wiggled into a comfortable position on the mattress.

"One more thing before you do." The sleet pinging against the windowpane matched the ice in Anna's voice.

Katarina's shoulders fell and she hung her head. "Did I do something wrong?"

"Never contradict or correct me in front of my servants again. It's disrespectful." Anna said.

"I'm sorry. It won't happen again." Katarina's eyes stung with tears. She hadn't meant to hurt her sister, but it was too easy to fall into childish patterns. Arguing and venting helped to ease the worry. But she knew it wasn't the Christian way. She also knew she shouldn't give her opinion unless someone asked for it. One was to defer to elders even if they were wrong and trust God to work out the details.

Behaving like an adult was hard. Katarina pulled the blanket over her head and worried about tomorrow. Somewhere, there was a lesson in this chaos. If nothing else, maybe God was simply teaching her how to trust Him in the storm.

~

THE GLACIAL WINDS almost took her breath away as she flew through the milky sky. Katarina hugged the sweaty, ebony body and snuggled her face into the silky black mane. Then a tug on her feet pulled her into the dark shadows.

Another tug, then a stroke on her arm. Katarina opened her eyes to see the familiar silhouetted figure beside her bed, shrouded in the flame of an oil lamp. "Is it time to get up already? I just fell asleep."

"Tak. You can sleep later. Olek is waiting. We walk to the top of the hill." Alyona adjusted the flame on the lamp and set it on the floor beside Katarina, then picked up Anna's quilt and folded it.

"Where's Anna?"

"She's already washed up and outside. It's your turn. Can you see? Take the lamp."

"Ja. I'll be but a minute."

"Watch your step. The drive is icy and snow-covered." She gathered up Katarina's blanket. "I have both quilts. Now hurry. Olek and I walk with Anna."

"Snow and ice are good," Katarina mumbled as she slid to the washbasin and rinsed the sand from her eyes. "Thank you, God, for hearing my prayers." She slipped on her sheepskin coat, wrapped the black wool shawl around her head and neck, and pulled on her leather boots that Alyona had set by the fire to warm. Once again, she applauded herself for the foresight of adding new soles and wool lining. They'd keep her feet toasty today.

When she opened the door, the sub-zero gust took her breath away. She sheltered the lamp from the wind with her hand and stood for a few seconds to get her bearings before shimmying to the drafty derelict outhouse beside the main building. But the flimsy door refused to shut, and the wind whipped through the space between the three thin wood partitions. She placed her feet into the two dugouts on either side of the hole and squatted. As she stood up, her foot hit a metal pail. Even with the lamp, it was too dark to see. "I wished I'd seen that earlier."

Katarina yanked up her collar and tightened the shawl around her face, then headed up the path, following the silhouetted trio moving up the hill under the glow of Olek's lantern. A snow-covered stony protrusion caught Katarina's foot, and she cried out, sailing forward and hitting the ground with a hard thud. The lamp went flying and the flame died. She looked up, hoping someone had noticed and would come to her rescue, but the entourage was too far ahead. A sharp pain shot through her left hip. She stood up and rubbed it vigorously. The kerosene lamp was nowhere to be seen. "Onward Christian soldier," she said aloud, forgoing the light as she limped up the hill. "Let Sergei have it."

She reached the sleigh and crawled in beside Anna, while still rubbing her hip. "I guess I got what I prayed for," she mumbled sarcastically.

"Yes, Thank God for the new snow. And for Olek's attention to the horses. I don't know what we'd do without him. Or Alyona." Anna passed Katarina a quilt.

"Ja. We're very fortunate. I'm thankful, too. Hopefully, he can pull us out of today's disasters." Katarina wrapped the blanket around her legs and took a deep breath of the nippy air. A sharp pang of cold hit her lungs.

"No more tough days. Let's think positive. God is with us," Anna said.

I hope so. As the sleigh pulled away from the tiny farm-house, Katarina looked back. Except for the whiff of smoke coming from the chimney, the lone pine tree at the top of the hill was the only marker of the small farm's existence. The white landscape had swallowed the buildings.

18

THE HANGING SIGNS

AGAINST THE PINK HAZE OF EARLY DAWN, THE TOWN'S twinkling lights illuminated thick, yellowish-gray clouds hovering over the factories. Steam billowed from tall chimneys and the air reeked of burnt grain and Sulphur.

"Olek, is that Schoenwiese?" Katarina pointed as Olek redirected the team across the frozen field.

"Da." Olek switched into Russian. "See those tall buildings? Those are the factories — where the riots happened. Five people died." He looked over his shoulder and winked at her. "Don't worry. We don't go there. We circle east around the city. It's time to pray and keep our eyes open for soldiers."

Katarina bit her lip and scanned the fields. There were few trees in this agricultural valley. Nothing to protect them from being noticed. However, at this early hour, the area seemed peaceful. "Olek, do you see any signs of war?"

Olek shook his head. "Nyet."

Katarina removed her sheepskin mittens and tightened the wool scarf around her head, then pulled up the mink collar of her sheepskin coat. Despite her heavy clothing — the layered silk underwear, two long skirts, new wool-lined leather boots, a heavy coat, a thick shawl, a horsehair blanket, and a second quilt — the damp cold still seeped into her aching bones. Spring couldn't come soon enough. Today was especially frigid. But she had prayed for snow and cold and God had answered. So, she stopped grumbling and chose to trust divine protection.

After the incident at Sergei's house, Katarina worried about Olek's trustworthiness again. He'd been much too casual about the forgeries and dismissed the seriousness of both the illegal activity and the lying. In her world, lying was akin to stealing, which was akin to murder. They were all violations of the holy commandments. The only exception was shrewdness. It was both acceptable and admirable. Being shrewd wasn't lying. But Katarina hadn't yet learned how shrewdness and lying differed. However, she was fairly certain forgeries fell into the category of lying. But it would be wrong to accuse Olek of being a liar without more proof.

Based on what she'd learned at Sergei's house, Olek had a secret past that didn't quite fit with his high profile at the estate. What was he hiding? Did it have something to do with his relationship with the royal family? Or his political leanings? Katarina desperately wanted to whisper her suspicions to Anna, but her sister had laid her head against Alyona's strong shoulders.

Katarina took a deep breath and pushed away her uneasy feelings. Olek was an excellent servant, and he was taking great care of them on this trip. God had obviously positioned Olek here to keep them safe. She should stop being so judgmental and be more grateful. "Everything works together for good," she whispered to herself. She settled back on the bench and allowed the swaying of the sleigh to lull her into a hypnotic sleep.

❧

AN HOUR LATER, Katarina jolted from a sharp jab to her ribs. She opened her eyes to see Anna staring at her.

"Katarina. Wake up. You're not supposed to be sleeping. One of us must keep our eyes open."

Still feeling dazed from being woken so harshly, she started apologizing, then stopped herself. "What?"

"Olek says we're approaching a busy area. The soldiers could be anywhere. We must stay alert," Anna said. Her voice squeaked as the sleigh bounced over a small hill and the metal runners screeched over the stony surface.

Olek turned his head and spoke to them over his shoulder. "We need a carriage soon. The horses can't keep dragging us like this."

Katarina rubbed her eyes. They had passed the industrial section, left the grass, and were now driving on a packed gravel road. "Good grief. What happened to the ice and snow?"

"Melted. Our prayers didn't work. What are we going to do now?" Anna sighed and relaxed her grip on the bench as the sleigh straightened out.

"Pray for something better," Katarina said sarcastically under her breath.

Anna pointed across the field to a small wooden house with a thatched roof. "Olek, should we stop there?"

Olek nodded. "Da. There's no smoke in the chimney but I'll go check." He steered the troika off the gravel road and onto a wet grassy slope, stopping the team by the property's fieldstone boundary fence. "Stay here. I'll wave if it's good."

Katarina shivered. "I hope this doesn't turn out to be another long day. Meeting Sergei was fruitless."

"I wouldn't call it fruitless. We still have the papers, just in case we need them." Anna smirked as she removed her sheepskin mitts to retie her hat under her chin.

"You kept them?" Katarina said, disbelieving. "Why would you do that?"

"Of course. I paid for them. But Olek is carrying them, not I." Anna shrugged.

"Anna!" Katarina's jaw dropped. "Now we're complicit. Do you have any idea what will happen if we're caught with forged papers? The Bolsheviks will shoot Olek. And maybe us too. Or worse."

"Katarina, you're being overly dramatic. Settle down." Anna waved her hands in a dismissive gesture.

"Settle down?" Katarina squealed. "Innocent people are dying in this war. But you've just given the armies ammunition to kill us. What are you thinking? Besides, we must keep ourselves spotless before God, not be tarnished with the sin of this world."

"Katarina, I've told you before. Despite what the church says, the world isn't black and white. We must be prepared."

"Of course, things are black and white. There's right and there's wrong."

"But when black meets white, things become muddied. There are many shades of gray, Katarina. This is one of those times when things are not clear cut." Anna patted Katarina's hand in a patronizing gesture.

Katarina immediately withdrew her hand. "I disagree. This action is clearly sin. And I, for one, don't want to be a part of it. Yet you've put me in this position where I'm contaminated nonetheless. I hope there's enough time to ask for forgiveness before the gun goes off." She sat back and crossed her arms.

"Katarina, stop upsetting yourself. Trust God. Everything will work out." Anna jutted her chin to the sky.

"But if we trust God to watch over us, why do we need to align ourselves with illicit activities? God expects us to be moral and upright."

Anna patted Katarina on the arm. "Look. I know it doesn't look good. But I'm following Olek's advice. And David said to trust him for everything."

"Well, if that's the case, why don't we just go over the bridge, then? We can use our illegal papers and cross over without all this bother. If I'd known that you were going to be this callous and irreverent —"

"Katarina, the papers are our last hope. Not our only hope." Anna pointed to the lone figure heading their way. "Here comes Olek."

"That was quick."

Olek waved as he approached. "Da. A box cart with wheels, but no seats. And a broken wheel. I can fix it. You can rest in the house. The soldiers are gone."

How did he know the soldiers had been here? Katarina wrinkled her brow.

"No seats?" Anna said. "I can't sit without support."

"Shall we spend the night here?" Alyona interrupted.

The sisters swiveled to stare at Alyona. The maid flushed and turned her face away.

"This comes from spending too much time with us," Anna whispered in Katarina's ear. "She's becoming too familiar."

"Ja," Katarina grunted. Although Alyona had interjected into the conversation without an invitation, she'd addressed Olek and not them. Regardless, it wasn't the right time or place to argue with Anna.

"I can't say." Olek rubbed his nose, then looked at the ground and kicked it with his boot. "I must fix the wagon first."

Katarina narrowed her eyes. The servant was hiding something. "What do you mean the soldiers are gone? How do you know?"

Olek acted as if he hadn't heard her question and pointed

to the driver's seat. "Alyona, sit there. I walk in front with the horses."

Katarina gawked — first at Olek, then at Anna. The nerve of him! He'd just dismissed her. And without an apology. Something was definitely off. And to add to the slight, Anna wasn't correcting him.

Alyona climbed over the railing to take the driver's seat. She held the four sets of reins while Olek grabbed the center harness and guided the animals across the slippery pasture.

"The horses have been so good on this trip," Anna said, breaking the silence.

Katarina grimaced, swallowed her pride, and refocused. Everyone seemed on edge today. There was no point in digging into Olek's attitude now. "Ja. Thankfully, the horses had good energy, and none has sprained a limb. And everything else has gone well, too," Katarina said quietly. "I sense the angels have gone before us."

"What do you mean?" Anna dropped the quilt from her shoulders.

"The snow's been enough, not too much or too little. There've been no catastrophes, and our journey has been diverted from hazards. Whenever we stopped, provision met us there. It's been cold, but not deathly so. Even last night's ice storm gave us the start we needed this morning."

"Well, we must be doing something right then."

"Maybe." Katarina bit the corner of her bottom lip. "Although, I keep waiting for the other shoe to drop. Sooner or later, we're bound to run into either soldiers or rebels."

～

OLEK STOPPED the sleigh in front of a small white stucco house with blue-painted windows and a thatched roof. He pointed to the chimney. "Alyona, do we still have hot coals?"

The maid hung her head. "Not enough."

"What?" Anna stared at the servant. "Why not?"

"I fell on the ice and the pail of coals spilled on the snow. The bricks for the foot-warmers were hot." Alyona rambled nervously. "Olek said to hurry. There was no time to go back to the house to get more. I thought we could manage. After tea, I put bark in the samovar. There was still smoke. I thought the coals would last for the day."

"But?" Anna prodded.

"No coals now. Only ash." The maid looked at the ground and held her lips between her teeth.

"I can't believe you did this to us." Anna's face tightened and she gawked angrily at her maid. "Our survival depends on fire and water."

"Enough." Katarina interrupted. "There's no point flogging a dead horse." She turned to Olek. "Do we have matches or flint?"

Olek nodded. "Da. But we need coal or wood."

"The house can't be without fuel," Katarina said. "We'll find some."

"I'll feed the horses in the barn and fix the cart." Olek pointed to the building behind the house.

"We'll settle inside. Alyona can find firewood and start a fire." Anna accepted Olek's hand and exited the sleigh. "Bring the foot-warmers, Alyona. We'll heat the bricks inside."

Katarina suspected Olek hadn't checked the property thoroughly. He hadn't been gone long enough to do so. She stood in front of the house and scanned the exterior. The front door hung awkwardly from a single hinge. Broken glass lay on the snow-covered grass beneath the windows. The property appeared both neglected and abandoned. She could see why Olek hadn't bothered to look further.

Alyona scurried by, juggling the two foot-warmers in her

arms. She stopped in front of the door and set them on the ground.

"Wait." Katarina pointed at the frame. "The door is hanging on by a thread."

"Good eye, Kat. Let's be careful opening it. We don't want to get bonked on the head." Anna put her hands on her hips and looked around the yard. "Where did Olek disappear to so fast? We should ask him for advice."

"Around the corner, to the barn." Katarina pointed sideways while studying the flimsy panel in front of her. "Let me at it. Stand back." She waved the women away. Bracing her hip and one hand against the door, she grabbed the handle and pulled. The door groaned and shifted, then tore from the frame and slammed on the ground. When she stepped back, it toppled against her. She yelped as she fell beneath the weight, landing on her sore left hip and her old, injured shoulder. "OW!"

Alyona dropped to her knees and pushed at the panel. Katarina wriggled out from underneath it and slowly stood up. A searing pain passed through her side. She clamped her lips between her teeth and turned her face to keep from screaming.

"Are you alright?" The whites of Anna's eyes widened like saucers.

Katarina held up her hand to indicate she was fine. When the immediate pain passed, she chuckled. "I believe I just found our firewood."

"Oh, thank God. Goodness gracious, Katarina. You shouldn't have done such. You could've been seriously hurt." Anna pulled her scarf away from her mouth. "You should've let Olek or Alyona manage this."

Katarina dusted herself. "This coat has good padding. I'm not hurt. Come. Let's see inside." She rubbed her hip and stomped up the two rickety stairs.

"You are so hurt." Anna grabbed Katarina's elbow. "Don't lie to me."

"I'm just bruised. It's nothing." Katarina assured her. "It's more from falling on the ice earlier ... at Sergei's."

"You were already injured? Why do you take such risks?" Anna whispered sternly. "We have servants for a reason. What would I do without you?"

"Without me, *they'd* look after you. That's what you pay them for," Katarina whispered back.

Anna's jaw tightened, but she dropped the subject.

The late morning light streaked through the darkened portal and cast moving shadows in the entrance. Katarina stopped inside the bare mud room to allow her eyes to adjust to the light, then climbed the two steps into the main structure.

Typical of most peasant houses in rural areas, it contained one large, single open room. Torn pieces of blue and white wallpaper fluttered from the walls. Small bullet-sized holes, smeared reddish-brown stains, and two head-sized indentations decorated the plaster. A stack of newspapers flapped beside the coal stove. The late morning sun flickered through the bare branches of an apple tree outside the house, projecting dancing shadows through the large, shattered window.

The place was cold and damp, as if there hadn't been a fire in days.

Anna and Alyona hovered at Katarina's side as they scouted the interior together. "It looks like a war zone," Anna murmured.

"I guess Olek was right. The soldiers have come and gone. But why such destruction? Have the soldiers no respect for property?" Katarina surveyed the room, shocked by the devastation.

"I hope the soldiers don't destroy the estate like this," Anna said. "We'll have our work cut out for us."

"When the owners return, they'll be mightily discouraged." Katarina took a deep breath and blew it out slowly. "The air stinks of rotting mice."

Alyona plunked the box of bricks beside the stove, then straightened up, put her hands on her hips and stretched her back. The black woolen shawl slipped off her head, revealing the gray streaks in her dark hair while the lambent light emphasized the lines around her mouth and eyes.

Even though they were all tired from the grueling, bumpy trip, Alyona worked without complaining. Katarina admired the maid's stoicism, but she could see that the servant was aging before their eyes. She wondered how they would ever manage without her.

Across the room against the far wall, a thin straw mattress lay doubled up on the plank flooring beside a single wooden bed. Next to it, another single bed lay flipped on its side with a busted frame, the rope supports removed, and the mattress torn apart. Alyona set the good mattress on the sound bed and invited Anna to sit down.

A small wooden table sat next to the coal cookstove in the center of the room with the remnants of two chairs and their broken legs strewn around it. "We have firewood," Katarina said. She checked the chimney and the ceiling above it and found them both intact. It was safe to start a fire.

She picked up the top newspaper from the pile beside the stove and checked the date. "Last week's edition. The owners obviously had money for newspapers." She quickly scanned the headlines. "The Rada signed a treaty with the central powers but now the Bolsheviks have taken Kyiv. The council has abandoned its post and fled north. This sounds like mass confusion." She looked up and sighed. "Is anyone protecting us? It seems the Land of the Mennonites is forgotten."

"It would be better if we *were* forgotten," Anna said as she scrutinized their surroundings. "But instead, Lenin's Bolsheviks seek our utter destruction."

"The world is at war and Russia is divided," Alyona added. She took the newspaper from Katarina and rolled it into a tight tube so it could be used for fire starter.

"Ja. And here we are, three women alone in the middle of nowhere trying to find a warm place to lay our heads," Katarina said.

"Well, let's build a fire before I give birth in the cold. I already feel like the Virgin Mary. About to have a child, but no place to lay my head. The Bible is making more sense to me every day. I now understand how she felt." Anna rubbed her hands together and stomped her feet on the plank flooring. "And I fear I have frostbite."

Katarina scanned her sister's face. "The tip of your nose has a tinge of white."

"Oh, dear. Even though I covered up like a Turkish maid, yet" Anna sighed. "Then my nose will peel as it heals. I hope no one important notices."

Alyona checked the coal box beside the stove. "The box is empty." She opened the stove and began scooping the ash into the tarnished metal bucket lying beside it. "There're no hot coals. The fire's been out for a while."

Katarina tapped her fingers on her hips. "We can use the furniture, but we need an axe. I'll go and check the barn."

"Check the root cellar, too. There must be one somewhere outside. Maybe they stored the coal there. The soldiers can't have taken it all," Anna said. "And keep an eye out for food while you're at it. We don't have much left."

"Will do."

～

KATARINA TIGHTENED her wool scarf and went outside, thankful to leave the foul-smelling bungalow, if only for a few minutes. Like many peasant buildings, the small barn was tucked directly behind and perpendicular to the house in an 'L' shape formation. She scanned the yard for something resembling a root cellar — a stone structure with a door built into the earth. Finding nothing, she headed into the barn. The heavy, sliding door was ajar.

At the scent of dusty hay and horse sweat, she sneezed, then coughed. Her lungs prickled, warning her of an impending allergic attack. She retied the scarf over her mouth and nose to filter the air and continued into the dark belly of the barn. She found Olek bent over the wagon, hammering on the wheel. Dappled light shone through the vented roof and between the gaps of the plank framing, casting murky shadows throughout the cavity. A large, dark spot near the rafters blocked the light from one side. Katarina blinked and squeezed her eyes to adjust to the dimness. "Olek, have you seen any coal? Or did you notice a root cellar somewhere?"

"FRÄULEIN KATARINA. NO!" Olek dropped his tools and jumped up. "GET OUT NOW!"

She waved him off and took another step. "I'm fine. I've covered my nose."

"NO!" Olek raced towards her. "TURN AROUND! DON'T LOOK. DON'T LOOK."

But it was too late. As her eyes adjusted to the darkness, she glanced up at the shifting shadows and spotted the silhouettes of the two figures hanging there. Her eyes glued to the scene while her mind grappled to understand what she was seeing. Then, when the awareness came, a garbled scream escaped from her throat. Her hands flew to her mouth and her knees weakened. Silent tears coursed down her frozen cheeks.

Olek grabbed her by the shoulders and twirled her around to face the exit. "You shouldn't have come."

Katarina dropped to her knees.

He knelt beside her and wrapped his muscular arms around her, rocking her as she sobbed. "You shouldn't have come," he said again. "You can't unsee this."

When she settled, he guided her outside to a nearby tree stump. "Sit here. I'll look for coal and firewood. Dry your tears. Go inside when you've settled. Don't tell anyone. Your sister must not know. Act like all is fine."

"But?" She removed her mitts and brushed her wet face with the back of her hand, then blew her nose against her fingers and wiped them against her coat. "Anna will know. She'll see my face and she'll know."

"Stay here until you are calm. You can't go inside while you're shaking like a leaf. We must not frighten your sister. She can't deliver the baby here."

Katarina pointed to the barn. "Shouldn't we ...?"

"What? Cut them down? For the wolves to eat? Nyet." He shook his head. "The ground is frozen, and we have no time."

"But it seems so ... cruel."

"Nyet. They're dead. We can't help them now. Listen to me, Fräulein." He grabbed her chin between both hands and forced her to look at him. "I'm getting the cart ready as fast as I can. But I need help moving the benches. I need Alyona. But if I go inside, they'll ask about you. And your sister must not be left alone. Shall we go together?"

Katarina nodded, then shook her head. "No. No one else should see this. I'll help you."

"It's heavy work. And the horses are inside. Your allergies. You can't breathe well in there. Are you sure?"

"Ja." She wiped her nose again. "But we still need coal."

"I'll go look for a cellar or coal bin. Only ..." his voice trailed.

Katarina sensed Olek's fear. If there were two dead, there could be more. He didn't want to put his head in another cavern to find out. And neither did she.

Olek stood up straight and rubbed his scruffy chin. "We must do what we can. Frau Penner must not be cold."

"She's already cold. We all are." Katarina laughed despite her tears.

He patted her on the shoulder. "I know. Stay here."

Olek disappeared behind the barn and returned a few minutes later with an armful of firewood. "This is all there is. The coal cellar behind the barn is empty. The cabbage barrels dumped out. Not even a potato or a carrot. The whole place stripped." He gestured to the logs with his chin. "From under the stairs. Good for a small fire. But not enough for cooking. But it will keep you warm. "

Katarina nodded. "There's paper in the house to start the fire. This will help. We must hurry, Olek. We need to get to Chortitza as soon as possible."

"But now we're too far from the bridge. We must cross at the rapids. Fräulein Katarina, please keep praying for protection. I fear more problems ahead."

KATARINA WAITED while Olek went to the house and started a fire. When he returned to the barn, she went to work, helping him reorganize supplies and repair the cart. Olek reconstructed the interior, removing the long storage box and the bench from the sleigh and repositioning them inside the wagon, using the wood from the sleigh's hull to brace the sides. Katarina acted as Olek's second pair of hands, closely following his instructions with lifting, carrying, and positioning.

Despite using her scarf as a filter from the dust and horse

dander, her face and eyes itched, and she sneezed constantly. When her breathing became labored and her throat tightened, she sought temporary relief in the frigid outside air. Each respite allowed her to keep working for a few minutes. Olek grimaced each time she left and shook his head when she returned.

"You should quit. Ask Alyona to come help."

"I'm fine," Katarina insisted — despite the scratchiness in her voice. "I don't want anyone else to see this horror. Can we open both the back and front doors to improve the ventilation? It may help."

"We can try it. But there's not much wind." Olek took off his mittens and blew on his hands, rubbing them together as he walked to open the rear doors.

The light cross breeze dropped the temperature further but cleared the air enough for Katarina to keep working. The heat from the horses' bodies helped to warm the barn. Thankfully, there were no other animals adding to her allergies; but a framed section of chicken wire and the rotting manure in the pens pointed to the recent presence of fowl and bovines.

Katarina avoided ogling the hanging reminders of war. She found a pitchfork to fill the wagon with hay and straw. Not finding clean stuff, she took the fodder underneath the hanging couple. The possibility of embedded bodily fluids made her retch, but she convinced herself that the coats and blankets would offer protection from the germs. She determined that if Alyona could work without complaining, so could she.

She prayed for the mental strength to keep the truth from Anna. This secret would be hers and Olek's alone. And once they left, she'd block the memory from her mind. She could note it in her diary, she thought. Then she'd close the book on the grotesque story and never open it again. But how could one forget such a thing?

Olek's voice interrupted her musings. "Let's get the mattresses from the house and put them here on the straw." He drove the last nail into the wood and put away his tools. "For David's Frau to rest."

Katarina agreed, croaking through her restricted throat as they transferred their belongings to the new vehicle. She stood back and eyed the makeshift bench. "There's not much room, but Alyona and I will sit on the bench. Anna can lie down in the back."

"It won't be for long. We'll cross the river before dark. Maybe a couple of hours."

"And then?"

"We'll find your sister, Frau Maria's, farm. It's closer. We can rest there for one night."

Katarina threw her arms around his waist. "Thank you, Olek. What would we do without you? God has placed you in our lives to protect us through this terrible time. I'm so grateful."

Olek returned the hug with one arm and kissed her forehead. "It's my job, Fräulein. Besides, you are my family. I have no other. I'll always be here for you."

Katarina pulled away and stared at his round face. The flecks of gold flickering in his brown eyes spoke of a longing to belong. *Family.* He'd called her family. She'd never thought of him in that way before. Yet, she realized as she pondered his words, Olek did fit into the clan as if he had always belonged there. For lack of better words, he was their next of kin on this trip. In that respect, perhaps the forged documents weren't altogether false.

Olek broke the awkward moment by clearing his throat. He patted her on the back. "Come, let's get those mattresses and be on our way."

19

REINHART AND MAX

1952 JANUARY. MUNICH, GERMANY

"Ten Nuremberg and three Knackwurst." Reinhart pointed to the designated sausages in the display case. "Danke."

"Is you still feeding that cat of yours?" Max, the butcher jested from behind the meat cooler.

Reinhart shrugged and smiled sheepishly. "He's old. He won't be around much longer. I let him eat what he wants."

"It's yer money. When they get that old, I think they should wander off to the ruins and join nature."

"I could never do that." Reinhart grimaced. Why were non-pet owners so flippant about the end of an animal's life? Couldn't they understand an owner's emotional attachment to a helpless thing? If he didn't keep it alive, no one else would.

The thought of the defenseless creature triggered the hideous memory from Warsaw. In the middle of the street, in broad daylight, he watched his fellow soldiers torture the young woman. He could still hear her earth-shattering scream

171

and see them tear at her clothes. He'd wanted to stop them and wanted even more to kill them. Instead, he'd stood there like a frozen statue, staring at the blood pooling on the ground beneath her while they devoured her like rabid dogs. He'd been a coward. He shook his head to push the memory away and refocused on the butcher in front of him.

"Like I said, it's yer money." Max tied the brown paper package with a white string and slid it across the counter. "Anything else?"

The bottle on the shelf above the vintage wooden cash register caught Reinhart's eyes, and he stared at it for a long minute. It looked exactly like the one Peter had brought over to his office. He pointed to it. "That's an expensive bottle of whisky."

The butcher laughed, "Ja. It's not for sale."

"I don't remember seeing it there before."

"I moved it. It was part of the Christmas decoration. There were two bottles. Did ya see the large basket with the canned ham and sausages? One was in the basket, the other on the red cloth." Max pointed to the window and shaped the scene with his hands.

"Oh. Now that you mention it, I do — vaguely. Why did you change the display?"

"It's time for something new. And I gave away the second bottle. There was no point in keeping it anymore," Max said softly as he rang up the order.

"Huh. That sounds like an interesting story." Reinhart fished a bill out of his pocket and paid the butcher. He didn't want to pry, but he wondered if there was a connection between Max and Peter.

"Ja. It is, I suppose." The butcher gave Reinhart his change. "Before the war, I had a partner of sorts. A great employee. Very dedicated. You know the type. He enjoyed working here — really wanted to help the business grow."

Since the shop was empty of customers and Reinhart was in no hurry to leave, he stood by the counter and played with the coins in his hand. "And?" He said to encourage Max to say more.

"He was an immigrant — a refugee from the Great War. So he worked extra hard to prove himself," Max explained. "I decided to sell him half the store. To help him and his family." He pointed to the whisky. "We were gonna sign the papers the next week at a special dinner. Together with both families. I was so excited to have a real, honest partner. I bought the two bottles to celebrate — one to open then, and the other for our ten-year anniversary. But it never happened."

"Why not?"

"He died. The Saturday before our big event."

"Oh, no. How?"

"A fishing accident. The coroner guessed he leaned over too far and fell out of the boat. It flipped over and hit him on the head. He drowned." Max shook his head. "I still can't believe it."

Reinhart froze. This story was very familiar. Chills traveled down his arms. He blinked several times and considered his words. "I'd like to hear more. Can I buy a soft drink?"

"Sure." Max jerked his chin at the cooler behind Reinhart. "Help yourself."

Reinhart tossed him a coin and pulled an orange soda from the cooler. He sat down at the red and chrome table near the cash register. "So, what happened to the other bottle?"

Max folded his arms across his chest and leaned his hips against the counter, his gaze focused on the souvenir. "Back then, my friend's son worked here part-time on weekends. They were both named Peetar. I called the boy Junior. But only when his Papa was around. After, I only called him Peetar. Properly like, to be respectful of his loss." Max shifted and turned around to face Reinhart. He waved his hand in the air, dismissively. "Anyway, I thought it only right to give the kid a chance to prove himself. Back then, he had attitude — like most teenagers. Full of superhero juices and no common sense. Always arguing. He was excited about the war talk. Believed the Nazi propaganda. Said he was gonna join the Luftwaffe and make a difference. 'I'm gonna help revive the old Germany,' he said."

Reinhart toyed with the soft drink, listening intently and not wanting to interrupt.

Max walked around the meat counter and joined Reinhart at the table. "One day I said to him, 'Listen, Peetar. You can stay working here. Keep this store going. Your Papa and I had grand plans for this place. I wanna give ya the chance to keep his dream alive. We can build a restaurant in the back. Maybe add a bakery.'

"'No,' he said. 'The war's coming, and I'm gonna fly those airplanes through the skies and bomb the enemy. The sooner I volunteer, the less chance I'll end up on the front lines.'

"'Don't be crazy,' I said. 'We can't have another war. Look how many died in the Great War. The world won't let it happen. And frankly, after what your parents went through to get here, I'm surprised you'd want to take part in such ugliness.'" Max stood up, went to the cooler, and pulled out a *limonade*. "The family went through the Great War and the Russian civil war. The boy's birth parents both died there." He popped the bottle cap on the soft drink with a metal opener attached to a ring of keys on his belt. "'Peetar,' I said to him. 'Didn't ya hear the stories? It was murder and mayhem over there. War is a terrible thing. Don't lower yourself. Do something positive with your life. Something your Papa would be proud of. Keep his memory alive.'

"But he wouldn't listen. He joined the Luftwaffe. But he had problems. He never became the great pilot he wanted to be, like the Red Baron, Manfred von Richthofen. It was all fanciful thinking on his part. Like most kids." The butcher sat down at the table across from Reinhart. He shook his head slowly from side-to-side. "Not that it would've mattered, in the end. Considering his age. Hitler destroyed that whole generation. Especially the kids."

"And the whisky? How does that fit in?" Reinhart probed. He guessed the rest of the story, but he wanted the facts from the butcher. Peter's strange visit to his office was beginning to make sense.

"I've stared at those two bottles for years. Wondering what I should do with them. Waiting for another perfect partner to come along. But I'm getting old. Maybe I should sell the place. I don't have the energy anymore. And Germany's still in a mess. The clean-up from the war never ends. Inflation is crazy. And the Americans walk around like they own this place, telling us what we can do and where we can go." Max's shoulders sagged as he stared out the display window. "Hitler destroyed our beloved Deutschland, and we all let it happen. The country will never be great again. At least not in my lifetime. The world will make sure of that."

"And the bottle. What happened to the second bottle?" Reinhart insisted, impatiently.

The butcher turned back to Reinhart and nodded. "The son comes in every so often. We're friendly. He works at the university now. Helping some professor of history, I think. It's a good job for him. I'm happy for him but sad for me."

Max sucked back the fizzy drink, then wiped his brow with the rag tucked into his waist. "He doesn't come around as much as he used to. But a few weeks ago, he came in on his birthday. I always remembered that date because he was working here when his Papa died, and his birthday came two weeks later. That first one was hard. He had trouble concentrating on his job and I sent him home early. I was afraid he'd hurt himself on the saws. He refused to celebrate his birthday for years after that. I guess the memory was too painful."

Reinhart ran his thumbs over the condensation on his soda bottle. "Why did he take it so hard?"

Max gulped his soda and nodded. "Ja. If I remember it right, on the day Peetar, the senior, died, the two of them were having a tiff. That wasn't unusual. They argued a lot back then. Sometimes they'd go fishing to talk it out. That day, Peetar the kid wasn't where he was supposed to be at the right time, so his Papa went fishing alone. The boy blamed himself. Said that if he'd been there, maybe his Papa wouldn't have died. I think the guilt ate him up. He couldn't work here much after that."

"That makes sense." Reinhart reflected on Peter's mood swings and the cloud of shame that seemed to hang over him. Maybe the war hadn't bothered Peter that much — like it had done to him. Perhaps his father's death was a heavier weight. Katarina's demise likely triggered that earlier pain. "But what about the whisky?" Reinhart asked again.

The butcher chuckled and held up his hand. "I'm getting to that. A while back, he came in to buy a roast. Just then, I was standing here holding that bottle in my hands and trying to figure out what to do with it. He walked in, hanging his head, looking all forlorn, carrying the weight of the world on his shoulders. I decided — right then and there — that the bottle really belonged to his father, so now it should go to him. Partnership or no partnership.

"'Peetar,' I said. 'Your Papa and I wanted to expand this place together. I always hoped you'd join me and carry the dream for your Papa. But ya didn't wanna. That's fine. Ya deserve to work at a job that makes ya happy. I understand. But for all these years, I've kept this bottle of whisky in memory of your Papa. We were gonna open it on the official day of our partnership. And then, we were gonna keep the second bottle for our ten-year anniversary. Well, both those dates are gone now. And so are both your parents. So here.' I handed him the bottle. 'Drink this with your wife or a good friend and toast your Papa for me. Think about him and his dreams and all the good times ya had.'"

"How did he respond?" Reinhart sipped on his soft drink and stared at the table, avoiding eye contact with Max and pretending he knew nothing.

"At first, he refused. Said he couldn't accept it. Then, he said. 'My wife's pregnant. She's not drinking these days.' I thought, what a strange thing to say. The bottle has nothing to do with his wife. But I said, 'Congratulations. Then why don't you keep it until the child is born? Celebrate your parents' grandchild for them.' Peetar shook his head, like he was going to say no again. But then he took the bottle. There were tears in his eyes, and he choked up. He could barely thank me. But before he walked out the door, he said, 'I'm sorry I couldn't take over the shop, Max. Thanks for everything you did for my parents. I'll remember this always.' He hasn't told me yet how he celebrated, and I haven't asked."

So that was the dark secret eating at Peter's soul and keeping him up at night, Reinhart thought while nodding at Max's storytelling. Peter had also fought with Katarina just before she left for the war for the last time. He'd wanted to make amends but never got the chance.

Reinhart wondered if Peter was trying to absolve himself by reconstructing the diary. Or was he searching for proof of parental love within the pages of history? Either way, finding the truth about his roots might help him feel more stable or ease his pain. Maybe then he could set clearer goals in his life and become more productive and happier.

Reinhart nursed his soft drink, feeling a tad dishonest for not admitting he knew Peter. He set the drink down and passed his hand over his jaw, gazing intently at the old butcher. "Max, I need to tell you something."

The man's eyebrows furrowed. "Tell me what?"

"I know Peter. I've been giving him some professional advice with his mother's diary."

Max's eyebrows shot up. "Oh? Well, then you know the whole story."

Reinhart shook his head slightly. "No. I don't think so. Though he's told me some."

"But it's incredible, don't you think?" Max leaned forward. Tears welled in his pale gray-blue eyes.

"What is?" Reinhart frowned at the butcher's emotional reaction. What was he missing?

"First, his biological mother dies and his biological father goes missing in the civil war. Then, his adopted father dies, and his adopted mother goes missing in the second war. What's the chances of that? In one family? And to one person. Both sets of parents, gone. Each pair with one confirmed dead and the other presumed so under mysterious circumstances. The poor kid. No wonder he's so screwed up."

The drink slipped from Reinhart's hand and dropped on the table. The orange liquid bubbled out of the bottle in a fizzy blob. Max whipped off the towel around his waist and picked up the glass and swiped at the liquid, absorbing it all with one quick stroke. "It's humid today. The glass is slippery. It happens all the time. Don't feel bad."

Reinhart rubbed his lips together as he watched the butcher clean up his mess. The whole story was preposterous, and yet suddenly, the entire saga was crystal clear. How had he not put two and two together? Peter had implied as much on multiple occasions. It was the reason the man was struggling with his mother's diary. "I agree. Who wouldn't be confused? I also have trouble accepting that these are coincidences."

"So, what do you think?" The butcher crumpled the towel into a ball and tossed it across the room. It landed neatly in the porcelain sink behind the cooler.

"Huh? What do I think about what?"

"Could either of them still be alive? Katarina, or even David? I don't want to dash the kid's hopes, but I've wondered, too."

Reinhart's heart sank. "I think it's wrong to give him false hope, Max. So many soldiers never came home from the Great War. Thousands disappeared; their bodies left in shallow graves in the open fields. The families never knew what happened to their loved ones or where they were buried. It was the same during the Russian civil war. And lately, we've heard stories about the camps in Russia, people being shipped to Siberia and Kazakhstan. The father could have ended up in any of those places."

"Or none."

"Or none," Reinhart repeated. "There's little chance the father is still alive. Too much time has passed. And as for Katarina — again, too much time has gone by. Soldiers disappeared during Hitler's war, too. Katarina was a translator for the SS, so if the Russians caught her, they'd have executed her as a spy. Or she could be sitting in a Russian prison right now. But my guess is she's dead, as the government said."

"That's my take on it, too. But there's one thing that bothers me." Max tapped his finger on the table.

"What's that?"

"Katarina asked for special assignment. She wanted to go back to Ukraine. She lost a baby there during the civil war — while alive, not dead. And Peetar's father David disappeared then, too. Katarina had more than one reason to go back there. Could she have gone AWOL? And blended in with the locals so she could look for them?"

Reinhart's eyes widened. "That's a good question. She was

fluent in the language and the culture." He pushed his chair back and walked back to the cooler to get another soft drink. "This is astounding, although entirely speculative. We can't know anything for certain." He plopped down on the chair and handed the drink to Max to open.

"The trouble is, if they caught her, she could be anywhere right now." Max snapped the cap off the bottle and gave it back to Reinhart.

"Dead or alive."

"Exactly. And this is Peetar's dilemma. Can ya help him?" The butcher urged.

"Help him?"

"Ja. Help Peetar find the needle in the haystack that he's looking for. The clue that shows where she might have gone. Or, if she disappeared on purpose."

Reinhart pushed the empty glass to the side. "The diary. He's convinced the secret's in the diary."

"Ja," exclaimed the butcher. "I agree. It must be."

"But where?"

"Start with the babies. It must begin with the babies."

"Which one? Peter or Jacob?"

"Does it matter? Comb them both. If there's a nit on the hair, he'll have the proof he needs."

"The nit on the hair?"

Max patted Reinhart on the hand. "You know. The tiniest detail can make the difference. Pay attention to everything. Look closely."

20

CROSSING THE DNIEPER

**1918 FEBRUARY (JULIAN CALENDAR). THE LEFT
BANK OF THE DNIEPER RIVER, NORTH OF
ALEKSANDROVSK, UKRAINE**

AFTER THE HORSES WERE HITCHED INTO THEIR THREE-
abreast formation and the supplies transferred to the wagon,
the group headed towards the shimmering gray ribbon on the
horizon. Katarina and Alyona took turns sitting on the bench
and keeping Anna company on the straw mattress in the
back.

The wagon bounced and swerved around the icy corners
of the rutted country roads. Olek snapped the whip repeatedly — urging the team onward — seemingly oblivious to
women's discomfort. Anna's face paled with every slippery
turn and Katarina and Alyona hung on for dear life.

"Olek, please slow down. We'll upset." Katarina cried out
when she could take it no longer.

He pointed at the sun's descending position. "We must get
to the other side of the river before dusk. These are

dangerous roads. We can't take shortcuts across the fields anymore. But if Frau Penner can't manage, I'll slow down."

However, the serene white landscape defied danger. The gray clouds meandered lazily across the winter sky and the hills sparkled with fresh blankets of snowy white. Wagons carrying travelers, tarped supplies, or household goods crossed their paths from time to time. Everyone nodded and waved to each other as if there was no war. Katarina wondered if they were through the worst of the chaos.

Then, in the distance, a series of gunshots rang out. The image of the two bodies swaying from the rafters flashed through Katarina's mind. She wondered who the victims were and why they'd been hanged; and prayed for friends or family to find them before they rotted on the ropes.

Olek interrupted her dark thoughts, pointing to the horizon. "Vot on" — there it is.

Katarina spotted it, too. The mighty Dnieper — peppered with tiny tree-topped granite islands — sparkled like a silver ribbon with lacy edges. A foggy gray blanket hovered over the surface and misty drops hung in the air. Icy fingers had carved the riverbank into impressive designs worthy of an artist's palette, but the white-capped waves warned about the dangerous rapids.

Olek stopped the wagon at the top of the hill so they could enjoy the scenery for a few minutes before descending to the riverbank.

Katarina jumped into the back of the wagon and woke Anna. "Look. You've got to see this."

Anna shifted to sit and grabbed onto Katarina's arm for support. "Incredible. I've never seen it like this before."

"Nor I," Katarina said. "It's like a living storybook." She shivered and rubbed her arms, inhaling deeply of the damp freshwater air. Her skin tingled. For the first time in many days, she felt alive and invigorated. "It's like God came down and carved the riverbank and breathed on the water."

"Look over there, Katarina." Anna pointed at the abutment on the shoreline. "There's the old ferry crossing."

Next to the tiny, decrepit shack, charcoal puffs wafted from the smokestack of a long flat barge positioned at the wharf.

"That's no little ferry. We've got real transportation!" Katarina said excitedly, clapping her hands. "God has met us again!"

"Ja. Only a few more hours until I can sleep in a proper bed." Exhaustion resonated in Anna's voice.

"It's been so long since I've seen the river. I've forgotten how massive it is. I feel like a little child seeing it for the first time." Katarina babbled, unable to control her enthusiasm. "Do you remember when we used to go swimming at the beaches, Anna? I can almost see Chortitza Island."

"Mm. I remember visiting the graves of our ancestors there and having picnics under the old oak tree. And roasting fish over the open fire. Those were the best times." Anna's face lit up, and she rubbed her belly. "We should plan a vacation after the war ends. I'll talk to David next time he's home."

"Ooh. Ja. Smoked fish. I can't remember the last time we ate that." Katarina's stomach rumbled, reminding her that she'd skipped lunch again. "We should find a local fish shop. There should be one on the other side."

Olek interrupted their musings and pointed to the barge on the shoreline. "I hope we have enough money." The tension was gone from his face, replaced by a huge smile.

Maybe the worst really was behind them, Katarina thought.

"I've more cash if you need it," Anna said.

Olek held up the wad in his pocket. "Sergei returned the

Kerenka. He said we'd probably need it for emergencies on the road."

Katarina understood why. Anna wanted to dispose of the despised currency, too. She'd hidden the more valuable Duma notes in her undergarments.

"You see," Anna said, referring to Sergei, "He really was a good man."

"The salt of the earth." Katarina nodded. "Yet not a Christian. How is it possible that one so foul and without faith can still be so kind?"

"It's man-made goodness, Katarina. Those without God depend on their own strength to control their character. But when they meet us, they are ashamed of their shortcomings. Their guilt controls them."

"Huh." Katarina pondered on Anna's comment. "But we never spoke about our faith to him."

"We don't need to," Anna said. "Our religion speaks for itself."

OLEK MANEUVERED the troika to the old ferry dock and handed the reins to Alyona before jumping off the wagon. As he headed to the simple wooden hut on the shoreline, a short figure in a heavy brown coat and wearing a knitted wool hat stretched over his ears, exited the wheelhouse of the barge, and greeted Olek with a handshake. After a brief discussion and much finger-pointing, the man shook his head. Olek produced a wad of cash and peeled notes from it, offering them to the captain one by one. After a lengthy negotiation, the man nodded, and they shook hands. Olek returned to the wagon and explained.

"All is good. He complains of expensive coal. Armies take everything, even fuel. But money solves many problems. Even

Kerenka." Olek rubbed his hands together and blew on them before putting his mitts on. "Now we wait one hour for good steam. The wheelhouse is warm. Come." He walked to the back and removed the lumber holding the tailgate in position, then offered the sisters a supporting hand as they slid off.

"I need a good stretch." Anna yawned. "I'm stiff, tired, and hungry."

"Me, too." Katarina welcomed the permission to stand and stretch her legs. They hooked their arms together as they walked towards the boat. "I can't wait to get to Maria's and enjoy a real home-cooked meal." Katarina redirected Anna around a glob of slush on the platform. "Be careful. It's icy here."

"You haven't eaten yet?" Anna seemed surprised.

Katarina stretched a stiff smile across her face. "No. I wasn't hungry earlier." Had Anna forgotten how she turned down Alyona's offers of sausage and rusks? After seeing the hanging couple, she'd had little appetite. But she also worried about running out of food. "Besides, I'm tired of eating the same thing over and over. Anyway, there's probably not much left. I can wait."

"If there is, it's likely frozen by now. I know I am. I can't feel my toes anymore." Anna rubbed her arms, went up and down on her tiptoes, then shook her feet from side to side.

"Me, too. My warm boots aren't warm enough. The river looked so pretty and inviting from the top of the riverbank. But this damp cold is no picnic. I feel like I'm standing inside a pail of ice." Katarina stomped her feet. Her voice still croaked from being exposed to the dust and dander in the barn. She was thankful the allergic attack hadn't been worse.

They stood on the deck watching the Troika plod onto the barge. The lead horse balked and stepped backward, startling the other two and forcing them to retreat. Olek yelled, yanked on the reins, and snapped the whip, but the horses became confused and turned into each other. Leather straps and chains became entangled, and the entire venture came to a standstill.

The boat master held up his hands and shouted at Olek to stop fighting with the horses. He walked up to the center lead, calmly took control of the team, and led them onto the platform.

"He's obviously done this a few times before," Katarina said as the horses succumbed to the masterful guidance.

"Olek must feel embarrassed to be outdone like that." Anna nudged Katarina with her elbow. "Come. Let's head to the wheelhouse. I'm freezing."

A SMALL CAST iron cook stove radiated a welcoming warmth as they stepped inside the cozy cabin. As the heat quickly soaked through their frozen fingers and woolen layers, the sisters shed their outerwear and collapsed on the lower bunk — using it as a couch.

"Sit Alyona. Come warm up with us." Katarina pointed to the single chair beside a tiny table.

The maid shook her head. "You should eat. I'll go see what's left in the box." She turned and left the wheelhouse.

Anna looked around. "Does he live here all winter? There's not much stuff lying about."

"Maybe it's tucked away by the engine."

"It must get awfully lonely."

Alyona returned with a sack of rusks and a jar of water. "There's only one ring of sausage left. If you can wait a bit, I think it's best we pace ourselves.

"But we'll be at Maria's by dusk." Anna eagerly chomped on the toasted bun. "There's no need to save food now."

Alyona stared at the floor, her lips clamped together in a

straight line. Katarina sensed the maid's reluctance to disagree with her mistress. "Anna, I think Alyona's right. We don't know what's ahead of us yet."

Katarina tried to remember when the servants had last eaten but couldn't. Since Alyona had already been caught unprepared with the empty kettle, she wondered if the maid was worried about the food supply. But was it more than that? Was Alyona worried about encountering rebels? Although they'd heard the rumors about Makhno's control of the Dnieper's right bank, they hoped the gossip was false. Such a confrontation could be deadly.

While recalling the day's events, Katarina stared at the jar of water, and then at the stove. "Alyona, please get the samovar. We have coal."

Anna's face lit up. "Tea. We can have tea again. Do we still have herbs?"

Alyona didn't need prodding. She raced out of the wheelhouse and returned a minute later with the kettle. Setting it down on the hot stove, she grabbed the tongs hanging beside it. She removed several red-hot coals from the belly and dropped them into the chimney of the samovar. Then she scooped a handful of fresh, dry coals from the storage box and stuffed them into her pocket.

"We should ask the shipmaster," Anna said as she watched the theft. "Coal is expensive."

"I'll tell Olek," Alyona said as the boat jerked from its sliding position. "When I serve him with tea." The motion of the boat threw Alyona off balance and she slapped the wall for support before plunking down onto the only chair in the room.

"And we're off," Katarina announced with a loud cheer. "I'm warm now. Let's go watch." She stuffed the last of the toasted crust into her mouth, washed it down with a swig of water, and handed the jar to Anna who promptly guzzled the rest. After putting on her coat, she pushed her toes into her toasty warm boots, then helped Anna dress. "One more night, Anna," she said. "After this, our feet will never be cold again."

"Huh," Anna snorted. "I won't hold my breath waiting for that to come true."

~

THEY EXITED the wheelhouse and wandered to a partially covered area on the deck where they could overlook the deep gray water swirling beneath them. As the boat maneuvered between the islands, patches of snow-covered ice floated alongside it.

Alyona delivered tea to the sisters, then went back to the wheelhouse to refill the teapot from the samovar. She returned with a steaming pot and two cups and brought them over to Olek. The two servants sat together on a small bench at the far end of the platform, conversing and drinking tea. When the western shore emerged into full view, Alyona gave a high-pitched joyful shout and pumped her hand in the air above her head. Olek slapped the railing enthusiastically with both hands.

"What's that all about?" Anna whispered. She hugged her baby bulge with both arms, one hand rolling back and forth across the top and the other supporting it at the bottom. "I can't hear what they're saying."

Katarina dropped her eyes to the dark churning water and pretended she couldn't hear. She wasn't about to admit to eavesdropping. "Look at the riverbank, Anna. Doesn't it look like a giant, dirty blob rising from the water?" She pointed at the shoreline. "Almost like a scary sea creature coming up from the depths."

"Honestly, Katarina. Your imagination is working over-time again," Anna scoffed. "But I can see that Olek was right about this. There's only a skiff of snow. The sleigh would never have made it." She turned to Katarina. "How did he know?"

"From Sergei, I suppose. Or Alyona. Her family lives nearby. She knows this river like the back of her hand."

"She does?" Anna glared at Katarina. "And how do *you* know so much? You *are* eavesdropping again. I can tell. What are they saying?"

Katarina shrugged. "She's hoping to see her children and grandchildren."

"She has children?"

"You didn't know?" Katarina asked, surprised.

"No. Maybe? I don't remember." Anna's mouth twisted to the side. "She's never talked about them. I always assumed she had none. When does she see them? She only takes two weeks off in the winter."

"Did you ever ask about her personal life?" Katarina despaired. Despite Anna's ongoing charity work for the church, her sister showed little interest in, or compassion for, those who worked for her. It seemed hypocritical to her.

"No, it's not my business. Alyona came with the house, so why do I need to know more?" Anna's voice shifted into a matter-of-fact tone. "Tradition holds that we keep distance between ourselves and our servants. If we get involved in their personal life, they'll take advantage. Provided they do their jobs properly, there's no need for intimate conversation."

"And there, my dear sister, is a part of the reasons for the Bolshevik uprising. Because the kulaks do not honor the hardship of the peasants, they contribute to the inequity of society." Katarina gave her sister a sour look.

"Kulaks? Wealthy peasants." Anna screwed up her face. "That word smacks with such disparaging weight."

"Anna, in their opinion, we *are* the guilty rich — making money off the backs of the working class while they suffer to keep us in our luxurious surroundings. According to them, we're not entitled to our own property."

Anna rolled her eyes. "Well, that sounds like jealous talk to me. We've worked hard for everything we have. But, nonetheless. I'll do right by Alyona. As soon as we're settled, I'll give her a week off to visit her family. Since we're here already, she doesn't need to travel far."

"Oba y Oba," Katarina mocked. "That's so generous of you."

"If we're stuck at Mutter and Papa's for a while, we won't be needing her, anyway. I may even allow her a longer leave. However long it takes for this Red skirmish to be over with, so we can go home."

Katarina glared at her sister through narrowed eyes. Did Anna really expect the world to revolve around her? Or was the traditional hierarchy so ingrained in her mindset that she couldn't see the unfairness and the obvious inequities in their society? There was no point in explaining now. Her sister wouldn't understand, and the talk could go badly. So, she clamped her lips between her teeth.

WHEN THE BARGE grated against the shoreline, the shipmaster barked at Olek. He turned and beckoned the women to climb on. Katarina and Alyona helped Anna settle on the mattress in the back before climbing up to the front bench.

Olek stood in front of the troika, holding on to the center harness until the barge was safely anchored, then guided the team off the deck. The horses balked as they hoofed onto the slippery shoreline and the wagon shifted sharply to the left. The front wheel caught the edge of a pile of ice and disappeared underneath the lip of the barge. The ferry master retrieved an axe lying on the shoreline and brought it over to Olek. He pointed to the steep embankment ahead, the deeply rutted road, and the slick patches of ice.

Olek grimaced and turned to the women, "Can you walk to the top?"

Katarina looked at Anna. "I can. But can you? That's a straight-up climb."

"This baby is getting very heavy in the groin. It's hard to walk," Anna said, shaking her head.

Katarina groaned. She'd heard that heaviness in the groin was one of the last signs. It meant the baby had dropped and was positioning itself for the birth. But they still had to travel for a few more hours. They couldn't risk Anna going into labor yet. "Anna, you should stay on. Alyona and I will walk."

"Thanks." Anna rolled her hand over her stomach and lay back on the mattress.

Olek opened the tailgate and helped Katarina and Alyona off the wagon. "Olek, that looks like a very steep climb. Please go slowly." Katarina whispered. "We mustn't jostle Anna so much."

"If we can go at all." Olek secured the tailgate, then walked back to the wheel and stared at the icy obstruction.

"Can we free it?" Katarina hunched to peek under the wagon.

"This was the broken wheel. It's not strong." Olek took off his hat and scratched his bald spot.

"Can we back up and re-angle the wagon?"

"I'll chop at the ice. Then we try again."

Katarina glanced up at the sun. Its low position warned they were running out of daylight. As dusk deepened, rebels would be on the lookout for easy targets. She turned and met Anna's questioning stare. "We should've kept the sleigh," Anna mouthed. Katarina nodded. But it was too late now. They had to make the best of it.

"Pray." It was the only answer she could think of. Pray for help. Pray they'd get somewhere safe in time before Anna had the baby. Pray they wouldn't freeze to death in the damp cold. If God cared about them personally, wouldn't he rescue them? She reflected on the verse.

This is the confidence we have in approaching God: that if we ask anything according to his will, he hears us. [1]

Her faith wavered. *'According to his will.'* What if God had other plans for them? How could she know God's will? Was this what the pastor meant by trials and tribulations — a spiritual test? If so, more dark times would lie ahead.

1 1 John 5:14

21

THE OTHER SIDE OF THE RIVER

1918 FEBRUARY. NEAR EINLAGE, UKRAINE. FORMER FREE LANDS OF THE ZAPORIZHIAN COSSACKS ON THE RIGHT BANK OF THE DNIEPER RIVER.

OLEK HACKED AT THE FROZEN SLUSH WHILE THE shipmaster led the horses back and forth, trying to maneuver the wagon out of the icy obstruction. Finally, they crammed wooden slabs around the stuck wheel and it rolled up the ramp. Olek checked for damage, then looked up with a wide smile and gave a thumbs up.

Katarina and Alyona hiked up the steep embankment behind the wagon, while Anna secured herself on the floor of the cart. As the Troika headed up the slope, the cart tilted to the left. Anna shrieked and Katarina held her breath, her eyes glued to the vehicle. But Anna waved to say she was fine. Then, when the pathway rose more sharply, the wagon pitched almost straight up, and Anna let out an ear-piercing scream. She sailed down feet first towards the bottom of the wagon's box.

Katarina and Alyona stood open-mouthed as Anna's arms flew in the air and her head disappeared. At the sharp crack of Anna's feet slamming against the tailgate, Katarina screamed and sprinted towards the wagon. "Anna! No! Are you safe?"

Alyona was two steps behind her. "She's good." The maid grabbed her arm. "Olek put lumber across the bottom. It can't fall open."

"Thank God." Katarina held her hand over her racing heart. "I pray she's not hurt." When the wagon crested the embankment, it jerked left, then right, then slipped over a large hump and stopped. Olek waved his hat to say all was well. Katarina and Alyona cheered and ran to catch up.

"Thanks for the excitement, Anna." Katarina joked as they climbed aboard. "You gave us quite the fright."

"I gave you a scare?" Anna mocked as she wiped the tears from her pale face. "You weren't the one falling out!"

"Well, you said you couldn't walk. Did your baby complain?" Katarina croaked. Her lungs ached from running too fast in the frigid air and she collapsed on the straw beside her sister, coughing.

"Not yet. He's too scared to move," Anna sniffed. "But I'm not doing very well."

"Well then, we need to calm you both down. Should I sing a tune or two?" Katarina asked.

"Yes, please. I need a pleasant thought to take away this awful shock." Anna hugged her belly. The color was slowly returning to her previously ashen face.

"As soon as I get my breath back." Katarina rubbed her chest to encourage her heart rate and breathing to settle.

The late afternoon sun glinted deceptively on the peaceful, snow-covered fields. War and civil strife seemed implausible and distant. *We're so close to home. Nothing can go wrong now.*

Except ... No. Katarina refocused. "Do you remember the Christmas when we got stuck on the road on the way to Tante Annie's?"

Anna gave a weak smile and wiped her nose with a monogrammed linen handkerchief. "Ja. You were about seven then. I was nine. Papa took the horse to get help and the rest of us walked home with Mutter. We were all there — you, me, Maria, Helena, and our brothers David and Heinrich — all bundled up like Egyptian mummies and trudging home in the middle of the snowstorm singing Christmas carols and throwing snowballs at each other. By the time we got back, we didn't care about the storm anymore."

"And Katya had hot cocoa waiting for us because she worried so." Katarina reflected on the nostalgic memory. "Let's sing a Christmas carol." She thought of an easy tune to erase the fright of the moment that wouldn't exhaust her lungs.

Anna beamed and pumped her hand in the air. "Yes! Let's pretend we're little girls and it's Christmas again."

"I'll start." Katarina hummed a note and invited all to join in on a rowdy rendition of the old Christmas carol.

O Tannenbaum, o Tannenbaum,
   wie treu sind deine Blätter!
   Du grünst nicht nur zur Sommerzeit,
   Nein auch im Winter, wenn es schneit.
   O Tannenbaum, o Tannenbaum,
   wie treu sind deine Blätter!

~

AS THEY DROVE up the rutted road and passed through a narrow strip of frozen, marshy swampland, Katarina tried to ignore her growling stomach, which was getting more demanding by the minute. At the entrance to the mixed forest, she stopped singing and gazed at the snow swirling across the treetops and the sparkling icicles hanging from the bare branches. Sinister shadows flickered through the trees. The back of her neck tingled, and goosebumps rose on her arms.

Olek spotted the upturned wagon in the ditch first. He slowed the team and swiveled in his seat. "Do you want me to check?" He asked Anna, pointing.

Katarina caught a flash of red. "Something or someone's there."

"No, don't stop. It could be a ruse." Anna's eyes narrowed with suspicion. "And we don't have time. We must get to Maria's."

Olek nodded and snapped the reins.

"Wait," Katarina yelled. "Stop. Something doesn't look right."

Olek yanked on the reins.

"Katarina, what are you doing? There could be rebels in the bush. This isn't a safe area." Anna signaled to Olek. "No, don't stop Olek. Go, go."

Olek hesitated. Katarina followed his concerned gaze until she saw it, too. "No. Stop." She pointed to the accident scene. "Anna, look. There's a child standing there."

"I don't see anything. Where are you looking?" Anna peered into the trees.

"There, behind the cart. Now I see two children."

"Katarina, I don't trust this situation." Anna grabbed her arm.

Olek stopped the Troika. "I see the children, too."

"I'm getting off." Katarina crawled to the tailgate and threw her leg over the panel.

"No, Katarina, please don't. This isn't a good idea."

Katarina waved off her sister's worries and jumped off. As she ran down into the gully, two short figures emerged from behind the upturned wagon, crying and waving frantically. "Please help us!"

"What happened here?" When she ran up to the children, she glimpsed a swollen, purplish foot poking out from under the wagon. She shivered and squeezed her eyes shut — wanting to know, but not wanting to see the carnage.

"They killed our parents."

"Who did? Do you know who did this?"

"Robbers. Bad men."

Katarina held her hand over her mouth and fought the urge to vomit while she quickly scanned the grisly scene. The dead wore no outerwear and footwear, the woman's legs were bare and splattered with blood. The scene was too gruesome to bear. Her insides screamed. Every muscle in her body wanted to flee. She crouched behind the wagon and retched. *What is happening to this country?* She wiped her mouth with her sleeve, then turned her back to the horror and focused on the children.

"When did this happen?"

"This morning."

Katarina guessed the pretty girl with the glistening round amber eyes and blond hair to be about eleven or twelve years of age. Her lashes were the longest that Katarina had ever seen, and she couldn't stop herself from staring at them.

"We have no food." The boy — Katarina pegged him to be about eight — scratched the caramel brown hair beneath the oversized gray cap. The gray wool scarf wrapped around his long, narrow face almost hid the bloody smears on his cheeks.

"We're hungry. And thirsty." The girl shivered uncontrollably. She pulled the red scarf away from her mouth. The bluish cast to her lips proved the girl was dangerously chilled to the bone.

Katarina guessed the gunmen had ambushed the family and left them for dead. "What're your names?"

"I'm Yuliya and this is my brother Anatoliy."

"Where do you live?"

"Seleney-Lug." Yuliya tugged on her gray double-breasted wool coat. An embroidered hem of black roses on a red background from the underneath dress peeked out the bottom.

Katarina recognized the name of the village on the river but was unsure of its exact location. The children were too well dressed to be vagrants, she concluded. Either they came from a working-class family, or the mother took great pride in appearances.

"What were you doing here?" Katarina gazed over her shoulder into the trees. How could it be that no one had noticed them until now? Or had others — fearing the danger — passed them by?

"We were visiting my sister in Einlage. She works here."

"And shopping," Anatoliy added.

Katarina raised her eyebrows. There wasn't much shopping in the village, except for specialty cheeses and meats in the local Mennonite butcher shop, and a renowned fabric store beside the tavern. She held out her hand, "Come. You can't stay here. My sister lives close by. We'll get you some food and a warm bed."

The children took her hands and together they trekked up the snow-covered bank. Alyona stood by the tailgate, waiting to help boost the children onto the wagon. "Scoot over there by my sister," Katarina said as she crawled on after them.

"What happened?" Anna asked in German, her eyes wide and her eyebrows knitted together in one straight line.

Katarina shook her head as an icy shiver traveled down her back. How should she explain it? The spectacle was too gruesome to describe.

Alyona tucked her quilt around the boy's thin shoulders. "Here. Let's get you warm."

Katarina wrapped her horsehair blanket around the girl. Her hands still trembled from the shock of the scene, and she rubbed them on Yuliya's back. "We'll be safe soon. We don't have much further to go."

Yuliya wiped an unkempt mop of vanilla hair from her oval face, and she looked up to meet Katarina's gaze. Frozen tears hung in the girl's upper lashes and fresh ones slipped down her cheek. She pulled the blanket tightly around her lean frame.

"Do you want to talk about it? Can you tell me what happened?" Katarina asked in Ukrainian, expecting that the children wouldn't understand German.

Yuliya rubbed her eyes. "They stopped us when we came around the corner. They were hiding in the trees with guns."

"They started shooting, and the horses got scared. Then the wagon broke away and flipped over and rolled into the ditch." Anatoliy's brown eyes flickered. "The horses ran away."

"Mama screamed and said her leg was broken. And then our *Tato* crawled out and grabbed his gun. But he couldn't get it ready fast enough." Tears rolled down Yuliya's ruddy blood-stained cheeks.

"They circled us, and Mama screamed for us to hide. We ran into the trees." Anatoliy dramatized with his hands.

"They were shooting. They stole everything. When they left, we came back and found our parents." Yuliya's chin trembled. "But we were too late. The bad men killed them."

"No one stopped to help. Except you." Anatoliy's voice croaked. Tears cascaded down his face.

Anna whispered in German. "I don't like this situation, Katarina. This could be a trap. I've heard that the rebels use children as bait. They're probably watching us right now.

Next, they'll pounce on us and accuse us of kidnapping. Besides, it can't be true. Guns are illegal now."

Katarina bit her tongue at her sister's insensitivity. "Don't be ridiculous, Anna. They're not making this up. Look at how cold they are. The attack happened hours ago. Their parents are dead. I saw the bodies. I'm surprised these two haven't frozen to death by now."

"How do you know that was their parents? That could be anyone lying there. Either way, we'll get blamed. Tomorrow, there'll be a warrant for our arrest. They'll accuse us of murder, too."

"Nonsense," Katarina scolded. "After what we've been through over the last couple of days, now you're worried about our reputation? After you paid for forged documents? What's wrong with you? Don't be so quick to attack others before knowing the whole story. There's right and wrong, Anna. Helping them is the right thing to do."

"You're right. We don't know the facts. But surely a local would have come by to save them, eventually. Someone who knew them." Anna's eyes darted around the landscape and down the road.

"But no one did. And they've been there all day."

"So they say."

"Good grief, Anna. Be reasonable. Look at their expensive clothing. They're obviously not homeless waifs. Can't you see? They were attacked and robbed, they're not the ones doing the robbing. Besides, these children can't look after them-selves. They're not adults. Look how cold they are. If they could have gone for help themselves, they would have. Don't be so quick to judge."

Anna tightened her lips into a forced smile. "Maybe so. Well, what's done is done. We'll make the best of it. I just hope you're right." Anna switched to her coarse Russian to address the children. "Don't worry. You'll be nice and warm soon. There's a hot meal waiting at our sister's house. We're almost there."

Alyona twisted around on the bench and began speaking to the children in Ukrainian. Whether or not she'd understood the German, she didn't show, but she focused on the children and avoided Anna's glare.

"Our Tato injured his hand in the army, so he came home to recover," Yuliya said.

Perhaps that explained the gun, Katarina thought. But for which side? If the bandits had known who he was, he could have been a target.

"And what does your Mama do?" Alyona asked.

It was odd hearing that question posed to a child. In the Mennonite world, no one would ask a child such a question. Women were mothers, helped their husbands with farm labor, and did charity work at the church. Some poor women worked outside the home, but it wasn't common. Yet, Alyona seemed to take it for granted.

"She's a seamstress. She has a shop in our house." Ice fell from Yuliya's long lashes, and she rubbed her face with the blanket.

Katarina glared at Anna. "See? A proper family."

"But which army?" Anna whispered.

Katarina looked up at the sky, rolled her eyes, and took a deep breath. Anna served at the soup lines and organized charity drives. How could she act one way in the community but be so different here? The hypocrisy shocked her. She bit her lips between her teeth lest she provoked another argument.

~

AT THE ENTRANCE to George and Maria's farm, Olek stopped the team and pointed to an empty snow-covered field a short distance from the slate-roofed, two-story red brick farmhouse.

"There, look."

Katarina followed his finger and found the blotchy, red patch near the dairy barn. The bottom of the wide Dutch door was missing as if someone had ripped it from its hinges. She scanned the unusually stark and quiet yard. No animals roamed inside the fenced winter pasture. "Anna, this doesn't look right."

"Where're all the cattle? The bull isn't in his usual place. They've moved him over there." Anna pointed. "And the pens are empty."

"Except for the buildings, it doesn't look like Maria and George's farm at all." Katarina squeezed her eyes and blinked, trying to remember what the farm looked like when she last saw it.

"The farm was always so busy. They had four or five field-hands. Where is everyone?" Anna's brows wrinkled. "Something's not right."

"Olek, what do you say?" The hair on the back of Katarina's neck bristled. Had something happened to Maria and the children? She wrapped her arms around the orphans, praying they wouldn't see another tragedy today. She'd seen enough horror to last for her lifetime.

Olek tempered his voice as he pointed. "Judging by the blood over there, there's been some butchering. I'll keep my eyes open. But it's too late now to find another place to rest."

"Even if the hired hands are gone, Maria has the boys to help while George is away at war. I can't see her selling all the cattle." Katarina's eyes met Anna's. Anna mouthed the word "Makhno."

An icy finger traveled down Katarina's spine. She shivered under her heavy sheepskin coat and tightened her arms around the orphans' shoulders. Could it be that the murdering anarchist and his burgeoning army with the black flag had been here? The mere thought of his name was enough to curdle her blood.

"Go slowly, Olek," Anna ordered. "We can't turn back now. We must find our sister."

22

MARIA'S HOUSE

NEAR EINLAGE, RIGHT BANK OF THE DNIEPER RIVER, UKRAINE

OLEK STOPPED THE WAGON BY THE FRONT STAIRS BUT HELD his left hand in the air in a stop sign and the index finger of his right hand over his mouth while he eyeballed the perimeter of the farmhouse.

Katarina ignored his warning and kicked at the wooden beam blocking the tailgate. Olek swiveled in his seat and gave her an exasperated look before climbing down. Before he'd reached the back, she'd lifted the lumber away and jumped off.

"Kat, what's gotten into you? That's not very lady-like." Anna's petite face screwed up in a disapproving frown.

Katarina winked, "Why not me? I'm strong enough." She held out her hands to the orphans. "Come meet our sister and cousins. They'll be excited to see you."

Anatoliy's brown eyes widened, and he drew back as Katarina helped him off the cart. "But they don't know us."

Katarina chuckled at the child's shyness, and she ruffled his hair. "Strangers are friends you haven't met yet."

When Yuliya jumped off the wagon, she ran to her brother and threw her arms around his thin shoulders.

"There's nothing to be afraid of," Katarina reassured them both. "This is my family."

The lace curtains on the dimly lit windows fluttered and small faces peeked out, then disappeared. Seconds later, a buxom yeasty woman in a navy dress and white pinafore opened the door and scrutinized the visitors. Upon recognizing her sisters, Maria wrapped a knitted black shawl over her ash-blond hair before flying down the stairs. "What on earth are you doing here?" She chortled in her usual bubbly way. "It's nice to see you, but this is such a surprise." Her strong arms enveloped Katarina in a bear hug.

Katarina was relieved that, despite the farm's bleak appearance, Maria appeared in good spirits. She returned the embrace and whispered, "Say nothing to the children. The Bolsheviks are razing Halbstadt. We escaped before they got to the estate. We've been on the road for three days. Don't ask for details. It's been an awful trip."

Maria pulled back. As her sky-blue eyes met Katarina's, the broad smile faded. Her mouth opened and closed as if she wanted to say something but was afraid to. Then her lips tightened into a straight line, and she inhaled deeply through her nose and blew out slowly through her mouth. Her breath hung in a frosty circle around her face, then slowly dissipated into the crisp, winter air. Her smile returned as she greeted the others.

Even though Maria seemed happy about their unexpected visit, Katarina detected worry in her older sister's demeanor. However, whatever the problem was, she assumed they'd learn about it shortly.

"Anna, sweetheart, you look ready to pop." Maria threw

her arms around her pregnant sister and kissed her on both cheeks.

"Yes, any day now."

"You shouldn't be traveling like this."

"We had no choice."

Maria gave a sympathetic nod, squeezed Anna's shoulders, and turned to the children. "Who's this?" She bent down and held out her hand to the boy.

"This is Anatoliy." Katarina spoke in Ukrainian for the children's sake and introduced the children in the proper order — boy first, then the girl. "And this is Yuliya."

"Well, so nice to meet you. My youngsters love company." Maria's fluency in the local Ukrainian dialect paralleled that of her youngest sister. She turned around and beckoned the faces peering through the window.

Ten-year-old twins, Sarah and Helen burst through the door. Eight-year-old Mary was right behind them. "Tante Trina, Tante Anna!" they yelled as they streaked down the stairs in stockinged feet.

The twelve-year-old twins, Hans and Gerhard, waved from the door as they restrained three-year-old Marta from running onto the cold deck without shoes on. Seven-year-old Wilhelm scooted past them and dashed into Katarina's arms. His wide, toothy smile stretched from ear to ear. "Nice brush-cut, Wilhelm." Katarina rubbed his shaven head while waving to the others.

Mary wrapped her arms around her aunt's waist.

"Mary, you look like such a little lady with that pretty kerchief," Katarina said while thinking it odd that the girls were wearing head coverings at home. She wondered if they'd interrupted evening plans.

She waited until her young cousins were busy chatting with Anna before whispering to Maria, "These children were attacked down the road, near here. The parents are dead."

Maria gazed sympathetically at the two orphans. Yuliya shivered uncontrollably and her sad eyes darted between the children, the adults, and the yard. Anatoliy stood close by his sister's side while yawning and rubbing his arms. Katarina noticed the frostbite on his pinched face.

Maria saw it too. "You must all be cold and hungry. It's freezing out here. Come. Let's get you inside where you can have a warm bath and something to eat." She turned to Alyona. "Take these two through the back door. My maid, Olga will help you get them cleaned up and fed."

"I need a hot bath, too." Anna rubbed her stomach as she ascended the stairs. "And a hot meal."

"First, these children must be washed up and checked for lice and other diseases," Maria said in an uncharacteristic sharp tone. "Once they're cleaned up, you'll get your baths."

Anna's eyes flashed dagger-like at Katarina. Katarina interpreted the mental message to say, 'We shouldn't have brought those waifs here. Now we've inconvenienced our older sister.'

Katarina bit her tongue. As far as she was concerned, they'd done the right thing, not the easy thing. Their parents would be proud. Or so she hoped.

As Alyona and the orphans disappeared down the snow-covered pathway, Katarina remembered Olek was still waiting for a thumbs-up for him to leave for the stables. She turned and waved. He nodded and immediately drove off. She didn't have to ask where he'd be sleeping tonight. After the incident with the orphans, he'd be protecting the horses from his straw bed inside the tack room.

Once inside, Maria invited the sisters into the sitting room. Her brood tagged along and the small space became crowded quickly. "Go now," Maria ordered. "The women need to talk. Your new friends will join you soon."

"But we want to visit, too," Mary whined.

"Supper is almost ready. You can visit later. Now shoo." She dismissed them with a backward wave before addressing her sisters. "Sit down. Please." She pointed to the couch. "You must be hungry and thirsty. I'll get some tea and snacks."

"I've never seen Maria so snippy," Anna whispered while fidgeting with her coat. When it dropped to the floor, she ignored it and plopped down on the wing chair beside the couch.

Katarina snatched up the coat and hung it on the hook in the front hallway. "Do you think we came at a bad time?"

"I wondered the same." Anna kicked her heels against the plank oak flooring. "Kat, please help me with my boots. I can't bend over anymore."

"What would you do without me?"

"Based on the past three days, I don't think I'd survive," Anna quipped.

Katarina refrained from giving a witty comeback. Tonight, her sister's comment wasn't so far from the truth.

Maria rolled the butler cart into the room with a pot of hot tea and a plate of pasty-looking cookies. "Our maids are washing up the orphans and preparing supper." She stopped in the middle of the room chewing on the corner of her bottom lip. "I'm sorry about your difficult travels, sisters. I wish I could offer you safety here, but you've probably noticed that we're having troubles, too."

"We saw the empty pens. What's going on?" Katarina got up from the couch and poured tea. "Did you sell all your cattle?"

Maria stepped to the large front window and surveyed the yard before sitting down in the corner wing chair. She sighed and put her swollen feet onto the embroidered footstool. "Bandits. They're here all the time. They've made this their home away from home."

Anna's eyes went wide as saucers and her jaw dropped. "Lord, have mercy."

Katarina detected Maria's guarded tone. She held her cup in mid-air. "What do you mean?" She slowly set the cup down on its saucer.

"I can almost guarantee this gang attacked your orphans. They practically own the area. We never know when they'll show up. They play with their guns like they're toys — shooting them in the air, pointing them at our heads." Maria pointed to the scattered holes in the ceiling. "We're afraid for our lives. My brood is sick with fear."

Anna paled. "Will they come while we're here?"

"Here?" Katarina studied the walls and ceilings. The place was a disaster. The bullet holes and torn wallpaper were frighteningly reminiscent of the house with the hanging couple. How had she missed seeing this when she first walked in?

The news smacked like a bad nightmare. "They come here?" She repeated after Maria nodded. Had they walked into a trap? "What do they want?" The cup rattled against the saucer in her lap. She stood up and returned it to the cart.

"Food, mostly. At first, they came for guns. They searched the place and found George's hunting rifles. Now, they say we owe them because they didn't turn us in to the authorities. We cook for them and do their laundry. But the threats continue. Sometimes they stay for days. They've stripped our entire larder." Maria pointed to a head-sized hole in the wall. "And they have no respect for property or people."

"Lord Jesus, keep us safe," Anna prayed out loud. Her eyes bulged and fixated on her older sister.

Katarina tried to swallow, but the lump in her throat locked in place and her chest tightened. The room swam, and a sneeze formed in the back of her nose. *Horses.* "Achoo!"

Maria acknowledged the sneeze with a brief "Bless you,"

before continuing. "We're praying they'll move on. But they keep coming back, helping themselves to the livestock and everything else. They say we have more than we need, and others are starving. We're obligated to help, but both the barns and the cellar are nearing empty. Is it true? Is the country destitute? We don't dare leave to find out."

The red patch by the barn. They've been slaughtering the animals. "Do you have enough food to last through the spring?" Katarina glanced at Anna's belly. *Dear God, please don't let the baby be born here. Not now. Give us one more day. Another week would be better.*

"I don't know. We have basics — cabbage, root vegetables, apples. Without the extra mouths to feed, we could last a few months. But these men don't care about our survival. Only theirs. But if others are dying —"

"What about grain and flour?" Anna interjected.

Anna, don't you understand? The Bolsheviks are burning the eastern villages and Makhno's army is terrorizing the west. They're taking all the food. There's nothing left for us. We're doomed. The words screamed in Katarina's head, but she couldn't push them through her mouth.

Maria's voice cracked. "After the first raid, we dragged sacks of corn, potatoes, and flour to the attic and hid them behind old furniture and blankets. They haven't looked up there since they last searched for the guns. I'm praying they won't. Those bags are both food and seeds for the spring. Without seeds ..." Her voice trailed. "And they've confiscated our vehicles. I can't get to town to buy flour and sugar. The neighbors bring supplies when they can. But they've had trouble, too. And the animals must be fed. There's not enough to go around. Every day I pray for help."

"Thankfully, you live by the river. The boys can go fishing," Anna said dismissively. "You won't go hungry. This nonsense will end when law and order returns."

"And when will that be? And what should she do in the meantime?" Katarina retorted, glaring straight-faced at Anna.

Maria ignored the acrimony. "I wouldn't dare send them by themselves. The old ferry station and the riverbanks are gathering places for the radicals. They'd harass the boys for sure. Frankly, I'm surprised you got through without an ambush."

"We've had no problem with ruffians." Anna sipped tea in the fine China cup, holding it in a lady-like fashion with her little finger pointing straight out. "Except for finding the orphans. But nothing bad happened to us."

"Thank God you didn't come earlier. You would have run right into them. They were here this morning. For all I know, they could be back tonight. I wish we could leave, but I don't know where to go, or how. And I'm terrified of what they'll do if we try."

"We saw the blood by the barn," Katarina said hesitatingly.

"Ja. They slay the animals by the barn with no respect for proper health practices. The entrails stain the meat. We clean it as fast as we can and hope no one gets sick. They throw the entrails to dogs and pigs."

"Yuck." Katarina and Anna said in unison.

There were respected procedures for killing livestock — proper ways to drain the blood and hang the meat: carefully removing the organs and viscera and cleaning the insides with fresh water. Such waste was buried and kept away from domestic animals. Failing to follow health guidelines invited sickness. Didn't everyone know this?

"What happened this morning?" Anna pressed.

"Today's loot was a small sow and two chickens. I collect the bones and leftovers for stock to make soup. If I didn't, there wouldn't be enough food," Maria explained. "We keep everything in the summer kitchen where it's cold. The iceman hasn't been by this winter."

"How many feeders do you have left?" Anna referred to the young pigs grown specifically for food.

"Anna?" Katarina glared at her sister. The question was highly inappropriate as far as she was concerned. Couldn't she understand Maria's desperate circumstances?

Maria answered as if she hadn't noticed Katarina's attempted intervention. "A dozen or so. But if they keep killing the young, we won't have enough to reproduce later." Maria toyed with the handle of her teacup and her eyes flicked to the window. "But considering the shortage of feed, it probably won't matter."

Maria spoke in a matter-of-fact tone — as if she'd been talking about the laundry. Katarina guessed that the situation had been going on for so long that Maria had become accustomed to the terror. She scratched at her palms, wondering how they could help.

"Well, thank God you're alive and well. At least they haven't hurt you or the children." Anna beckoned Katarina to pass the cookie plate. "You'll get through this. We all will. Spring will be here soon. These hoodlums won't have time to cause chaos when planting season arrives."

Again, Katarina's eyes widened at Anna's callousness. She got up from the couch and poured herself another cup of tea to avoid screaming at her pregnant sister.

"This is a new kind of war, Anna." Maria's gaze drifted back to the window. "The restlessness of the locals goes far beyond youthful boredom. They're specifically targeting the Mennonites. The neighbors say as much. I fear spring won't save us this year." Maria sniffed and brushed the brimming tears away with the back of her hand. "And more fear hovers in the shadows and waits to strike. God help us." She paused and lifted her chin. A small, forced smile stretched across her face. "But God protects us still. Look how He's brought you here. As sure as The Word says, His hand covers us."

But Maria's guarded tones, the constant frantic glances out the window, her nervous gestures, and the dark circles around her eyes told Katarina that her sister was under terrible stress.

"I need a good night's sleep," Maria said, crossing and uncrossing her ankles. "The babies aren't getting enough milk. Everyone's cranky. The boys ask for their father."

Katarina brushed a golden strand from her face. "Have you heard from George?" Her hand drifted to the old bump on her arm. The events of the past three days were like a bad dream and a muddy mess. She wanted to scream. *God, where are you? Why are allowing this? My sister is suffering so, and we are all alone.*

"His last letter said he was leaving Berdyansk for the mountains."

"Where? The Caucasus? In forestry? Or as a medic?" Anna's eyebrows drew together in curiosity.

"Nay ... veterinarian support. For a General Denikin. The Czar's army." Maria pushed the footstool away and put her feet flat on the floor.

"They must be making progress." Anna murmured.

Katarina slammed her cup down on its saucer. "This whole war thing has gone too far. How do they expect us to operate the farms with no men? Do the women have to do everything?"

Anna and Maria burst out laughing. "It seems so, doesn't it?" Maria sneered. "We must produce even more than before, we're told. To support the war effort."

"The government takes our grain and forgets to pay the bill. It's thievery." Anna tapped her fingernails against the cup. "There's unfairness everywhere."

"Russia cares nothing about our hardship." Maria's voice

edged with defiance. "And this new Ukraine government is too disorganized. The local officials say old men have experience and young boys can be taught. And as for this farm ... since I have three growing boys, they insist I have plenty of help." Her tone softened. "Thank God Olga has stayed on — bless her heart. She's just as strong as any man."

"Even so," Anna protested. "Your boys are not old enough, nor knowledgeable enough, to manage the farm equipment. What will you do in the spring if the men are not back by then?"

"I could ask you the same question." Maria flicked her hand in the air.

Anna shook her head. "Olek will never leave. And our field hands still sleep in the shacks."

"For how long, Anna? This war carries on and the country is short of men," Maria snorted.

"Olek's over fifty. They won't recruit him." Anna wiped the cookie crumbs from the corners of her mouth with her little finger. "Besides, he'll run to Denikin's army if they try. As you said — our helpers are old men and young boys. We're making do."

Maria's nose flared. She raised her eyebrows and sipped her tea but her gaze drifted back to the window.

Katarina tapped her fingers on the wooden arm of the settee. "Where are your farm hands, Maria?"

"Dispersed between the various armies — like every other able-bodied man. The neighbor's boys help when they can. Nine- and ten-year-old boys doing a man's job while the grown men fight in a war that no one can possibly win." Maria sighed. "There're no capable men left to work the fields or the barns. And my greatest fear is that George will never return."

Katarina met Anna's eyes. "I dread the same," Anna said. "About David."

The room fell silent. Katarina reached for a cookie, took a bite, then put it down. It was as flavorless as sawdust. The war rationed everything these days, including sugar and spices. The Mennonites adapted their recipes, using home-grown honey on everything from sore throats and cuts to infant formulas. It tasted great on their favorite summer treat of *roll kuchen* with watermelon. But sugar cookies needed sugar, not honey. The texture just wasn't the same.

Katarina flicked her tongue over the crumbs. Something else was off. Lard, butter, or oil? Her sister had just mentioned the shortage of milk. Which meant there wasn't enough cream to make butter. Besides, butter was a commodity to sell, not to use frivolously at home. Every-thing was confiscated for the war, it seemed. Even lard. Sunflower seeds? And there it was. A nutty taste. Both in the flour and the fat. She took another bite. There was one other oddity. Soured milk. The entire recipe was strange. Evidently, Maria and Olga were experimenting in the kitchen.

As she thought about the food shortages, she wondered about Maria's youngest, and she looked around the room for the cradle. It wasn't in the room and neither was the newest member of the family, Gerta. Katarina mashed the rest of the curious cookie against her teeth and washed it down with the pale herbal tea. "Where are the babies?"

"In the attic closet. They're safer there."

Katarina wasn't sure she heard right. She gaped and blinked several times. "Huh?"

"What?" Anna's cup clattered on the saucer.

"Oh, not to worry. They're fine up there. Their siblings bring them out to play and they tell me when the baby needs feeding or changing." A pink color crept up Maria's neck. "Don't look so shocked. I've got eight kids. When the bandits show up, I don't have time to shuffle two babies and six youngsters into the stairwell. I do what I can to keep everyone safe."

Katarina palmed her mouth and studied their older sister. She swiveled and made direct eye contact with Anna, then turned back to Maria. "Maria, you will not do this alone anymore. You're coming to Mutter and Papa's with us."

Maria threw her head back and laughed. "You think it's any safer there? Makhno's people are everywhere. They practically control these steppes now. Look what happened to the parents of these two you picked up. And they are Ruskies, Katarina. We are German Mennonites, supporters of the Czar. They scorn us."

"But we can't go home," Anna exclaimed. "The Reds have set fire to everything."

"You can't stay here, either." Maria's voice was firm and emphatic. "It's too dangerous."

"Maria, I don't think you understand," Katarina said. "The Bolsheviks were blowing up Halbstadt as we left. Anna's right. They're probably burning the estate as we speak. We either stay here or we go to Mutter and Papa's. Besides, there's safety in numbers. We need to stick together."

"Ladies, I don't think you understand. If you stay here, those men could do something far worse to you. Katarina you're a single woman, and Anna you're about to give birth. You're both in harm's way. You must leave. We can't. They know who we are. If we try to leave, they'll follow us and then we'll put others at risk. Besides, those rebels took our horses and our wagons. We have no transportation." Maria put her hands over her face and bawled. "I'm sorry for crying. I'm trying to be strong. But truth be told, I don't know how much longer I can last."

"God won't leave us desperate, will he?" Katarina's eyes widened. "The Bible promises us that God will provide. Is that not true?"

Silence descended on the group. Katarina toyed with her thumbs. Finally, Anna spoke. "Our faith is being tested. There is always a solution. We simply must find it. Now, let's think this through. If Makhno's Black Army controls the right bank and the Reds are controlling the left, where are our men?" Anna held her cup and saucer up in the air and smiled weakly at Katarina. "Sorry, I can't reach. I am also helpless now."

Katarina set her sister's cup on the serving wagon while Anna rambled on. "David can't be far away. Weren't all involved in that battle in Kyiv? He's on the hospital train helping the injured. He must be nearby."

"Anna, there's war everywhere," Katarina said. "In that newspaper we found yesterday — I read that General Denikin has control of Crimea and the Sea. That's not far from here. And up north there's a General Kolchak leading the charge with the American and British allies. The article said nothing about an Imperial regiment being in Kyiv. In fact, if the governor and the members of the Central Rada have run away as the article suggested, then who was, or rather, *is* overseeing this new Ukraine? The paper also said there's supposed to be a cease-fire, but the battle in Kyiv took place in the middle of peace talks between Russia and Germany. Ukraine had a voice at the table, but now the Bolsheviks have silenced us and moved the command center to Kharkiv. So, their rampage against the Land of the Mennonites makes no sense."

"They're retaliating against Germany and the Czar by attacking us," Maria exclaimed. "They consider us German colonists."

"Of course." Katarina slapped her forehead. "They must be losing at the negotiating table and blaming us for it."

"Will they rescue us?" Anna looked quizzically at Katarina.

"Who, the Czar's government or Germany?"

"Either," Anna said.

Katarina shrugged. "Your guess is as good as mine. We can't know which government or country we can depend on."

"Or which army, I presume," Anna added.

"Katarina, are you saying that war surrounds us?" Maria's voice trembled.

Katarina nodded and considered the Bible verse: *We are troubled on every side. Persecuted, but not forsaken.*[1] She looked up at her sisters and felt the color drain from her face. "We're living in the end of times. This is the Tribulation."

"Then Christ will save us yet. But where do we fit into this Biblical prophecy? And where shall we go while we wait?" Maria stared at the floor. "Do we give up and do nothing? What will happen to our children?" she asked softly. "What can we do?"

"The prophecy says seven years," Anna said. "The war has carried on for over three. We must bear four more."

"Then worse horrors are promised," Maria said softly.

"May God help us to endure to the end," Katarina added.

1 2 CORINTHIANS 4:8-9

23

STONE SOUP

Katarina spotted Alyona standing beneath the archway. The woman had changed her clothes and cleaned up. Her gray hair was slicked back into a neatly braided bun, and she wore a white apron over an embroidered white vyshyvanka[1] and brown skirt that she'd borrowed from Maria's maid, Olga. Despite Alyona's tidy appearance, fatigue showed in her weathered face and bloodshot brown eyes.

We're all tired to the bone. And yet this woman works without complaining.

During a gap in the conversation, Anna acknowledged her servant.

"The orphans are cleaned. And supper is served," Alyona said.

"Come. Let's fill our bellies before it gets too late." Maria pushed the footstool aside and stood up. "After that, you two can bathe and rinse out your clothes and we'll figure out what to do next."

The false bravado in Maria's voice and the forced smile didn't conceal the tension in her face and the sad expression in her sky-blue eyes. Katarina wished she could snap her fingers to a perfect tomorrow. Although the foreboding in her soul said there was more trouble to come, she knew it was a sin to dwell on fear. The scriptures commanded believers to encourage each other. But how did one spur another to hope when the future appeared dark?

"I'm hungry," Anna stood up and clapped her hands. "Food clears the mind and warms the soul. It can solve a multitude of problems."

"Ja," Katarina agreed. Except, she doubted that food would solve anything tonight.

Yuliya and Anatoliy met them at the doorway of the dining room with wide grins on their scrubbed faces. Dressed in identical white shirts and black pants, and with their damp straight hair perfectly parted in the middle, they could have passed as Maria's boys. Yuliya's only female identifier was her long hair.

"There were no dresses that fit," Alyona whispered to Anna. "She's too tall, too skinny, and already developing at eleven."

"Not even the skirts?" Anna looked alarmed.

"I'll scrub her clothes tonight and put them by the fire. They'll be dry by morning." Alyona answered.

"But she'll need another," Anna said. "It's not possible for a girl to have only one skirt."

"If our seamstress is still in Chortitza, we can get a dress in a day or two," Katarina said softly in German.

"Nonsense. I'll spare no such expense. The church has a charity closet," Anna snapped. "They're orphans. And locals. Second-hand is good enough for them."

"Have these children eaten?" Maria asked her maid, Olga. When the matronly servant nodded, Maria leaned into the woman's shoulder and whispered hoarsely. "Was there any disease or lice?"

Olga shook her head. "Ni. They are healthy."

"Wonderful. Then they can join the others."

The servant nodded and guided the children out of the room.

"What's all this concern about disease?" Katarina asked after they sat down. She scanned the sparse table settings with mismatched silverware and dishes. *Where's the Delft and Mutter's silver? Are we not deserving?* She examined the chipped glass, then looked up and met Anna's gaze. Anna shook her head slowly from side to side. *Don't ask.*

Maria tucked the white linen napkin inside the neckline of her blouse. "You haven't heard?"

"No, I must have missed it." Katarina picked up her spoon and toyed with the soup.

"The armies — they're all infected with lice, typhus, and other unmentionable illnesses. It's rampant. We've already had our share of contamination here." Maria removed the black kerchief covering her gray-streaked ashen locks.

Katarina and Anna gasped simultaneously. Anna's spoon clattered to her bowl. Maria's crudely chopped hair was as short as a man's. Butchered would be a more accurate description, Katarina thought.

"Oba. Nay." Katarina's eyes brimmed with tears. The girls' kerchiefs and the boys' brush-cuts made sense now.

"I had to keep the orphans separated until we knew for sure. I can't take any chances with my family," Maria explained.

"Well, of course. We understand." Anna picked up her spoon and studied her soup.

The subject was too awful to discuss, but the silence was equally awkward. Katarina slurped at the borsch. It had cabbage, onions, carrots, potatoes, and a pork base, but the aroma was off, and the flavor more so. "The soup — it's missing dill. It's a bit bland." She cringed at hearing herself speak her thoughts out loud. Every day, she sounded more like their mother.

"Ja. I'm sorry. It went bad over the winter." Maria blew on her spoon, then sucked at the edge. "But thankfully, Mutter isn't here to notice. And the children don't complain."

"But pickles make a suitable substitute. You said you had some. Or did I misunderstand?" Katarina asked. Now it sounded like she was whining. She didn't mean to.

Daggers shot from Anna's eyes. Katarina grimaced.

"I apologize for the simple meal, sisters," Maria said. "We're trying to be creative with what we have. I keep the pickles for the children's snacks. They help with hunger. Besides, it's not wise to tantalize the gangs with garlic and dill. They'll suspect we're hoarding food. If my cooking tastes too good, they'll want more."

"Ah." Katarina found the strategy amusing and chuckled. "Not such a silly idea. If the food is lousy, they'll quit hassling you and go elsewhere."

"Exactly. Such is my hope, as lame a solution as it is." Maria slurped from her spoon.

Pickles. Katarina suddenly craved a pickle and cheese sandwich. "Do you have enough to share? The bandits aren't here now. Surely, they won't notice a few missing pickles?"

The stunned looks told Katarina she'd gone too far. Tears welled in Maria's eyes, and she cupped her forehead. Anna gave Katarina the death stare.

"I'm sorry. It was selfish of me to ask," Katarina stammered, twirling her spoon in the soup. "How are you managing with other spices?"

Maria's shoulders sagged, and a tear slipped down her cheek. She sucked her lips between her teeth. Exasperation showed on Anna's face.

Stop. Katarina forced a spoonful of borsch down her

throat. "It's a good thing I'm so hungry, I could eat a dead horse."

At this, Maria burst into tears and covered her face with her hands.

"Katarina, please let it go. You're making things worse." Anna whispered.

Silence descended as the three women supped. Katarina picked a small bone out of her soup and set it aside. Her mind wandered back to their arrival and the empty condition of the yard. The dogs hadn't announced them. That was odd. "Are the dogs still here?"

Maria shook her head.

"They took them, too?" Katarina asked in disbelief. What was that meat floating in the soup? She suddenly felt sick to her stomach. She looked up and met Anna's glare. "Well, I can't just sit here and say nothing," Katarina exclaimed.

"Then change the subject to something more pleasant," Anna scolded.

"Fine." What could she talk about that was pleasant? "Say, remember when we got fresh lemons from Georgia?"

"And the oranges from Palestine at Christmas," Anna chimed in. "And remember those gypsies with those amazing spices?"

"What I wouldn't give for fresh peppercorns," Maria sighed. "I can't let myself think about that. It makes me miss our sausages. Those bandits took everything, including the Delft and the silverware. I can't even offer my sisters a nice meal." She dabbed at her eyes with the linen napkin.

Ouch. Katarina's heart twinged. She'd been so ungrateful and insensitive. "I'm sorry, Maria. I didn't understand how much you've suffered. This whole situation is so incredible and hard to believe. By the way, how are the neighbors? Earlier you said they were attacked, too?"

"Ja. It's tough. But I must be strong for the children,"

Maria sighed. "The neighbors haven't been by in a few weeks, and we can't go anywhere. During the first attacks, they robbed all the neighborhood smokehouses. Now they go after the livestock, too. I'm praying for relief from this horror and dearth."

"Well, not all is lost. As long as there's flour, eggs, and milk, we can make vareniki. These are good, even without the sausage gravy." Anna bit into the doughy pockets filled with cottage cheese and potatoes. "Although, I suppose the rebels are banging at the door for these, too." Her voice faded as she realized what she'd just said.

Katarina narrowed her eyes at her sibling. *Can we enjoy nothing tonight?*

Anna shifted her focus to her plate. A pink flush rose from her neck.

"Ja. By God's grace, we have enough to feed all. I don't wish any to starve and I don't mind sharing the little I have. But these arrogant and selfish attitudes disturb me." Maria's tone rose, and she shook her head repeatedly. "They have no sympathy, and they think they're entitled to everything. The day before last, we boiled the milk for cheese and set the curds outside to chill. They found the jars of whey. I begged for the children. I had to barter for the morning's milk. Can you believe it? They don't even care about the little ones." Maria's voice croaked.

Barter? What did you barter with? Katarina shuddered. She didn't want to know the answer. "How many cows are left?" she asked, then realized her question was irrelevant. Maria had described enough.

It was clear the attacks were deliberate, not coincidental. This farm was a victim of something bigger. Starving citizens wouldn't resort to such inhumane tactics — terrorizing women and children with repeated and insane demands — leaving only enough food to keep them alive, then threatening to take it all away. These rebels appeared at will, allowing their prey temporary reprieves between surprise attacks, and intimidating the women and children before they left so they felt captive and helpless. These were strategies of madmen or political cunning, not starving peasants.

Katarina tapped her fingernail on the table. Hadn't Lenin written something about the necessity of agitation to empower the peasants and workers? That explained the riots and strikes at the factories. Destroying farms further disrupted the food supply and had far-reaching repercussions. According to both Lenin and Makhno's manifestos, social changes included a collective redistribution of wealth and land, where each had only what they needed. But implementing this ideology involved brutal tactics. Like the Bolsheviks, Makhno's anarchists terrorized ordinary citizens but one-upped the Communists' strategies with their friendly enemy approach — gaining entry to homes cordially, and then slowly dismantling the farms, and preying on the landowners' guilt and worry for their neighbors.

Katarina chewed on her bottom lip. The burning of Halbstadt, the depletion of Maria's livestock, even the murder of the orphans' parents — it was all a political agenda. None of this violence would end soon.

"We still have two milk cows," Maria said, answering Katarina's question. "And they haven't shot the bull yet. I think they're letting us keep them so that we have enough to feed their army."

"Oh? Do they expect noodles and vareniki, too?" Anna scoffed. "What happens when the flour runs out? If they burn the fields, there won't be wheat to harvest."

Katarina's mind raced. The answer was redundant. They'd be killed. As German colonists, they were the enemy.

"Ha," Maria snorted. "He knows Mennonite women are great cooks. That's why they keep showing up at mealtime. I feed the children early so they're finished before the thieves show up. But my plans don't always work out."

"Maria, just prepare a few pails of extra meals for the day and have them ready at the door when they arrive. Then they'd be less of a nuisance. Kill them with kindness, I say," Anna said with a resigned tone. "They just want to eat. Eventually, they'll stop harassing you and leave."

"You must have missed what I said earlier, Anna. We don't know when they're coming or how many will show up. I can't plan meals for fifty men every day. There's not enough food."

"Fifty?" Anna's fork clattered to the plate.

"I told you — they're an army. The group that comes here, they're just a remnant. I was serious when I said the flour won't last the winter."

"Dear God." Katarina breathed a prayer as she pushed away her bowl. "I can't imagine living like this."

"We must be grateful for what we have." Maria sounded resigned.

Katarina scraped back her chair and crossed her arms. "It's not like this everywhere Maria. These men have tortured you for so long that you've become used to it. You and the children need to leave before you run out of food. As you said earlier, we can't stay here with you. But neither can you remain here."

"But how can I leave with my big family? We're trapped here. We have no transportation, no way out." Tears rolled down Maria's cheeks. She picked up her napkin and blew her nose. "I keep praying for answers, but there are none."

"Maria, do you remember that killing in the eastern villages last year where thirty-eight died? The newspaper said Makhno and his men did it. You know the old saying — once a dog has a taste for blood, it doesn't stop. The rumors are rampant. Men, women, children, and even animals are slaughtered in the fields and left to rot. Everyone knows Makhno has a vendetta against the Mennonites. If these militants are linked to him, they won't stop at only raiding the farms. By feeding them, you're giving them an open invitation to keep marauding."

Maria dabbed at her puffy eyes. "But Katarina, we have no way of leaving. They took our horses and wagons. We can't just walk away. And they'll stop us if we try. And you're right. We're afraid they'll kill us. But we're prisoners in our own homes. It's hopeless. We can't get out. Maybe some of the children. But not me, and not the boys. They know us too well."

"Maria, we'll get you and your family out of here. Somehow. You must come to Mutter and Papa's with us. Papa may have other answers. Even if this vigilantism is widespread, at least he's there to protect us," Katarina pleaded.

"I agree." Anna massaged her stomach in slow, concentric circles. "It's best we all stick together. Let's get out of here as soon as we can. Before dawn breaks. I can't risk having my baby here."

"But how can we leave? It's the middle of winter and we have no transportation. And you don't have room for us in that box cart." Maria's face flooded with fear.

"We'll figure out a plan," Katarina said. "As God is my witness, Maria, your story will not end in terror."

---

1 Vyshyvanka: an embroidered Ukrainian blouse

24

EVERY CHILD MATTERS

"ANOTHER EARLY MORNING. I DON'T KNOW HOW MUCH more of this I can stand." Anna moaned as she climbed into the bed of the rickety wagon. "I can't imagine how Mother Mary did it — on a donkey, no less. For a week or longer. Four mornings of these early wake-up calls and bum-numbing rides and every fiber of my being wants to scream. This baby won't wait much longer."

Katarina met Maria's worried eyes. It wasn't like Anna to complain so. "We'll be at Mutter and Papa's before nightfall. Tonight, we sleep in our old beds."

"With God's help, I'll meet you there tomorrow. It will be like old times. The three of us taking over Mutter's kitchen." Maria's face lit up. Her tone was more upbeat than last night.

"And with the house full of screaming kinder. Poor Mutter." Anna chuckled as she wriggled onto the straw mattress.

"She'll grumble about the noise, but she'll hide a big smile behind her morning coffee," Katarina quipped while helping Sarah and Helen onto the wagon.

"Prips," Anna corrected. "The only coffee in Russia these

days is made from roasted cereal grain." She motioned to the twins. "Come sit over here."

"Prips is barely tolerable. It has the aftertaste of burned toast ... although no side effects like coffee." Maria picked up eight-year-old Mary and gave her a quick kiss before setting her onto the wagon. "You be good for Mama, ja?"

Mary scrambled over to sit beside Anna. "I'll miss you, Mutter," she said waving to her mother.

"It's just one night. I'll see you tomorrow." Maria smiled stiffly and turned her head, pretending to eyeball the pre-dawn horizon as she wiped a tear from her eye.

"I remember getting the jitters from coffee." Anna wrapped a blanket around Mary's shoulders. "Prips is much easier on the nerves."

"What kind of grain is used to make prips?" Katarina asked. "The air around Schoenwiese stank like burnt toast. But according to the newspaper, there's a shortage of cereals." She boosted Yuliya onto the wagon. "Find a warm spot, young lady. The wind can be very cold." Yuliya snuggled in beside Anna and Mary.

"Usually barley, oats, and chicory." Maria rejoined the conversation. "But who knows? They could be using weed seeds for all we know. The recipe probably changes daily."

"Don't they use the same stuff to make beer? Maybe that's what we were smelling. Men can't seem to live without beer or vodka." Katarina said as she boosted Wilhelm onto the cart. He stood hesitatingly at the back — searching for the right place to squat.

"A healthy boy like you should be able to manage the corner," Katarina snapped. "Just cover up well so you don't freeze. The winds can be brutal."

Wilhelm's eyes widened at her snippy tone, but he obediently scooted over to the corner.

Katarina barely cared about her timbre or choice of words

this morning. In the last two days, she'd said too many wrong things, expressed too many wrong opinions and offended her sisters too many times. Between the anxiety, lousy sleep, scant food, and days of traveling on bumpy roads — she was over-tired and overwrought, and every muscle in her body ached. But since Anna had it worse, she had no right to gripe. Thankfully, this dark journey would soon be over.

She couldn't wait to crawl into her comfortable childhood bed for a decadent good night's rest without worrying about early morning wake-up calls. She looked forward to gorging on home-cooked meals prepared by her mother and Katya — the family housekeeper and Katarina's childhood nanny. After this, she'd never be tired or hungry again.

Katarina hadn't realize how much she missed her child-hood home until now. Although the idea of traveling the world had held her fancy for years, today she'd give anything to feel safe and secure. She was tired of looking over her shoulder to see what terror was about to unfold next. She planned to re-evaluate her goals when they returned to Halbstadt.

Anatoliy stood shyly beside the wagon. Alyona scooped him up, set him on the straw, and tossed him a wool blanket. He crawled over to his sister. "Ni," Alyona scolded. "Boys sit in the back." The brown-eyed child grabbed his warm covering and sat down beside Wilhelm.

"Dawn's breaking. We must hurry." Katarina scanned the murky horizon for signs of trouble, but a grove of evergreens broke her line of sight. The back of her neck tingled. "Maria, what time do they usually show up?"

"I told you, they're unpredictable," Maria said.

"Maria, we'll keep you in our prayers all day and night. Until we are all together at Mutter and Papa's. This nightmare will be over soon." Anna slipped her arm around Yuliya's thin shoulders and pulled her close.

"Sisters — you're an answer to my prayers. God be praised. I've been so worried about my brood. They've almost lost their innocence from the things they've seen," Maria said. "But don't fret about me. I can wait one more day. The bandits probably won't even notice half my brood is missing. If they do, I'll tell them they're visiting relatives or neighbors."

"Well, you won't even have to lie to say that!" Anna exclaimed.

Maria jerked her chin towards the front of the wagon. "Anna, your family must've treated Olek and Alyona very well. They're like angels of mercy. Such self-sacrificing loyalty is hard to find. You're in good hands." Tears brimmed in her sky-blue eyes as she watched the children settle into the wagon.

"Ja. We are blessed," Anna nodded.

"Thankfully, we don't have much further to go today," Katarina said. "Olek fixed the wheel, and these little ones don't add much weight. He'll be back with Papa's carriage tomorrow after he delivers the orphans to their sister. Unless —"

"— He'll make it," Anna interrupted. "Katarina, stop adding to angst."

Katarina bit her lip. She couldn't help but worry about their happy-go-lucky sister's welfare. Maria was the encourager, the motivator, the one everyone else went to for cheering up. But she wasn't so jovial anymore. And her hugs had felt mechanical, too. It was obvious she was suffering terribly. Katarina said another prayer for her elder sister.

Olek circled the wagon a final time, double-checking the horses and supplies. He offered Katarina a helping hand before closing the tailgate and securing it with a strip of lumber. Then he went to the front and climbed up to the driver's seat.

"Time to go," Anna said briskly. She stared at the golden sliver of first light in the morning sky. "If we don't go now, we may not get another chance."

Maria white-knuckled the rickety planked side. "Helen, Sarah, Mary, Wilhelm." Maria called out each name as if she was reciting a funeral dirge. "Please be good for your Tantes. I don't want to hear about any trouble when I see you tomorrow. Do you understand?"

Heads bobbed up and down in unison.

"Does everyone remember why you're going to Oma and Opa's?"

"For cookies," Mary declared.

Maria chuckled, "Ja. Oma is baking her special cookies for you. And tomorrow night, we'll have a big party with vareniki and Oma's famous cookies for dessert. And maybe even sausage ..." Maria's voice trailed.

"And there are no bad men at Oma's," Helen said confidently. "We don't have to be scared anymore."

Maria's blue eyes flickered. She inhaled deeply and blew a long stream through her mouth. "Kinder, there's one more thing that I need you to do for me. This is very important. Are you listening?" The bundled bodies stopped wiggling and all eyes turned to their mother. "If those bad men stop the wagon, do not, I repeat, do not speak to them. Do you understand?"

"We know." Wilhelm's voice edged with annoyance.

"If they ask where you live, don't answer. If they think they know you, don't say anything. Let the adults talk. Even if it doesn't sound right to you, let the adults say what they think is right. Do you understand?"

"We must be seen and not heard," Sarah said sarcastically.

"This isn't funny, Sarah. These men can hurt you. Don't forget all the terrible things they've already done here.

They're not nice, even though they sometimes pretend to be. They're not your friends."

"And they're not family," Helen added. "Never trust anyone who isn't family."

"Right. Bad people are sneaky like wolves." Maria reached into the box and squeezed Helen's shoulder.

"What about Alexei? He seems nice." Wilhelm's thin blond eyebrows knit together.

"No, Wilhelm. He's a wolf pretending to be a sheep. But he's really a wolf." A pink color flushed through Maria's cheeks, and she bit her lip. Her eyes darted back and forth between each child. "That man cannot be trusted. Don't tell him anything."

The boy threw his hands in the air. "Fine."

"Fine," Maria repeated sternly before she stepped away from the wagon. Worry etched her lined face. She turned her back to the group.

"Don't stress, Maria. This will all turn out fine," Anna said.

Maria pivoted and whispered. "Sisters, what if our parents are in the same spot as I am? They've been attacked before."

"If things are not well there," Anna said, "we'll send a message. But regardless, someone will be back to pick you up. I promise."

"And if all else fails, we can always leave a message on the Chortitza oak," Katarina joked.

"Like the olden days." Anna chuckled.

"Exactly. And then, we'll all come together under the old oak tree." Katarina sang the phrase from an old family hymn.

It seemed appropriate to mention the ancient oak tree on Chortitza Island where their Prussian ancestors had camped after arriving on the Steppes in 1789. The seven-hundred-year-old sentinel was almost as revered as the religion itself. Every summer, the descendants made their annual pilgrimage to reunite and share a meal under its massive canopy. Although they enjoyed the gatherings, the sisters had felt the glorification was much overdone. It was, after all, just a tree. Yet today, the historical landmark seemed appropriate as an emergency beacon.

"As it was back then, it shall be again." Anna wrapped her arm around Mary's shoulders and hugged her closely as they sang.

The song was both a sober reminder of the challenges their ancestors had struggled through and overcome, and an encouragement to persevere. Today's crisis was another test to be added to the history books — one that their descendants would discuss for generations to come. But only if they endured and prevailed while maintaining their honor and dignity. Integrity under fire was all that mattered now.

Katarina thought of that ancestral challenge and reflected on their current dilemma. "Maria, yesterday you said we're not the only family in this position. So, we should take comfort that we are not alone. We'll band together with them and help each other. And as for us, one way or another, we'll always find each other. And no child will be left behind." Katarina added the final note of reassurance hoping it would ease her sister's pain.

"If the rebels take the land, there's always Germany," Anna jested, then quickly changed her tone when Maria turned her back and started sobbing. "Although I'm sure it won't come to that."

Olek adjusted his cap and turned around in his seat. "We have to go now." His voice strained with urgency.

Maria blew the children a kiss and stepped away.

"Ya, yah!" Olek snapped the reins and cracked the whip.

~

As THE WAGON lurched over the frozen soil, the children cuddled together, tucking blankets around their legs and shoulders. The boys yanked their ear flaps down over their ears and the girls tightened their kerchiefs over their heads. Wool scarves covered everyone's mouths and noses.

"You are all so bundled up. You look like Christmas presents. I can't tell who you are," Katarina joked. She wished she could snap her fingers and change the trip into a festive winter hayride for old times' sake, but her gut said more trouble lay ahead. She pulled Helen close and regarded Anna lying on the straw mattress with her hands cupping her pumpkin-sized belly.

At that moment, the grave responsibility for the trip suddenly dawned on Katarina. Seven vulnerable souls — not including her own or the servants — were relying one hundred percent on her, their two servants and one flimsy wagon to bring them to safety. The sense of responsibility overwhelmed her.

She meditated on the heavy feeling. No one had ever explained the transition from childhood to adulthood, nor described the moment when they'd made that leap. She'd always assumed it was a progressive thing, not a sudden jolt. But here she was ... And yet, according to some, she still wasn't truly an adult because she wasn't married. Although that, too, would probably come one day. And then, her status would be official.

Katarina took a deep breath of the frosty air and studied the orphans. Anatoliy and Yuliya already knew that everything could change in a heartbeat. Earlier, Maria had said that her girls had already seen too much. Katarina hadn't asked her to explain. She couldn't put her finger on why she didn't want to know the details, only that she sensed something sinister in Maria's words.

An icy pang shot through her lungs from inhaling too

deeply of the subzero air. She rubbed her chest and scolded herself for brooding. As an adult, it was her job to encourage the children and lift their spirits. She'd take a lesson from Maria. Her elder sister always kept a positive attitude in the face of difficulty and never let her children see her worry. Right now, they should be playing word games or singing hymns.

As the wagon carrying the ten lives rolled into the naked wilderness, the golden sphere peeked over the horizon and cast shadows on the serene white landscape. Frosty clouds from the horses' breath hung motionless in the windless frigid morning. The jingling of their bells and the stomping of their hooves against the frozen earth echoed in the stillness. The peaceful countryside belied the horrors that Katarina had seen over the past week. She prayed for freedom from fear and for the war to end.

25

BARTERING FOR BABIES

THE FLICKERING LIGHTS IN THE WINDOWS ANNOUNCED residents rising to greet the day, but no one noticed the wagon full of nervous passengers as it passed through the sleepy streets of the tiny Mennonite village.

Katarina wondered if these simple farmers, day laborers, and fishermen also suffered under the regional anarchy, or were they — like Grushka and Pylyp — supportive of the political unrest? The chaos in the country was confusing. If the government was corrupt or incompetent and the corporate structure unfair or abusive, why terrorize the average citizen?

And how did Makhno fit into the bigger picture? His burgeoning Black Army was a darkening curtain hovering over the region, and his unpredictable actions were putting the Mennonites on edge. Were his acts of violence a necessary evil in the Ukrainian fight for independence, or was he simply carrying out a vendetta against the Mennonites for some perceived childhood injury? Ukraine was now officially a sovereign nation, so why wasn't he quitting his Robin Hood raids against the wealthy? He should turn his anger against the Bolsheviks. But he wasn't.

When it came to politics, some agreed that both Makhno's and the Bolsheviks' policies to equalize wealth were good ideas. However, others felt this policy should be voluntary, not forced. Still, others disagreed, insisting the former Imperial ways were best. Hence, the struggle between the Reds and the Whites boiled into war. But their enmity differed from the fight for power and land raging between the Central Powers and the Allies. And Makhno's battle seemed personal.

Katarina realized her unanswered questions were only causing her more angst. But after the last few days, it was tough not to be afraid. Earlier, she'd asked Anna for her viewpoint. But her sister told her to stop wasting her energy on something that was unexplainable. "It's the way it is, Katarina. Who can understand the hearts of evil men? One day the violence will end, and life will be sacred again." Except it didn't seem to be ending.

If only she could talk to her cousin and boss at the newspaper — Regier. He understood war and politics. She missed him terribly. She prayed he'd escaped the fires and the violence and made a mental note to write to him tomorrow.

AFTER PASSING THE QUIET VILLAGE, Olek pushed the horses into a full gallop. The wagon teetered dangerously as it careened around icy curves and sailed over bumps. During a sideways slide and a violent lurch, Katarina tightened her grip around Sarah's shoulders; Yuliya and Mary screamed, and Anna's face paled. The wagon jerked left, then right, before straightening out.

"Are you going to make it?" Katarina asked Anna. "You don't look so good."

"I must." Anna hugged her belly with both arms.

"It will all be over soon." Katarina meant both the drive and the birth.

Anna nodded. "Two more hours," she said, referring to the distance.

The stability of the wheel and the chances of meeting up with rebels worried Katarina. She prayed they'd arrive at their parents' home without incident, but her heart went out to the orphans. How would their lives change? She hoped they wouldn't end up at a disreputable orphanage. She studied the six pairs of eyes peeking out from between the wool wrappings. *Two sets of brown. The rest are all blue. They will know us by our eyes.*

After the wagon slipped sideways around another glassy curve, Katarina bit her lips and gave Anna a cat-eyed stare, hoping she'd read her mind and tell Olek to slow down. Even though he was an expert Troika driver, skill alone could not outsmart nature. One wrong turn could send them airborne and sailing into the trees. If it hadn't been for the children present, she would have screamed at him. But she didn't dare violate Anna's rules of order in front of them. She'd made that mistake once too often during this trip.

Olek shoulder-checked the wagon's positioning and caught Katarina's anxious look. He shrugged, raised one eyebrow, and twisted his mouth as if to say *I don't know if the wheel will hold.*

When the vehicle straightened, Katarina blew a long stream through her mouth and relaxed her grip around Sarah. Then, several piercing whistles split the air above them and three loud pops came from behind.

"No," Anna cried. "Not now. We're so close."

The bundled heads turned to watch the riders chasing them.

"Olek, we've got trouble," Katarina yelled.

"I'm going as fast as I can. But we'll never outrun them." Olek snapped the whip again.

"Guns, guns!" Mary screamed as more gunfire erupted.

Tears slipped from Sarah's blue eyes. "Are they going to kill us?"

Yuliya sobbed and pulled her scarf up to cover more of her face. Anatoliy crawled to her. "Yuliya, they're coming for us again."

"No, Anatoliy," Katarina said as goosebumps rose on the back of her arms. "They're not coming for you. They just want our stuff." She wanted to gather the orphans in her arms and reassure them but there was no time. She'd comfort them later and then prayed there would be a later.

"What can we do?" The whites of Wilhelm's eyes bulged between the woolen layers.

Another gun fired as the gang closed in. A deep voice boomed, "Stop, or we shoot."

Olek shifted to look back at the posse, then pulled on the reins to stop the team.

"What are you doing?" Katarina screamed. Her arms tightened around Sarah. "We can't stop now." They were doomed. She was sure of it.

"Olek, do not stop." Anna cried out with a trembling voice. "They will kill us."

"Don't worry, we'll be fine," Olek said firmly. "Trust me." He raised his hands in the air in open surrender.

Katarina's heart sank as the bandits approached the wagon. Now she understood why they'd been driving so fast through the wooded area. Olek had anticipated problems.

The fashionably dressed troop, wearing modern sheepskin coats and traditional Cossack hats, swarmed the vehicle on both sides. Katarina stared at the expensive clothing. Except for the black flag proving membership in Makhno's army, the gang looked like common thieves. She glanced at Yuliya and Anatoliy. *Are these the robbers that killed your parents?*

A wiry man with a thin face and a V-shaped beard, with his ear flaps of the *papakhas* hat tied underneath his chin, circled the wagon on his chocolate steed before approaching Olek from the front. "Where are you going?"

Katarina recognized the dialect as local, and she winked at the children. Olek usually spoke Russian, but he was equally fluent in Ukrainian. He would get them out of this mess.

Olek's mouth twitched. He opened and closed it like a fish out of water, then sucked in his lower lip before answering. "Can't you see our dilemma? That woman is about to give birth. We have no time to waste. The situation is dire. Please let us pass."

At that cue, Anna screamed.

"You see," Alyona piped in. "She's already in labor. We must get her to safety."

The leader lifted his sidearm and aimed it at Alyona. "Who are you, woman? What are these children to you?"

Katarina recognized the small weapon with a long, thin barrel like the one David owned. *German guns. Stolen from the colonies.*

"These are my family. We are traveling south to see my sister," Alyona lied. "You must know my son. Ivan Ivanovich Yurchenko. He has the fish house beside the river in the village."

The man squinted, then pointed the pistol at Olek's head and cocked the trigger.

"What do you have to say, driver?"

Anna screamed again.

Katarina hoped her sister was only acting. Anna's eyes squeezed shut and her face screwed up as if she was in terrible pain. A chill passed down her spine. *Dear Lord, please don't let this be real. Not yet. We're so close.*

Olek held up one hand and pointed to the box beneath him. "Thank you so much for stopping us. The horses were out of my control on these icy roads. Can I offer you a gift of gratitude for saving our lives?" He stood up slowly, pointing at the box beneath him.

The corner of the ringleader's mouth tweaked into a smirk. He brought his horse alongside the wagon, but the gun remained aimed and cocked.

Olek crouched and opened the lid and produced a bottle of brandy. The man released the trigger, lowered the gun, and shoved the bottle into his saddlebag. "What else do you have?"

Anna screamed again.

Olek glanced at Anna anxiously, then motioned to Alyona and pointed at the pail.

Alyona removed the lid and tipped the pail upside down. One frozen ring of sausage slid out. She handed it to Olek, and he offered it to the bandit. Katarina bit her lips to keep from laughing at the man's delighted expression as he grabbed the meat and sniffed. "This is quality meat from the Mennonites. Where did you get such?"

"It was a special purchase. Please enjoy," Olek said.

The bandit backed up the steed, paraded around the wagon, then signaled to his entourage. Two men with long guns strapped to their shoulders dismounted and strode towards the wagon. They ran their hands along the end and sides, then stooped to inspect the undercarriage.

"Is this your vehicle?"

"No. We borrowed it from a friend. I'm just a poor man taking these women to visit their families and celebrate the new birth. Please let us pass."

"Where are you from?"

"Tokmak." Sweat beaded on Olek's forehead.

Katarina cringed. The town was on the other side of the river.

"You're a long way from home. What are you doing here? The man leaned forward on his horse and toyed with his pistol.

"There's war on the left bank. Bloodshed everywhere. We were lucky to get out. We thought we'd be safer here, in *Ukrainian* territory."

Katarina guessed Olek emphasized the word Ukrainian in an attempt to impress the gang leader, making him think he was on their side.

"Are you one of the Mennonite slaves?" The gunslinger asked Olek while leering at Anna.

"No, no. These women have little money. Believe me. I'm a simple working man. I work only for myself."

Neither truth nor lies would change the outcome, Katarina reckoned. They were trapped, their future completely in the hands of the rebels.

The children sat like frozen statues with their eyes glued to the floor. Katarina prayed they would stay silent. One wrong word could put everyone in jeopardy. *Don't move, and whatever you do, don't speak.* She sat on her hands and pleaded to the children with her eyes.

The remaining riders closed in, forming a tight circle around the wagon. A funky wave of horsey stench assaulted Katarina's sinuses. Her eyes watered, her chest felt tight, and the inevitable pounding beat in her skull grew louder. She pulled the scarf over her nose to filter the air, but it was no use. A wave of heat washed over her. She tried to swallow, but the lump in her throat wouldn't leave.

The first sneeze rose with a violent "Achoo!" Her hand flew to her face as she tried to contain it, but it was too late. Then another, and another.

The bandits stopped their inspection and ogled Katarina with suspicious eyes as she gasped with rattling inhalations and loud wheezing. She covered her face with her hands and tried to hold her breath, but the series started again. Her upper back prickled with a hot flush.

Anna stopped moaning and gawked with horror. The whites of the children's eyes widened. Katarina gazed at Olek with a look of sheer desperation. *Help!*

Her panic triggered a flashback to the orphans' parents' bloodied corpses lying in the snow. She squeezed her eyes and prayed they would not meet the same fate. The sneezing gave way to dizziness, a racing heartbeat, and a pounding headache as the color drained from her face.

"What's wrong with her?" The leader asked Olek.

"She's allergic to horses."

He pointed to the troika. "You have three. Isn't she allergic to those, too?"

"She keeps her back to the wind," Olek explained. "Her throat closes when they get too close."

The man studied Katarina. "She's not much good to us, then." He motioned to his gang and drew a circle in the air.

Two scrawny boys — who in Katarina's opinion didn't look a day over fifteen — climbed into the box and ordered everyone, including Anna, to stand. She protested with a painful scream, pointing at her belly.

"The woman is giving birth," Alyona scolded the youth with a motherly tone. "What's wrong with you? Are you animals?"

The boys backed off and resorted to rifling through the rest of the contents.

When they gave their bags a cursory examination, Katarina froze, remembering she'd forgotten to put on her grandmother's locket. She prayed they wouldn't find it. Then, the boy spotted the samovar and he kicked her bag aside.

"Look what I found." He handed the heavy silver kettle to the leader who studied it with a critical eye.

"Beautiful detailing. Look at the sunflowers twisted into a rope design. And what is this? A family crest? It's even signed by the designer. A real collectors' item. Our leader will cherish this gift. Good job, Misha."

The boy beamed at the compliment.

A man with beady black eyes and a skinny unshorn face with a dark goatee leaned over the edge of the wagon and wiggled a finger at Anna's poorly fitting sheepskin coat. "Nice tailoring. Where did you get it?"

Katarina guessed that the bandit's expensive-looking double-breasted tailored wool coat and fur hat had been stolen from some other unsuspecting victim.

Anna bit her lip, screwed up her face, and grabbed her stomach, whimpering, "It hurts."

"Pick up the pails and check those boxes." The leader circled the wagon again, peering into both the interior and examining the frame. "If you're hiding guns, I suggest you hand them over before we find them."

The second hoodlum looked at Wilhelm. "Hey, don't I know you?" He went to pull down Wilhelm's scarf, but the child jerked away and turned his head.

"Leave him alone," Mary yelled before she slapped her hand over her mouth.

The bandit turned and studied each of the children and then the women. His fingers toyed with the gun. "I think these young ones are from our favorite farm."

Katarina froze. *Please God. Blind their eyes and ears.*

"Ah. They all look alike. They're probably related." The man with the black goatee riding around the wagon chuckled. "Tak. Our ledi can't leave."

Our lady? Does he mean Maria?

"Where and when did you cross?" The gang leader pointed his gun at Olek again.

"At the barge. The old ferry crossing."

"The barge? With this piece of garbage?" He pointed to the cart. "Or did you sell your good one to buy a spare horse?"

"Ah, yes. You have me there." Olek chuckled. "The old mare wasn't doing so well. She needed help."

"I've never seen a contraption like this before: all three horses tied abreast on a single frame. Is it hard to drive?"

"Tak. Very complicated. But very fast."

"Huh. Not so fast from what I saw. But they're nice looking. And well cared for." The leader toyed with his mustache. His eyes flicked over the passengers and stopped at Anna who continued to moan. Alyona hovered over her, adjusting, and readjusting the blanket, making it appear as if Anna was in active labor.

Katarina covered her face with her scarf as she struggled to breathe the musky air. *Please don't take the horses.*

"So, you say you crossed at the barge. That costs a fortune. Where did you spend the night?" The man's eyes glinted wickedly as he fired questions in rapid sequence.

"A farmhouse near the crossing. An old couple offered their help. We didn't even have to pay them. Now, please, let us go." Olek pleaded. "You can see the state of this poor creature with the baby about to be born and the other gasping for air."

The bandit chuckled. "I think you're lying. You had money for the barge. These are precious horses. You have special training to drive this rig. Those two women wear expensive clothes." He pointed his gun at Anna and Katarina. "You come from one of those fancy estates across the river. Do you think I'm stupid? Where's the money?"

"We only have enough for food and lodging for one more night."

"Hand it over. And the guns, too. Where are you hiding them?" He cocked his weapon and waved it at Olek.

"Ni." Olek shook his head and removed the money pouch from his inside pocket. "Money, yes. Guns, no."

The leader grabbed the pouch and opened it. "Kerenkas and kopecks. More than a little." Sneering, he removed the cash and tossed the wallet on the deck; then waved his gun at his troops. The two youths jumped out of the wagon and returned to their horses.

"Because of her," he pointed to Anna, "I won't take your horses today. But tomorrow, they're mine. You can go now, but I'll find you later. And remember this. These lands belong to Ukraine, not to Russia. Freedom costs money. Next time you bring payment to cross."

Olek nodded. "Da. Tak. Dyakuyu. Your graciousness is honored."

Katarina flinched at Olek's verbal stumbling as he switched between languages. She hoped the ringleader didn't notice.

"Get out of here. By the way," the gang leader backed away from the wagon, "your front wheel is missing a spoke." He turned his horse around and rode back to his troops.

Olek stared straight ahead with his chin clenched and his narrow mouth firmly set in a straight, tight line as he snapped the reins.

Katarina inhaled sharply of the frigid air and coughed. She felt dizzy and weak, and her body trembled uncontrollably. She curled up beside Anna and hugged her knees. The air rushed back into her lungs in wheezy gasps.

Anna sat up and sobbed into her hands. Maria's children wiped their wet faces with their scarves. Yuliya and Anatoliy buried themselves in each other's arms.

After a minute of crying, Anna looked up with glassy eyes and scanned the group. "We are safe. We are alive. All is well."

She dried her face with her palms. "Are you alright, Katarina? You're so pale. I worried."

Katarina gave a small upside-down smile and croaked, "I'll be fine in a bit."

"Kat, I'm sorry I dismissed your allergies before. I didn't understand how serious they were. I've never seen you suffer so." Anna turned back to the children and clapped her hands. "We're safe, everyone. God has protected us once again. Let's say a prayer of thanksgiving."

Yuliya stifled a sob. "I thought we were going to die. Like our Mama and Tato."

Anna stroked her hair. "That will never happen, Yuliya. God protected us from evil. And that means he has a better plan for our lives."

The girl's eyebrows knit together, and she cocked her head. "Does God know who I am?"

"Of course, he does," Anna said. "He knows everything about you."

"Ja." Mary nodded with assurance. "That's true. My Mutter says so."

Tiny eyes sparkled behind the layered coverings. "Did we do good? We stayed quiet the whole time," Wilhelm asked.

"Except me. I'm sorry," Mary said.

"Everyone did fine. Even you Mary. There was no harm done. Thank you all for being so obedient," Anna said.

"We're alive," Katarina croaked. "That's all that matters."

"Alyona, where did you hide that last ring of sausage?" Anna asked, "I was so sure it was all gone yesterday."

The servant grinned. "I keep for emergency."

"You did well," Anna added.

"And Olek, too." Katarina cleared her throat. "You were so smart to pack the brandy."

Olek chuckled, "I, too, carry for emergencies."

"Well, then. I guess we had our one – and hopefully only –

emergency today," Katarina murmured. Although she still felt weak, she'd stopped shaking and her heart rate was returning to normal. Her voice would clear in a few hours.

As an animated din rose from the group, Katarina shut her eyes and focused on the rhythmic swaying of the wagon, inhaling the crisp winter air with slow, deep breaths. Soon, they'd be home. All was well.

26

THE TRUTH ABOUT YULIYA

1952 FEBRUARY. MUNICH, GERMANY.

"Peter, your supper is on the table." Heidi crossed her arms and tapped her fingers on her biceps. Today, only three empty beer bottles sat on the side table. At least Peter was trying to cut down on his drinking. She'd give him that. But the pile of papers on the couch beside him wasn't getting any smaller. She took a deep breath and counted to three. "I ate without you."

"Later. I'm not hungry now," Peter said, without looking up and his eyes glued to the book in his hands.

"Beer is not food," Heidi said as sternly as she dared without losing her temper. It was taking all her self-control to not pick a fight with him today, but her patience was wearing thin. "You should eat."

"I'll eat when I'm done."

"Fine. Eat it cold, then. I don't care." Heidi plopped down in the wing chair and retrieved a ball of wool and a pair of knitting needles from the tapestry bag under the coffee table. "What has you so absorbed?"

Her question met with more silence. Why was he deliberately ignoring her? She deliberately clicked the knitting needles together several times — hoping for a reaction. But Peter didn't flinch.

"Well, if that's the way you want it," she muttered under her breath. She picked up a stitch at the end of the row, but it dropped from the needle. "I guess nothing's going right for me today." She counted her stitches, then unraveled the row and started over. *Knit one, purl one, knit one, purl one.*

"Oh, you've got to be kidding me." Peter's head jerked up and his jaw dropped. He stared straight ahead at the wall.

"What?" Heidi glanced up, hoping for a meaningful conversation. When she realized that Peter was talking to himself, she shook her head and resumed knitting. *I've got to finish this baby blanket.*

"Yuliya." Peter's finger ran along a line in the book. He looked up and stared at the wall, unblinking, as if deep in thought.

"Who?"

"Yuliya. I knew her." Peter picked up a pencil and tapped the page repeatedly.

"Are you talking to me now?" Heidi scowled as she set the knitting down in her lap. "You keep muttering under your breath. I never know."

"Something's been bugging me about this story for months. I couldn't put my finger on it. But I've got it now." Peter shifted to face her.

Here we go again. Another sign. Or a dead end. "Is this about Katarina's diaries again? Let me guess. You've found a clue," Heidi said sarcastically. She crossed her arms and glared at him.

"Sort of. Listen to me. Before Hitler's war, Mum had this friend, Yuliya. Living here in Germany. How many women do you know with that name?" Peter waved off Heidi's open mouth as she went to answer. "They usually change it to Julia. But she didn't. She kept it as Yuliya. And Mum said they saved each other's lives in Russia."

"Is that in the diary?" Heidi raised an eyebrow. Maybe this time, Peter was on to something. "How they saved each other's lives?"

"Ja. Yuliya's parents were killed in a bandit attack and Mum rescued them. Don't you see?" Peter's face lit up.

"Don't I see what?" She didn't. Peter wasn't explaining himself.

"It's a clue, Heidi. This is the first real connection that I've found to Mutter's life here in Germany."

"I'm still not following." Heidi stretched out her legs and crossed her ankles, waiting for a more detailed explanation.

Peter pushed aside the book. "Listen. The regulations against the Jews began tightening long before the war broke out. One day, Yuliya shows up at our apartment. I remember her so clearly. She was this drop-dead gorgeous blond with amber eyes and legs that went on forever."

"Now, you're trying to make me jealous," Heidi smirked and uncrossed her arms.

"I was seventeen. Of course, I noticed beautiful girls." He waved his hand in the air again. "Never mind that. Listen, Mum told me to go for a walk because the two of them had something important to discuss. The following Sunday, I had to go along to a 'special' service at a church we'd never been to before." Peter made quotation marks in the air around the word 'special.' "At least, not a church *I'd* ever been to. A famous guest preacher, who'd been to America was there preaching against the new regulations and telling everyone to fight against injustice. In the middle of the service, the police came in and arrested him. After the church cleared, Mum and Yuliya had another very secret discussion on the walk home."

"What was it about?" Heidi pulled in her knees and leaned

forward. "The discussion, I mean. Between Katarina and Yuliya."

"I couldn't hear it." Peter waved his hand in the air. "But here's the thing. I'd never seen the two of them together in public before, until that summer. If anything, Mum deliberately crossed the street whenever she'd see Yuliya. It was almost as if she was embarrassed to be seen with her. I noticed it, because, as I said, the woman was a knock-out. Until then, I always thought Mum was envious of her."

"And?" Heidi probed.

"I learned later that Yuliya's mother was Jewish. And when her boss at the clothing store found out, she lost her job. And to make matters worse, the woman was divorced. Her reputation was, as they say, tarnished."

"So, she couldn't get another job because of her ethnicity. And she had no financial support," Heidi clarified.

"Ja." Peter nodded. "She was in dire straits."

"Was she asking Katarina for help?"

Peter nodded again. He stared at her with a blank expression on his face, as if searching his memory bank.

"But why?"

"Mum said she owed her."

"I'm confused. Katarina owed Yuliya? But I thought you said, Katarina saved Yuliya's life."

"Correct. But at some point, Yuliya saved Mum, too." Peter flicked the pencil against the book, then dropped it on the coffee table. He sat back on the couch and crossed his arms.

"And what's that story?"

"I don't know, yet." Peter shook his head. "But I've got a feeling it's a much bigger tale."

Heidi's blond eyebrows knit together. She twisted her mouth to the side and tapped a finger on her thigh. "So why did Katarina avoid Yuliya after they were both in Germany?"

Peter picked up the pencil and tapped the table. "That's exactly my point. How come? I need to figure that out. But here's the thing. Mutter worked for the *National Translation Service* then. She had a lot of connections. I thought Yuliya was asking her for help to get a job. After all, Yuliya was also fluent in at least three or four languages."

"Let me guess. Now, you're thinking it was something else."

"Ja. It just came to me now. The forgeries."

Heidi shook her head and groaned. "Now, you've just lost me again."

Peter tapped his index finger on the book. "Mutter learned about forgery in Ukraine from this guy, Sergei. She knew it was possible. All those papers I found in her dresser when I was searching for my identity documents — there were duplicates with slight changes. Dates, places — little things that an average person may not notice."

"But an official would."

"Exactly."

"But she was so religious. Didn't you once say that Katarina and Anna argued over such moral technicalities? From everything you've told me, her thinking was black and white."

"Ja. And she talks about that here, too. But for whatever reason, Anna hung on to those papers, and later Mutter kept them."

"What does this have to do with Yuliya?"

"Again. I'm still trying to piece things together here. I know nothing for certain, yet. But my guess is that at some point, those papers, or others like it, came in handy.

"Now skip forward to 1937. Over the previous fifteen years, Mum's cultivated a vast network — good and bad alike. And now Hitler's in charge. And things are happening in Germany that are very reminiscent of the upheaval in Russia. Don't forget, the Germans were persecuted there. They were driven out, their land taken away. Many were murdered at point-blank range. Mum knew what bigotry felt like. In Germany, the Jews were being attacked and their freedoms were destroyed. They were in harm's way — just like the Germans in Russia."

"Oh. I just got chills." Heidi rubbed her arms. "But Peter — your Mutter was working for the SS. They were the worst of the worst. Why would Yuliya ask for help from someone in that organization?"

"Not then, she wasn't. She was still employed by the *National Translation Services*. She contracted with the SS later."

"Willingly? She willingly worked for them?" Heidi cocked her head and squinted.

Peter shrugged. "Come on, Heidi. You know that the average person didn't understand Hitler's plans or believe the rumors. Even I voted for him then. For Mum, it was just a government job."

"But at some point, she would have found out."

"Ja. But my guess is she was in too deep by then. I remember she jumped at the chance to go to Poland. 'I'm going home to the old country,' she said. 'I'm going to look up our ancestors' churches and search for the ancient homesteads. I'll bring back some amber for Marta. It grows on the Baltic beaches there. Maybe I'll be lucky and find some.'"

"Did she?"

Peter contemplated the question and frowned. "What? Find amber?" He shrugged. "I don't know. I had no interest in jewelry. It was all girls' stuff in my mind."

"I don't mean amber. The homesteads." Heidi shook her head and waved a hand in the air to dismiss the question. "Never mind. Did you see her after that?"

"Maybe two or three times. I remember Mutter being very sober-minded and reflective after the first trip to Poland.

And guarded with her words. The next time I saw her was in Marienburg." Peter chewed on his bottom lip.

"You've mentioned this airport before. Why does it gnaw at you, so?"

Peter nodded. "I don't know."

"What does Yuliya have to do with any of this?"

"Again, I don't know. I will tell you what I do know, though. I only saw Yuliya a few times after that – and then she vanished. Poof." Peter made the explosive gesture with his hands.

"Poof? To where?" Heidi knit her eyebrows together.

He leaned in. "I don't know. But I'm confident Mum had something to do with it."

Heidi blinked several times. "Interesting. You said this Yuliya was Jewish. Do you think she was arrested, or did she escape?"

Peter picked up the pencil and flicked it around in his hand. "Her brother."

"What? She had a brother? What happened to him?"

"Anatoliy." Peter sat back and shook his pen in the air, then slapped it against his palm. "He lived in our building. Why did I never make the connection before?"

"What connection?"

"He lived down the hall from us. Mum used to send food over to his apartment. Anatoliy was a cripple with a wooden leg. He lived with this old Babushka — that's what we called her. She was half-deaf. The volume on her radio was always cranked loud enough for everyone in the building to hear. No one else needed one. When I wanted to listen to the news, I'd take my morning coffee and stand in the hallway to get the daily update. She'd screech, too — with this high-pitched squeal that would make your ears ring. Mostly, she yelled at him. Poor man. I often wondered why Anatoliy stayed living with her, but I just assumed they were family.

"Anyway, Babushka cleaned the hallways in exchange for reduced rent; and she'd usually leave their apartment door open with the radio on while she worked. When I passed by, I'd see him hunched over the table with a newspaper. He'd look up and nod. I'd smile and nod back. I never talked to him, though. He was a shy man, maybe ten years my senior."

"What happened to him?"

"And that's the thing, Heidi. About the same time that Yuliya disappeared, so did Anatoliy and Babushka."

"But it wasn't an arrest?"

"No. At least, not that I noticed." Peter flicked the pencil between his fingers.

Heidi stared into space. "So, you think Katarina had something to do with this?"

"I do."

"And you think this all has something to do with Ukraine and the civil war there?" Heidi tapped the wooden arm of the wing chair.

"I think so."

"Peter, if she was caught helping the Jews ..."

"They would have shot her."

"Except you're certain she went to Ukraine with the SS."

"Ja."

"And now you're back at the beginning." Heidi shook her head and picked up her knitting.

He stared back at her with a questioning look. "What?"

"Peter. You're driving yourself crazy trying to figure out if Katarina is dead or alive. You haven't answered one of your own questions." Heidi pulled a strand from the ball of wool, then picked up her knitting needles and clicked them together.

Peter sighed. "You're right. All that I know is that Mutter helped a couple of Jews she once knew in Russia."

"I think you're looking for a needle in a haystack, Peter.

And you're searching for something that doesn't exist. You should give up."

He chuckled. "Except, Heidi, I'm learning something about Mutter. She had a good heart."

"All Mutters have good hearts, Peter. Even the bad ones love their children. But some struggle to show it." Heidi held the ball of wool in the air. "I'm showing love to our little one right now by making one blanket for him or her. I'm a terrible knitter, but I'm determined to learn."

27

HOME AGAIN

1918 FEBRUARY (JULIAN CALENDAR). CHORTITZA COLONY, UKRAINE.

THE EXCITED CHEERS OF SMALL VOICES WOKE KATARINA from a deep sleep. She rubbed her eyes, wiped the drool from her chin, then sat up and brushed the straw from her coat and hair. Taking a deep breath, she squinted at the serene, frosted landscape. The crisp air held a familiar earthy aroma of spruce, wood smoke, and manure. "Are we home?" Her voice cracked, the huskiness from the allergic reaction still evident in her tone. "What happened to the plantation? Did I miss it?"

"Yes, you slept through it," Anna said. "All the pretty green covered with sparkling white. The trees looked like they were wearing diamond studded shawls."

Katarina cleared her throat and stretched. "Drat. I didn't want to miss it. Why didn't you wake me?"

"The kids were having too much fun making sport of your snoring. I didn't want to spoil it for them."

Eight-year-old Mary cupped her hands over her mouth and giggled.

Katarina wrinkled her nose at her niece. "Thanks a lot."

"You were noisy!" the child proclaimed, laughing.

"Look, I can see the farmhouse." Anna pointed ahead to the conifer-lined drive. Just then, the wagon jerked and the front of the box tilted left. "No, not now," she cried. "We're almost there."

Arms and hands flew as the passengers scrambled to keep from sliding. Olek stopped the troika and jumped off. He checked the undercarriage. "The axle is broken. Now, we must walk. Do you wish to stay until I get back?"

"I'm not spending another hour in the freezing cold waiting for a ride when I can drink hot milk in front of a roaring fire. Please help me down," Anna ordered.

"This way." Katarina leaped over the side without waiting for Olek to open the tailgate. Her feet sank into a knee-high snowdrift, and she lost her balance; then landed on her right side. She rolled over and gazed up at the cerulean sky. They were home! After four terrifying days and three nights, they'd arrived safely. She wriggled her legs, pounded her heels into the snow, and screamed. But her ragged voice delivered only spasmodic, screeching sounds.

She jumped up, pointed to the tree-lined drive, and beckoned to the bedraggled youngsters. "Follow me for cookies and milk."

The children tumbled from the wagon and raced past her, embracing the day with playful innocence as if it were a winter holiday and no awfulness had ever happened. White balls emerged from handfuls of wet, sticky snow, and shrieks rang out while each tried to dodge the others' round weapons.

Katarina delighted in the shenanigans, but her soul twinged with a pinch of jealousy, wishing she were ten again.

She ran to join in the sport, but her lungs throbbed with a knife-like pain, and she collapsed and dropped to her knees.

She inhaled deeply of the familiar farm smell and soaked in the brilliant scenery with its snow-dusted towering spruce trees and ice-encrusted blankets. The evergreens, planted by her great-great-grandparents when first they arrived from Prussia, were taller, denser, and prettier than she remembered. The comforting peacefulness warmed her soul and quelled the damp cold that had settled into her bones.

So much had happened in the past two years. She shivered, remembering the trauma, and prayed the black stallion had forgotten her.

Following the accident, the tense bond with her mother became insufferable. Upon relocating to Anna's, she echoed her sister's adolescent outburst, vowing never to return home. But slowly, her relationship with her mother softened. Perhaps the passage of time and the physical distance had helped. Regardless, today she felt like a prodigal and wondered whether she'd be welcome here. Would her mother, Lena, view her as the grown-up she'd become, or would she still treat her as a child in need of supervision?

All things considered, she didn't want to be here. But there was nowhere else to run to. Besides, this was the safest place for Anna to give birth. That took priority over any other personal feelings. Running away wasn't an option this time.

Katarina set her face like flint and walked down the long, circular driveway, watching the tired, red brick farmhouse loom ever larger with every step. Fresh piles of snow marked the shoveled pathways to the front and rear doors. The three chimneys dotting the centerline of the shingled roof puffed foggy gray billows into the azure winter sky. The expansive covered porch — that stretched along the full width of the house and welcomed visitors during the hot summer months

— was swept clean. The yeasty aroma of fresh bread and sweet cinnamon mixed with the yard's pungent farm scent and produced a sweet and sour earthy fragrance. Katarina guessed Katya was baking breakfast breads in the outdoor stone oven.

The carriage sat parked by the summer kitchen with its tongue buried in knee-deep snow. Katarina froze, her eyes glued to the vehicle while fearing the inevitable confrontation with her unaffectionate mother. Her heart pounded in her head — its beat matching the drip, drip, drip of the icicles melting from the roof's overhang. They dented the snowdrifts beneath it into toothy mounds of dirty white and added to the building's dated appearance.

Katarina stood and waited for Anna to catch up to her.

"We're home, Katarina. Can you believe it? We made it." Anna puffed. She carried her belly with both hands as she trudged through the ankle-deep base.

"Ja. We did." Katarina pointed to the carriage. "*They're* home."

"After everything we've gone through, I feared what we might find here. But the property looks normal. Thank God."

"Since when do you worry about anything?" Katarina shortened her step to sync with Anna's.

"I'm not worried. I'm just tired. And everything hurts. I remind myself that Mary rode to Bethlehem on a donkey and gave birth in a stable, so I should be able to walk this short distance." Anna analyzed the footprints and picked one set to follow.

Katarina kicked at the snow. "Except you're not the Virgin Mary. You don't have to act so brave."

"Yes, I do. Attitude is everything in bad times. When we look for the silver lining in the dark clouds, they don't seem so scary."

"That's hard to do when you have no compass and you're

surrounded by ominous uncertainty in the middle of a moon-less night."

"It's always darkest before the dawn. And daybreak is guaranteed." Anna stopped. "Katarina, can you please take smaller steps? The snow is so deep. I'm trying to walk in your tracks."

"I'll try. I didn't realize my stride was so much longer than yours."

"Yes. And so are your big feet. Which makes it easy for me to follow."

"Ha. You want to watch me make the first misstep, so you can avoid the potholes." Katarina said.

"Exactly."

"Then I shall lead. And you can pray I don't trip."

They turned the corner and entered the shoveled path alongside the house.

"Does everything look the same to you, Anna? I can't tell. I haven't been back in so long. Or maybe my judgment is tainted from the last few days."

Anna wrinkled her nose and squinted while surveying the exterior. "The bandits could be hiding, but I don't see any fresh tracks in the snow." She turned and winked, "Relax. All will be fine."

Katarina's knees knocked as she climbed the first step. It was from the allergy attack, she told herself. A hot bath and a good sleep would fix that. She listened to the happy screams of the children as they greeted their grandparents, then stopped on the second stair and took a deep breath of the comforting piquant aroma of cloves, garlic, and dill wafting through the open door. A black dress with a white pinafore flashed past the entrance — Katya.

At the top of the landing, the familiar click-clack of steel heels against a wood floor and the swish of petticoats under the mid-calf navy dress announced Lena. Her gray hair was covered with a white kerchief tied behind her neck and she'd thrown a black knitted shawl over her plump shoulders. Her arms opened wide, and Katarina melted into them.

"You're home," Lena said softly. "I always knew you'd come. Papa wanted to march into harm's way to find you, but I told him to wait. I figured you girls would run here if you could."

"We didn't know where else to go." Katarina gazed at her mother's sallow face. The crinkly lines around Lena's icy blue eyes and those around her mouth and forehead were deeper than she remembered.

"You're safe now." Lena kissed Katarina's cheek, then took her face in her hands. Her eyes filled with watery pools. "Welcome home."

"Did they come here?" Katarina croaked, her limbs trembling. "The soldiers. Makhno? The Reds?"

Lena loosened her grip and turned away to greet Anna waddling up the stairs. "We're fine. Better than most. And we still have food. The world is a crazy place right now, but as long as we have each other, we can get through anything."

28

ONCE A CHILD

THAT NIGHT AT SUPPER, THEIR FATHER, JOHANN, COVERED his cup with his hand as Katya approached with the teapot. "Bring the dessert, Katya. We must celebrate the safe return of our prodigal daughters."

Katya nodded but continued serving tea to the women. She wasn't ignoring her employer's request, but rather deferring it enough to irritate him.

Katarina smirked at Katya's snub. It was a familiar passive-aggressive game designed to add humor and deflect tension during difficult family discussions.

Katya winked at her former charge, indicating the game was on and there was more to come. Anna, who resented Katarina and Katya's affableness, narrowed her eyes at the secret messages. According to her, friendly relationships with the servants only led to mischief and laziness.

The maid had worked for the family since first being hired as Katarina's nanny. As their bond grew, Katarina shared both deep feelings and dark secrets with the servant. Katarina found Katya to be a unique source of womanly wisdom.

The fact that Katya and Katarina shared the same

moniker of the Grand Duchess endeared them to each other. While most families had pet names for their children, and Katya was a variation of 'Katharine,' it was too confusing for both the nanny and her charge to share the same identifier. When Katarina voiced her opinion and requested to be known by her Christian name, the family agreed.

But Anna hated being excluded from Katya and Katarina's special relationship. She retaliated by stealing the limelight at home and becoming the shining example of the perfect child. She was always one step better than Katarina, one step more well-behaved, and one step more Christian in every way. And definitely prettier. Her high-profile marriage cemented their mother's high esteem of her second youngest. Anna succeeded whereas Katarina failed.

Although Anna's need to be the center of attention irritated Katarina, Lena's constant comparison between them bothered her more. Anna was the yardstick and Katarina could never seem to measure up. Over the years, she learned to accept that Anna was perfect and she was flawed, and that was that. Although she wanted her parents to be proud of her, Katarina had no interest in following in Anna's footsteps. Therefore, earning her mother's admiration seemed impossible.

While living in Halbstadt, Katarina thought she'd moved past the need for parental approval. She'd spread her wings and become her own person. She and Anna had both grown up.

But now, sitting at the family dinner table, she suddenly felt like a ten-year-old little girl waiting to be chastised. And her childish reactions followed. When their father referred to them as prodigal daughters, Katarina covered her face and rolled her eyes.

Even though Johann was joking, the descriptor felt like a

put-down. Was he insinuating that she and Anna had strayed away from the strict confines of church and family?

The fact that they worshipped at a different denomination from their parents didn't make them heathen. In Katarina's opinion, the rules of conduct between the two sides of the river were not identical, but similar enough.

However, her parents had their own views of politically-correct geography and religious rules of order. And since it was not her place to judge them, Katarina bit her lips, put her hands in her lap, and smiled as if his words were complimentary.

They'd just been through a tough week. Maybe she was just overtired and overthinking. She shouldn't be so sensitive.

≈

THE CLATTERING of Anna's cup against the saucer interrupted Katarina's brooding. "Is there news yet? Is the estate still standing?"

"The reports are trickling in. Nothing's been said about your husband's place yet. That's a good sign." Johann's pale aqua eyes followed Katya as she left the room. "But we've heard half the village burned to the ground."

"Where are the displaced?" Anna raised one eyebrow. "Please tell me all escaped the fires."

"Few deaths, thank the Lord. But many are homeless. And therein lies the challenge." Johann tapped his thick fingers on the table. "Rebuilding takes time. And with so many away at war, labor is in short supply. The winter storms are making things worse. The destitute must be fed and housed now, not six months from now. And the shortage of food is adding to the crisis."

"I heard the armies decimated the livestock and left carcasses rotting in the fields!" Lena exclaimed. "Whole cows and horses left for the wolves. How could they be so inhumane? What will people eat?"

Johann stroked his long salt and pepper beard and nodded. "The winter is already lean. Spring will be worse. Every household must tighten its belts and dig into its larders. Everyone must learn to do with less and share with their neighbors. If we work together, no one will starve."

"And where are our men? Dietrich hasn't written in weeks." Lena said referring to their youngest son who was three years older than Anna. "When did you last hear from your husband, Anna?"

"The mail doesn't always get through," Johann said. "Bandits rob the trains and steal the mail."

"We got a letter last week, Mutter. David's fine. He triages the injured soldiers in the fields and brings them to the doctors on the hospital train. I think 'triage' means they prioritize who gets treated first. But I don't want to know the gory details, so I don't ask more."

"It sounds gut-wrenching awful. I don't want to read specifics either," Katarina said, recalling her discovery of the hanging couple and the orphans' parents. The memory made her stomach churn.

Katya returned to the room with a cookie platter. Instead of offering it to Johann first as was the custom, she set it beside Lena's elbow. Johann's jaw twitched.

Katarina's and Anna's eyes met across the table and they both sucked in a grin. Katya was definitely provoking Johann. The two probably had a spat. Maybe Katya neglected to put away the pitchfork and Johann had tripped on it. Or she forgot to clean his favorite shirt. Whatever it was, the two would pick at each other for a day or so, until the sin was forgotten. In the meantime, the tiff was a pleasant distraction from the hell they'd just gone through.

"Ja. Thank God we were spared," Lena took a cookie and

passed the platter to Katarina. "Katarina, pass the cookies to your father." Lena waited until Johann had the platter in his hand before taking a bite. "We're blessed to have you girls home."

"Katarina and I are both happy to be back, even though it's under such unfortunate circumstances," Anna said. "Although, I worry about the work waiting for us in Halbstadt. As chair of the women's welfare committee, I'm responsible for assessing housing and food needs. I've started a to-do list, but now I realize we've no information on the numbers." Anna turned to Katarina. "Can you help research how many are affected?"

At first, Katarina was flattered by Anna's attempt to include her. But then, she was puzzled. Anna was on the committee, not her. It was inappropriate for her — as a single woman with no status — to make inquiries of the church leaders. She raised her index finger in the air to ask for clarification, but Anna ignored her and kept rambling.

"Never mind. We'll billet what we can. And I suppose a hundred can sleep on the floor in the sanctuary. We'll move the pews and use the school rooms. But we need a more permanent solution." Anna rubbed her belly in circular motions, matching the pace of her quickened speech. "And we must speak with the senior men to find out how many homes need rebuilding. And when they'll be ready. I must speak to the leadership. There's so much to do."

Lena scraped back her chair and went over to Anna and wrapped her plump arms around her shoulders. "Anechka, this is not the time to worry about such. Right now, your priority is the baby. Everything else can wait. There are others who can run the committees. You don't have to do it all."

Katarina clenched her fists to control the jealousy rising in her veins from Lena's admiration of her sister. However, it was true that Anna was the driving force behind both the church's charity drives and the town's social calendar. The committees would notice her absence during the recovery phase. But they'd find someone else to take charge of the humanitarian relief until Anna returned.

But when would that be? Not for a month or two, or until Anna recovered from birthing. *Two months or longer?* But what about her jobs in Halbstadt? A twinge of panic shot through her. If they had to stay here, what would she do with her time? Reintegrate with the local church social groups? Being single, she'd stick out like a sore thumb among her married peers. There would be public scrutiny and twittering. Katarina took a deep breath and sighed. Why was nothing ever easy?

Regardless of however long it took before they could go home, Katarina didn't want to spend the time just embroidering or enduring her mother's inevitable accusations of laziness. The local missions needed help, too. She'd work here. So, she asked: "Papa, what's the situation here in Chortitza?" Referring to the charities.

But Johann's mind was on politics. He stuffed another cookie in his mouth; his long mustache wiggling as he chewed. "No deaths here. Thank God. Although there was torture of other kinds. The Red Guards passed through quickly en route to Kyiv. But brutally so. There was little mercy. Our past loyalties to the Czar have cost us dearly, I'm afraid. I pray daily for our continued safety." Johann shook his index finger in the air. "Our forefathers were right when they told us to remain neutral. If we had stayed true to our faith and completely separated ourselves from worldly affairs, we would not be in this mess."

Katarina wondered about the swaying bodies in the barn. Who killed them? The battle at Kyiv was between the Bolsheviks and the Ukrainians. Was one side more brutal than the other? "Papa, we're not the only ones affected. The locals suffer, too. We saw things on our trip." She paused and glanced nervously at her sister, suddenly realizing she'd already said too much.

Anna tilted her head and frowned. "What do you mean, Katarina? The lack of food at Sergei's house, or the empty coal bin? There's a shortage of food everywhere."

"Ah ... Ja. And ..." Katarina stuttered. Olek had made her promise to keep the upsetting incident a secret. He'd tell Johann later. But he insisted they protect the others from the truth.

Katarina bit her lip and dug her fingernails into her palms to stop herself from blurting out the rest of the story. Keeping this secret somehow felt akin to lying. Her heart pounded and sweat beaded on her forehead. She probably looked as guilty as she felt.

All eyes turned to her now. Anna's one eyebrow raised in a question mark. Lena's icy blues twitched as they gazed across the rim of the cup. Johann tapped his thick fingers on the table. Katarina scrambled to deflect suspicion.

"Papa, are we not permitted to fight back under any circumstances? Are we not called to protect our fellow man? The soldiers are burning our homes, destroying the fields, pilfering foodstuffs, and threatening lives. No one is stopping them." Katarina raised her voice to stress her point. "There must be something we can do to defend ourselves. Non-resistance seems irrational under these circumstances."

"Calm down, Katarina." Johann slammed his fist on the table. "God has a plan for Russia, and we must not interfere. Whatever happens, we must trust Him. He knows the end from the beginning. If we die, we'll be in Heaven with the Lord. If we live, God's purpose continues."

Anna and Lena nodded simultaneously as Johann preached. "As for the locals, the Russians, and the rest of the world, that's not our concern. If they wish to kill each other,

our conscience is clean. We don't take part in their folly."
Johann picked up the white cloth napkin and dusted the
crumbs from his graying beard.

"In other words, do nothing and die — let God sort it
out," Katarina sighed and rolled her eyes at the ceiling.

Lena gawked with wide eyes. "Ja, Katarina. Whether we
live or die — that is up to God. But if there is something else
that can be done — well, that's up to the men to decide. It's
not for us women to know now. However, we shall all pray
and ask God to guide us." Lena's icy stare sent a shiver down
Katarina's back.

Once again, Katarina clenched her fists under the table.
Her mother's passivity drove her crazy. In her opinion, Lena's
interpretation of the spiritual order as blind obedience to her
husband made her look weak, indifferent, and emotionless.
Katarina vowed to never be as submissive as her mother.

Despite Lena's deference to the male sex, Katarina
noticed that her mother respected Anna's opinions, but
discounted hers. But then, she felt Anna was often treated
differently and given more privileges. Was it because Anna
embraced tradition without questioning it? Or did her sister's
marital status make the difference?

*I'm less than because I'm a woman. I'm less than because I'm
single.* Katarina swallowed the tears welling up in her throat.
Am I also less than because I wish for a career? If that was true,
then she'd never be fully accepted until she followed the
traditional path. But that meant giving up her dreams. Her
shoulders sank from the weightiness of her own startling
conclusions.

29

WORRIES ABOUT MARIA

JOHANN CLEARED HIS THROAT. "NOW, LET'S TALK ABOUT our more immediate worries. What's going on with Maria and her brood?"

He'd changed the subject again.

Katarina put her face in her hands and glowered at her father between her fingers. When Johann decided a conversation was over, then it was done. And it was never appropriate to criticize one's faith. Ever. As the head of the family, Johann controlled — among other things — the content and direction of the dialogue. The women were expected to listen and obey — never argue. He was right and that was that. But Katarina enjoyed debates. She hated being shut down just when the discussion was getting interesting.

"You shouldn't have left Maria and the boys there. Your maid and those orphans would've managed just fine."

"Papa, Maria assured us she could handle the gangs. Her concern was for the orphans' survival. She insisted on staying behind. It was her choice." Katarina swallowed the lump in her throat and glanced furtively at Anna. Had they done the right thing? She prayed Maria wouldn't face the same fate as the couple in the barn.

Anna interjected. "Papa! We couldn't possibly leave the orphans to the fate of the rebels. Granted, the decision was heart-wrenching. All lives have value. What else could we do?"

Triage, Katarina thought. They'd performed triage just like David did on the train with the injured. They'd chosen life over death for the orphans and risked Maria's — believing their sister could wait.

She silently cursed the damp cold as she rubbed the old, inflamed bump on her arm. Her upper back prickled with tension. She could barely keep her eyes open, and everything hurt. It had been a long day and a dreadful journey. After supper, she'd search for Grandfather's secret clove and mint liniment in the ancient medicine chest. Then, she'd sleep for a hundred years.

"I understand," Johann continued. "But you're both wrong. Maria is your sister. She and the boys are your primary responsibility. Your servants would have protected the orphans until help arrived." He wrinkled his nose and pulled a handkerchief out of his pocket.

Katarina bristled. What did their father expect from them? She met Anna's eyes. Clearly, Johann didn't understand the circumstances. Should they tell him about the attack on the road? Anna's slow headshake sent the message, *Let it be*.

Johann wiped his face with the handkerchief, then blew his nose with a loud honk. "Now, tell me the plans. If I must jump into this hornet's nest, then I want to be prepared." He blinked several times as if he was about to sneeze but returned the cloth to his pocket and wiped his watering eyes with the back of his hand. "Well? Don't just sit there and gawk with your mouths hanging open. Tell me how we're going to rescue your sister."

Katarina took a deep breath and stammered. "Olek is leaving at daybreak. First, he'll find the orphans' sister and drop them off with her. Then, he'll take Alyona to her son's place near the ferry crossing. After that, he'll go back to the farm and pick up Maria and the other children."

"That's mighty brave of him, considering the rebels are roaming in broad daylight *and* he's driving through the most dangerous areas. What happens if he doesn't get there tomorrow? If anything happens to her, there'll be another eight orphans to feed." Johann paused. An incredulous expression spread across his face. "What were those parents thinking? Taking their two brats on such a trip under such conditions? They must have had more money than brains."

Katarina clamped her jaw shut. She glanced at Anna for permission to tell the rest of the story, but her sister stared at the table and rubbed her baby bulge with slow, determined circles.

"Olek may be a smart man with a few tricks up his sleeves, but few dare to venture out now. The countryside is mighty dangerous. Frankly, I'm shocked you made it here without trouble." Johann shook his head.

"Ja." Katarina reached for a cookie from the platter in the center of the table and snapped it in half. This time, she caught Anna's eye and sent a plea for help.

"I trust his judgment, Papa." Anna picked up on Katarina's cue. "He knows the area, understands the culture, and speaks the language fluently. I'm sure he'll manage. He has connections."

"Huh." Johann snorted and crooked his index finger at the cookie plate. "What connections?"

"Locals, I assume," Katarina said, shrugging. "But he also said he'll take the long route past the ferry crossing. He won't be driving through those dirty villages along the riverbank."

"But he has to go through that area to get to Maria's," Johann frowned.

"Yes, he can't avoid that," Anna said.

Johann took two cookies and stuffed one in his mouth. "I'm going with him."

Shock and horror passed over Lena's face. "You'll do no such thing. The rebels will shoot first and ask questions later."

Johann chuckled at his wife's reaction. "I've heard the name-calling. We are the kulaks — the unworthy wealthy. They say the word with venom in their mouths. As if they are snakes, and we are the rats. Our lives are already at risk."

"Papa, Mutter is right. You can't be throwing yourself in harm's way," Anna pleaded.

"Girls, girls. Don't worry about me. There's nothing a few bribes can't solve. Brandy and tobacco buy both honest men and desperate criminals. Olek and I will fill the benches."

"I think they prefer money." Katarina removed the empty cookie platter from the table and handed it to Katya who'd begun clearing the table.

"Cash is in short supply these days," Johann continued. "Bartering is more efficient. Besides, our currency is probably going to change again if these negotiations are signed. Nobody trusts the new Ukrainian Karbovanets; and those Kerensky rubles may be worthless soon, too."

"Another currency change? From which side? Ukraine? Or Russia?" Katarina and Anna both leaned forward simultaneously. "What negotiations?"

"Germany and Russia are meeting at Brest-Litovsk, finalizing details to end the war."

"Finalizing?" Katarina held her breath. What had she missed in the past few days? "They've been in talks for months. Have they signed? Is the war over?"

A smug look passed over Johann's face. He leaned back in

his chair and crossed his arms over his chest. "Let's put it this way. The newspapers are going crazy. If it's true, Mother Russia has conceded much. The Ottoman gets some land. Germany gets a lot of lands, including Ukraine. And we become an independent state under the control and authority of Germany."

"Meine Liebe. Is this for certain?" Anna stared at her father; her eyes wide.

"Our men will come home soon!" Happiness resonated in Lena's voice.

"Life will return to normal," Katarina exclaimed. "The trains will run again. And the schools will get new books." *Books!* Her skin tingled with the promise of a better life without the uncertainty of the last four years. "If Germany is in charge, will the schoolbooks be in German? Will I instruct in German instead of Russian next semester?"

"It's been a hard four years," Anna added. "We've done without lace, chocolate, and black tea. If we hadn't raised our own meat and milk, I don't know how we would've managed."

"It's not official yet," Johann explained. "They must still sign the papers. But the news says they're very close. It should be any day now."

"If Ukraine becomes part of Germany, will we become German citizens?" Anna asked.

Johann pushed his chair back, crossed his legs, and rubbed his beard. A smile peaked out from under his thick mustache. "Wouldn't that be nice?"

"There are rumors. If it's so ..." The news felt like a too-good-to-be-true dream. Katarina wanted to pinch herself.

"Tsk, tsk, Katarina. Don't you know more than rumors? You're a schoolteacher and you work for the newspaper! *You* should be telling *us* the latest facts." Lena's chin jutted to the ceiling.

Katarina flinched. The sarcasm hit like cold water against

her face. She gritted her teeth. Why did her mother need to scoff at her education and employment? What sin was she committing?

Anna patted Katarina's arm under the table indicating she'd also noticed the insensitive slight. The touch reminded Katarina that their mother didn't mean to be rude or arrogant. Lena was just a blunt person by nature, and her crude attempts at humor were often misplaced. Katarina knew this, but it hurt nonetheless. She took a deep breath and exhaled.

Katya conveniently interrupted with a second tea service. When the former nanny refilled Katarina's cup, she whispered in her ear, "Be careful. You can't win this." The servant could still sense the mood shifts of her former charge and knew her triggers. Katarina grimaced. Both Katya and Anna were right. Arguing was pointless.

Katarina swallowed the sharp rebuttal sitting on the tip of her tongue and cleared her throat. "Mutter, I try to stay on top of political news. But I've been away from it for the past week. Things change. There's a lot to keep track of. I know about the ongoing negotiations. Everyone does. There's been a cease-fire for two months. I didn't know the countries were ready to sign the treaty papers. That's different from rumors." Katarina spoke slowly, controlling her tone.

The parents' eyes met across the table. Johann's looked sternly at his wife and Lena's mouth twitched. She turned her face away.

Anna broke the awkward silence. "Well, I hope this means we'll get some law and order back and those bandits on the road will be arrested for their poor behavior."

"I doubt we'll see instant results. But an organized military action by Germany will push out the riffraff." Johann snapped his suspenders to announce he was tired of the conversation.

Anna either missed the signal or ignored it. "What about the Red Terror? Will it end with this treaty?"

"Of course. They'll have to leave."

"And what about Makhno and his troops? He doesn't play by the law. He makes up his own rules as he goes along," Anna said.

The unpredictability of the growing anarchist army gnawed on Katarina's mind. The raids on the local farms, the murders in the eastern villages, the dead dog, the couple in the barn, the orphaned children, and yesterday's ambush — the horror had become mind-numbing. Whether the responsibility for the crimes belonged to the Red Guards or Makhno's ruffians, it didn't matter. They were both using terror as weapons of control.

"I don't think we can depend on Germany to get rid of him," Katarina said. "He'll only disappear into the woodwork until the excitement settles. Then just like that, he'll jump out of the forest and strike with both fists. He won't accept another country controlling these lands. He's determined to eliminate any who try."

"They should have arrested him a long time ago," Anna added. "Is there no law and order left in the land?"

"Let's leave Makhno to the authorities and not speculate about him. We have the treaty signing on our doorstep. Let's pray for peace and focus on the facts in front of us." Johann pushed his chair back. "God has not given us a spirit of cowardice," he said, quoting the Bible verse.[1] Let's remember that we are not in charge of these events." He stood up. "Now, I'm going to the barn to talk to Olek. I must bring my daughter and grandsons home."

Katarina messaged Anna with her eyes. *Tell him!* Anna's gaze darted from her father to her mother and back to Katarina. She slowly rolled her hand over her belly, then looked directly at her father. "Papa. There's something you need to know."

Johann pivoted on his heel and studied Anna. "What is it?"

"On the way here, we were ambushed." Anna bit a corner of her lip, and her eyes froze on his face.

"What?" Lena's deep-set eyes widened like saucers.

Johann grabbed the wooden armchair. His large rough fists tightened around the intricate carved backrest. "All right. I'm listening. What happened?" He glared at Anna with an unwavering gaze. She flinched and turned to Katarina. "You tell him."

Chicken. Katarina rolled her eyes. "They came out of the woods with guns and held us up."

"Where?" Johann's aqua eyes flickered.

"About an hour north of here. By a long section of forest."

"Who were *they*?" His voice tightened — the tone firm and commanding.

"We don't know. But they wore expensive coats. Probably stolen. The leader carried a black flag. They spoke like locals." Katarina rubbed her lips together.

"Were you robbed?" Johann's tone softened.

"Were you hurt?" Lena interrupted.

"Robbed, ja. But we weren't hurt. They took David's family samovar — the good, silver one. And all the money."

"Well, not all." Anna patted her belly and chuckled. "I was lying on my money belt."

"And somehow, they missed the jewelry at the bottom of my bag," Katarina added.

"Maybe it was the sausage." The sisters looked at each other and burst out laughing.

"Oba, ja. A ring of Mennonite sausage stopped them from looking any further," Katarina roared.

Lena slapped the table. "That's it, Johann. You're not

going with Anna's driver. Everyone is staying home until this scourge has left the area."

"Lena, you and our girls will stay home where it's safe. I, however, will do what I feel needs to be done." Johann's jaw flexed.

"But if they kill you, what will happen to us? We are only women. We can't take care of this place ourselves. And if they march onto the farm, what kind of defenses will we have?"

"Lena, stop this mindless fretting. If they raid the farm, give them what they want. Food, clothing, and a warm place to sleep. Then they'll be embarrassed about their behavior and they'll leave. It's the most logical solution to this nonsense. There's a shortage of food. When the war ends, this craziness will all go away. Don't put evil in your head by worrying about things that haven't yet happened."

"But Papa, what if they come here and try to kill us? They murdered the orphan's parents." Tears welled in Anna's eyes.

Johann threw his hands in the air. "Again, with the what ifs! Ladies, please. Let's not exaggerate this. You didn't see what happened to that couple. My guess is that they tried to protect themselves with their own guns and then there was a shootout. Now, be mindful that one gun invites another to the fight. Our faith teaches that we're safer without weapons. This incident proves that. Besides, if you are destined to die this way, then you'll be in heaven. What concerns you about death? Make sure your spiritual life is clean, then you have nothing to worry about." Johann pushed his chair into the table and snapped his suspenders again. "If that's it, then I'm going to the barn." He jutted his chin at Katya. "Bring me two pies. Olek and I will eat our sweets together in the stables like real men."

Johann stomped down the hall to the mudroom. Lena traced the pattern on the oak table. Anna stared into space and rolled her hand over her belly. Katarina's heart sank into hers. Why was every conversation laden with fear and fore-boding, and every day filled with worries about the future? As far as she was concerned, peace and safety couldn't come soon enough. Germany was the only hope they had.

1 2 Timothy 1:7

30

IF MENNONITES HAD GUNS

THE NEXT DAY.

"I'M RELIEVED YOU MADE IT HOME ALIVE." KATARINA pushed the rolling pin across the thick dough, stretching it into a long rectangle. "I worried you'd be attacked on the road. How did you get through without being noticed?"

Maria chortled with a half snort. "It must've been your prayers that sustained us, sisters. But let me tell you, we were mighty anxious. The boys and I were up half the night coming up with half-true stories to tell the rebels if they stopped us. It was nerve-wracking. I quick-chewed[1] my nails."

"Half-true stories, huh?" Katarina chuckled. "I wish I'd been there for that." *Especially for the quick-chewing.*

"Well, I was worried sick, too. Mutter almost threw a fit when Papa insisted on going along with Olek," Anna said.

"Ja." Maria cracked an egg into the bowl. "Thankfully, Olek talked him out of it. Mennonite men are too obvious. They would never have made it all the way there and back without getting stopped. What is it? The German accent, our proper clothes, or the clean speech?" She dotted the eggs with salt and pepper and jabbed the yolks with a fork.

"Maybe we just look like money," Anna said sarcastically.

Maria chuckled. "Ja. Maybe. Anyway, the rebels know we don't fraternize with the locals. So, it's obvious to them that the driver is a servant and that he's there to defend us. And then they search for guns. And if one tries to stop them, they shoot."

"Did Olek say anything about problems on the way down? I worried about the bandits ambushing again. Those poor orphans. They must have been terrified." Katarina stopped rolling the dough and removed the paring knife from behind her apron ties.

"He didn't say. I only asked if all went well, and he said it did." Maria picked up two forks and whipped the eggs.

"I'm surprised Olek refused to take Papa's gun. Although, I'm more surprised Papa has one. I thought the Bolsheviks confiscated them all." Katarina scrutinized the dough. If there weren't a shortage of flour, she'd use a glass to make perfect circles for the *vareniki*[2]. But now, every scrap of dough was precious. Cutting it into squares left nothing to throw away.

"When we left Halbstadt, we heard the munitions depot explode. Anna said there're more guns around than we realize. *Eich*. I can't keep up with the secrets and deceit in this war," Katarina said as she carved the dough into imperfect squares.

"Lately, rifles come from Germany. But they mostly land in rebel hands," Maria added. "The authorities keep searching our farms for our hidden stash."

"Guns. And lies about guns. It's hard to know what to believe anymore." Anna added flour and salt to a bowl. "The politicians are encouraging dishonesty."

"The gun laws are ridiculous. Papa buried his in the pasture before the inspections passed through. He wouldn't

take a chance even though it was strictly a hunting rifle."
Maria stopped whipping the eggs and set the bowl aside.

"That was a dangerous thing to do," Anna said. "Men were
shot for less. But David and Olek did the same. I was terrified
during the inspections. I ran to the church with my knitting
and hid there with the other women. I didn't want to be put
in the position of lying to the authorities. Sometimes it's best
not to know everything."

"Thankfully, I wasn't home then." Katarina stopped
talking as Lena walked into the room.

"That's right, ladies. The less one knows, the less trouble
one gets into." Lena scanned the table. "My, my Katarina. The
dough looks perfect. We'll make a fine wife out of you yet.
The water's boiling. Do you have any ready to cook?"

Maria handed a plate of the prepared dumplings to her
mother. After Lena left the room, she snickered, "Ja, Katarina. You'll make a fine wife soon. By the way, do you have
someone in mind who may be interested in sampling your
wares?"

Anna burst out laughing, "I know of one who has bright
blue eyes."

Katarina narrowed her eyes. "Shush." Her neck warmed.

"What's this I hear?" Lena re-entered the room. "Does
Katarina have a man in mind? If so, we must invite him over."

"No. It's not like that." Katarina tapped the rolling pin on
the table. "It's not possible. He fights for the wrong side."

Lena's eyebrows knit together. "What do you mean? Is he
not one of ours?"

"Oh, yes, he is," Anna said with gleeful enthusiasm. "But
he's conscripted to the Bolsheviks as a horse trader."

Katarina stared at her sisters with an incredulous look.
"Are there no secrets in this house? Am I not allowed
privacy?"

"Who is he?" Lena asked again.

"Our dear cousin from Vitebsk. The veterinarian's son, Peter." Anna fluttered her eyelashes. "Our second cousin, once removed. Distant enough to be legitimate husband material."

Katarina felt the heat wash over her face a second time. She gave her sister a dirty look. "Anna, that's not fair. It's not your story to tell."

"Well, then. It seems we have work to do." Maria's face shone with amusement. She stepped into the middle of the room, crossed her arms, and tapped her fingers on her elbows. "How shall we begin this? A seasonal party, perhaps? We could coordinate this with a church function. Mutter, what's on the local calendar next month?"

Lena's narrow lips pressed together into a tight, thin line. "Peter from Vitebsk? I'm afraid not. It's too late for that."

"What do you mean?" Maria frowned.

All eyes turned to their mother. "Young Peter is courting Gertrude Wiebe. I'm told it's quite serious."

"Surely not." Anna's mouth dropped open. She cocked her head towards Katarina and gave her a sympathetic frown.

Katarina's eyes bulged. "Gertrude Wiebe? That milk-toast? He's fallen for her?"

"Milk-toast? Whatever do you mean? Gertrude's a lovely young lady. She's very well-behaved," Lena said.

"Exactly my point. She's as bland as baby food. She has no personality. None. Why would he want such a pushover?" Katarina's dusted her hands on her apron and plopped into a chair. *Just my luck.* She could feel every eye hovering over her. *Now, they all know.* She wanted to melt into the floor.

"Ooh. I think I hear jealousy," Maria crooned. She returned to the table and started kneading the dough.

"Well, I'm happy for the young man. I believe he's chosen well. That young lady is properly groomed for marriage. She'll make a wonderful wife," Lena added. "Every man should be so fortunate."

Is she insinuating that I'm not marriage material? Katarina glared at her mother. *She is. She's saying I'm second potatoes to that bland Gertrude. I can't believe she'd think that of her own daughter.*

"Yes, she's a very sweet girl," Anna said. "But they're not engaged. There's still time for him to change his mind."

Katarina scowled and narrowed her eyes at Anna.

"That's right. It's not too late," Maria's voice perked up with a note of enthusiasm. She passed the ball of dough to Anna. "You could write him a letter, Katarina. Tell him how you feel."

Katarina gawked. "I shan't do any such thing. He'd never respect me if I started chasing him."

"She has a point, Maria. The man's never shown interest in our sister. It's best to leave it alone." Anna fingered the dough.

Katarina's heart sank. *How does she know he was never interested in me? Why? What's wrong with me?*

"Well, don't be too discouraged. These things don't always work out as planned. The war isn't over yet." Maria walked over to Katarina and gave her a one-armed hug.

"It doesn't matter." Katarina waved a hand in the air. "With my horse allergy, it wasn't possible, anyway. He's obviously not 'the one.'"

"Don't let such problems stand in your way, Katarina. Love can solve any challenge." Anna smirked and fluttered her eyelashes.

"It obviously isn't fixing the war though, is it?" Katarina retorted. "The husband store has many bare shelves these days. Even yours aren't available. What makes you think there's anyone left for me?"

Anna dropped her gaze and smacked her lips together. "Ouch."

"Katarina, the war turns boys into men. When they return, your checklist will be full of possibilities." Lena picked up the empty bowl from the table. "But I'm so proud of you for choosing wisely. He'll make a good husband."

"For someone else," Katarina snorted as she slapped a new batch of dough on the table and smacked it with the rolling pin.

"Nonetheless, it's wonderful to see that your mind has turned to more Godly pursuits and you are putting away those childish dreams. It's every woman's calling to be a wife and mother." A rare smile lit Lena's face. "Thank you, Lord," she mumbled as she left the room, "she's normal after all."

Katarina stared at the dough and shook her head. "I never said I was ready to marry."

"You didn't have to. The fact that you're interested in a man makes her happy. Maybe she'll leave you alone now," Anna whispered.

"Don't assume that," Maria said. "It could have the opposite effect. Now she'll be scouring the countryside looking for a match."

"Oh, please no. It's bad enough that Tante Susz is searching." Katarina rolled her eyes.

"Well, they are sisters. I'm sure you're a big topic of conversation at the sewing circle," Anna said. "You're at that age. You best get married before you're too old."

Katarina threw her hands in the air. "I hate being pushed into a corner like this. Everyone wants to plan my life for me. Why can't I figure it out myself?"

"Because you are to take advice from the older and wiser women who've had experience. You can't know what's best for you when you've never been married," Anna explained.

"Ridiculous. I'm perfectly capable of knowing what I like or not. I'm not a child." Katarina attacked the dough with renewed vigor. "I should be able to make my own decisions."

"Well, you can," Maria said. "We're just guiding you."

Katarina narrowed her eyes and waved the rolling pin in the air. "This is no different from the Bolsheviks and their stupid gun laws."

"Now that's a stretch, Katarina," Maria snorted but accepted the bait to change the subject. "Although, I agree the government is treating us like children — forcing us to keep secrets. Next, they'll be expecting us to spy on one another."

"You see?" Katarina stabbed the dough with a paring knife. "It's just like this family. Keep your mouth shut or face the inquisition."

"No, it's not the same. We care about each other. The government doesn't give a hoot about us," Maria said.

"Well, honesty is still the best policy, as far as I'm concerned," Anna said. "And I'm proud of Olek for how he handled both trips. If he'd had any weapons on him, the bandits would've seen him as a threat. We could've all lost our lives." She brushed a blond strand from her face with a flour-covered hand, leaving behind a streak of white across her pale cheeks. "It's a good thing they loaded the benches with bribes."

"Men must see alcohol and tobacco as a secret handshake of sorts. It's a weird thing, isn't it? It would never work with women." Katarina wiped the knife and put it back in her apron.

"Nay, but they can manipulate us in other ways." Anna dropped a spoonful of filling on the prepared dough. She looked up and frowned. "Do you know where Papa keeps the gun now? We should know, just in case."

"Girls, it's none of our business. The less we know the better." Lena set a pot of hot potatoes on the table and returned to the stove.

"Better for whom?" Maria slammed the metal masher into the pot.

"Katya told me it's behind the lower supports in the hayloft," Katarina whispered as she folded the dough squares over the filling and pinched the edges. "It's in the crawl space. Unless someone knows where to look, they won't find it."

"How does she know?" Anna asked in a hoarse whisper.

"Papa showed her. He trusts her with our lives."

"As long as she doesn't spill the secret to those blood-thirsty rebels." Anna leaned back in her chair to peer into the kitchen and check on Lena's whereabouts.

"Exactly. If things continue for much longer, we may need to hunt for our daily meat." Maria dumped the cheese curds into the potatoes and stirred. "We also need guns to protect our stock from wildlife. The wolves and foxes are awfully bold these days. There's nothing for them to eat, either."

Anna checked the seal on Katarina's dumplings and moved them to the tray. "But we mustn't hunt in the spring when the deer are having their young. The babies can't raise themselves. The wolves will kill them before they can grow up. Then we'll have a shortage."

"Oh, Anna. Babies, babies, babies. That's your maternal instinct talking." Lena ducked back into the room and surveyed the table. "Rabbits and deer populate far faster than we do. God designed it that way to feed us. Leave such matters to God and men. Keep your mind on your own young. If times become more desperate, you won't think of such nonsense. You'll be eating whatever God puts in front of you." Lena picked up the prepared tray and exited the room.

Katarina smirked and winked. "Ja, Anna. It's just your mothering instinct."

Anna rolled her eyes. "I'm too liberal with my ideas, I suppose."

"Not at all." Maria dusted her hands and sat down. "I

think caring about nature is an admirable trait. Although we have more important matters to consider now."

"Yes, like those poor children. I can't stop thinking about how terrified they must have been going past that scene again," Anna sighed.

"No doubt. Their young minds are injured for life," Maria added.

"We must keep them in our prayers," Katarina said. "Although I wish we could have done more."

"Ja. Fortunately, they're safe now ... we hope." Maria peeked around the corner, then rolled her eyes and sighed. "I don't believe this. Mutter went upstairs and left the pot boiling. I'll be right back." She scooted to the stove.

"Mutter seems awfully forgetful lately." Anna frowned. "Did you notice?"

Katarina shrugged. "Maybe she's not sleeping well again. She complains of hot flashes."

"Ugh," Anna groaned. "Womanhood is full of complications. First, our bodies announce the beginning of womanhood with shocking discomfort, then we suffer the pain of childbirth. And in the end, we lose our minds."

"It's the curse of Eve. If she hadn't bitten the apple ..." Katarina sighed.

Maria returned with a bowl of hot vareniki. "Careful, this is hot. I think I burnt my hand when I drained the pot."

"Quick. Plunge it into the water bucket in the mudroom. It's icy cold." Anna pointed to the door.

Maria examined her hand and flexed it. "It'll be fine."

"Then put some butter on it," Anna scolded again.

Maria made a face. "I'm fine. I don't need fixing."

Anna's eyes narrowed at the verbal slap. She blinked several times, straightened her shoulders, and cleared her throat. "I hope Alyona doesn't have problems with the trains.

Those orphans need to get to Tokmak to find their grand-parents."

"It will be a while before we see Alyona again. They'll stay at her daughter's until they allow regular passage. The cars have little space for civilians with the armies taking up most of the seats. And she must change trains twice before finding her way back to Halbstadt." Katarina squared the corners of the last piece of dough with the rolling pin. "In retrospect, the orphans should've stayed here."

"Yes, well, we assumed they had more family living close by. How were we to know the sister couldn't take them in? They're a bit young to live on their own. I'm surprised the grandparents live so far away." Anna held up the butter dish to Maria. "Take it. Grease your hand."

"I said I'm fine." Maria took the butter dish and slammed it on the table.

Katarina grimaced and sliced the dough into squares. "I suppose people go where the work is. But I wonder how common that is among the locals? Siblings, their parents, and extended family drift apart because of jobs. Surely people don't choose to live this way."

"It's the war," Anna said. "The rising cost of living breaks families apart. People make desperate choices to survive. Even our families are scattered. Look at David's family. He has cousins in the Kuban, family in Yalta, and even in Canada."

"Speaking of scattered family, has anyone heard from Justina and Heinrich?" Maria asked.

"I did," Anna said. "Our sister Helena's letters from Eichenfeld have been too sporadic. Mutter begged them to go check on things. Why they agreed on such a venture in the middle of winter is beyond me. Especially with all this mayhem in the countryside. God forbid they run into trouble."

"If Mutter doesn't get a letter every week, she worries. Although, she denies it. But it makes sense to travel now while the roads are still frozen, and the ground is hard." Katarina dusted her hands, plopped down in a chair, and announced, "That's it for the dough."

"When will they be back?" Maria started clearing the table.

"A few weeks. Before the muddy season arrives," Anna said.

The back door slammed, and a draft of icy air blew through the kitchen. The stomping of feet on the mudroom floor followed the grating sound of boot soles rubbing on the scraper.

"Where's Papa?" Katarina's eyebrows knit together.

"He's taking a nap," Maria said with a guarded tone.

"And Mutter?"

Anna pointed to the hallway. "She went upstairs. She's probably helping Katya clean."

"Then who's here?" Goosebumps formed on Katarina's arms.

An object slid across the floor and bumped the wall. "It's not Olek. He wouldn't enter unannounced."

"Somebody thinks they're at home," Anna whispered.

Heavy steps announced themselves on the stairs. All eyes turned as the door creaked open.

---

1 Slang for chewing one's nails to the quick.

2 Vareniki is the Ukrainian term for boiled dough pockets. The filling is mostly made from cheese, potatoes, onions, or cabbage, but may also be made with seasonal fruit or meat. Outside of Ukraine, these are commonly known by their Polish name — perogies.

31

DAVID AND ANNA

KATARINA'S MOUTH WENT DRY. SHE SUCKED ON HER CHEEKS and swallowed. Anyone walking in through the mudroom had to be family. But since all were accounted for, who was this?

Lena ran down the stairs and burst into the room. "What are you girls gawking at? Is no one getting the door?"

"They came in through the mudroom, not the front." Katarina pointed nervously behind her. Maria and Anna stared at the door, their faces frozen, their eyes wide with fright.

Lena threw the kitchen towel at Katarina and hurried to the mudroom entrance. "You girls have too much fear in your heads."

The door scraped against the plank flooring before Lena could reach it. A tall, bearded man with broad shoulders wearing dirty, tattered clothing stepped to the threshold.

"Well, I'll be ..." Lena gasped and moved aside to let the bedraggled stranger enter.

Anna's mouth gaped and her eyes bulged. The spoon dropped from her hand and clattered onto the table. Tears rolled down her cheeks as her expression shifted from disbelief to awe. She squealed with delight, pulled her bulk from the chair, and quickly waddled into David's outstretched arms. He planted a kiss on top of her head and wrapped his arms around her petite shoulders.

"How did you get home?" Katarina asked, staring wide-eyed at the dirty man that was her brother-in-law.

"How did you know to come here?" Maria, also dumb-founded, held her flour-covered hands in the air.

Lena rubbed her hands on her apron, then pulled the cloth over and over her hands as if she couldn't clean them enough.

Although the voice was David's, this filthy, disfigured man didn't match the well-groomed one that left them months ago. While the rest hesitated to hug him, Anna buried her face in his chest and allowed him to squeeze her into himself. It must be true love, Katarina thought.

David threw his head back and laughed with a deep, hearty guffaw, revealing yellowed, tobacco-stained teeth. "One question at a time, ladies." The skin on his face draped around his cloudy blue eyes and the ragged, unkempt beard almost masked the bony cheekbones that peeked above the facial hairline.

Katarina was curious why David wore ordinary civilian clothes instead of a soldier's uniform. But she reasoned that — considering the varying political stripes roaming the countryside — perhaps it was best not to identify with one side.

"Come, sit down. I'll bring tea," Lena beckoned him to a chair. "And something to eat. Katya, it's time for *faspa*.[1]" She signaled to the servant and pointed to the samovar. "Katarina, go wake your father. Tell him we have guests, but don't tell him who it is."

"Never mind." The light from the hallway silhouetted Johann's broad frame in the doorway. "I already heard the ruckus."

David eyed the table full of prepared vareniki. "It looks like you're waiting for me. Are we having a party?"

"Supper, but no sausage," Katarina pouted, deliberately sticking her bottom lip out in a childlike fashion.

"The rebels got all the sausage again, did they?" David gave her an exaggerated upside-down smile. His cloudy eyes now sparkled with their former sarcastic humor. He plunked down on a kitchen chair and pulled Anna to his side.

Johann joined his son-in-law at the table and motioned to Lena, pointing to the dirty, cluttered table. Then he shot a disapproving look at Anna as she wrapped her arms around her husband's shoulders and kissed him on the lips.

"Life is simple these days. We are making do with what we have." Johann rubbed his nose and gave a sour glare at the flour-covered table.

"We're cleaning as fast as we can, Papa," Katarina said, removing the mixing bowl in front of him. "The smoking room is clean. So's the dining room." She hoped he'd take the hint and remove the smelly man from their prep area.

Lena shot her a dirty look. "Katarina. Don't be rude. It only takes a minute to clean up. We all want to visit."

David grinned. "Yes, indeed. It's good to be home. I sure missed your great home cooking, Mutter. Like I told my buddies on the field — Mennonite women can cook shoe leather and make it taste good."

Katarina rolled her eyes. *Yuck.* "I hope I never have to eat that," she said under her breath.

The compliment made its mark as grins lit each woman's face. "Our girls are the best cooks on this side of the river. Don't let anyone tell you otherwise," Lena's face beamed with pride.

David chuckled and nodded, "I say they're the best on both sides of the river, perhaps even in all of Russia."

Adoration radiated on Anna's face. She stood at his side

rubbing his shoulders and gazing at her beloved's face. "It's so good to have you home, David. You must tell us everything."

He wrapped an arm around his wife's waist and patted her bum. "It's not a pretty story. But I'll give you the highlights."

After they'd wiped down the table, Katya returned with a tray of zwieback, pickles, cheese, and cold pork roast. Katarina grabbed two Delft cups from the hutch in the formal dining room, while Lena made lemon balm and peppermint tea. "Katya, please fill the samovar. It's almost empty," Lena ordered as she filled the teapot.

The pattern of the women serving the men was a natural one learned in childhood. No one ever questioned whether it was right or wrong. Even Katarina understood it was a woman's place to anticipate a man's needs and meet them before he asked.

David grabbed a bun from the tray, slathered it with bacon grease, and stuffed it with meat, cheese, and pickles. The sandwich disappeared in two bites, and he reached for a second before he swallowed the first. The women stood nearby, wide-eyed, and open-mouthed, silently watching David stuff food into his mouth like a starving man. Which he probably was, Katarina thought.

"Can we bring you anything else?" Lena asked. She turned to the maid and whispered. "Katya let's prepare the dining room. Put out the good silver. We must celebrate David's return."

David waved his hand in the air dismissively, before grabbing another roll. "This is a great snack. But I'll happily wait for supper. Which, by the smell of it," he pointed to the stove behind the partial wall, "must be almost ready."

"We were just finishing up as you walked through the door." Anna moved behind her husband's right shoulder and brushed the loose hairs from his collar. She turned, wrinkled her nose, and made eye contact with Katarina. "He needs a bath," she mouthed.

Katarina nodded, jerked her chin towards the kitchen, and slipped out of the room. She found the maid beside the stove. "Katya, David needs a bath and a change of clothes. Shall we burn them? They look beyond washing."

Katya scooped the dumplings from the boiling water. "Tak. He could have lice. I'll ask Olek to find the kerosene and nit comb. He can help David shave. After supper, I'll move the children from Anna's room to the attic and stairwell. The couple will want privacy."

"Go ahead, Katya. I'll finish cooking supper. I don't want to be in the room with him right now. He stinks too much. What do I need to do?"

"Slice the roast and put it back in the oven to finish browning." Katya pointed to the pot of boiling water. "And cook everything. The men will want at least a dozen vareniki, each. Make gravy and fry onions."

"With what fat?"

"Yesterday's goose grease. The beef is too dry. This cow didn't get enough to eat." Katya changed her cooking apron and tied it around her waist.

Katarina glanced at the cutting table. "Are there no other vegetables besides cabbage and onions?"

"It's the end of winter and markets are bare. There've been no shipments from the south in weeks," Katya said. "Not even pepper. It's the war. It affects everyone. But we have vinegar and mustard." The smile left her face. "Katarina, your parents helped many families this winter. At a sacrifice to themselves. The larder is lean. I didn't tell them, but they know. Your Mama checks these things."

"Is this what being poor feels like? Portioning everything and worrying about not having enough tomorrow?" Katarina scooped the dumplings from the broth.

Katya rubbed her lips together. "There are others in much worse shape. Be thankful. And don't complain. If your Mama hears, she'll get upset with you. Act normal. Keep the peace."

"I know. I know. I don't want to upset her. She worries enough." Katarina turned to her former nanny and gave her a quick hug. "I've missed you so much, Katya. It feels strange to say this, but I'm actually glad to be home. The family is together again. As best we can, amid this crazy war. It's been a long time since I've heard laughter at the table."

"Leave the worries for tomorrow, Katarina. Today, we celebrate."

---

1 FASPA: A late afternoon snack usually consisting of meat, cheeses, pickles, and breads. Usually served with strong coffee or tea.

32

WAR-TALK

DRESSED IN TRADITIONAL BLACK PANTS AND WHITE SHIRT; and with a clean-shaven face and head, David barely resembled the man who entered the house a few hours earlier. Nor did he look like the muscular broad-shouldered man who left for the war seven months ago. Johann's oversized utility clothes, which were once a size too small for David, now clung awkwardly to the younger man's large frame. The skin sagged under his square chin and the hollows under his angular cheekbones emphasized his dramatic weight loss, making him look much older than his twenty-seven years.

Katarina mused over her brother-in-law's scrawny appearance. Didn't he get enough to eat in the army? The Soviets were confiscating the grain to feed their soldiers. Were the Czar's regiments not entitled to the same rations? Even though Russia was torn apart, they were all grown men fighting for the same country. Was Lenin trying to starve the Whites? The idea seemed irrational and inhumane.

David's sudden arrival threw off the usual staggered schedule of feeding the children an hour before the adults. The women organized the children at the breakfast table in the kitchen and the two married couples in the formal dining room. Katarina, Maria, and Katya assumed meal service duties.

Katarina quickly discovered the almost impossible task of eating and serving at the same time. She succumbed to standing beside the stove and gulping forkfuls between tasks. The gummy potato and cheese-filled pockets grew cold and tasteless quickly, and she lost her appetite and shoved the plate aside. She decided to eat later when she could join the others during the dessert course.

She couldn't believe how Maria managed the hectic pace. Her older sister flitted back and forth seemingly unperturbed by the chaos of eight screaming children in one room and four demanding adults in the other, all the while remaining cheerful, energetic, and enthusiastic. Katarina guessed that God provided mothers with extra wisdom and energy.

When she'd finished cooking, Katarina brought the pies to the dining room buffet and quietly slipped onto a side chair just in time to see David empty the large serving bowl for the third time. Johann sat at the head of the table with his empty plate pushed to the side after finishing his meal and toyed with his silverware while updating David on politics and farm matters.

Anna sat next to her husband, watching him eat while stirring the spoon in her teacup for an interminably long time, her eyes wide like saucers. Lena scraped all the leftovers into another dish and pushed it toward David. Katarina had never seen anyone eat so much. There was little left for her.

When David finally declared he was finished, it was almost anti-climactic. He wiped his mouth, picked at his teeth, and threw the napkin on the plate. "What's for dessert?" He asked.

"Pies," Lena said, trying not to smile. "Apple or pumpkin."

"Both," he announced firmly as the Kroeger clock chimed

eight. And with that, the entire family moved into the formal sitting room for desserts and tea.

~

JOHANN UNLOCKED the hand-carved filigree cabinet above the Kroeger clock and removed a brandy bottle. He filled two snifters and handed one to David.

David put his nose to the glass and inhaled the heady aroma before taking a sip. He sat down in the floral wing chair in the corner, his face aglow with ethereal happiness. Anna parked on the settee across from him, with her eyes glued to his face, transfixed on his every word.

Katarina was slightly embarrassed by the couple's blatant intimacy. Under normal circumstances, she'd leave the room and give the couple privacy. But she envied their shameless adoration for each other and wondered if she'd ever experience such a fire.

Lena invited the children to join the adults in the sitting room. They scrambled for prime spots around their uncle's feet and peppered him with questions about the war. But before he could say a word, Johann and Lena launched into an educational diatribe on the evil of alcohol.

Strong drink was reserved for special celebrations or medicinal purposes, they explained, and this was such an occasion. But it was exclusive to men since only their constitutions could handle the potent effects. Johann opened the King James pulpit Bible on the side table to the proverb declaring the evil of drunkenness. "That's why a man should never drink alone," Lena stated firmly. "Otherwise, he won't know when to stop."

Johann concurred.

Katarina squirmed and bit the inside of her cheek, guiltily recalling her first taste of the sweet-tasting medicine following her frightening encounter with the black stallion. She remembered the burning sensation when it trickled down her throat, and how quickly it had calmed her nerves and relieved her pain.

During the sermon, the children yawned and fidgeted, while Katarina focused on the floor to keep from rolling her eyes. In her opinion, the lecture was entirely unnecessary and inappropriate. She looked up and noticed Maria and Anna also staring at the floor, stone-faced. Meanwhile, David chewed his cheek — but his eyes twinkled and a smile toyed with the corners of his mouth.

After the preaching stopped and the somber atmosphere lightened, questions poured from the floor. "What was it like?" Ten-year-old George pulled on the arm of the wing chair. "Did you see lots of bad guys?"

"Did they try to kill you?" Mary yanked on David's pant leg.

"Did you have to shoot anyone?" Helen screwed up her face as she tried to picture the scene.

A thin, contemplative smile stretched across David's face. He raised the glass to his mouth, swallowed, then pursed his lips and deliberated before answering. "I shot no one. My job was to help injured persons."

It was a simplified explanation of his work, Katarina realized. She'd read enough war reports at the newspaper office to know there was no glory in the gore of war. The stories of tragic deaths and chopped-off limbs were better left untold. Children's minds needed protection from such horror.

She carefully composed broad questions to divert the probing. "We heard the war's almost over. Is it true? We know there's a cease-fire, but ..." Katarina wanted to ask him how he got home and why he wasn't wearing a soldier's uniform. Her instincts said things were not as simple as they seemed.

David's gaze dropped to the floor. He nodded, slowly.

"They gave me temporary leave because of the cease-fire. But I can't stay long. The hospitals are overwhelmed and there's a shortage of help and volunteers. Many are too injured to travel home. The mental strain disables more."

He looked at Anna. Sadness flickered across his face as he continued. "There is hunger and disease everywhere. Ordinary citizens scour the countryside for safe refuge and food. Their homes are destroyed or usurped. I wish I could say that the end of the war is good news. It is. But people are starving, dying from hunger and cold. The horror won't end when the fighting ceases. It will take years for hospitals to empty, homes to be rebuilt, and families to recover. Crops must be planted. People need food. I must do my part to ease the pain where I can."

"You're going back?" Anna choked. "Am I to lose you again?" A tear dribbled down her cheeks.

David nodded. "In a few weeks. After I've verified the damages at home."

Anna's head dropped to her chest. A hush fell over the room. No one moved. Goosebumps rose on the back of Katarina's arms. She caught Maria's eye and jutted her chin at the children. Maria nodded.

"Come, kinder. Let's go to the kitchen for some warm milk before bed," Maria said. "You can visit with Uncle David tomorrow."

After the children had left the room, David continued, "Have you heard much about the conditions? How is the estate?"

Anna shook her head, clamped her lips between her teeth, and hugged her belly.

"The Bolsheviks seized the grain storage and set fire to several towns," Johann said, pensively. "I've heard nothing about your place, David. But the reports from the region aren't good."

"What about my family? Are they safe?" David's eyes swept his wife's.

Anna nodded and massaged her belly methodically with small circles. "Your brother, Johann, his wife, Agatha, and their little ones left for Canada after Christmas. We haven't received any news in over a month. Your older siblings took your mother to Yalta for the winter. As for the others ..." She shook her head and tore her gaze away from his. "David, I'm sorry. We fled through the tree plantation as soon as we heard the guns. We couldn't go into town, or even to the other side of the estate. The fires were blazing behind us. I've sent a letter, but I've not yet received word."

David sucked his lips between his teeth and squared his long legs, "When I heard about the fires, I feared the worst. But I thank God you're here alive and well." He turned to Johann. "You already know this, but the Reds have control of the train station at Aleksandrovsk, which means they're practically at your doorstep. I'm sorry to sound the alarm, but everyone should prepare for the worst." His eyes flicked over Anna's belly. "If Germany arrives and they refuse to leave, hellfire will follow. Leaving the country is still possible, but dangerous."

"We're aware. But we're not leaving. This is our home." Johann said firmly while rubbing the sides of his brandy glass.

"Well, thankfully the conflict between the Blacks and Reds is at a standstill. For now," David said.

"How did that happen?" Johann asked.

"Apparently, Makhno thinks he has the Reds in his back pocket. But they believe he's in theirs. They're playing with each other right now. When the game ends, this entire area will go up like a powder keg. Unless ..." David held his glass in a mid-air salute. His eyebrows shot up and his head cocked to the side. "... Germany saves us all."

Makhno. Katarina's stomach tightened. Would the vigilante never disappear? The Ukrainian was like the proverbial fly that was forever escaping the flyswatter.

She reached for a sugar cookie from the tea table and snapped it in two. "Where were you positioned, David?" She tried to remember the maps pinned to the wall in Regier's office when she saw them last. He'd explained to her that the position and movement of the regiments determined the strength of the front lines.

"I mostly worked on the hospital train out of Ekaterinoslav, but I've been in a few places over the last few months." David smiled reassuringly. "I was rarely in harm's way."

Johann shifted in his chair. "Ekaterinoslav? Isn't Makhno's friend Arshinov camped there?"

"Ja. The Black Army controls the city and the surrounding area, but his people left us alone. They knew we were there for the injured, not war games."

"So that explains the plain clothing," Katarina mused out loud. "I wondered why you weren't wearing a soldier's uniform."

"Ja, I didn't want to be shot walking home." David swallowed the last of the brandy in his glass. "There are too many sides to this war. It's hard to know when the uniform is safe or dangerous. The situation is as fluid as the Dnieper is long." He gave the glass to Maria, who immediately poured him a cup of hot tea.

Katarina wondered about Peter's forced conscription to the Red Army. "Did you ever have to change colors?"

"The Red Cross armband shows neutrality. We take no sides. Our job is to save lives and treat the injured, although sometimes we must choose one life over another." David wiped his brow with his palm. "It's different among the soldiers. There's a certain callousness in battle. Their job is to kill and avoid being killed."

"What do you mean — you had to choose one life over another? How could they put you in such a position? Deciding who lives and who dies? That's not right," Lena exclaimed. "Only God should decide. All deserve to live."

Katarina stared at her mother in disbelief. Had Lena already forgotten how her daughters had just been in a similar situation with the orphans — triaging the most vulnerable, but second-guessing their decision after the fact?

"Ja. But in the middle of a battlefield, one's own survival depends on both skill and wit. And God's fortune. During those times, I set aside my personal beliefs. I saved the life in front of me, regardless of the situation."

"Well, that was the right thing to do. But I think one should always stand up for their beliefs, regardless of the circumstances." The cup clattered in the saucer as Lena set it on the serving table.

Katarina shivered as a chill passed through the room. David's storytelling made the war much too real. Although she didn't want to believe it, she knew it to be true. While most women remained sheltered from the politics of war, their news came from their husbands or the sewing circle gossip. Thus, it was often inaccurate. She only knew this because the newspaper office censored the war data it gathered. Since she couldn't discuss the confidential information, she composed her question carefully. "David, Lenin is putting increased pressure on the German ethnics to leave Russia. Did you have problems because of our culture?"

Anna interjected before David could answer, dismissing Katarina's question with a wave of her hand. "I can't imagine what it must be like — to sleep in ditches and work around foul-mouthed locals while bullets fire around you. How did you keep yourself untainted?" She spat the words with disgust.

"I keep my head down and try not to antagonize anyone.

Our little cluster held morning Bible readings and evening prayer meetings — when we could. Although it wasn't always possible. I mostly closed my eyes and ears to the ugliness as best I could and prayed for peace." David's eyes flicked over his wife as she adjusted her posture.

"Didn't you protest against the war while you were there?" Lena asked with anger in her voice. "Surely you met someone with influence — who could help change the course of things. It's all so wrong. So very, very wrong. Innocents are slaughtered. People are starving."

David's eyes bulged and his mouth dropped open — as if it was the silliest thing he'd ever heard. "Protest? Nay. I carried broken bodies to the medical facilities. I had no power to complain. If I defied orders, they would have killed me."

"But by helping, you are complicit in their evil," Lena argued. "Someone must stand up for the vulnerable. Defy the injustice."

"Nay, Mutter." David palmed his mouth and coughed in amusement at his mother-in-law's confusion. "By helping, I saved souls from dying. My job was to keep men alive."

"But by helping the killers, you aid the killing. You heal them and then what? They go back and kill again? We should not be involved in this drama. It is best to let God handle it." Lena stood up, walked to the serving table, and refilled her teacup.

"Mutter, you must understand. When the uniform comes off, the sides of war no longer exist. Red, white, black, or green. It doesn't matter. There are only suffering people. I don't pick and choose the injured. And ... there were women and children too. Not all who get hurt are killers. War destroys. We save as many as we can."

"But God expects us to stand up for our faith in these trials. By pretending to be one of them, you deny Christ."

David's eyebrows shot up and his back stiffened. He folded his hands in his lap and toyed with his thumbs then lifted his eyes and scanned the face of each adult. "With all due respect, Mutter, other than food and labor shortages, this village has not experienced the travesty of war. I pray you never do. But *if* and *when* it happens, you will understand why I made the decisions I did. I bear no regret. I committed no sin. I am at peace with my soul."

It was obvious to Katarina that Lena didn't understand the complexities of war. Neither did she — even though she'd been close enough to know she didn't want to see more. She looked down at the crumbled cookie in her clenched fists and dropped the remnants into her napkin. Then she dusted her hands against her skirt, stepped to the serving cart, and poured a glass of water.

The truth was too awful to bear. Although they'd escaped the firestorm in Halbstadt, war was everywhere. Hundreds of thousands had already died. More were still suffering. And still, good people were forced to take sides. None of it made sense. The war needed to end soon. Katarina prayed for peace.

33

PETER'S BIRTH

1918, 1 MARCH / 16 FEBRUARY. (THE CALENDAR CHANGES FROM JULIAN TO GREGORIAN)

Run, Katarina, run. Take the horse. Hurry. The fires are coming. Look over there. Watch out for the bodies. Run. There's another. Don't stop until you're far away from the river.

Katarina shot up in bed, gasping. Her heart pounded in her chest and a loud whooshing pulsed in her ears. Was it a dream, or did she really hear Anna's screams? The fire was so real, she could almost smell the smoke. Were they being attacked again? She pushed her damp hair from her eyes and exhaled the tension. *It was a dream. Go back to sleep.*

She wiped her face with the edge of the sheet and lay on her side, staring across the room at the barely visible stars twinkling through the filmy lace curtains. A faint glow heralded the onset of sunrise. She moved her arm across the rumpled sheet, expecting to feel Maria's warmth, but the bed was cold. Startled, she rolled over and felt again, then squinted into the darkness. Either she'd disturbed her sister with her noisy nightmare or Maria was nursing her youngest. She snuggled back into the pillow and closed her eyes.

A long wail jolted her upright. *Anna.* This was no dream. Katarina jumped out of bed, grabbed her robe, and dashed down the hall.

Lena came out of Anna's bedroom with an empty pitcher in her hands and thrust it at Katarina. "Here, go fill this with water. Hurry."

As she started down the hall, she bumped into Maria coming out of the storage room — her arms laden with linens. "All hands on the plow," Maria chortled. "It's baby time."

Katarina stopped mid-stride. "How long has she been at it?"

"A few hours, now. Half the night."

"Why didn't you wake me?"

"And do what? Hold her hand? Mom and I've been taking turns. Everything's under control. I need you fresh to watch my little ones. We're getting close." Maria juggled the pile of towels under her chin. "When this is over, I want to sleep without them climbing all over me."

"Did someone call the midwife?"

"Olek picked her up at midnight." Maria's voice faded as she entered the bedroom and kicked the door closed.

Katarina stared at the door and muttered to herself. "I guess I'll get water."

As she passed the converted bedroom underneath the attic stairs, her three nieces greeted her from the doorway. "What's going on, Tante Trina?"

"Tante Anna's having a baby. Go back to sleep."

A chorus of cheers broke out. "She's having the baby, she's having the baby! We're getting another cousin today!"

"May we watch?" Helen's face lit up in eager anticipation.

Katarina groaned. *How does one say no to that face?* "Nay, sorry. Go back to bed. It's still early."

"Aww." Pouts and frowns replaced the gleeful expressions.

"That's not fair," Mary barked and stomped her foot. "We know about babies. We watched the baby goats get born."

"This is different." Katarina hoped they wouldn't ask how. She'd never explained the facts of life to a child before and wouldn't know where to begin. Like them, she'd seen farm animals mate and give birth. But a human birth was different. It was ... intimate — although she hadn't actually witnessed one.

Last year, during Margaretha's arrival, Anna's water broke over teatime. Alyona quickly took charge and shooed Katarina away. Then, everything happened so fast — the mid-wife barely arrived in time. Katarina had patiently waited — accepting her place in the order of things.

This time, she was definitely old enough to help. But again, she wasn't allowed. Wasn't birthing a natural part of womanhood? Something she was supposed to aspire towards? It wasn't fair that Maria could be in the room and she couldn't. Katarina wrestled with the feelings of envy and rejection.

Granted, she understood that Anna deserved privacy. It wasn't a place for curious onlookers. And someone needed to monitor the children so they wouldn't create problems at the most critical time. It was only logical that this task fell to her.

Katarina resigned herself to her assigned duties. After filling the water pitcher, she brought it to the bedroom. The door was ajar, and she softly announced herself.

Maria ushered her in and pointed to the washstand. "You can say hello, but you can't stay."

The scene wasn't what Katarina expected.

The brilliance of four oil lamps lit up the room like broad daylight, while the soft, golden glow of the early morning sun pierced the ice crystals on the window glass through the opened curtains. Shadows danced through the stained-glass ornament hanging from the curtain rod. The room was alive with the celebration of birth.

The scents of lemon, lavender, and rose and the headiness of feminine energy filled the room. Anna lay with her knees drawn up beneath a thin, white sheet, her large belly protruding above it. She stared at the ceiling, panting in short, rapid breaths. Rivulets of sweat dripped from her reddened face. Maria rinsed a lavender-scented cloth in the ceramic washbasin and placed it on Anna's forehead while humming a hymn.

The midwife, Frau Toews, sat on a kitchen stool at the foot of the four-poster bed, her eyes glued to the pocket watch in her hand while Lena wiggled clean towels underneath Anna's bottom.

Katarina had assumed the room would be dark and sober, but despite Anna's distress, it was full of joy and light. She tiptoed to Anna's side and put her palm on her sister's. "How are you doing?"

Anna snapped through a clenched jaw and raised a fist in the air, "I'm tired and I want to quit."

Katarina's jaw dropped in shock. *Quit?* The room exploded in laughter. Confused, Katarina stared at the other women. How could they laugh at a time like this? Her sister was in terrible pain. Could Anna take a break? Then, realizing her own naiveté, a warm flush rose up her neck. She turned to the midwife, "How much longer?"

"The baby takes as much time as he or she wants. Only God knows the time," Frau Toews smiled up at her, then looked down at the watch, and jotted in her notebook.

"Can I do anything?" Katarina rubbed her fingernails with her thumbs.

"Ja," Lena looked up and nodded. "We are all hungry and thirsty. Go to the kitchen and make us something to eat. And wake Katya up. She needs to start the bread."

They're so calm. Everything must seem normal to them. Katarina bent down and kissed Anna's cheek, then left the room. As she headed down the hallway, Anna screamed. Katarina deliberated whether to run back but then realized she'd just be in the way. Anna had more experienced nurses in the room.

Helen poked her head around the corner. "Are you sure there's nothing we can do? She sounds like she's hurting awful."

Katarina smiled at the innocent face. "Ja, she is. But you can pray this all ends quickly." She hesitated to say more. These girls had seen too much ugliness and faced too much fear. God only knew what insanity was yet to come. They needed wonderful memories to overshadow the bad. Could she do that — give them a happy day to remember?

The reality of her responsibility hit as clear as the blue winter sky. She could make this a day that none forgot. Then, the entire household would share in this memory forever.

Katarina turned her head in time to spot Helen's mischievous eyes glued to Anna's bedroom door. The child was waiting for an opportunity to sneak in. *Not on my watch.* "Girls, do you want to help?"

"Ja." Helen's head bobbed vigorously. Sarah and Mary squealed, jumped, and clapped their hands.

"Then put on some clothes. Come downstairs, and you can help me make breakfast," Katarina said.

"But we want to see the new baby," Mary whined while twirling in her nightdress. Her white-blond hair floated aimlessly around her chubby face.

"And you shall. But there's nothing to see right now. Tante Anna is resting. Oma and your Mama have been up all night, getting everything ready for the baby. Now, they're hungry and want to eat. I'm going to make them a nice breakfast. Can you help me?" Katarina asked.

"Ja." The girls shouted in unison, happy to be enlisted into kitchen duties.

"Get out of those night clothes and meet me downstairs." Katarina mentally patted herself on the back for preventing an unpleasant squabble.

As she walked past the attic stairs, the trapdoor opened. Wilhelm shuffled out, yawning, and rubbing his eyes. "What's going on? What's all that noise? Who's screaming?"

"Tante Anna's having the baby," Sarah yelled at the top of her lungs.

"Oh." He turned and retreated into the attic.

Boys.

KATARINA PADDED to the kitchen where she found Katya punching down the bread dough. "You're awake already?"

"With all that hollering, who can sleep?" Katya slapped the dough into the bowl.

"The men and boys don't seem to have a problem." Katarina selected a dozen eggs from the egg basket, rinsed them under the tap, and retrieved a large bowl from the shelf.

"Ha. The boys maybe. David and your Tato are milking cows."

"Papa and David are up?" Katarina asked, shocked. "It's not even sunup yet. Am I the only one who slept this night?"

"Maybe they sleep in the hayloft." Katya oiled the bread dough, covered it with a towel, and set it beside the warm stove.

"That must be cold." Katarina shivered at the prospect of sleeping in a barn in the middle of winter, thankful they hadn't needed to resort to such on their journey.

"No doubt. But they're very busy lately." Katya wiped the

flour from the prep table. "They're building a new cellar under the greenhouse."

"Why? Are we short of storage space?" Katarina cracked the eggs into a large bowl and checked for stray shells. "Why not wait for spring? It's still the middle of winter." After adding milk and salt to the eggs, she began whipping them with two forks.

"It's not my place to question. If your Tato says we need another cellar, then it's so." Katya said. "It's wartime. Everybody's nervous. There's no trust and much suspicion. There's no law, no order, and too many guns." She rinsed her hands in the sink. "Your Mama says to have faith, but to me, blind faith is ignorance. And God doesn't want us to be ignorant. Your Tato makes plans. But quietly, to not raise trouble."

Katarina took a deep breath. "Ja, God calls us to wisdom. And wisdom says to prepare for hard times. And we are living in the worst of days." She clenched her jaw and whipped honey and flour into the mixture. The black stallion galloped through her mind. *Makhno, go away*.

"Maybe. But things may get worse still." Katya leaned back against the counter and crossed her arms, watching Katarina attack the pancake batter.

"Are you making egg bread?" A smirk toyed at the corners of the maid's mouth.

Katarina looked up, "Ni, why?"

"You're beating like you are. What are you making?" Katya pointed at the bowl.

"*Rhei Ei*."

"Stir the flour, don't beat it. You'll end up with tough scrambled pancakes." Katya removed breakfast plates from the shelves and set them on the prep table.

Katarina groaned, "It's too late. What do I do now? We don't have enough eggs to start over."

Katya shrugged. "Add cream and more sugar. Throw in a

couple of chopped apples. Fry it with lots of fat. Everyone is too tired and hungry to notice."

"Sugar? We have sugar? I'm using honey." Katarina's eyes darted around the kitchen.

Katya clucked her tongue. "Ach. I forget. This shortage of food is driving everyone crazy."

"If the armies keep stealing our animals and grain, the entire country will starve soon." Katarina retrieved two apples from the bowl on the table, diced them, and tossed them in the batter.

"It's true now. My family in Tokmak have problems. No money. Little food. They tell me to steal. To help them." Katya grabbed the cutlery box from the shelf and put it on the kitchen table.

"Good grief. That's awful." Katarina waved her hand over the element to check the heat before setting down the frying pan. She retrieved a log and shoved it into the stove's belly. When the temperature rose and the frying pan was hot, she added the lard and swirled it around the surface. At the first sign of smoke, she dumped in the batter. But the edges frayed instantly in the overly hot grease. Katarina slapped the counter and moaned, "NO!" Now, the stove was too hot and the dish was bound to burn. She had to make this work.

She chose an iron trivet from the drawer and set it underneath the pan to lower the heat. "Why do you stay here, Katya? It sounds like your family needs you more."

"Your parents treat me well, Katarina. Maybe I'm only a common Little Russki. And I support a free Ukraine. But I hold no anger toward the Germans or the Mennonites. You work hard like us. You expect others to do the same." The servant put one hand on her hip and watched her young charge with a mentor's eye. "I'm not stupid. Food only comes to those who work for it. But envy controls many. They say your people are not deserving. But I don't say such."

"Why don't we deserve what we've worked for?" Katarina stirred the frying mixture and poked at the bubbles.

"Because of your alliances with the Czar and your devotion to German ways," Katya said in a matter-of-fact tone.

There was something telling in the maid's voice. What was it? Disrespect?

Katarina felt as if she'd been punched in the stomach. She whirled to face Katya. "Do you support Makhno?"

"He is one of my people. I don't like his ways, but he wants a free Ukraine. That's good." Katya removed cups from the cupboard and set them on the table. "Who am I to disagree?"

Katarina stared at her childhood confidante's back. "But why did he attack our farm — twice?" She slid the pan from the hot element to the warmer.

Katya ran her hand along the edge of the prep table and scraped bits of dough from it with her fingernail. "He didn't. One of his gangs did. They took food from here. They didn't hurt you on purpose. It was an accident."

"So, *you knew* about the raid," Katarina said, disbelieving. Tears welled in her eyes, and she blinked rapidly to hold them back. "You knew. You could have stopped it." Her breath stuck in her chest and her knees wobbled. She grabbed the counter for support.

Katya brushed away the mousy brown strands from her face and hung her head. "They warned me. But I couldn't stop it. I'm only one woman, Katarina. I have no voice."

As Katarina swallowed the sour lump in her throat, an exuberant female chorus sang from the doorway, "We're ready. What can we do?"

Katarina turned and pasted a smile on her face but glared at Katya through narrowed eyes. How much did the maid know about the rebel raid at Anna's wedding? Why didn't she warn them? Katya claimed loyalty to the family, but was she still trustworthy?

She thought of Dmitri, the stableman, who'd rung the bell when the fire broke out at the mill. She'd suspected him of staging the event. Shortly after that, he'd disappeared. Her father said he was fighting in the war. But for which side, she wondered. Were the servants in cahoots? Were any trustworthy anymore?

War was fluid, Russia was imploding, and the locals were shifting sides as fast as a drifting sand dune in a sandstorm. The only thing certain in this war was uncertainty.

34

HEIDI AND PETER

1952 MARCH. MUNICH, GERMANY

THE CUSSING FROM THE LIVING ROOM WAS LOUD ENOUGH to cause Heidi to stop folding the laundry and storm out of the bedroom. She turned the corner just in time to see Peter smack the book on the coffee table. "Did I hear cursing? What's going on? Are you having another crisis at work?"

But when she noticed Katarina's diary, she knew. And then she saw the beer bottle by his side. Only one today. That was an improvement from the past two months, but the day was still young. Something was triggering Peter's drinking and fueling his frustration. And she doubted it was his job — although it could be a contributing factor. The only other thing could be the diary.

Well, let's see where this goes. She leaned against the door-frame between the bedroom and the living room and clicked her fingernails impatiently on the wood, watching him fuss.

Peter picked up the book, waved it in the air, and slammed it down on the table a second time. "One line! One! Damn!"

"One line about what?" Heidi gritted her teeth. As far as she was concerned, whatever the problem was, it didn't justify the expletives.

"It's a boy. That's it? There's all this build-up to my birth. But she writes 'It's a boy. They named him Peter after David's father.' That's as excited as she can get? It's like poof — I'm born. Yawn. Next." Peter looked as crestfallen as a little boy with a smashed birthday cake.

Heidi rolled her eyes. "So what? You're not Katarina's biological child, Peter. And you weren't her first nephew. Were you expecting more drama? Why? Because she raised you?" Heidi returned to the bedroom to retrieve the basket of laundry and carried it to the living room. She set it on the floor beside the chair and resumed sorting.

"When I was a kid, she talked about my birth day plenty," Peter explained. "She said the entire family came together, and they had this huge, week-long celebration. The neighbors brought cakes and cookies, cheeses, and even sausage. Everyone was so relieved that I wasn't born in a barge in the middle of the Dnieper or in a snow-covered ditch. I arrived when I was supposed to. And the bonus was that my Papa was there. Everyone worried because of what Anna went through with my sister Margaretha's difficult birth. They expected me to arrive early — like she did. But instead, everything went perfectly."

"So, Katarina talked to you about it. That's something at least." Heidi folded a towel and gave a half nod to sympathize with Peter's overreaction.

Peter sighed and stuck the pencil behind his ear. "Ja. But I'm surprised she didn't write more about it."

"She was a teenager keeping a journal, Peter. She wasn't writing a memoir for you to read thirty-four years later." Heidi folded a towel and sighed. When would he give this up?

Peter brushed the chestnut curl from his forehead and rubbed his face. "I don't know why I keep torturing myself."

"I wonder the same thing, Peter." Heidi slipped onto the wing chair and began separating the remaining laundry into piles to be ironed or folded. "I sense that you're searching for a connection to your roots, but you keep getting lost in this story. Your parents are gone. You can't bring them back."

"I know that, Heidi. I wish I could go back there — to Russia — but I know I can't. Even if I could, I probably wouldn't find the graves. From what little I've heard, Stalin's made sure of that." Peter took the pencil from his ear, tapped it against his palm, and slouched back on the couch.

"I don't understand what you'd prove by doing that. That they're dead?" Heidi picked up a shirt from the pile, examined it, then threw it back in the basket. "Peter. Quit. Enough already. I don't know what's worse. Your drinking, or this diary. They're both addictions and they're both driving me insane." She stood up and put her hands on her hips. "We have had this discussion more than once. You promised to leave this alone and focus on work. You're spinning your wheels in the mud and getting nowhere. If you continue like this, then I'm leaving. I can't live like this."

"I'll stop drinking. If that makes you happy, I will. But I can't stop transcribing. Not yet." Peter tossed the pencil onto the coffee table, then leaned back and crossed his arms over his chest. "It calls to me."

"It calls to you," Heidi mocked. "What calls to you more? The beer or the book?" She snagged an undershirt from the pile and folded it.

"Heidi, please stop it. I'd like some support here." Peter shifted his legs and put his hand in the air.

"Support? Seriously?" Heidi looked at her husband, aghast. "Peter, I'm the one who needs taking care of here, not you. If you haven't noticed, I'm pregnant and I'm scared of how our relationship is deteriorating these days. When the baby arrives, I want you to be here for me. I'm worried about you drowning your sorrows in a bottle while I'm trying to care for our little one. I don't want to cry myself to sleep every night." Heidi's voice croaked as the tears welled in her throat. She clasped her chest. "Peter, please, I'm begging you. Stop this craziness. Smarten up."

The dagger of words hit its intended mark. Peter shot back in his seat and his deep-set blue eyes flickered. "Heidi, please calm down. You're exaggerating things. I'm just frustrated right now. You're right, I suppose. I am spinning my wheels."

"That's the truest thing you've said yet. But you're still turning down every suggestion I make. I don't know what else to say." Heidi stood up and rubbed the small of her back. At the end of the second trimester, the pregnancy was already taking its toll on her body. Her organs felt squished, her ankles were swollen, and running to the bathroom every hour was becoming tiresome. Overall, she felt like a blimp. Maybe her husband wasn't attracted to her anymore. She'd understand if he wasn't.

Peter's thick, dark brown eyebrows knit together in one long line. His eyes followed her as she paced in circles around the room. "What am I missing?"

"I've told you before that you should write your sister." She stretched back and stared at the crack in the ceiling.

"Why?" Curiosity now replaced the earlier annoyance in his voice.

"It may help you figure out what you need to know," Heidi said, softly. She gazed at the chiseled jaw, the deep-set blue eyes, and the single lock of curly hair that she loved to touch. She wanted him more than anything. But more than that, she wanted him to want her the same. Why couldn't he understand that?

"She knows nothing. She was only thirteen when she left Germany." Peter shook his head and ran his fingers through his hair.

"I'm not saying she'll have answers for you. But the act of writing may help you find closure." Heidi eased down in the chair and pulled at her side. The baby had settled in an uncomfortable bulge and was kicking against her kidney. She massaged the spot and manipulated the little feet, then groaned when they kicked again.

Peter stared at her, his face blank, oblivious to her discomfort. "You think I should do a *grieving* exercise? I'll have you know I stopped mourning years ago. That's not what this is."

"Are you sure? After my parents died in the war, someone said 'Grief is like an ocean. The waves come when you least expect them, and they never stop. They just get smaller. But every once in a while, a big one still crashes in.'"

Peter pursed his lips and frowned, "Heidi, this isn't grief. My mother's son is somewhere in Russia. If she'd brought him to Germany, we would have been raised as brothers. I would have called him my brother, not my cousin. But the only thing I know about him is that his name was Jacob. I believe with all my heart that she went looking for him during the Second War. I want to learn more.

He pointed his index finger at the book and tapped it three times. "Look, I'm sorry if I get a little emotional about my own story. Somewhere I fit into this saga, too. It's taken an entire year of transcribing to find my name in this historical record. But I haven't yet read anything about Jacob."

Heidi frowned and chewed on the inside of her cheek. There was something off about this story. Either that or Peter didn't have all the facts. "Peter, tell me something. Was Jacob your Papa's child?"

"What?" Peter stuttered, and a stunned look passed over his face. "What do you mean? Why wouldn't ... How?"

"Was Katarina married to someone else? From everything you've read so far, she was reluctant to marry, but she always liked your Papa. But didn't you once tell me they married in the camps ... in Riga? When was Jacob born? Did your Papa ever mention him?"

"No, he didn't. Maybe I'm not remembering right." A blank stare came over Peter's face. He reached for the bottle and held it to his lips. Finding it empty, he set it down on the side table and picked up a red marking pencil. "Heidi, you may be on to something here. That means there's more to this story. Much more." He looked up at her and grinned. "If Jacob wasn't my adopted Papa's son, then there must be a clue about *his* Papa somewhere. This gives me another trail to follow." He scribbled in the notebook beside him.

"Ach du Lieber!" Heidi rolled her eyes. "This is all you need, Peter. More rabbit trails. And brick walls. Tell me, is there no one left in Ukraine who's related to the family? Someone you can write to?"

Peter shrugged. He swapped the red pencil for the leaden one and checked the nib. "I don't know who's dead or not. And I don't have addresses."

"Why don't you send a letter to the local post office there? Maybe it will reach someone who knew your family."

"Oh, so now you want me to risk some stranger's life by sending a letter to communist Russia?" Peter shook his head and held both open palms in the air — telling Heidi he thought her question ridiculous.

"What do you mean? How would that hurt?" She asked.

"Heidi, I was born in Little Russia and now I live in Germany. Think about the implications. If I send a letter to ... let's use Katya, for example. If I send a letter to Katya at the old local post office in Ukraine, and the authorities find out — which they will! The MGB reads everyone's mail. Surely, you've heard about the redacted letters that come out of there. What do you think happens when mail from here goes there? They scrutinize all contact from the West. If Katya's still alive, they could arrest her for being a German spy and throw her in the gulag — just for receiving a letter from the West, and from a defector, no less — me! It doesn't matter that I was a child when I left. They'll consider me a defector just because I was born there and now live in the West. And I'll never know whether she gets my letter. Because they won't let her write back. And worse, she could die because of me."

Heidi felt the color fade from her face. Her eyes widened. "Ach du meine Gute! I never thought of that. Then — are other old-timers not in touch with their relatives still living there?"

Peter shook his head. "Before Hitler's war, I knew many who tried to stay in touch with their families and friends in Russia, but then the news went dark. I read some of those heavily redacted letters. It was hard to understand what was happening. We guessed things in Ukraine were not good. After I got back from the war, the old-timers that used to live in our apartment or near us had either moved away or died. As you know, bombs decimated Munich. Our street was nothing but rubble — still is." Peter's eyes drifted to the kitchen. "But the old butcher shop where my Papa worked survived. You know the one. I'm there every few weeks."

Heidi smiled and mentally reviewed the supper menu. "Those sausages are fantastic. I like it when you go there. You're always in a better mood when you come home."

"Ja. I enjoy visiting old Max, my Papa's friend. Max still runs it, just like he always did. But since the clean-up, the Americans patrol the area. The neighborhood doesn't have the same vibe." Peter picked up the empty bottle and took it to the entry closet, put it in the cardboard box; then returned to the couch and closed the book. "You're right. I'm probably chasing rabbit trails."

"Oh, don't give up, yet." Heidi felt a pang of sympathy for Peter's confusion. "Say, I have an idea. Do you think some of the Russian Mennonites from your old building are still shopping at that butcher shop? Would Max know them? Or better yet, would Max know the story about Jacob?"

"Papa and Max were close friends. I never thought of asking him." Peter twisted his mouth to the side and tapped the pencil on his palm. "Huh. Maybe I should."

Heidi buried her face in her hands. "Why do I let you suck me into this?"

"What do you mean?" Peter frowned.

"The selfish part of me wants you to give up this search, put it away, and focus on building a family life. But, my love, I want you to be happy. I want us to be happy. But I sense you won't be until you find these answers. Every time we talk about this, I feel like we're walking down this never-ending delusive winding road that leads nowhere! How can we make plans if we don't know where we're going?"

Peter shook his head. "Heidi, that's not true. We have plans. We're having a baby. I promise I'll get another job that pays better. I know I can't make a living from translating my Mutter's diaries. But one day, it will be a book. Then I'll sell it to a publisher. I've talked to Reinhart about this. It can be done. But I must do the grunt work first. This could take years. I know that."

Heidi put her hands on her head and pulled on her hair. "Oh, Peter. This is so frustrating. This is your pipe dream. You're all over the map and I can't keep up. First, you like your job. Then, you don't. Katarina's dead. Or maybe she's not. You're writing a book. But you must translate it first. At first, it would be months. Now, it's years. You want to know about your past, but you can't find the right road to figure it out. You are lost, Peter. Lost. Give it up. Straighten your path.

Do one thing and do it well. Accept history as it is. The past is dead. Focus on the future."

"Heidi, sweetheart, listen to me." Peter rose, walked over to his wife, and took her face in his hands. "I love you. I want my child to know the family stories about my parents, my sister, and about Jacob, too." He winced. "Well, the Jacob piece would be a pleasant bonus. I'd like to solve that mystery." He leaned over and kissed her on the mouth. Then, he walked over to the adjoining tiny kitchen and filled the kettle.

"You need expert help, Peter. You must look elsewhere besides the diaries. What about your Aunt Justina? Surely, she would know something."

Peter set the kettle on the stove and lit the element. "Uncle Heinrich is my uncle — the eldest son in the family. Justina is his wife. I don't know them well. They left Riga before we did, and they emigrated straight away to Canada. You've seen the letters. They're mostly superficial. 'Hi, how are you,' that kind of thing. She talks about Marta's family and the weather in Canada. And the sunflower harvests. To be honest, I hadn't thought of asking her about Jacob. I'm afraid to."

"Why? Does it frighten you?" Heidi massaged her baby bulge and studied the cockeyed look on her husband's face.

"I don't know. And now that we've discussed it, I'm wondering why myself. And if Marta knows, why hasn't she said something in her letters? Was Jacob a secret? A love child perhaps? If so, I can see why the family preferred to keep him in the closet." Peter added the tea leaves to the teapot and removed two cups from the cupboard.

"Oh, dear," Heidi grimaced. "A love child during wartime? I hope you realize horrible things happened to women during wartime. Have you considered where this trail could lead? On second thought, I don't think you should turn these pages, Peter. This could be a dark journey."

Peter grinned. He poured the tea and brought a cup to his wife. "I'd rather travel a darkened road than none. At least, the adventure will be an entertaining ride."

"Thanks." She accepted the tea and took a sip. "I can think of better vacations. And finding skeletons is not my idea of a fun time. Besides, this hidden secret could affect our child's future." Heidi's eyes widened as she considered the implications.

"Well, Mutter did enjoy genealogy." Peter remained standing in the middle of the room, tapping the side of the cup with his middle finger.

"Did that include her own?"

"Especially her own. So, I'd like to make her proud and research this completely."

"Gute Trauer. Next, you'll want to dig up graves, too." Heidi put her cup on the coffee table, then stood up, walked over to him, and wrapped her arms around his waist. "But I still love you."

He squeezed her shoulders and kissed her forehead. "Who knows where this will lead? But whatever happens, Heidi — I want you with me."

35

A NEW LIFE, A NEW CALENDAR

1918 MARCH, GREGORIAN CALENDAR.
CHORTITZA VILLAGE.

THE SCRAWNY FLAT-FACED GOVERNMENT CLERK SNORTED and tapped a long, bony finger at the document. "Humph. Church registries are no longer proof of birth." He slid the certificate across the desk, then dipped his pen into the inkwell and scribbled a line in the notebook.

Anna looked at Katarina and rolled her eyes. Katarina bit her bottom lip and shook her head. She didn't know what to say, either.

Anna faced the clerk again and cleared her throat. "We were told to register the birth with civil authorities, according to the new law. That's why we're here."

"Do you have any medical documentation?" The clerk said without lifting his head. He continued writing.

"I had a midwife. Wait. Katarina, can you take him?" Anna loosened Peter's baby blanket and handed the infant to her. "She gave me some papers." Anna fumbled in her bag. "Will this do?" She passed the scrawled document to the stern-faced man.

The clerk pushed the wire-rimmed glasses up his narrow nose and squinted at the printing. "It's in German. It must be in Russian." He pushed the note back across the desk and returned his attention to his notebook.

"What does it matter?" Anna scowled as she clawed back the paper. "Isn't Germany supervising Ukraine until the new government is organized?"

The clerk's nose rose upward, and his pale thin lips turned down at the corners as he pointed at the telephone on the wall. "Nothing is official until I'm duly informed by the authorities. Until then, the Ukraine territory is still under the management of Russia. Today, all paperwork must be in Russian." His finger slid down the page of his notebook to the next numbered line. He made another mark, examined it, and frowned.

Anna blew at a honey-colored strand hanging in her face, shook her head in exasperation, and blinked back the welling tears.

Katarina rubbed her lips together and took a deep breath while carefully considering her words. "Is this really necessary? My sister is doing her best to follow the law, but you're making this very difficult."

The beady black eyes flashed and zeroed in on Katarina's face. "Are you defying the government?"

Katarina blanched and stepped back. She repositioned the infant and patted his back to keep him from crying. "No, I'm sorry, kind sir. We're just trying to get some clarification. Surely, this isn't the first Mennonite birth you've registered."

The flat face hardened. "The Mennonite faith has no validity with the new Russian order." The clerk dipped the pen in the inkwell a second time, wiped the nib, and scanned the journal. "I suggest you change your tone. I could have you arrested." He hunched his shoulders over the notebook and leaned forward, revealing the bald spot on the back of his pointy skull. "Come back when you have the proper papers."

Katarina looked at Anna, shrugged her shoulders, and mouthed, "Let's go."

Anna stuffed the document into her bag and headed for the door. Katarina trailed behind her, hiding her face behind the infant's blanket as they exited the tiny office. They maneuvered through the large foyer in the government building as quickly as they dared, hurrying past the long, gawking queues at the post office's wickets and the bank lines.

When they arrived at the outer exit, the middle-aged Russian guard opened the door and politely touched his hat. His left fist rested on the sheath of a knife tucked into his waistbelt and a long gun hung from his right shoulder. Katarina couldn't help but stare — first at the weapons, then at him. He caught her eye and winked.

Katarina startled, gave a stiff smile, and quickly turned away. Her heart pounded in her ears, and goosebumps formed on her arms. How had their world changed so fast? When the army invaded the village, the Russian government officials began treating local citizens like common criminals. Every soldier seemed poised to use their weapons. Was there no trust left? And no belief in goodness? She chewed on her bottom lip and tightened her grip around the fussing baby.

Anna stomped past with a defiant expression, her nose flared and her chin pointing to the sky. She ignored the soldier and walked directly to the carriage stop.

"Are you alright?" Katarina asked as she returned the infant to his mother. "That was scary."

A tear slipped down Anna's cheek. "I wish David had come with us. I don't know what to do now." She patted baby

Peter's back and kissed his head. "Will they arrest me if I don't register within the week? I don't want to break the law."

"I suggest we talk to your midwife, Frau Toews. She lives close by." Katarina peeked back at the soldier — his fingers toying with the barrel of his long gun. He was still studying them.

"I suppose," Anna whispered, "This whole military thing is spookish. Let's get out of here."

"Olek's down the street at the general store." Katarina pointed at their buggy. "It looks like he's loading supplies. He's not seeing us."

"Give him another minute. I hope he got sugar today. I rustled up as many ration cards as I could find." Anna rubbed the baby's back. "But even money means nothing when there's no stock."

"If there's no sugar today, we still have honey," Katarina sighed. "All is not lost."

"Oh, my goodness. Look at that." Anna pointed her chin at the wagon loaded with a heavy machine gun driving up the street. "A *tachanka*. And more soldiers."

They shrank beneath the wooden overhang outside the clapboard government building while the parade passed. Four white horses with braided manes pulled the armed open cart with its heavy machine gun and three soldiers. One man held onto the equipment's controls while the other two stood on either side of the artillery, with their backs to the gun, scanning the desolate streets. Behind the wagon, a commanding officer's booming voice shouted orders to rifle-carrying cadets with red stars on their jackets and red bands on their gray-green *papakhas* hats. Their high black boots pounded the muddy pulp beneath their feet.

The guard standing behind them saluted to the military fanfare. "The soldiers seem so young," Katarina whispered. "Except for the officers."

"No more than twenty, I think," Anna murmured. "Like us."

"How can they understand war, Anna? I can't imagine what goes through their minds when they murder someone."

"I wonder the same, Kat. The guilt and shame of what they've done must cause a lifetime of nightmares. Do you think they're the same troops who set fire to Halbstadt?"

"Maybe. It's only been a month."

When the regiment disappeared down the street, the building's sentinel lit a cigarette and relaxed his posture. Katarina waved at Olek and caught his attention.

He raised his hand to acknowledge he'd seen her, then flicked his cigarette away before driving the buggy across the street. "Where to next?" Olek jumped down and helped them aboard.

"We need to go to Frau Toews's house," Anna said, her voice laced with irritation. "Do you know where she lives?"

Olek's eyebrows shot up. His mouth opened and closed as if he wanted to ask a question, but then seemed to think better of it. He pulled down the earflaps of his *ushanka* hat, climbed up to the driver's seat, and snapped the reins.

The vehicle turned down a vacant-looking side street rutted with snow and debris-encrusted puddles. "These homes look empty," Katarina said as they passed one shuttered house after another. "Where did everyone go?"

"It's because of Lenin's policies. He's pushing all the German ethnics out of the country." Anna's voice trembled and tears welled in her eyes. "And encouraging violence against us." Baby Peter squirmed and whimpered as she hugged him close.

Katarina swallowed the lump in her throat. "We must have faith, Anna. Lenin's power will disappear soon. Ukraine is independent now. And Germany is coming to help." But the military threats, the empty store shelves, and the shuttered homes and businesses said otherwise. She wished she'd gone to Canada in December when David's brother Johann and his wife Agatha left. They'd pleaded for her to join them, but she'd chosen to stay with Anna because her sister was pregnant with Margaretha.

"But the damage has been already done, Katarina," Anna said. "Lenin's policies and an anti-German sentiment have already taken hold. Makhno holds landowners at gunpoint, forcing them to relinquish their property while Lenin brainwashes the Slavs to turn against us. When Germany arrives, the locals will revolt and violence against us will increase until law and order are restored. Those who've left for safer lands won't return until we can reassure them that all is well." Anna's voice edged with bitterness. "I fear worse war is coming."

"Anna, please, let's not speak of such. Things must get better when Germany arrives. Not everyone buys Lenin's lies. It's not possible for one man to change the beliefs of an entire country." She tried to sound reassuring, even though she wasn't entirely convinced herself.

"I certainly hope that you're right."

Katarina tore her eyes away from the desolate street and turned to her sister. The black hat — with the estate's white roses emblem stitched on the brim — sat at a crooked angle and strands of gold hung in tiny ringlets around Anna's neck. Lines were already forming at the corners of her cornflower-blue eyes. Despite her disheveled appearance, she looked as elegant as a Madonna with the baby at her breast. Yet the fear showed. "Do you worry about the estate?"

The infant wriggled and Anna adjusted his quilt. "David and Papa are taking a group of men to check things out. They say the Red Terror will end with the signing of the peace treaty. Then, Russia's soldiers will leave. Replaced by Germany's, I suppose."

"Ja. But right now, the countryside isn't safe. How will the men cross the Dnieper and get to the estate when there are *Makhnovshchina* and Red militia around every corner?"

Anna shuddered. "Don't think it. I fear losing my husband. And our father. David assures me that his Red Cross armbands will protect them. I hope that's true. I pray for their safety."

"Ja, I do as well." But Katarina had read the terrifying statistics in the newspapers. The names of the recent dead filled pages of white space. It made her wonder if God was listening to anyone's prayers.

~

"WE'RE HERE." Katarina pointed to a crooked white picket fence marred by too many winters. The gate stood ajar; the base wedged in a frozen mound of March slush. The tired blue and white stucco house sat in the middle of the tiny yard, with a triangle of gray snow resting at the base of its silent brick chimney. Loose shingles on the overhanging eave threatened to give way and icicles dripped from the edges.

"There's no smoke coming from the chimney. I'll go check if she's home." Katarina lifted her gray wool skirt above the ankles and side-stepped the mounds of melting snow and muddy puddles along the pathway. She ducked under the draping edge and bounded up the stairs, then pounded on the scarred wooden door with her fist.

A curtain fluttered before the door cracked open.

"Ja. Vas is los?" A tiny woman with her head and shoulders covered by a thick, black woolen shawl and wearing several layers of dark skirts poked her thin face through the opening. The body wrapping disfigured her petiteness and made the widow look like a morbid triangle.

Katarina smirked at the midwife's cartoonish appearance.

"The government won't accept the papers." She held up the signed birth certificate.

"Why not?"

"Because they're in German."

The woman scowled and snatched the paper from Katarina's hand and beckoned her inside. "Stupid Bolsheviks. Wait here." She pointed to the multicolored rag rug on the battered plank flooring and pivoted on her heel. The heavy black skirts swirled into a balloon-like shape behind her as she stomped around the corner.

Katarina shivered in the damp cold and watched the wet snow drip from her boots. Her eyes drifted around the chilly, stark room and settled on the pot-belly stove in the center. A large container sat on the element, but there was no condensation on the side nor any steam rising from the surface. The coal box on the floor held thin strips of glazed kindling — resembling chopped-up furniture.

The ghoulish figure reappeared and a slender hand wearing black fingerless gloves shoved the paper in front of Katarina's face. "Here, this should satisfy them."

"Wait, there's a different date here," Katarina said, examining the certificate.

"Ja. If they want Russian, they probably want the new Gregorian dates, too. But maybe I should put both? If I'm wrong, then they refuse you again. They keep changing their minds. Today, it's one thing. Tomorrow, it's something else."

"Nay, Oba. This is ridiculous. Why can't they give us a straight answer? I don't want to bother you again."

"Ja. And then, you'll be in trouble for harassing them. The Reds shoot first and ask questions later." The midwife looked up to the ceiling and smacked her lips, then turned back. "Wait, I have an idea." She ripped the papers from Katarina's hand and flitted around the corner again, reappearing moments later with two more sheets of paper.

"They number the certificates at the printer and the government checks them. They'll notice the discrepancy. I'll have to explain." The midwife shrugged. "But there's not much I can do if they keep changing the rules. Here's one with both dates. Now you have three to choose from. One should be right." She sucked on her bottom lip. "Katarina, please let me know which one they accept so I can mark the others as errors on my register. Otherwise, they'll arrest me for falsifying records."

"Nay, Oba. I can't put you at risk like this." Katarina tried to read the tiny scrawl, but the print blurred in her shaking hand.

The midwife raised her thin shoulders to her ears. "I'm an old woman. They shot my sons and my husband. I have no one left. If Anna doesn't have the right papers, they'll arrest her, or take the child. Better they take me than the little one." She yanked on the decorative ends of her knitted black shawl. "Catherine the Great must be rolling in her grave. I pray our children will live long enough to restore the glory. Otherwise, the world is doomed."

Corpses and guns flashed through Katarina's imagination. She glanced at the unlit stove. "Do you have food? Or do you need coal? I can send our driver back with supplies."

The old widow's pale lips tightened into a thin line, "I have no chickens left, but the neighbors share their eggs. The mill has no flour, so I can't bake bread. I have no money for coal. If you can spare some ..."

"Oba, ja. Absolutely. I'll send Olek back with supplies tomorrow ..." Katarina blinked away the brimming tears. Was this what Katya meant by the desperate conditions in the countryside? The midwife had delivered Anna's baby. She deserved help. "Would you like to come and stay with us? We have lots of space. And a warm kitchen."

The thin face crinkled with a smile. "Thanks for the kind

offer, Katarina. But I'll go to my sister's when the Bolsheviks leave town. Germany is coming soon. They'll save us from this Red scourge. I can manage for a few more weeks. I have potato soup today. It tastes good cold. And if you send coal, I can cook the rats."

"Rats?"

The thin shoulders under the black shroud rose up and down. "It's meat. They're plentiful."

Katarina palmed her mouth. Even though she could see the desperation in front of her, the woman's circumstances were hard to fathom. A wave of guilt washed over her as she remembered pouting like a spoiled child when the sausage was gone.

AFTER PAYING the midwife for her service, Katarina returned to the carriage. Anna sat in the dark corner, nursing the infant.

"Well?" Anna barked. "What did she say?"

"We have three birth certificates," Katarina said, still reeling from what she'd just learned.

There was no point in explaining the rest. Later, at home, she'd ask Olek to bring supplies to the Frau. Then, she'd tell her mother and Lena to check the church's benevolence list. If the widow chose not to register, she could still receive food by volunteering at the soup lines. All church members knew the rules of charity. Plus, she could get help from her neighbors. Katarina doubted the woman would starve.

The carriage jerked forward and she braced her feet against the floor.

"Why?" Anna asked.

"Huh?" Katarina blinked and refocused. *The papers.* "Oh.

It's not only the Russian and German language in dispute here; it's also the calendar."

"The calendar?"

"Russia has switched to the Gregorian calendar only. The Orthodox calendar is no longer in use. Officially."

"Oh." A puzzled expression passed over Anna's face and her thin, blond eyebrows knit together. "So, what is the correct date?"

"March 1, according to the papers."

"What happened to the previous two weeks? When do we celebrate Peter's birthday?"

"That's up to you. But I suggest you keep all paperwork as consistent as possible. For the government."

Anna threw her head back and laughed, "This will be quite the story to tell this little one when he grows up."

"No doubt."

"Humpf! He won't believe it," Anna rambled. "I shall keep all three papers to prove it to him."

Katarina shook her head in disbelief. "What is this obsession you have with holding on to false papers? You're inviting trouble into our lives."

Anna's cornflower eyes twinkled, and her tiny pink mouth formed a round circle. "So says the fiction writer who decorates my house with books."

"That's different. Books are my escape from the horror of war that threatens to swallow our lives."

"Well, Katarina. I'm hanging on to the truth so it doesn't become fiction. Consider it my contribution to the family's legacy. When my children are older, I shall regale them with our frightening stories of survival during these dark times."

"What a lovely thought, Anna," Katarina snorted. "You're already thinking of scary stories to give your brood nightmares. I wasn't aware of this sinister side of your personality.

Please warn me before you begin the storytelling so I can triple-sheet the children's beds."

Anna laughed. "Well, Katarina, you're forever seeking genealogical data. This will make for a very interesting history."

"Indeed."

Olek brought the coach to a stop beside the post office. "Shall I park down the street again?" He motioned with his chin. "The army is gone. But I don't want to infuriate the guards and steal some government official's valued parking space."

"It's better to be safe than sorry," Katarina said. "We won't be long."

Olek jumped down, opened the carriage door, and offered them his supporting hand. Anna passed the infant to Katarina before hoisting her skirts above the ankles and skipping down the three metal stairs. She side-stepped the muddy puddle beside the wagon, then turned to retrieve the baby from Katarina.

When Katarina passed the boy back to his mother, she tried to copy her sister's agile descent. But her heel caught on the lower rung, and she lost her balance and stumbled into the mud. The cherished papers fluttered out of her hands towards a slushy pile of melting snow.

"No!" Katarina flailed forwards to snatch the papers before they landed. But her toe snagged the hem of her skirts and she sailed into the supporting post of the building's wooden overhang and smacked her head into the sharp edge. Dazed, she collapsed on the ice-covered gravel walkway.

Anna echoed her sister's 'No!' with her own shrill scream, waking the infant in her arms who added his lusty cry to the mayhem. She covered his ears and yelled, "Katarina! Are you alright?"

Before Katarina could answer, the rat-a-tat-tat of gunfire

down the street followed the sound of a ringing telephone inside the government building. Men raced to their vehicles, and a chaotic multi-directional stream of horses, carriages, and wagons competed for space in the narrow street. Pedestrians with perplexed expressions froze in the middle of the traffic.

Katarina rubbed the bump on her head and slowly stood up, holding on to the post while waiting for the dizziness to pass. "What's going on?"

"I think they got the phone call," Anna grinned. "I suspect Germany's in charge now."

They stood on the wooden sidewalk and stared at the erupting disorder. A small crowd poured out of the large government building and onto the street.

"So, what do we do now?" Katarina waved the papers.

"Let's find out." Anna snuggled the crying baby against her shoulder and proceeded toward the post office. The door opened before they could reach it and the Russian guard — who'd previously been stationed outside — exited. He ignored them and furtively glanced up and down the roadway before dashing to the adjoining dark alley.

Katarina's hand smacked the heavy door before it closed.

They traipsed through the empty lobby and straight into the government office. The clerk was busy filling a box with contents from his desk.

"Going somewhere?" Katarina asked.

"The treaty is signed. Ukraine is now under Germany's control. I'm no longer employed by Russia." The former government employee buttoned his gray wool coat.

"What about the birth registration?"

"Not my problem. Take it up with the next management." The scrawny man put on his hat, grabbed the box, and walked out the back door. "Good luck to you."

Katarina and Anna stood with their mouths gaping and their eyes wide.

"Now, what do we do?" Katarina asked.

"I guess we go home," Anna said.

36

REINHART AND HELGA

1952 APRIL. MUNICH, GERMANY.

REINHART EXTENDED HIS HAND AS HIS SODDEN GUESTS
stepped into the apartment. "Heidi and Peter, welcome. I'm
so glad you could make it. Please let me take your coats. You
must be soaked."

"Ja, and freezing. It's one step above snow out there. The
rain is practically ice pellets." Peter helped his wife wriggle
out of her coat before removing his.

"It won't last. The forecast is for a warm evening." Reinhart hung the coats on the wooden rack in the corner. "The
sunset will be glorious — if the clouds pass."

"Thanks for inviting us." Heidi returned Reinhart's handshake. "But I should warn you, these days I use every invitation as an excuse to get out of cooking. As Peter will attest,
I'm sure."

Peter chuckled. "She's not joking. I'm losing weight living
on soup and sandwiches."

"Oh, you lie. You're just naturally skinny." Heidi slapped
his arm. "Besides, you like my soups and breads."

Reinhart turned to the tall buxom blond at his side. She bumped his bicep with her elbow while tying a black ribbon over her straight Baltic hair. "And this is my wife, Helga. And I can assure you she doesn't allow anyone to get away with not eating."

Helga's icy sky-blue eyes crinkled at the corners and her square face lit up as she laughed. "The pleasure is all mine. I love impressing my guests." She shook their hands and pointed to the open sitting room. "Please come in and have a seat."

"It sure smells good, Helga. Is that roast pork and fennel?" Peter asked.

"Ja, it is. I didn't want to inundate you with strange food on your first visit." Helga's eyes met Reinhart's and she nervously brushed a stray blond strand from her face. He patted her on the waist before escorting the couple to the living room.

"I appreciate that. I'm not a picky eater ... most of the time," Peter said as he sat down on the aqua velvet couch.

Heidi stood in the middle of the room, her eyes scanning the cozy apartment. "Can I help you in the kitchen, Helga?"

"Certainly, if you wish. Although, it's very small. Barely enough room for two. I've already chopped the vegetables. But follow me." Helga said. "You can pull up a dining chair and watch me work."

Reinhart waited until the women had entered the kitchen and were out of earshot before slipping into the salmon-colored wing chair. "How are things at the university, Peter?"

"I don't know, Reinhart." Peter leaned back and laced his fingers behind his head.

"What do you mean? Please tell me you're not having problems with this new professor, too. You've only been there a few months." Reinhart frowned. The man's instability and moodiness concerned him. He hoped he wouldn't be sorry for tonight's visit.

"Ja. I like him, and I appreciate the job. But I'm not convinced this is where I should be. Heidi thinks I'm going through a phase." Peter pulled his arms down and smoothed the wrinkles on his brown pants. "I'm having trouble focusing. Everything bugs me."

"A phase?" Reinhart echoed before surmising the likely cause of his friend's restlessness. Whenever Peter discovered an irregularity in his mother's diaries, he'd mull over it for weeks. "Let me guess. Katarina's diaries. How's the translation going?"

Peter grimaced and toyed with the crocheted coaster on the end table. "Slowly. Mundane but curious."

"What do you mean?" Reinhart silently applauded himself for recognizing Peter's dilemma.

"Well, I came across this part where they meet this forger, and he provides fake transit documents so they can cross the Dnieper. Then later, I learned the story about my three birth certificates. And it got me thinking." Peter ran his fingers through his chestnut hair.

Reinhart held up his right hand. "Wait. Mennonites and forgeries? Three birth certificates? That is curious. Why was Katarina carrying around fake documents?"

"The forgeries weren't used, from what I can tell. There was some kind of confusion or misunderstanding. However, they must have had some importance. Why else keep them? Although ... I don't know if this is relevant but ... I don't know if Mutter trusted the church completely. I think she struggled with her faith. She said, 'We had to make tough decisions in the war. The church would've disagreed, but we did what we had to do.'"

"That's understandable. It's hard to believe in a loving God when times are tough." Reinhart nibbled on his lower lip, considering his words. He really didn't want to stray down a religious rabbit trail. Beliefs were as personal as politics. But Katarina's Mennonite faith was as relevant to her wartime experiences as her German ethnicity. "Religion is composed of man-made rules that don't always fit with reality, Peter. But faith is hope. It keeps us going through the awfulness."

"I suppose." Peter cocked his head quizzically. "But if God cares about us, why do bad things happen to good people and vice-versa? The things we saw in the war ..."

"That's a tough one, Peter. Both good and evil are omnipresent. We choose one over the other every day." Reinhart shifted in his chair. "But sometimes the difference is muddy. Religion is supposed to help us make those distinctions. But it doesn't always ..."

"I agree. I still can't fathom how we got duped into participating in Hitler's craziness. But that was different from what my parents went through in the civil war. They weren't believing lies. They were just trying to survive."

"Ja. Both wars were battles of good versus evil. Fear and chaos reigned, and bad decisions were made. While your mothers faced lawlessness in the Great War, we struggled with illogical and inhumane laws during Hitler's war. Not to dismiss what you and your parents went through, Peter — but consider the terror of the camps. Such horror. Why didn't God intervene? I was there. I saw enough to become highly skeptical of the existence of a supreme being." Reinhart waved his hand in the air. "Let's change the subject. The question about why bad things happen to good people and why evil exists is redundant and futile. I apologize for rambling."

Peter grinned. "Ja. Faith is complex."

Reinhart waved at Helga as she peeked through the serving window. "Helga, please bring that bottle we've been saving."

He turned back to Peter and clasped his hands in his lap.

"Let's discuss the forgeries. Here's my take on it. In both wars, freedom of movement was restricted. Forged papers came in mighty handy. But if caught, the legal consequences could be fatal. As members of a patriarchal faith that underscored submission, your mothers would have experienced some serious conflicts of conscience."

"I never looked it at that way, Reinhart. But now that you mention it. I remember something about 'men carry the voice of God. Therefore, women are to defer to a man's wisdom.' But there was a hierarchy among men as well. The elder male in the family always had the last word — unless the church overruled. But my mothers were traveling without that leadership. Their naivety increased their vulnerability." Peter ran his fingers through his hair. "Good grief. They'd likely obey any man present."

"Ja, Peter. It was a very dangerous situation for them. You know ... as a man, it's nice to have total control, but all that responsibility can be oppressive, too. A patriarchal system only works for women if everyone follows the rules and there's no disruption to the order. In such a world, men protect women from wrongdoing by other men. Now, let's remember that women's right to vote was only beginning to be recognized in some countries. Culturally speaking, women were still the property of their husbands and fathers. They were not people."

Peter nodded. "Ja. Even now, in 1952, many churches don't allow women to vote or even to be full members." He pointed across the room to his wife. "Heidi often says, 'I'm a person, too. I have a right to my opinion.' She rages that it's barely acceptable for a woman to work, impossible to get promoted and men earn double that of women doing the same job." Peter jerked his thumb towards his wife. "But when it comes to having children — we both suffer. Women sacrifice their jobs to have children. Supporting them is our job. There's a lot of pressure on us, too."

"Ja, Peter. I agree."

Helga interrupted the conversation with a bottle of Riesling and two glasses. "Please help yourselves. Supper will be another thirty minutes. Heidi and I are getting to know each other and talking about babies. I doubt you want to listen to our babbling."

"Thanks for your consideration. Those days are over for us, I hope." Reinhart winked at his wife. He gazed lovingly at her backside as she returned to the kitchen, then looked over at Peter. "Care for a glass of wine?"

Peter's eyes flicked over to his wife perched in the doorway between the dining room and the kitchen. He bit the corner of his lip. "Ja, sure. Say, Reinhart, speaking of babies, where are your girls? I was expecting to meet them."

"They're on a camping weekend with their scout troop. Learning about survival training and such."

"An awfully cold weekend to be doing that. Aren't you worried about them?"

"Not at all. They have warm tents and good leaders. They'll be fine. Besides, this will encourage them to have a bit more respect for my war stories when they get back. I'm secretly thrilled by this weather challenge. They need a little hardening up." Reinhart chuckled as he popped the cork. "And to be totally honest, I'm relieved by their absence. There's too much bubble gum in this place when they're home. I try to spend as little time here as I can."

He poured two glasses of wine and handed one to Peter. "Not that I don't love them. I do. Very much so. But men aren't welcome in some conversations. And unfortunately, this discomfort increases as they get older. At nine and eleven, they're discovering the intimate truths of womanhood. And that's not my domain. So, I escape as much as I can."

"I wish I could relate, but I can't. At least not yet. My sister left at thirteen, and Mutter never talked to me about such delicate matters. I had to learn the hard way." Peter sipped the wine, then set the glass down on the crocheted coaster. "But back to the forgeries. The diary entry made me wonder about the other documents I found when I was seventeen. While I was snooping for my identification papers."

"You've lost me. What other documents?"

"The three identical birth certificates had three different dates. But I found other documents written in Cyrillic and other languages, too. Reinhart, even if they needed forged papers at one time, why would she keep such incriminating evidence years later? Surely not for sentimental reasons. Did she expect to need them again?"

Reinhart raised his eyebrows and leaned back in his chair. "Beats me. I suggest you keep working on those diaries, Peter. The answer must be there somewhere."

Peter rubbed his face with both hands, then slapped his hands on his legs. "Maybe there's no reason. She liked to collect things. I'm probably reading too much into this."

"It's as interesting as an archeological dig, Peter." Reinhart bit the corner of his bottom lip. "Speaking of digging into the past, a couple of months ago, I had an interesting conversation with your friend, Max, the butcher."

"Really? You went to my old butcher shop? Isn't that a bit out of your way?" Peter's eyebrows shot up as he picked up the wine glass.

"The long walk does me good." Reinhart patted his middle-aged spread. "Besides, his sausages are much better than Fleischmann's up the street."

"Oh, I agree with that. You can't beat old Max's blends. I used to work there when I was a kid. I learned lots about sausage making. Although I was more of a cutter in those days." Peter perked up and his grin widened. "Once a month, they'd dedicate a week to stuffing the casings. It was my job to stoke the fire in the old smoker. The entire neighborhood smelled of roasted meat. People lined up around the block to buy his sausages. Mutter complained I stank like I'd walked through a fire when I came home. The ash on my clothes made a mess of her perfectly clean apartment." Peter threw his head back and laughed. "I can still smell the smoke."

Reinhart paled. Peter's description was too vivid. He couldn't stop the memory from flashing in front of his eyes. *Ash. It fell from the sky like snowflakes. White smoke. The sky was perpetually cloudy and smelled of burning meat.* A sour taste rose from his stomach. He'd never associated sausages in that way before. He set his drink down and stood up. "I'll be right back. I need to check on supper." Except now, he wasn't hungry.

He purposefully strode towards the kitchen, bulldozing past Heidi and inadvertently brushing her knees. It was too late to apologize. Helga turned from frying the spaetzle. Her eyes widened and she held the spatula in mid-air. Heidi was gawking at him, too.

"How are things coming here?" Reinhart barked. He quickly retracted his irritated tone with a nervous smile. His eyes landed on the roast sitting on the counter, tented under a tinfoil covering. The heavy aroma of cooked pork, onion, and fennel permeated the tiny space. His stomach heaved and he covered his mouth with his hand. "Smells good," He lied.

"Ah, fine." Helga said slowly. She tilted her head, studying him. "We'll be another fifteen minutes. Are you men starving? Do you need a snack before we eat?"

He shook his head, then nodded. Food was an excellent distraction. "Some bread, cheese, maybe pickles, too."

Helga pointed across the room. "It's on the table. Take a plate and help yourself."

"I'll get it for you." Heidi jumped into the conversation. "What would you like?"

Reinhart felt guilty for behaving poorly. But it was too late to apologize. He'd explain his actions to Helga later after their company had left. He'd tell her that he'd needed to distract himself from the disturbing memories. She'd understand.

Helga had her own memories about the war — the whistling bombs screeching as they fell from the skies and the strange odors in the air around her home in the forest. When she learned the truth, she'd been horrified.

They met in Munich during the war — before the bombing. He was a soldier, and she was a records clerk. After Germany's dark and humiliating ending, she and other physically strong women tackled the grim work of cleaning up the city. It hadn't been easy with two toddlers. But the country needed the help of every German.

At the beginning of the reconstruction, after the girls went to bed, they'd share a drink and commiserate. But their memories of the war were different. He'd seen things she hadn't. And regardless of what Helga did or said, the images in his mind flashed at the worst times. And sometimes it wasn't just the pictures in his head, it was also the loud sounds, the color of the air, or the stench of the food.

Like now. Only the smell of frying onions kept him from retching.

Reinhart rubbed his hands together, then pointed to the table. "Anything. We're peckish." The food didn't matter. The request was just an excuse to exorcise the demons toying with his mind.

"Here." Heidi handed him a plate filled with bread, cheese, and sweet pickles. "Nibble away and have another glass of wine. Supper's almost ready."

He accepted the plate with a smile. "I'm sorry I hit your knees there earlier. I wasn't paying attention."

Her round baby blue eyes flashed up and connected with his face as she eased down on the stool. "Don't worry about it. It's a small space. I understand. Our apartment's the same."

"Thanks. I'm used to tripping over the girls, but not our company. Again, my apologies." Reinhart strode back to the wing chair and offered the plate of appetizers to Peter. "Help yourself. Supper's almost ready. Do you want another glass of wine?" He was rambling now — plying his guest with food and drink in a weak attempt to divert the conversation and gain control of himself. He hoped Peter didn't notice.

"Thanks, Reinhart. I know my musings over my mother's diaries can be boring to some. And I really appreciate your insight. I've talked to a few historians at the university, but they lecture me with facts that I already know. You're different."

Peter's words stroked Reinhart's ego and brought his attention back to the present. "How so?"

"You don't take a black-and-white approach to the facts. It's more like ... you examine things with a microscope, but then you pull back and look at the globe, too. I appreciate that about you."

Reinhart choked on the compliment. Tears welled in the back of his throat, and he deliberately tensed his face so as not to smile. He shouldn't act proud. It wasn't proper. But the one thing he always wanted in life was to know he was making a difference in someone else's. Peter had just given him this gift. How should he respond? He didn't feel worthy. "Thanks, Peter. It's good to know that I'm not the stereotypical blunted German with a closed mind. Although, I admit to being critical. In that respect, I suppose you could say I'm typical."

Peter chuckled. "So you've said more than once. But I would describe you as an open-minded evaluator. You have your opinions, but you don't allow them to cloud your judgment."

"A skill I learned in the war; I suppose." Reinhart gripped the glass and swirled the drink absentmindedly as another memory flashed. "It's called detachment. Not allowing myself to become emotionally involved with my job. Unfortunately, this trait has the side effect of numbing all my emotions, to the point where Helga says I have none."

Peter's eyebrows knit together. "That's an interesting comment. Mutter said the war did the same thing to her."

Reinhart frowned. "I thought you said her emotions were erratic?"

"Ja." Peter nodded. "To the outsider, she appeared stoic and submissive. But at home, it was different. She said she couldn't feel anymore. But that wasn't true. She bottled her rage. When the cork came off, all hell broke loose. Afterward, she became depressed and went through the motions of living, pretending everything was normal. But it wasn't. The pressure would slowly build again. It was a never-ending cycle."

"How long did that take? Between the blow-ups?"

"Weeks sometimes. Even months. I'd get lulled into this safe feeling, believing it wouldn't happen again. But it always did. Papa and I never talked about it. We just danced around the issue and stayed busy. I guess that's why I wanted to run away to the Luftwaffe. Fly away from the pain. Papa worked long hours at the butcher shop and then went fishing to relax." Peter ran his fingers through his light chestnut waves and looked out at the sleet pinging against the window. "I'll think we'll need to take a taxi home tonight."

Reinhart sensed Peter's discomfort around the subject of his father. After speaking with Max, Reinhart understood. "About the butcher shop. Max said he offered you the chance to help manage the business."

"Did he? I don't remember his saying that." Peter frowned and set down his wine glass and helped himself to the appetizers.

"I got the impression that he'd still be willing ..." Reinhart said softly.

Peter popped a piece of cheese and bread in his mouth and leaned back on the couch, talking as he chewed. "I haven't worked there in fifteen years. I've moved on and joined the intellectuals. Why would I want to make my living standing on a cement floor carving up carcasses when I can read books from a comfortable chair?"

"I don't know, Peter. I'm only telling you what he said. Would you?" Reinhart watched a flicker of surprise pass over his friend's face.

"What? Go back?" Peter shifted his focus to the far end of the room where the lively female chatter and the clinking of dishes suggested the meal was imminent.

"Ja. Could you go back to cutting meat and stuffing sausages?" Reinhart stood up as Helga announced supper was served.

"That's a good question, Reinhart. But also, a scary thought. But thanks for letting me know about Max. I didn't realize he still thought of me with such fondness."

"You are the son of his late best friend, Peter. Of course, he cares about you." Reinhart motioned to Peter to go ahead of him. "From what he told me, you're practically family."

Helga clapped her hands. "Gentlemen. Let's eat."

37

THE VISITORS

1918 APRIL. THE FAMILY FARM NEAR CHORTITZA.

Katarina looked up from her embroidery stitching, "What are the men up to today? They're sure making a lot of noise outside."

"Gone." Anna set her handiwork on the table and scurried to the kitchen window. She pulled aside the lace curtains and peered out; then quickly closed them and pivoted sharply. Standing with her back to the portal, she stared at Katarina — her jaw clenched, her eyes wide.

"Gone?" Katarina narrowed her eyes and cocked her head. The back of her arms prickled. "They left? Where? When?" *Who's in the yard?*

"Early this morning. They went to Halbstadt to check on the estate. And the village. They'll be away for the rest of the week. Didn't you hear the big discussion last night?" Anna took a deliberate step sideways away from the window but kept her back to the wall.

Something was amiss. Katarina set down her stitching,

scraped back her chair, and went towards the window. "You thought wrong. I went to bed early. I heard nothing."

"You probably had your head in a book again." Anna shifted her stance and blocked the light.

"Move. I want to see." She shoved Anna aside.

"No, you don't," Anna's voice trembled. She stretched out her arm. "Don't open the curtains."

Katarina stared through the pinholes of the white lace. A throng of horses, gun-carrying riders, and wagons encircled the yard and trailed down the driveway. Goosebumps formed on the back of her arms and her mouth went dry. She sucked on her cheeks and swallowed. "Where's Olek?"

"He's escorting the men across the river. He'll be back in a day or two," Anna whispered.

"Who's looking after the farm?"

"Katya. And a couple of young helpers Papa hired from the village."

"Obviously no one expected this." She rubbed the old bump on her arm and flexed her fist. "How did they know to come here ... now? Who told them?"

"They must have been spying on the farm," Anna whispered. "Maybe they ..."

"What?" Katarina turned and came face-to-face with her sister. "Maybe they what?"

"Followed us." Anna's cornflower blue eyes met hers.

"They can't have. We've been here for more than a month." Katarina held her hand over her pounding heart. "Who knew the men were gone?"

"Katya would never betray the family," Anna read Katarina's mind.

"Well, somehow they found out." Katarina searched for another explanation. "Are they the bandits from Maria's farm?"

Anna screwed up her face and peered through the lace.

"Only she would know. But they're not the ones who met us on the road."

Katarina lifted a corner of the curtain. Anna squeezed in beside her, their cheeks touching. "Look," Katarina pointed. "Two tachankas. Like the ones we saw in town last week, but carrying black flags."

Anna inhaled sharply. "The front horses are organized by color — white, bay, black. These are not simple freeloaders. This must be Makhno's army! What do they want with us?"

"We're going to die." Dizziness washed over Katarina and her stomach revolted. She wanted to run, but her feet were frozen to the floor. She gagged and pulled the apron to her mouth. The small vomit was only water.

"Ja," Anna echoed, her focus glued to the scene outside and oblivious to Katarina's discomfort.

They both stood silent and awestruck, watching the unfolding spectacle. Ten gun-toting riders on horseback trotted beside the two tachankas. Each machine gun was manned by two armed guards and the wagons were pulled by a team of four horses.

Katarina searched for the black stallion. None of the black horses resembled the one that had knocked her down in the barn two years ago. That one had a white snip. And this group had a lot of serious-looking weapons that didn't resemble simple hunting rifles. Her legs trembled. "Anna, Papa's gun is in the hayloft. But we can't get it now. What are we going to do?"

"It wouldn't help us anyway. I have no idea how to shoot one."

"Neither do I."

"Violence begets violence," Maria murmured from behind. "Leave it to me. There are other ways. I've been through this before."

Anna scowled. "This better not be your fault, Maria. I don't know what you did, but I don't want to find out, either."

"We don't have much choice," Katarina hissed. "We're doomed." Her chest felt heavy and tight, her feet like two lead weights. The surreal scene was developing like a slow-moving picture show. Katarina pinched herself. It hurt.

Two guards jumped off the first armed wagon and strode over to a white mare with a braided and ribboned mane and a black flag strapped to the stirrup. A short figure with broad shoulders and laden with a bandolier and a saber dismounted and handed the reins to one of the gunmen. The small person shouted to the others and pointed to the barns and storage sheds. Four riders immediately took off in the assigned direction.

"Girls, get away from the window," Lena screeched from the doorway. "Anna, take your son into the attic. Maria, you, too. Save your children. Go now."

Like two obedient children, Anna and Maria stopped ogling and dashed away. A strong arm pulled Katarina from the window and spun her around. Her mother's deep-set icy blue eyes met hers. Fear resonated on her face and her jaw flexed with tension. "Katarina, go to the kitchen. Help Katya cook something to feed these villains."

Katarina blinked rapidly to regain her bearings and shook her head. "Feed them? Like what? We've barely enough to feed ourselves."

"Shush, Katarina. This is a test of our faith. We must show love under all circumstances. These are human beings who want to survive. If we feed them, they'll leave. We have nothing else they want. I'll prepare the dining room. And hide the silverware. And the Delft. Now, go to the stove. Quick. Pretend to cook, even if you're not." Lena rushed out of the room.

Katarina sucked at the air. Her mother was repeating what

her father had told them — that the vandals only wanted food, shelter, and guns. Her brain said Maria had lived through these attacks, so there was no reason to fear. But every fiber of her being shook and her knees threatened to collapse beneath her.

What if *he* — her attacker from two years ago — was among them? Would *he* recognize her? She clung to the wall and shuffled to the kitchen. Snatching the metal bucket from the shelf, she hung it on the hook beneath the new brass faucet and yanked on the tap. Rage surged through her veins.

"Take it easy on that new tap. We don't want to break it." Katya stood by the stove, scraping carrots into the refuse pail.

As she dumped the water into the oversized soup pot, Katarina ogled Katya with an evil eye. "Why are you bothering to clean carrots for these awful *Menschen*? Are you on their side?"

Katya blanched. "I'm just the cook. I'm not on anyone's side."

"You should be on ours. We deserve it," Katarina spat. She regretted the insult as soon as it left her mouth. But she couldn't take it back now. Besides, berating the maid might cause her to think twice about supporting the bandits.

She took a deep breath, threw a log into the stove, and tempered her voice. "What are we throwing in the pot? It's the end of winter and the vegetables are scarce."

"We have barley, carrots, and onions today. It'll have to do."

"Yuck. I hate barley."

"You don't have to eat it," Katya winked. "You are welcome to go hungry and leave it all for them." She jerked her chin towards the window.

As Katarina rinsed the grain and threw it into the pot, a cold draft blew in from the back door and raucous laughter resounded from the entryway. Her stomach tightened. They were here. Footsteps stomped through the mudroom and up the small flight of stairs. As the heel of a heavy boot struck the partitioning door, she jerked and her hand flew sideways, knocking over the bowl of chopped onions on the counter.

Katya dropped her knife on the cutting board and did an about-face. Katarina's fingers slid to the knife, but Katya slapped it out of her hand. "No," she whispered. "Stay innocent."

Two tall men in full-length fur coats and wearing the traditional ushankas — winter hats, with the earflaps hanging down — burst into the kitchen. Long knife sheaths flashed from inside the unbuttoned coats. Above the red britches, embroidered black waist sashes hung to their mid-thigh. Knife hilts protruded from behind the Cossack belts. Rows of *gazyrs* — narrow pockets designed as sleeves for individual bullets — were sewn into the chests of the off-white linen *kosovorotka* — the traditional long-sleeved peasant tunics. One man wore black, knee-high leather boots, while the other wore only wool-felt *valenki* — boot liners — inside his rubber galoshes.

Long guns pointed in their direction. Katarina's heart pounded in her ears, her knees shook like jelly, and her mouth went dry. She swallowed hard and stared at the guns, the protruding bayonets, and the ammunition belts. They were going to die. That much was certain.

"What's for supper, ladies?" they sneered.

Katarina sucked in her breath. The militants didn't look a day over twenty. What was it her father said about the rebellious youth — "Young people lack the wisdom of experience. If they don't want to listen to wise advice, don't argue with them. Only fools argue with fools"? She wished he'd instructed her on how to handle fools with guns.

Footsteps shuffled from behind the two men and a sharp heel cracked the floor. But the intruders stood steady, their eyes leering, their lips curled, and their fingers itching the trigger.

"Ooh, something smells good. But I think this kitchen needs a little more help." A female voice sang as Lena limped into the kitchen with a gunman at her heels. He held a pistol to the back of Lena's head and grinned at the owner of the voice standing behind the two taller gunmen. "Were you trying to get away, *Ledi?*"

Since Lena had been in the dining room, Katarina gathered that one gunman had entered by the front door when the others came in through the back. In other words, they were surrounded. Her legs wobbled and she gripped the counter for support. The knife poked her hand. She grabbed it and slipped it into her waistband.

An odd-looking stocky person of medium height dressed in a fox fur coat and matching hat emerged from between the two men. She was approximately mid-thirty with a narrow nose, a thin mouth, sunken cheeks, and one brown eye slightly larger than the other. Katarina squeezed her eyes, blinked, and stared again — dumbstruck by both the woman's ugliness and her command of the group.

"Is there anyone else inside?" The vigilante's shifty eyes darted between the three women. "Tell us now."

Katarina held her breath to calm the whooshing in her ears and the pounding in her chest. Katya stood rigidly beside her, chewing her lips, her hands clenched into tight fists. Lena appeared frozen in place — her arms hung stiffly at her sides and her face held a blank, stony expression.

The woman waved her pistol and jerked her chin at the open hallway. "Check the house."

The male slowly backed out of the alcove with his gun still pointing at the group, then turned and advanced up the hallway. The leader nudged the other man with her pistol.

"Follow him." As they left, another two soldiers emerged from the mudroom's stairwell and shadowed the woman.

The vigilante wandered back and forth, circling her three hostages — her shifty eyes continuously scanning their bodies while she twirled the pistol in her hand. "I am *Atamansha* Marusya — the General of the Free Combat *Druzhina*. Your home is now my headquarters. But there's no need to be frightened. If you listen to us, we'll get along fine. Do you understand?"

The women nodded simultaneously.

"Good. Now, where are the men who live here?" Marusya's gun clicked.

"They went into the city for supplies," Lena said quickly. "They'll be back soon."

It was the first time Katarina had heard her mother tell a lie and she cast her gaze to the floor so as not to raise suspicion. Her stomach tightened and she hugged her arms to keep from shaking.

"Tsk. Tsk. So unfortunate for you." She jutted her chin at the soup pot. "What are you cooking?"

"Barley stew," Katya said.

"Prepare the ovens. My hard-working men are butchering a lamb." Marusya toyed with the rotating chamber on her pistol. Her eyes swept over Katya. "Your days of serving the kulaks are over. From this day forward, you work for me."

Katarina wondered what the Atamansha meant. Was she planning to murder them?

The stew bubbled noisily behind her, but her feet refused to budge. Katya elbowed Katarina, then gently pushed her aside. Katya picked up the long-handled wooden spoon and stirred the pot.

Marusya brushed past her, and Katarina stumbled backward into the dividing wall, slamming her palms into the wood to maintain her balance. Her wrist brushed against the head of the knife tucked in her waistband.

"I hope you've made enough. There're twenty cold and hungry men outside." Marusya peeked into the soup pot and sniffed. Then she turned on her heel, stepped up to Katarina, and put the gun underneath her chin — pulling her so close their breaths mingled. The hypnotic brown eyes penetrated Katarina's, and the stench of garlic emanated from her mouth. "Have you learned to bake bread, Fräulein?"

"Tak, Madam." Katarina's heart raced. She clawed at the wooden counter behind her. The weight of the knife pushed against her waist. Behind Marusya, the gunman's eyes narrowed, and he pointed his long gun directly at Katarina. She hesitated. Using the knife now would get her killed.

"Then, you'd best get to work." Her voice softened and she passed the barrel of the pistol over Katarina's breasts. "You will call me either Marusya or Atamansha. I am not a madam." She reached up and stroked Katarina's cheeks. "What's your name? Are you married?"

"I'm ... Katarina." She shook her head. "No, I'm not married."

"Tsk, tsk. Such a shame," Marusya clucked. "Your mother must be so disappointed in you. You're a very pretty girl. Maybe it's your clothing." She took a step back and slid the pistol down to Katarina's stomach. "This dress doesn't suit you. You should wear brighter colors. Men like pretty girls in fancy dresses. Don't you own any nicer ones? With embroidery? And jewelry. Like the red beads our women wear." A sly smile crossed Marusya's face. "What is wrong with you Germans? You're so dull looking. Life should be a celebration of color! After supper, you will show me your closet. I'll help you find something nicer."

She pulled away and tossed her ushanka hat on the table, then slipped off her fur coat and finger-combed her crudely chopped, mousey-brown bob. Knife hilts poked out from behind the wide, heavily embroidered, red waist sash. The beaded and fringed ends hung to the knee. Similarly dressed like her four soldiers, Marusya wore the gray linen kosovorotka — a thigh-length men's peasant tunic with cuffs and a mock collar — over the *sharovary* — the wide, black harem trousers with narrow bottoms that were neatly tucked into the black knee-high boots.

Katarina gawked at the costume, envying the artistry. The belt would look gorgeous over her own dark skirts. The outfit aside, Katarina was astonished that any woman could both dress like a man and direct a military team. It was even more surprising that these men respected their female leader. If she hadn't seen it with her own eyes, she'd never believed it.

When Marusya spotted Katarina's ogling her clothes, she smirked, then winked. A hot flush rose up Katarina's neck.

The clunk of heavy boots in the hallway and the soft patter of little feet interrupted them. "Look what we found," a soldier announced as Maria and Anna came in with the infants in their arms and the other children trailing behind. Another guard marched at the rear, his long guns pointed at the children's heads.

"Well, well, well." Marusya tucked her pistol behind her colorful waistband and approached the group. "What do we have here?" She pulled back Peter's baby blanket and sneered, "And you said you had no meat? This little one is almost ready for the soup pot." She threw her head back and cackled, then looked at one-year-old Gerta. "And that one definitely is."

The three sisters stood terror-struck, their mouths gaping, their eyes wide. Anna and Maria tightened their grips around their babies. Lena's eyes darted between the soldiers, the guns, and her family — her jaw firmly clenched.

"No, you can't cook them," eight-year-old Mary screamed.

Marusya snickered, cocked her pistol, and aimed it

directly at the girl's head. "Haven't you heard of *Baba Yaga*? I am her. I eat small children for supper. You best be quiet, little one, or you'll be next."

Maria's daughters burst into tears and circled their mother, clinging to her skirts. The boys froze with fear.

Marusya threw her head back and roared. She rubbed the top of Mary's blond head. "Oh, such drama! There's no need to be frightened, yet. I'll wait to see what your cook has on the menu first. And you won't go hungry either. In fact, there're two cows here to feed you." She pointed the gun at Anna and Maria. "Your milk will have to do tonight." She leaned into Anna and whispered, "Don't worry, my men won't interfere. I try not to torture little ones, but sometimes I can't help myself."

Anna's eyes bulged and she pulled Peter into her breast.

Marusya turned to her soldiers. "Get them out of here and keep them out of sight. Park them in the attic. And send in Gregoire. He likes entertaining the little ones." She jerked her chin at Anna. "Take this cow. The other —" she pointed the gun at Maria "— stays here for now."

The soldier escorted Anna and the children down the hall while the other two men ran down the stairs into the mudroom. The backdoor swung open and slammed shut, letting in a blast of frigid air.

"Show's over." Marusya snapped her fingers. "Get to work. Stoke the oven. And find me some brandy. My men are hungry and thirsty. They need something to warm their bones." She laid her gun and saber on the table, plopped down on a chair, and pulled another forward — using it as a footstool for her muddy boots. "And don't lie to me. I know you brew your own medicines." She picked up her pistol and waved it at the women. "Now, schnell. Stop gawking. We don't have all night. We must get to Aleksandrovsk tomorrow.

Makhno is waiting for my highly-skilled snipers and machine guns."

Makhno. It was that dreaded name again. He was closer than ever. An icy finger traveled down Katarina's spine, and she shivered. Thankfully, this nightmare would only last one night. They would survive.

Katarina compared the vigilante to Sergei. They were both exotic and dangerous yet very different. Sergei would never kill her. Marusya might. And her soldiers definitely would. Katarina determined she wouldn't die like this — not without a fight.

She methodically picked up the bread knife and started slicing the fresh loaf. Then she stopped and stared. The paring knife was still in her waistband. Could she do it? If worse came to worst, could she kill? The images of the orphans' parents lying in the snow and the couple hanging in the barn flashed through her mind. Her stomach twisted. No, she could never end another's life. Perhaps she could injure. Maybe. But was that also sin? Even if it was for self-protection?

"There's brandy in the cold cellar," Lena said with unusual calmness. She pulled out a paring knife from her skirt pocket and pointed it at the small stone structure outside.

"Blessed brandy." Marusya flicked her hand at two soldiers now standing in the doorway. "Go find it. And tell the men to hurry up with the butchering. Then send in the others."

Katarina blanched. They didn't stand a chance against this woman and her army.

38

SOUR SOUP

THERE WAS BARELY ENOUGH OF THE POORLY-SEASONED barley stew to get through the first course. Since both Katya and Lena were accustomed to cooking for church dinners, Katarina thought it odd that they'd underestimated the raw ingredients. But she assumed it was intentional and likely instigated by Maria, who'd earlier disclosed the seasoning trick she'd used when the gang had stopped over at her farm.

When Katya cleaned up the spilled onions, Katarina heard Maria whisper to the maid, "If you don't want them to come back, make it as bland as possible. Omit the paprika, garlic, and dill. And leave out the salt and pepper, too."

The reaction was predictable.

"Tasteless porridge." Marusya spat on the floor and threw the Delft bowl across the room. It shattered against the plastered wall, scarring Lena's prized blue and white Belgian wallpaper. The glob of greasy residue clung to the lacy filigree edges, then slowly dribbled to the floor, leaving a long beige stain.

A short yelp escaped Lena's mouth before her hands flew to her face. The irreplaceable specialty wallpaper had been her pride and joy. Now it would be ruined forever. The matriarch stood with her hands over her mouth, her eyes glazed, staring at the mark.

When Katya knelt and picked up the broken ceramic, the men hooted and called her a 'German whore.' She left the room clutching the broken fragments in her bare hands — her chin trembling and hanging to her chest, her brown eyes brimming with tears.

Katarina retrieved a cloth to wipe up the mess and Marusya's spittle. While on her knees, she gazed at the sea of black boots under her mother's prized oak table and gritted her teeth. Maria was right about complying with the vigilantes. Survival was all that mattered now. She swallowed her fear and prayed silently while she wiped the floor and washed the wall. Upon standing up, she tucked the towel into her waistband and gave her elder sister a tight smile.

Maria caught her eye and held her hand to the side of her face, mouthing something that Katarina couldn't decipher. Then Maria rolled her eyes and made a funny face while slapping food on the rebels' plates. Katarina still couldn't interpret the gestures. So, she continued filling the water glasses, doing her best to avoid the moving elbows and roaming arms.

A few seconds later, a hand grabbed her buttocks. Katarina yelped and jumped back. Her instinct said to hit the lice-infested creep with the water jug. But she feared being at the receiving end of the insects he was picking out of his beard and drowning in the water glass. She caught Maria's eye again, raised one eyebrow, and pointed her chin at the man. Maria nodded — he was the subject of her warning.

Katarina wondered who raised such monsters. They were obviously products of heathen homes filled with disrespect and greed — with wife-beating drunkards, adulterers, or absent men for fathers. She silently recited Psalm ninety-one and pleaded to Heaven for a rescue.

"Yuri, did you find meat?" Marusya asked the scrawny man — with a thin brown goatee barely covering his narrow chin — sauntering into the room. When he pulled out a chair, Marusya's eyes darted between Maria and Katarina, then followed Lena as she transferred bowls and platters between the kitchen, the serving alcove, and the dining room.

"Da. There're full barrels in the cellar behind the house." The twenty-something man clawed a chunk of lamb from the platter onto his plate. He sawed at it unsuccessfully with a butter knife, then tossed the tool aside, reached into his waistbelt, and pulled out a serrated knife with a small hook at the tip. The pistol in his gun belt clunked against the back of the wooden chair. "There's enough to feed us for a few days."

Katarina took note of the name and appraised him. Yuri's clothing blended in with the others. All the men wore the same traditional thigh-length peasant tunics made from white or beige cloth, and distinctively embroidered black waist sashes — some fancier than others. Dressed similarly to Marusya, the fringes of their personally monogrammed Cossack belts hung to the bottom of the shirts or longer and accented the red or black harem-style sharovary pants tucked into their boots. Yuri and five others wore black leather vests with the traditional gazyr bullet pockets sewn on the front.

Ammunition belts varied. Some had bullet pockets sewn into their shirts or vests. Others wore extra leather ammunition belts on top of the belts or crosswise from their shoulders to their waists. Except for those minor differences, they were a unified group. In a darkened room, it would be difficult to tell the men apart.

"We're only here for one night, Yuri. We don't need to skimp. Get us something with a bit more flavor." Marusya glared at the women and clucked her tongue. "Is this how you treat your most important guests?" She pointed her knife at Lena. "Since you're in charge of this household, you must set an example for the others. It's bad enough that you tried to hide the Delft and the silverware. Did you really think you could get away with sloppy cooking?" Marusya stabbed the oak table with her knife. "My men are trained to spot thieves and Russian loyalists. Ledi, the days of Czardom are over. Czar Nicholas is gone, never to return. And we will not give away this free land to the Bolsheviks. Nor to Germany. Russia is no longer our dictator. This is a new Ukrainia." Marusya refilled her goblet with brandy wine, stood up, and raised her glass in the air. "In this new country, the land belongs freely to all. *Slava Ukraini!* Glory to Ukrainia!"

The group stood together, clinked their glasses, and shouted a resounding "Glory to Ukraine!"

While the Atamansha celebrated, Lena's face paled. In the dimming daylight, shadows from the kerosene lanterns on the walls accentuated her graying hair and pasty complexion. Standing against the dark paneling with her navy dress and white apron, she looked almost ghostlike. Her mother was aging fast, Katarina thought. It wasn't fair for her to go through this. It wasn't fair to anyone.

Marusya refilled her glass a second time, then addressed Lena directly. "Ledi." We are sacrificing our lives for our new country. Our very lives! Do you know how many cold nights we've spent in the wilderness? Or how many times we've gone without food? We deserve a little appreciation while we build our new country. Is it too much for us to ask for a hot meal, a glass of wine, and a warm bed?" Marusya picked up a knife from the table and stabbed the air. "Ledi, you've disrespected me and my men. Now you must pay. Tonight, you will learn what it feels like to be cold and hungry. You will sleep in the barn with the drivers and horses."

Katarina gasped. If the woman treated her mother so harshly, what would happen to the rest of them?

Yuri and his two helpers grabbed their coats and long guns

and scurried outside. They returned minutes later with bowls of soured cabbage and pickles, and a large shoulder of preserved beef retrieved from its hiding spot in the bottom of the pickle barrel. Vinegar splashed onto Lena's prized oak table.

Katarina and her mother locked eyes. Maria had warned them. But Lena had accused Maria of fear-mongering; then refused to listen to Anna and Katarina, who insisted that Maria was telling the truth. "It won't happen here," Lena had argued. "The men have everything under control. We've even built a new cellar under the greenhouse. No one will think of looking there."

But Johann had listened. He'd left a few full barrels beside the empty ones in the old cellar, together with a month's food supply. "Thieves are lazy. They want guns and food," Johann said. "We'll make it easy for them. In the spring, we'll dig a tunnel from the house to the new cellar behind the greenhouse."

Since the recent snowfall had covered the tracks to the greenhouse, the bandits went straight to the old cellar and assumed they'd found the entire food storage. The ruse had worked.

"Katya, tell me the truth. Is this all the food on this big farm?" Marusya asked suspiciously.

Katya averted her reddened eyes and shrugged as she set the last dish on the family's prized hand-carved oaken buffet. "I cook and I clean. What is here, what is not here, I don't know."

Katarina noted the maid's angry tone and stiff body posture. Katya didn't forgive easily. She would never forget Marusya's insult.

"And you two —" the vigilante picked up her pistol, cocked the hammer, and pointed it — first at Katarina and then Maria. "Lovely Ledi, you don't want my men to go hungry, do you?"

"Oh, no, General. We'll cook anything you want," Maria's bubbly voice broke the tension. "You're welcome to whatever we have."

Marusya seemed pleasantly surprised by Maria's friendliness. She un-cocked the gun and put it back in her waist. "My soldiers outside are waiting to eat. You will feed them while we retire to the drawing room for brandy and cigars. This pretty girl comes with me." She pointed to Katarina, but her gaze darted between the others. "Now, don't try any nonsense just because we're in the other room, or I'll do more than chop off these golden locks from your baby sister's head. Tonight, you make soup and bread for tomorrow. We want a good, hearty breakfast at daybreak. And plenty of food for our travels."

Marusya stood up and hooked an arm around Katarina's waist, then pulled out the paring knife in Katarina's waistband and casually tossed it on the table. One of the men caught it and tucked it into his belt. "No more work for today, precious one. Show me to the smoking room."

39

A BED FOR MARUSYA

KATARINA'S STOMACH TIGHTENED AND HER HEART POUNDED in her ears. All this time, Marusya had known about the knife. If she'd acted on her impulse to use it, blood would have spilled. And it probably would have been hers.

She looked over her shoulder. Where was the promised spiritual protection she'd prayed for — that the Bible promised? Surely, God was sending someone. Sweat pooled between her breasts and the bump on her arm ached. Maybe they were destined to suffer — like the character of Job. Katarina despaired, took a deep breath, and swallowed.

As Marusya put her arm around Katarina's shoulder and pulled her in, Katarina's skin crawled. It didn't feel like walking arm-in-arm with her sisters or school chums. This felt uncomfortably intimate, almost like her experience with Sergei, but more sinister.

"Sit here, pretty girl." Marusya pointed to the three-seater floral settee against the main wall in the sitting room. "You and I are going to enjoy some girl time."

Katarina had sat on this couch a hundred times or more since her encounter with the black stallion and every time, the old memory surfaced as vividly as if it was yesterday. She'd slept on this very spot during that fateful night, with Anna lying on the floor beside her — giving up her wedding night to shadow her like a guardian angel. For weeks after, Katarina suffered violent dreams and woke short of breath — as if she'd run a hundred versts. Then, she thought she was going to die. Now, as she sank down on the worn cushioning, she wondered the same.

The six leather-vested men followed Marusya and Katarina into the room and headed immediately for Johann's locked liquor cabinet. A tall, thin soldier — with a black goatee, a long face, receding hairline, and his black hair tied into a ponytail — smashed the seal with the butt of his pistol and grabbed the bottle inside. Another retrieved crystal glasses from the serving cart. They filled the tumblers with Johann's prized liquor and handed one to Marusya.

The Atamansha guzzled the drink and went to the oak buffet. She shoved aside the silver tray of goblets and wiped the space with her sleeve. Removing a small pouch from her belt, she sprinkled a white powder on the table, then rolled a ruble note into a tight cylinder and held it upright over the powder. She leaned down and snorted the substance through both nostrils, then passed the moneyed tube to the man with the black goatee, who did the same.

"Alexei," Marusya addressed her sidekick. "Join us."

The other men removed the remaining three bottles from the liquor cabinet, refilled their glasses, and sat down in a conversational grouping at the far end of the room. Marusya downed her drink, refilled the glass, and plunked down beside Katarina on the couch. Alexei sat on the floor beside them.

"Well, pretty girl. Let's get to know each other. Tell me about yourself." Marusya's rate of speech increased staccato-like and her brown eyes became glassy — the pupils dilated and the whites reddened.

Katarina found Atamansha's shift in demeanor confusing. But everything about this woman felt wrong. Her stomach and her nails dug into her palms. "What were you sniffing?" She stared at the residue still visible on the buffet.

Marusya threw her head back and roared with a hoarse cackle. She grabbed Katarina's hand, lifted it to her mouth, and kissed it. "It's for energy. It makes us feel relaxed and alive. Do you want to try it?"

"No." Katarina shook her head and pulled her hand away.

"Well, how about a drink, then? Alexei, pour this pretty girl some brandy." Marusya's hand trailed to Katarina's again.

"I don't drink alcohol," Katarina protested as she pulled her hand away again.

"How old are you?"

"Eighteen."

"Well, then, you're old enough. Don't worry about your mother and sisters. They're washing up and cooking food for tomorrow. They'll never know. Have a drink with me. You have my permission. Trust me."

Katarina turned in her seat to come face to face with the shifty-eyed woman. "Trust you? You broke into our home. How can I trust you?"

Marusya acted shocked. "I didn't break into your home. You welcomed us in with open arms and a full table. Besides, we are soldiers fighting for the new Ukrainia. It is your civil obligation to take care of us. Not to mention, in this new country, the land belongs to everyone. Each shares with all."

"But you kill people with your guns. And you were mean to my nieces and nephews. You frightened all of us. Why do you do this evil?"

"Oh, did I scare you?" Marusya threw her head back and roared again. "You're only frightened because you've never had soldiers in your home before. Get used to it. This war is just beginning. Look at all these men, pretty girl. Where do you expect them to sleep? In the open steppes in the middle of winter? They'd freeze to death. No, we're fighting for your freedom. Yours and every child of *Ukrainia*. You should be honored to take care of us. We are soldiers, not common beggars. As for the little ones, I sent them away so you could take care of us. The army comes first. Don't worry about the *malen'ki* — the little ones. They're safe."

"But the children need food, too."

"Everyone makes sacrifices in war." Marusya stood up and raised her glass to the room. "Glory to Ukrainia! Bud 'Mo."

At the sound of the Atamansha's voice, the six guards snapped to attention and jumped to their feet to return the toast. "Hey!"

Marusya repeated the cheer three times. Each time, Alexei refilled the glass. When Marusya sat down, she turned to Katarina. "There, pretty girl. Can you see the respect my men show me? A woman must have respect." She shook her index finger in the air. "Never allow a man to treat you as a slave. Hold your head high and be bold. Speak your truth. In the new Ukrainia, women will work side by side with men. This war will change everything."

"Which war? I don't know who's fighting for what anymore. There're so many different armies, it's hard to keep track," Katarina said.

"Now that —" Marusya took Katarina's hand in hers, "— is exactly right. You're a smart Ledi. Let me give you a lesson in politics."

"I know politics." Katarina stiffened her spine. "I'm a schoolteacher in Halbstadt and I work at the newspaper, too."

"Really?" Marusya raised one eyebrow and gave a cockeyed grin. "So ambitious! Most Mennonite girls don't care about such things. The boys must be intimidated! It will be tough to find a husband who respects your intelligence."

Katarina couldn't help but smile at the compliment. Her cheeks warmed. "Ja, I've been told that before."

"I had the same problem," Marusya whispered as she laced her fingers between Katarina's. "I'm smarter than all these men and they know it. But look how they respect me. And most would marry me in a heartbeat. But that won't happen."

"Why not?" Katarina looked at Marusya with awe. The vigilante's twisted viewpoints almost made sense.

"I'm already married. My husband, Witold, fights for freedom in Poland. We're both making sacrifices. But one day when the war is over, we'll be together. You see, pretty girl, Witold honors my desire to fight here, in my home territory, while he fights in his. He doesn't own me, he honors me. And he doesn't treat me as his slave like my father did. I don't respect men like that."

"Nor do I."

"There, you see. We agree on so many points." Marusya stroked the back of Katarina's hand with her finger. "I have an idea. Why don't you come and work for me? We need intelligent women in this fight."

"Absolutely not." Shocked by the suggestion, Katarina abruptly pulled her hand away and clasped her hands tightly in her lap. "I'll never carry a gun or shoot people. It's against our religion."

"Religion? Tak." Marusya chuckled. "I know of your convictions. But God does not want us to be bound in chains to the government, either. We were created to be free." She raised her glass to the room. "Bud 'Mo."

"Hey!" the men responded, "Free Ukrainia!"

"Hey!"

"A life is too high a price to pay for freedom," Katarina said.

"That's where you're wrong. One must be willing to die for their beliefs. Are you willing to die for yours, pretty girl?"

Was she willing to die for what she believed in? What did she believe, exactly? Marusya's military methods and her personal persuasions were strange, but her passion for independence was clear. Ukraine's separation from Russia made sense. "I don't know," Katarina said softly. "My family says it is God's will that I marry. They say my life is not my own."

Marusya put a finger under Katarina's chin and pulled it towards her. "Is that what you want?" The putrid stench of alcohol wafted from her breath. Her brown eyes drilled into Katarina's.

Katarina jerked away. "At some point, maybe. But I want to choose the right one."

"Good idea." Marusya's hand traveled to Katarina's thigh and squeezed. "Then, I shall give you some advice. If you wish to attract a good man, you must let him know what to expect. First, dress like a Ledi. Throw these dowdy clothes out the window. Don't you have something nicer?"

"Most of my clothes are in Halbstadt. I'm wearing my old things," Katarina said.

"Add some embroidery. Alter these stiff arms. Get rid of the high necks. You know how to sew, don't you?" Marusya didn't wait for an answer. "You need some color. What about jewelry? Does your mother own some red beads or maybe something more expensive? Pearls from the Sea, perhaps? Take me to your closet. Show me what you have." She gave her glass to Alexei, then grabbed Katarina's hand and pulled her up. "Come. Let's play dress-up before we go to bed. Then, we have a good night's rest before we meet Makhno."

We? Katarina's knees knocked as she stood up. What was this woman planning?

Marusya picked up the bottle of brandy and held it in the air. "To Makhno!" The room erupted in a resounding cheer.

The villain draped her arm around Katarina's shoulders and sniffed her hair. "Lovely. Do you wash with lavender?"

Katarina paled and her stomach retched. What could she do or say to this evil person? The pounding beat in her ears drowned out the buzz in the room. Her knees weakened and her body trembled.

Marusya's strong arm hugged Katarina's waist. "Where do you sleep, pretty girl? Take me to your room. Yuri!" She turned to yell at the guard with the thin, brown goatee. "Make sure each man gets a good night's sleep. We have a busy day tomorrow. Pretty girl and I are going to bed now."

40

HIDDEN SINS

TWO WEEKS LATER.

WHEN MARUSYA LEFT, SHE TOOK KATYA WITH HER.
Katarina worried constantly about her former nanny's well-being, but hesitated to mention it to her mother and sisters.
Lena had barely survived the night. No one told Katarina the details, but she guessed.

During the first few days after the attack, Lena refused to leave her bedroom. Then, she went to the sewing room and quilted non-stop — refusing to speak to anyone.

The doctor came by every other day for two weeks. He examined each woman but his treatment focused mostly on Lena.

Maria and Anna pretended as if nothing unusual had happened. They cleaned up the shattered dishes and broken furniture, scrubbed the walls and floors, and boiled the bedding three times.

Everyone seemed determined for life to return to normal. But it wasn't normal. Everything had changed. They'd changed. Terror had walked into their sacred spaces and upset their world.

For Katarina, the night had been a confusing blur — a surreal event that caused her to question her memories. Her emotions rose and fell like an ocean wave, moving between tears and anger and numbness and back again.

Fearing a return of the evil visitors, she surveyed the yard through the upstairs and downstairs windows three times a day — morning, afternoon, and evening. Every night felt unsafe. She was afraid to fall asleep, and when she did, her dreams darkened. The farm felt like a prison with violent reminders in every corner. She yearned to return to Halbstadt where life was more civilized.

After two weeks, the women still hadn't spoken about Katya's kidnapping, their mother's injuries, or their own trauma. But Katarina was tired of the pretense and silence. She needed to talk about it.

"Do you think Katya is still alive?" she asked timidly as she dried another plate and stacked it on the pile. She'd assumed Katya's place in the kitchen after the maid left. When she wasn't cooking or cleaning, Katarina helped with childcare.

In between nursing their mother and the infants, Anna and Maria managed the laundry and scrubbed the floors. The daily drudgery left little time for anything else. Even church attendance and community activities were forgotten.

Olek and the young farm helpers told well-intentioned, concerned visitors that the women and children were sick with the flu. They left gifts of sausage, kvass, bread, and pies.

"All we can do is pray for her safety," Anna said regarding Katya. She lifted her whimpering son from the cradle.

"If she escapes, do you think she'll come back here?"

"For Mutter and Papa's sake, I hope so. They need her now more than ever."

Maria breezed into the room holding her hands in the air. She elbowed her way past Katarina to the sink, turned on the tap with two fingers, and soaped her hands.

"I think we can safely say the lice are gone." She rubbed her hands vigorously, added a second layer of soap, and then scrubbed again. "It's only taken two weeks to clean up the stink. Now Papa can sleep in the house again."

"Good, it's about time. Soon we can go home." Anna unbuttoned her blouse.

"What do you mean? You are home. This is home. We all grew up here," Maria chortled. She blew at the sweat dripping down her nose.

"After what happened, this doesn't feel like home," Anna said. "Home is supposed to be a safe place. I'm no longer comfortable here. I want to go back to Halbstadt, sleep in my own bed with my husband, and get up in the morning for a relaxing coffee. I'm tired of sitting on pins and needles — worrying about gangsters breaking into our house." She positioned her son at her breast. He latched on and sucked noisily, then stopped feeding and looked up at her as she stroked his head.

"I agree." Katarina gazed at the mother and son from across the room. Their unconditional love was the one bright spot in the darkness — signifying a hopeful and happy future.

She turned back to stacking plates on the shelf. "My stomach's been in a knot ever since we left Halbstadt. This nightmare with Marusya and her army triggered all my old nightmares. I'm afraid to go to sleep. I want my routine back — to go back to teaching and writing for the newspaper. I'll never complain about copying church registers again."

"The war is supposed to be over, but these rebels still control the steppes. When will the German army arrive and chase them away? They're taking forever. I want my George to come home. And I can't bear the news of more killings. So many lives have already been lost." Maria dried her hands on a kitchen towel, then folded it thoughtfully and hung it on the rack. "God grant us peace."

"Papa says the war isn't over, it's just a treaty putting it on pause. The bandits are taking advantage of the situation. Even though Germany technically has control ..." Katarina mused. "We are like lost sheep without a shepherd."

"And vulnerable to wolves," Anna burped the baby over her shoulder, then repositioned him. His tiny hands grabbed her breast as his mouth eagerly attacked the nipple.

"With the wolves come lice, disease, and God knows what else." Maria clenched her fists in the air. "I am so sick of this shat — and there's no other way to describe it."

"You are so right, Maria. In this case, there's no better metaphor. I doubt our parents would disagree." Katarina went to the stove and stirred the soup.

"At least, the children didn't suffer much," Anna said. She put her feet up on a kitchen chair and crossed her ankles.

"Thank God for that. And thank the Lord they left after only one night. I had a gang at my house for a week back in January. In the middle of a snowstorm, too. It was horrible." Pain flickered across Maria's face. She crossed her arms and leaned against the counter.

Katarina laid the spoon down on the trivet. She turned and studied Maria. "I can't imagine going through that for a whole week."

"But that gang was more civilized than this one," Maria said quickly and turned away. She picked up the dishrag and wiped the counter with vigorous swipes.

Katarina stared at the older sister's broad backside. She considered asking Maria what she meant by 'civilized' but decided not to. Although Maria's behavior on that night bothered Katarina tremendously, she knew that judging a bad decision after the fact wasn't helpful. She suspected Maria was suffering intense spiritual turmoil and she didn't want to make her guilt worse.

Anna broke the awkward silence, "How's Mutter today?"

"Still sick. The doctor says it's an infection. He says she'll get better, but she'll probably never be the same." Maria coughed and cleared her throat. "Her insides are torn up pretty badly."

And you?" Katarina croaked and swallowed the lump in her throat. "Are you all right?"

"It's just a tickle in my lungs. The doctor isn't worried."

Are you sick because ...? Katarina wanted to ask.

"Katarina, what did Dr. Neufeld say about you?" Maria asked.

Katarina blinked and stuttered. A warm flush rose up her neck. "Me? Oh, I'm fine. Just nerves. He told me to drink chamomile tea so I can sleep better at night. Or warm milk."

Maria spun around. Her eyebrows furrowed. "Sleep? Is that your biggest problem? What about the rest of you?"

"Huh?"

"You know, down there." Maria pointed to Katarina's groin.

"I'm not sick there," Katarina said innocently. What was Maria suggesting?

"But didn't she ...?"

"What?"

"You know, hurt you there?"

"No."

"No?" Anna and Maria said in unison. They both raised their eyebrows and made eye contact with each other.

"Katarina, I was sleeping in the bed next to you. I saw you get up in the middle of the night. You had barely any clothes on." Maria's voice softened and she gazed sympathetically at Katarina. "You don't have to be afraid. We're your sisters. You can tell us the truth."

"There's not much to tell. Marusya made me try on some dresses, we talked about my wardrobe, and then she told me to come to bed. She wouldn't let me put on my night clothes. When she lay down beside me, she fell asleep almost right away. She was very drunk." Katarina was puzzled. What were her sisters getting at? "I thought she was protecting me from the men."

"Lord, have mercy. He spared our baby sister," Maria cried. She flew to Katarina and wrapped her in a bear hug.

"What could Marusya have done to me? She's a girl, after all ... Isn't she? She said she had a husband."

Anna's mouth dropped open. "Maria, I think we need to have a little talk with our baby sister."

"Ja, I agree. We need to talk. About everything. God forbid they come back." Maria wrapped an arm around Katarina's shoulders and hugged her a second time.

"Oba. Nay. Please don't say that it might happen again. This was a nightmare," Katarina whimpered. "I couldn't live through such again."

"But I have, my dear." Maria took Katarina by the hand and led her to a chair. "I don't wish for anyone to go through what I did. Sit down. I'll turn the stove off."

Katarina could almost touch the awkwardness in the air as she sat down. Anna cooed to the baby while Maria pulled the soup pot from the element. Katarina rubbed her palms on her dress. She felt like a young child about to be lectured by the school principal. But that was ridiculous. She hadn't done anything wrong.

Maria chose the seat across the table. "Sisters, I'm so sorry. I wanted so desperately to protect you. Thankfully, my prayers for you were answered. God shielded you with his feathers." Maria put her elbows on the table and covered her mouth with her hands. Tears rolled down her cheeks. "But the injury to Mutter was unspeakable. I wish I could have stopped it. I didn't know what to do when they sent her to the barn. I offered to go in her place, but they only laughed at me. Thankfully, I wasn't hurt worse."

"Huh?" Katarina couldn't hold back any longer. According to what she'd observed during the dark night, Maria was out-and-out-lying. It was time for the truth. "And why was *that*, Maria?" She glared at her sister through narrowed eyes.

"Whatever do you mean?" Maria looked up, surprised. Her face held no shame.

Katarina wanted to slap Maria. Instead, she squeezed her fists and spoke through clenched lips. "Why was Mutter hurt so bad, and you were not? I saw you in the middle of the night. You weren't fighting him off and I didn't hear you screaming." She reached for the pitcher at the center of the table and poured herself a glass of water.

Was she being too harsh? At the community sewing circle, women debated and challenged a victim's injuries. In such circumstances, one was expected to yell and struggle to attract attention from bystanders. If that wasn't possible, the innocent should be bruised or cut to prove they tried to help themselves. Like her mother did. That was the right thing to do.

Maria shot back in her seat, her chin trembling. She cleared her throat and glared at Katarina. "Mutter was hurt badly because she fought for her life. The more she fought, the more they hurt her. I told you before — I have experience. I let them do what they want now. I don't fight anymore. The faster these men get it over with, the easier it is for me. When these things happen, one must decide whether to live or die. I need to live. I have a young family."

Katarina blinked and her mouth dropped open. She was at a loss for words.

"Maria, I'm shocked and appalled," Anna snapped. "Are you suggesting that we lie down and enjoy it because we have no other option? The church doesn't teach this. We are to fight for our dignity or die trying."

"The church has never preached anything about such violence against women — from what I can recall. They cover their eyes and pretend it doesn't happen. When it does, they claim 'extenuating circumstances' and preach forgiveness." Maria exhaled loudly. "Besides, I never said I enjoyed it. I said I allowed it to save my life and protect my children."

"We should not put our children above our faith." Anna stood up with an incredulous look on her face. She burped the infant on her shoulder and paced. "God will protect them. We are to follow God in all circumstances."

Katarina's eyes widened at Anna's trite comment, but she chose to ignore it. "Maria, I was lying right beside you. You never screamed. I could have come to your rescue." As far as she was concerned, Maria had brought this on herself.

Maria snorted, "No, you couldn't. That woman would have shot both of us in cold blood, in a heartbeat. The man would have, too — after he beat you over the head with his long gun or cut your head off with his saber."

"How can you know that?" Anna sniffed. "That man was drunk. They all were. If Katarina had intervened, maybe you both could have knocked him out. Then you could have escaped and rescued Mutter."

"Sisters, I already explained this. I've been through this before. There's no way we could have helped anyone. If anything, they would have ganged up on both of us. And you, too." Maria removed the white kerchief from her head, revealing the short ashen strands — barely covering her ears after being shorn during the lice infection at her house.

"Well, maybe you have a reputation then ... since you've done it before. You're an easy target." Again, Katarina wanted to slap her sister. How could Maria be so stupid? Rage bubbled in her chest.

"You're wrong. I've never seen this gang before." Maria's shoulders shook and she clamped her lips. She got up and retrieved the dishrag from the sink and began furiously scrubbing the table.

"I don't believe you, Maria. They are all friends of Makhno. These rebels probably tell each other where the easy prey is. Besides, I heard Wilhelm ask you about Alexei when we were at your place. Then, when we were ambushed outside the farm, a man recognized your kinder. He was the same one you were sleeping with, so don't lie. Maybe you didn't know all of them, but you knew one. For sure, the gang was watching the farm, waiting to catch us alone." Katarina narrowed her eyes and glared at her sister. "Maybe Marusya was testing me to see if I'd give in — as you did."

While Katarina ranted and accused her senior sister, Anna paced around the room, rocking the sleeping infant. "How can you honestly say your life was in danger, Maria?" Anna scolded. "Maybe you gave in because you liked it? Are you using rape as an excuse for adultery? Are you lying to protect your reputation?"

Tears flowed down Maria's cheeks. "I am not an adulterous woman. God knows I was trying to protect everyone by doing what I thought was right." Her chin trembled and the tears poured down her cheeks. "How can you say such to me, Anna? I know what I did. And so does God. You have no right to judge me. I doubt that I'm the only woman in this community who's suffered so."

Anna ignored Maria's defense. "I find it odd that not one man tried to assault me. Not one. And I was alone with the children in the attic the whole time. One man brought us bread and water, but he left. The others could have easily climbed up the ladder and attacked me." Anna laid the baby in the cradle. "I'm sorry, Maria, but your story lacks credibility with me."

A million questions swarmed through Katarina's mind. "Adultery? Will you be accused of adultery? Will they shame me, too? I didn't do anything wrong ... at least, I don't think I did."

"Ha ha," Anna coughed sarcastically. She sat down beside the cradle and rocked it. "If the church suspects anything, the deacons will send in the inquisition for sure. This is not going away overnight."

"Unless they realize we had no choice," Maria whimpered as she palmed her flushed cheeks and toyed with her kerchief. "Besides, there will be others."

"You honestly believe other women have gone through this, too? In our communities?" Katarina's eyes widened. "What a horrifying thought!"

Maria shook her head. "Katarina, these gangs are notorious for these crimes. I can almost guarantee you — we are not the only ones."

"Then the church will understand and forgive." Katarina looked down at the floor. Why was this getting so complicated? They were just ordinary women who did their best to survive a life-threatening situation. The more she tried to understand it, the more confusing it was, and the faster her heart raced.

"I am not getting up in front of the church and confessing anything." Maria pounded her fist on the table. "If someone wants to judge me, then let them. I was a victim of a crime. They can't accuse me when they weren't here to see what happened."

"Well, I saw what happened and I'm still not sure," Katarina said softly. She wanted to believe Maria, but a part of her still doubted her older sister.

"And I was locked up in a freezing attic with a roomful of cold, hungry, crying kinder, so I didn't see or hear anything. I thank God for that. The only thing I know is that our Mutter got hurt badly and you didn't. I think you will be judged on that fact alone." Anna crossed her arms. Daggers shot from her cornflower blue eyes.

"Then I will trust God to reveal the truth to all." Maria scraped back her chair and walked over to the stove. She opened the firebox and forced an oversized log into the chamber.

"If God sees all, why didn't he stop it?" Katarina mused.

"Because God gives everyone free will to do good or evil. These men and that Atamansha had choices. They will be judged. In God's time." Anna unpinned her hair and toyed with the long honey-blond braid.

"But this sounds like we will be accused, too. Even though we're innocent."

"Ja. It does sound like that, doesn't it Katarina?" Maria returned to the table and plopped down in the chair. "But we are guilty until proven innocent."

"That doesn't seem right. It should be the other way around."

"The men make the laws. They decide how things will be," Maria said.

"That doesn't seem right, either. It sounds like men believe women are not trustworthy." Katarina drew her eyebrows together. The sexes were much too divided. How was harmony possible under such circumstances?

"The Bible says we must submit to men. As women, we are inferior beings," Anna said with a matter-of-fact tone in her voice.

Maria's mouth pursed into a tight knot and her jaw quivered. She looked up at the ceiling and took a deep breath. "We are not inferior, Anna. Just designed for different roles."

Would the church blame them for the attack? If even Anna didn't believe them, then who would? "Anna, with due respect, you didn't go through what Maria and Mutter did. You didn't even go through what I did."

"What does that have to do with anything? I'm only speaking truth." Anna cocked her head and gave Katarina a sideways glance.

"Anna, maybe God protected you and the children. Maybe he protected me by making that woman so drunk she passed out. But He didn't protect Maria and Mutter. And I don't understand that. The Bible says God rescues us, but it didn't happen that way for everyone, did it? Mutter was hurt awful. If we're all serving God, why didn't he protect us all?" Katarina put her elbows on the table and leaned her head in her hands.

"Maybe we're not all serving God as we should." Maria's shoulders sagged as she stared at the table.

"This is all so horrible. It's incredible that God allowed this to happen." Katarina didn't want to believe that her sister had deliberately sinned, and she fought the temptation to further blame her. "Evil is dividing us."

"Not just us. The colonies, too," Anna said. "Do you remember the attacks on Schoenfeld?"

"Ja." Katarina nodded. How could she forget that news item that clicked from Regier's printer that fateful day? Heinrich's report was gut wrenching. After reading it, she ran to the sink and threw up her lunch.

"Thirty-eight dead. For no reason. Who knows why God allows such horrific tragedies? We can't see the big picture, but He can. We must trust Him," Anna said.

"That's the age-old question, isn't it? Why do bad things happen to good people?" Maria dried the table with her kerchief. "How many sermons have we heard about the book of Job? He lost everything for no reason, except God allowed the test to prove his faith."

"In the end, God restored his fortunes and gave him

double for his trouble. But how does that apply to us, here? Today?" Katarina swallowed the lump in her throat. "Will we be rewarded for our suffering?"

"If this violence doesn't end soon, none of us will live long enough to find out." The baby whimpered in the cradle and Anna checked his diaper. "He needs changing." She picked him up and headed to the stairs.

"I don't blame you, Maria. Really, I don't," Katarina whispered. "Please believe me. I felt helpless, too. During that whole ordeal, I felt frozen — as if part of me was watching everything from outside my body. I can't quite explain it. And I couldn't predict what Marusya might do next, or what those men would do if I tried to fight her off. I don't know what I would have done if I'd been in your place."

"I pray you never have to make that decision," Maria said.

"I do, too."

41

OF THIS WE SHALL NOT SPEAK

ANNA RETURNED TO THE ROOM WITH HER BABY AND LENA'S hand on her shoulder. Maria jumped out of the armchair, offered it to their mother, and moved to the adjacent stool.

Lena slowly eased her plump frame into the chair, using the kitchen table for support. Pain flickered across her pale, sunken cheeks. The black kerchief tied under her broad chin — hiding her crude haircut — and the severe black dress amplified her somber appearance.

"Girls, I was listening from the stairs. I understand your confusion and fear, but this nonsense ends now. After today, we shall not speak of this again." Lena's eyes went to each daughter's face, stopping briefly before carrying on. "What we went through here, was indeed terrifying. I pray it's never repeated."

Clouds formed in Lena's deep-set pale blue eyes. "Maria, I don't know what happened at your farm, and I don't want to know. You will discuss it with your husband when he comes home from the war. It will be up to him to decide what should be done. The church has no need to know of private matters between a husband and wife.

"I heard you say — you willingly gave your body to a drunken, evil man because of what he or others had done to you before. And you did so because you were afraid for your youngsters. As I did. Because I was afraid for all of you." Lena inhaled sharply and she grimaced with pain. Her hands went to her lap and she squeezed her thighs. "Maria, I won't judge your decision. I only ask for you to be honest with your husband. Tell him the truth, as hard as it may be. He deserves to know."

Maria fidgeted in her seat and played with her shorn locks. Tears flowed shamelessly down her cheeks. She stared at the wall above Lena's head.

Katarina's heart broke to see her mother in such agony. She went to the tap, filled a glass with water, and brought it to her.

Lena met Katarina's sympathetic gaze and gave her a small smile. She took a sip and set the glass down — but promptly picked it up again and gulped the entire glassful. Then she took a deep breath and exhaled slowly through her mouth.

"Anna and Katarina." Lena's blue eyes scanned their faces. "God protected you both. Lord willing, you'll never experience such horror again. But please do not be judgmental of your sister for her misfortune when you haven't lived through what she has. I'm asking you all to never speak about this incident to anyone. Talking about such evil only encourages more pain. It's best forgotten. Today, we bury this memory in an unmarked grave."

Lena's swollen eyes burrowed into Katarina's. "Katarina, I beg you to not write about this in your diary. God forbid some stranger reads it. What happened here is too shameful. No one must ever know."

Katarina inhaled and held her breath. But she'd already written about the event. She'd had to. It was the only way she could process the evil and make sense of it. What should she do now? Tear it up? She went to the sink and poured a glass of water. She needed time to think. Except, that was all she'd done for the past two weeks — think about what happened and what should be done about what happened. Tearing the pages from her diary would destroy the truth and erase her feelings. Even though she'd been taught that her parents knew best, Lena's instruction didn't feel best.

A heavy lump sat in Katarina's stomach and her weak arm ached. She returned to the armchair under the window, rubbing both her chest and her arm while staring at the door, wishing for Katya's return. More than anything, she wanted her nanny's advice right now. Other than Anna and Maria, whom else could she talk to? Even *they* didn't want to talk about *this*.

On ordinary matters, she'd go to her cousin, Jacob Regier. She could talk to him about anything ... but not this. He was a man, and this was a woman's grief.

Thankfully, she hadn't been hurt to the same degree as Lena or Maria. Eventually, the fright would dissipate and become a muddy memory like her encounter with the black stallion.

Maybe tearing the pages out of the diary was the proper and holy thing to do. But not today. She'd wait for the right time — when she was ready to close the book on the recollection.

Lena looked up at the ceiling, deep in thought, chewing on her bottom lip. Maria toyed with the folds in her skirt. Anna stopped rocking the cradle and braided her hair. Katarina watched the others and clicked her fingernails on the water glass.

Finally, Lena continued. "When the men return, they must not know the depth of our sorrow. They cannot see the despair on our faces. If we show cowardice, the men will be distraught and blame themselves. There's nothing more pitiful than a man who considers himself a failure. As women, it's our job to give them hope. The love of family matters more now than ever. Daughters, please, act happy even if you don't feel like it. Never let anyone see your hurt."

"But we're not safe!" Katarina protested. "Maria and the children are not secure in their own home. Nor here. Neither are we."

"But we will be when the men return," Lena explained. "This terror happened because the men were not home. They won't leave us alone again. And from now on, you mustn't leave the house without a man by your side."

"That's no guarantee," Katarina protested a second time. "Look at the orphans. Their parents were killed on the road. The mother was raped, too. I saw the blood."

"Shush, Katarina. Don't compare our situation to some local peasants who traveled where they didn't belong. We're a God-fearing people and we will be protected by the Almighty." Lena's eyes flickered with pain. She inhaled deeply and squeezed her thighs. "God is with us when we walk through dark valleys. He promises light on the other side of sorrow. Today, God watches how we deal with this trial. Like our ancestors, we must persevere. Let us be a light to others who suffer."

Lena reached for the glass and took a sip of water before continuing. "Girls, you know the family history. Our people do not give up during tribulation. Our task on earth is not finished until death welcomes us into God's presence. On that day, I want to stand before the Lord and hear the words, 'Well done, thou good and faithful servant.' Then, I will have no more remorse for my sins, and I can rejoice with those who passed before me."

The morbid image of their grandmother's open casket flashed through Katarina's mind. She shivered. Lena's emphasis on the afterlife was her way of coping with suffering. Although her faith and determination were admirable, it was difficult to understand God's will in this event. If God really cared about them, why did he allow it to happen in the first place?

But Katarina knew the answer without asking the question — choice. Not hers, but the men who chose to live a perverted life. They'd brought evil into their homes and infected her family. Now, it was up to the soiled women to purge the darkness from their souls so it wouldn't destroy them. And for that, they needed God. And each other.

"My daughters," Lena sighed. "This is our wake-up call. God has roused us to the nation's problem. Today we can understand the concerns of our community. Russia's political turmoil is threatening our way of life. But worse than that, many don't have enough to eat. There are women and children who suffer much more than we do. Katarina, I'm so proud of you for rescuing those orphans. You stepped into a dangerous situation to save two young lives. That's what we're all supposed to do."

Lena's icy blue eyes crinkled, and a rare smile tweaked at the corners of her mouth. "And on top of that, Katarina, you've taken on the challenge to educate young minds in this changing world. You are braver than most. If God keeps you from marrying, he has a bigger purpose for you. I will trust him with that plan. But you must be diligent to protect yourself from harm. Stay strong, my daughter. And close to the Lord."

Maria and Anna's jaws dropped open, and their eyes bulged. Their gaze drifted from Lena to Katarina and back to Lena.

For Katarina, the compliment shocked and then overwhelmed her. But she restrained herself. She bit her bottom lip, sucked in a smile, and straightened her shoulders — proudly.

"Anna," Lena said. "When you and Katarina return to Halbstadt, you are responsible for her safety. Bear in mind that your wealth and privilege are a double-edged sword. For both of your sakes, be on guard. But stay humble. Be grateful God kept you and your newborn son safe. Always remember there are others less fortunate than you. Give grace to all."

WHEN LENA LEFT the room to rest, Katarina prepared and served tea. Anna returned to knitting while her son napped in the cradle beside her, and Maria embroidered. The only sound in the room was the tick, tick, tick of the one remaining Kroeger clock in the house — the only one the rebels hadn't stolen.

An hour later, Lena returned and took her same place at the table and Katarina brought her tea. "There's one more matter we need to discuss." Lena's gaze drifted between the sisters. "After thinking about what happened here, I've made a decision. But I need your support."

The sisters' eyes met around the table. Their mother never asked for their opinion, permission, or support. As the matriarch of the family, Lena said what she wanted. As dutiful daughters, they obeyed. The culturally interpreted biblical pattern of the family hierarchy permitted only the father to disagree or overrule the mother. Adult brothers could give advice — provided they were married and no longer living at home. But no girl child's opinion was ever seriously considered, even when they were adults. At least, the parents wouldn't admit to doing so.

"We're listening," Maria said humbly. "Whatever you want, Mutter. We're here to help you."

Katarina narrowed her eyes at the older sister, now acting prim and proper like an obedient daughter with a self-righteous attitude — as if she hadn't done anything wrong. Maybe she'd told the truth. But maybe she hadn't. Katarina couldn't forget what she'd seen and heard in the dark night. Maybe if Lena had seen or heard it too, she wouldn't be so forgiving now. *Be sure your sins will find you out, Maria. God's judgment is eternal.*

"What is it, Mutter?" Anna's blond brows knit together in a long straight line as she arranged the long braid in a neat bun at the back of her head.

"This is difficult for me to say, as I must discuss this with your father, too." Lena sipped tea, then cleared her throat. "Those vile deeds were done by men who were intoxicated. A sober man wouldn't have the courage to do what they did. Because they found drink on our premises, we share in the responsibility for their actions. More so, I take responsibility for my injuries and yours. I ask your forgiveness."

Katarina's jaw dropped and her eyes bulged. She couldn't hold her tongue any longer. "You can't be serious, Mutter. We're not responsible for any of this. Those men should have controlled themselves. It's not our fault."

Lena held up her hand. "Some weak-minded men lack the maturity to handle strong drink. And these were young men with little experience. We shouldn't encourage their vulnerability by having it available for their indulgence."

"What are you suggesting, Mutter?" Anna asked. "Shall we take the position of the *Brethren* churches and remove strong drink from our homes? Our men are responsible. They don't have such problems." She gawked at her mother. "For certain, David and his brothers will dispute this."

"I disagree, Anna. When the men hear our story, they'll understand. You may do as you wish in your home. I, however, will no longer tolerate such substances in mine. It will only invite more trouble. Until this scourge has been exorcised from this country, we must not open the door to temptation."

Katarina made eye contact with her sisters. "Actually, when you put it that way, it makes sense. Although — in my case — intoxication spared me from trouble. But if this helps to keep everyone safe, then I'm all for it."

"You don't have a husband to argue with," Anna exclaimed. "Your opinion doesn't matter here."

Katarina glared at her sister. "Perhaps I see the problem more clearly than you because I don't."

Lena slapped the table. "Let's not debate this. My decision is final. However, I'll defer to your Papa. He may think differently. In the meantime, before they return, I want you three to check the cellars, the barns, and the house for brandy or other alcohol. Throw everything into that new cellar in the greenhouse. Leave no trace for the thieves. We'll keep one bottle in the house for medicine. But that's all. Do I have your word?"

"Ja." The women nodded in unison.

"Now, girls, listen to me. Wisdom comes from overcoming hardship, and suffering teaches compassion. Through this experience, God has given us a new gift — the knowledge of intimate violence. Until now, I never understood this pain. Now I do. But God doesn't want us wallowing in our misery. He expects us to use this for good — to help others.

"We shouldn't focus on our personal tragedy when others suffer. There's so much need in our communities. Our souls will heal when we pour ourselves into service to others." Lena gulped the rest of her tea. "Now, I've nattered on for long enough. Let's not speak of this again. Instead, let's be heavenly-minded and sing praises to God for his protection through this dark hour.

~

As Lena ended her sermon, galloping horses and carriages thundered through the yard. Katarina and Maria jumped from the table and raced to the window.

Not again. Dear God, please. Not again. Katarina's heart quickened. The blood rushed to her ears, the hair on the back of her arms prickled and her knees shook.

Across the yard, two heavily dressed riders jumped off their steeds and raced to the barn. The double Dutch doors were wide open.

"Who's in the barn? I didn't hear anyone come on the yard earlier, did you?" Maria's voice trembled.

"It's Papa and Olek," Katarina said as Johann emerged from the stable.

"Who's with them?" Anna crept up and peered over their shoulders.

"I don't recognize him, but he looks vaguely familiar," Maria said.

"Are they cheering?" Katarina asked, staring at the scene. "They're patting each other on the back."

"They must have good news," Anna said.

"Wonderful. They won't even notice our despair." Maria turned to speak to Lena who was still seated at the table. "Can you manage it, Mutter? We must act excited to see the men and join in their happiness."

Lena pinched her cheeks. "Make more tea, Katarina. Bring a plate of cookies and put the soup on the stove. Let's make the house smell inviting." She clapped her hands. "Set the table. Hurry!"

As the sisters scurried around the kitchen, the back door slammed and the dull thud of footwear hitting the mudroom wall followed. Footsteps thundered up the stairs and the door to the kitchen flew open. Johann burst into the room.

"Look who's here!" He announced excitedly before stepping aside.

A tall, disheveled character with sandy-brown hair and a full beard entered. Katarina immediately recognized the deep-set blue eyes, the large nose, and the angular frame. She screamed with delight, ran towards her brother, and threw her arms around his waist. "Dietrich. When did you get back, and how did you manage it?"

"Never mind that," Dietrich returned the hug and announced with a big smile. "Did you hear? The war is over. Germany is in charge now."

"Ja. We heard about the treaty. It's been over for a few weeks now. Did you just learn about it?" Katarina asked.

"No, no," Dietrich shouted loud enough for the entire room to hear. "They're here — in town — right now. Germany is here. We've been rescued."

42

MARGARETA

1952 APRIL. MUNICH, GERMANY

"Are you sure you don't mind walking, Heidi? I can call a cab. It's more than three kilometers. Can you manage it?" Peter shook the umbrella and snapped it closed.

"Don't be ridiculous. I'm not going to waste this beautiful fog. You know how I love it. It's one of nature's rare treasures. If we drive home, then we lose the deliciousness." Heidi spread her arms wide, closed her eyes, and pirouetted.

"All right, all right. But if you get tired, I'll hail a cab. If I can see one. Or rather if they can see us." Peter loved Heidi's playful side. It was one of her many sweet characteristics that had attracted him during their courtship. But tonight, her exuberance was unusual. Normally, she'd be exhausted after an intense evening.

"Stop fussing, I'm fine. Besides, I need the exercise. The walk does me good." Heidi stuck out her bottom lip and hooked her hand in the crook of his arm.

Peter slowed his step to match hers and they paced together through the murky mist until their fingers trailed to each other's hands. "What do you think of them?" He squeezed her hand when it found his.

"Of Helga and Reinhart? Nice enough couple, I suppose. It's hard to say on a first visit." Heidi's soft giggle rose with the characteristic upward inflection at the end that defined her voice. "It takes time to get to know someone, you know. First impressions are hardly reliable."

"Ja, I know that sweetheart. But I like Reinhart a great deal. It's important to me that you do as well. Like his wife, I mean."

"I knew what you meant, Peter. Helga and I talked about having babies and cooking mostly. She shared her experiences with me. Giving birth is scary stuff for us women. There's always a chance something may go wrong. The *what if's* sit on our shoulders like the black angel of death."

"Really?" Peter stopped, turned to her, and clasped her hand in both of his. "You know I love you, right? I'll be here to help you through it all. I'm not going anywhere."

Heidi leaned forward and pecked him on the lips. "I do know that. But you can't do the hard work for me. I'm afraid of those final hours or minutes."

"Millions have done it and survived." Peter put his arm around her shoulders and pulled her tight.

"And some haven't, Peter. Not everyone survives this dark journey. Sometimes, not even the child. It's all very scary. There are no guarantees."

"True enough." Peter rubbed his lips together and stared at the murky shadows between the buildings. "You know my Mutter ... Anna. She lost a little girl. Margaretha. Do you remember my telling you?"

"Oh, that's right. I'd forgotten. Remind me. What happened to her?"

"An illness of some sort. She was only three months old."

"Did they know why?" Heidi's voice softened.

"The diary didn't say. Only that she had a bad fever."

"Well, they didn't have penicillin and sulfa then. So, they couldn't help her." Heidi's face brightened. "But we do. If our child gets sick, we have antibiotics. And I'm sure we have better doctors now than they did." The corners of her pink lips curled up into a full smile. "I'm comforted that our generation has many medical solutions. And the doctor says not to worry, too. He's assured me that everything is fine with the baby. But I'm still afraid."

"Getting a tooth pulled is painful, too. But we all get through it." Peter joked.

"Oh, stop." She slapped his arm playfully. "You're minimizing my fears. Getting a tooth pulled is nothing like having a child."

"How do you know? You haven't done it yet."

"Ask me in another month."

They crossed the street to avoid the mountain of war rubble where two American soldiers stood beside the streetlamps, lighting each other's cigarettes. As Peter and Heidi sauntered by, the soldiers stopped conversing with each other and eyed them. Their hands went to the barrels of their rifles while cigarettes dangled from their mouths. "Nice evening for a walk," one called out.

"Ja, it is," Peter yelled back. He gave a one-armed wave, pulled Heidi's arm into his, and increased his pace.

The soldiers watched the couple for a brief minute, then leaned back against their green jeep and resumed their conversation.

"Helga said she worked there," Heidi said referring to the debris pile.

"Really? As a *Trümmerfrau*? Good grief that's horrible work. For how long? Did she use a pickaxe and a jackhammer, too?"

"Ja. She did it for six months, out of loyalty to the country.

Everyone must help Germany get back on its feet, she said. Although we bear the shame of the world, it's still our fatherland."

"That's honorable. But moving all those rocks didn't pay enough to buy a loaf of bread. And she had babies then, too. How did she manage? I helped for three days, and it almost killed me. Then I drove the trucks for the next six months until I convinced Professor Braun to hire me so I could study at the university."

Heidi threw her head back and laughed. "After all your tough talk about joining the Luftwaffe and serving your country. In the end, you shirked your responsibilities and took the easy way out. I should call you a coward, but you're my husband. So I won't."

"When I said those words, I was a child. I grew up during the war."

"We all did. Hitler's war and his social policies changed every German. I pray the world never sees another monster like him."

"We'll recover. But every child must be re-educated to erase a decade of Nazi misinformation."

"Our child will grow up in the new Germany, Peter. A strong country with democratic values. We're starting with a new foundation with a bright future."

"I agree, Heidi. We're rebuilding the country one brick at a time. After we clear the rubble."

"Well, I'm glad I never had to pick rocks. When I showed up there, they told me I was too tiny for such hard work, so I was slotted for clerical duties at *The Telekom* until I got the telephone operator job."

"Ja, you were fortunate. Come this way." Peter guided Heidi across the street. "Be careful. This sidewalk is full of cracks and loose concrete."

"I wonder how many decades it will take to fix this city,"

Heidi mused. "They'll need a lot of strong Helgas for a long time. Did you notice her bone structure? She must have Viking blood. I wouldn't want to compete with her."

"Nor I. And I wouldn't want to be on the receiving end of that broad fist, either." Peter glanced up at the dark cloud moving in above them. "Was she working alongside the POWs?"

"I don't know. They weren't there in the beginning. All the women were called to contribute first because there weren't enough men to do the job."

"Ja, we're still outnumbered." A few drops splashed on Peter's face. He opened the umbrella.

"What do you think your Mutter would say if she saw Germany's mess today? She was in the SS. She must have had high hopes for The Third Reich." Heidi cuddled in under the umbrella.

"She'd be devastated. Although, I'm still not convinced she doesn't know."

Heidi let out a long groan. "Are we back to this again?"

"Ja. I have dreams where she's calling me from a distance. When I wake up in the middle of the night, I can swear she's sitting beside my bed. Wherever she is, she's not done with me."

"Hmm. Peter ... There's something I've wondered about but haven't asked," Heidi said hesitatingly.

"Go on," Peter raised his eyebrows. Heidi was unusually talkative tonight.

"Despite the rain and snow, the books were intact. Now, I realize it was a hand-carved box. But still, there was no damage to the contents."

"Beeswax on the book covers. And the box — my Papa was an excellent woodworker. It was his gift to her."

As they turned another corner, the dark cloud burst and showered the street. The couple picked up their pace.

"Well, I suppose that makes sense. But, as I've said many times before, if Katarina is alive, she'd have contacted you by now." Heidi squeezed his arm.

"I know you're right, my love. But she was in the SS. Maybe she's still in hiding."

"If that's true, she's avoiding criminal charges. But I don't want to think of my mother-in-law as a war criminal. And if that's the case, then it's best she doesn't show up. I couldn't deal with it. Besides, the government declared her dead. You should accept that."

"But we never had a real funeral, Heidi. Not with a body, anyway. I live in limbo waiting to hear that they found her, dead or alive. I can't move on."

"Oh, Peter. That's not true." Heidi yanked on his arm. "You have moved on. You married me and we're having a baby. Your sister is married, too, and she has four kids. Life continues. This is a mental thing with you. It's not reality."

"I hear you, my love. But the questions keep buzzing in my head. I can't focus. The past affects everything. I must work, but I keep messing up because my mind wanders. I know I drink too much at times. But it helps me forget." Peter pointed back to the cordoned area with his thumb. "I know that there are no more answers in that mountain of debris. I must find peace. But I feel numb, Heidi. You're the only joy in my life. I don't know what I'd do without you." Peter looked up at the sky as the shower stopped. "I believe the rain's done for tonight." They turned right and shuffled down a narrow unlit alleyway. "Be careful. It's slippery here."

"You be careful, too. It will be hard for me to find another husband in this economy," Heidi jested.

"If I'm such a rare commodity, then I should make more demands in this marriage," Peter returned the verbal jab.

"Tsk, tsk. There are plenty of strong Helgas looking for a

cheap room and board in exchange for housekeeping. I won't be lonely."

"Egads. You would do such?" Peter stopped and unhooked his arm from Heidi's and closed the umbrella. "Do I need to worry about you?"

"Oh, relax. I'm just having sport with you. I'm not going anywhere." Heidi pointed at the sky. "The fog is lifting. Look, there's the quarter moon."

"And we're home. How do you feel?"

"Tired. I'd like a warm glass of milk and a foot bath please."

"Coming right up." He tapped the umbrella on the steps and climbed the first stair.

Heidi stopped at the landing and rubbed her stomach. "This child is kicking fiercely tonight. This isn't normal." A worried expression flooded her face. "Peter, I think you should call that cab now."

PETER FELT the gut punch before the doctor spoke. He'd anticipated a big smile and a shout of congratulations. Instead, the serious expression on the physician's face said things had not gone as expected. He tightened his grip on the floral arrangement and stared at the man in the white coat. What went wrong? And with whom?

"I'm sorry, Mr. Krahn. She was blue ... the cord was wrapped around her neck. We did what we could, but we couldn't save her. Your wife is sedated and sleeping now. I suggest you go for a walk, maybe grab a bite to eat, and come back in a couple of hours."

She? Was ... is a girl? He didn't even congratulate me. Blue baby. There're no congratulations because there's no baby ... Heidi?

Peter's knees buckled and the room swam in a blurry mist.

The glass jar filled with pink lilacs, white cherry blossoms, and purple hyacinths fell from his hands and shattered on the pale green linoleum flooring. He dropped to his knees — oblivious to the shards beneath him and only vaguely aware of the staring eyes of curious bystanders in the emergency waiting room — peeking at him from behind the newspapers in their hands.

Heat washed his neck and face as shame flushed through his mind. *Weakling. You're such a girl. Almost fainting from bad news and dropping the vase. Get yourself together, Peter.* His hands flailed, searching for support.

"Will you be all right, sir? Would you like a glass of water?" The doctor helped him to a chair and then signaled to a nurse at the desk. "I'll get someone to clean this up. There's broken glass around you. Stay here. Don't move."

Peter held up his hand and nodded. "I'll be fine. I just need a minute."

"Please don't move. We can't risk more injuries." The doctor reiterated, waving to an attendant before walking away.

Peter sucked at the saliva pooling in his mouth and swallowed. A sharp item pricked his chest. Absent-mindedly, he rubbed it, and the cherry blossom twig stuck in his lapel fell to the floor. *Heidi. Was she ...?* No, he reassured himself. The doctor said she's fine.

He wiped his nose and mouth with his fist and scanned the crowd. The spectators had returned to reading their books and newspapers. Across the room, the doctor engaged and laughed with two nurses. One glanced in his direction. Were they joking about how he fell apart? He shouldn't have reacted so.

Peter reached for the handkerchief in his jacket pocket and blew his nose, only noticing then that his cheeks were wet. "Ridiculous," he mumbled. "It was a shock. Any other man would react the same. Heidi's fine. We'll get through this. Nothing else matters." Talking to himself felt strengthening but silly at the same time and he quickly checked the faces nearby. The absence of peering eyes reassured him. No one thought he was crazy. He took a deep breath to calm his quivering insides.

After the attendant cleaned the floor, Peter left the hospital through the main door and stood on the new concrete steps to pull his thoughts together. He wiggled and tugged at the uncomfortable pant leg that refused to straighten, then looked down at it. Blood oozed from between the shredded threads sticking to his knee. He hadn't noticed it earlier, but now the wound stung. Should he return to the desk and request medical attention? No. He was still too shaken, and he didn't want to start crying again. He needed to pull himself together.

His thoughts scrambled. What should he do first? Heidi would be distraught. He had to do something to cheer her up. Flowers. The ones he'd clipped from the neighborhood trees were thrown out with the broken glass. In the weeks ahead, she'd need lots of cheery, fragrant colors to brighten her mood. The parks and streets were full of blossoms now. He'd pick some every day — until she felt better. But today, he'd buy some.

He whispered to himself, trying to motivate his stunned and sluggish body to move. "What else will she need? Cake? Ja! A huge torte with chocolate filling. She'd like that. The doctors will tell her to eat to regain her strength." He scanned the names of the shops across the street and stumbled down the steps. "Walk, Peter. Pull yourself together. There's got to be a bakery around here somewhere."

After finding a bakery and a florist, he headed back to the hospital, laden with an armful of flowers, a large chocolate torte, a box of Belgium chocolates, and two bottles of *limonade*. The white-suited attendant, who'd helped the janitor clean up the earlier mess, blocked him as he entered.

"Sir, may I help you? Where are you headed?" The man reached for the flowers. "Let me help you."

"It's fine. I'm better now." Peter jerked away from the man's touch but allowed him to take the flowers. "I'm sorry about earlier. I had some bad news."

"No need to apologize. It happens often. That's why I'm here. It's all cleaned up now." The man bent down and whispered. "But just to be on the safe side, I'll go with you. Which room are we going to?"

The question smacked him with another gut punch. Was she still in the same room? Surely, they would have moved her.

"She was in 305 earlier." His voice trembled. "I don't know if she's still there."

"Ah, the maternity wing. Up the stairs and to our right. It's a big room with six beds. Congratulations. This must be an exciting day for you."

No, it's not. His stomach twisted and the mind-numbing surreal fog returned. The man obviously didn't know. He should explain. *My daughter died. My daughter. My. Daughter.* But the words stuck in his throat. Instead, he asked, "Will she still be there? In the same room. With the new mothers and babies?" Tears crested and his voice broke as he spoke.

A puzzled look passed over the attendant's face. "Yes, if she had a baby. Was there a problem?"

Adrenalin surged through his veins and tears gushed from his eyes. He raced up the stairs and burst through the third-floor door. "*No!* Oh, poor Heidi. How can they be so cruel? Even chocolates can't fix this."

FINDING CLOSURE

A MONTH LATER

HEIDI DUSTED THE DIRT FROM HER PINK SKIRT. "I'M GLAD we decided on the lilac shrub, Peter. It's a beautiful memorial."

"Mutter said the Mennonites often planted common lilacs at the gravesites in Ukraine. She said if I ever go back there, I should look for the lilacs. Even if there aren't stones, there will be trees." Peter gazed at the small marker beside the newly planted shrub. "Thanks for agreeing to name her Margareta. It keeps my sister's name alive. Now, they're all together in heaven — Margareta, my parents, and my sister, Margaretha."

Heidi hugged his arm. "Is this a type of closure for you?"

"What do you mean?" Peter studied his wife's thin, pale face. The puffiness of pregnancy had been replaced by tiny crow's feet lines around her eyes and mouth that curled up whenever she smiled. She was still the most gorgeous woman he'd ever laid eyes on. Even though her analytical, probing questions irritated him and forced him to examine his soul, he'd still love her forever.

Their child had died, but as far as Peter was concerned, it was Heidi who needed to say goodbye, not him. She was the one who'd developed a deep, intimate connection with the unborn child during those eight months. She'd felt the kicks, massaged the tiny body through hers, even sung to it. Heidi's loss was more physical and profound than his. He'd only lost the dream of becoming a father. It wasn't the same as hers. And yet, it felt strange burying a daughter he'd never known. He should feel something more than disappointment and sympathy for his wife. But he didn't. In fact, he wasn't sure how to describe how he felt. And he didn't know what he should feel. He only knew his job was to listen and comfort her.

During the initial phase of mourning, Heidi had screamed through the days and nights, her wails rising and falling like ocean waves. Feeling helpless and not knowing what else to do or say, he wrapped her in his arms and held her tightly as her body trembled violently. And he felt guilty for not feeling the same. He wondered if he'd ever cry like that — with such deep, intense sorrow that shredded the soul.

Later, when her screaming lessened to whimpers, and her outbursts to questions that started with 'why' and 'what did I do wrong' — he'd been dumbstruck. All he could say was, "You didn't do anything wrong, Heidi" and "There are no answers, no reasons. These things just happen."

Then she'd begged God for another chance, but soon changed her mind. "No," she'd prayed. "I don't want to ever feel this pain again." So, she'd gone to church and prayed for God to take the hurt away. He'd waited for her at home, reflecting on his own losses. When she came back, she seemed more settled.

Her reactions and responses caused Peter to wonder

about his mother Anna's pain — when her infant daughter, Margaretha, died. Katarina had grieved then, too. Later, during the civil war, Katarina lost her infant son, Jacob — but how, he didn't know. *Mothers and babies. Mothers losing babies. Children losing mothers.* How many were separated because of war — never to find each other again?

"Does this make you think of those who died?" Heidi said, clarifying her question. "The graves you can't visit because of the Iron Curtain. Does it help you grieve?"

"Heidi, my search for my mother was never about finding closure. And naming our daughter Margareta, after my sister, reminds me that she lived. This honors my Mutter, Anna." Peter rubbed his chin. "Both my mums would have appreciated our name choice."

Heidi pointed to the adjacent grave containing Peter's adoptive father's remains. "Margareta is with her grandfather now. I picture him holding her in his arms as he presents her to Jesus. Can you envision them?"

The marker triggered memories of the argument that caused Peter to avoid the fishing trip on that fateful day. If he'd gone, maybe his father would still be alive. Then, Katarina would never have gone back to Ukraine. Or served in the war. But it was too late now. He had to live with his guilt. Forever. No human solution could ever bring closure. Somehow, he had to learn to forgive himself.

Peter pushed the regrets into the dark shadows of his soul and refocused his attention on the present. He wrapped an arm around his wife and kissed the top of her head. "Margareta is perfect in every way. Cooing and giggling with her *Omas* and *Opas* and all those who came before." His voice croaked. "Although maybe not my *Vater*, David, and Katarina. Perhaps it's only my adopted Papa and my Mutter, Anna, who are in heaven. We don't know for certain if the others are dead or alive."

Heidi wrapped her arms around Peter's waist. "It must be hard, this not knowing. And I'm sorry it still haunts you. Does coming here help? Some say cemeteries are places of healing."

"No, Heidi. Being here stirs things up and reminds me of what I don't know. I hate it here. I haven't been back since the year after Papa died — for the one-year anniversary — with my Mutter, Katarina. I couldn't go back after that. The memories were too bitter. And then the war was on. So, I pushed them to the back of my mind."

"What about our baby girl? Will you visit her?"

Peter grabbed his wife by both shoulders and kissed her hard on the mouth. "I know you mean well, sweetheart, but please stop with the questions. It hurts too much. I don't want to feel the pain."

"I'm only trying to help." Heidi's bottom lip curled into a flirty pout.

"Well, you're not helping. You're poking at smoking coals. And I don't want to get mad at you. So, please stop. I should be asking you how you feel." He stroked the small of her back.

"I want another baby." Heidi's round baby blue eyes crinkled at the corners and a small smile stretched across her face.

"What? So soon?" Peter's jaw dropped. "Only a few days ago, you said you never wanted to go through this again. How can you change your mind so fast?"

"If we don't, I fear we never will. It's the only way I'll get past this." Heidi said, emphatically.

Peter picked up the pail and shovel. "Come on. Let's get out of here. I can't deal with this anymore. Births, deaths, and pregnant women. It's too much. I need to go to work and earn some money to pay the bills."

His long, determined strides forced Heidi to trot beside

him. "Now you'll have time to work on Katarina's diaries again," she said.

Peter stopped mid-stride and twirled around. "How can you do this?"

"Do what?" Heidi stumbled and bumped into his shoulder.

"Think about normal life at a time like this? Why aren't you falling apart — lying on the couch binging on a bucket of ice cream? Isn't that how women grieve?"

Heidi giggled. "Peter, we just buried our daughter and planted a tree to remember her. Our job here is done. Besides, I did cry. Lots and lots. I'm still sad and I know I'll cry, again. I carried Margareta for eight precious months. That time was a gift and I want to cherish those memories. I don't want to waste my life stuffing my face in front of the television. I want to live with joy and thanksgiving. It's what she would want."

Peter stopped at the car, dropped the tools on the ground, and kissed the top of her head. "I know you're right, Heidi. And I'm proud of you for being so strong. This whole thing is so surreal." He fumbled with his keys. "I'm sorry I took down the nursery before you got home. I was trying to spare your feelings." Peter inserted the key into the trunk lock and cleared his throat — trying to stop the tears threatening to swallow his voice. "The whole time I was dismantling the crib and the shelving, I bawled like a little baby. I wanted this baby, Heidi. More than anything in the world. I wanted to have a real family. And losing her is just another reminder of what I lost in the war. Good grief, Heidi. I was a soldier. I saw people die. I should be tougher than this."

Heidi brushed away the blond strands floating around her face. "There's nothing wrong with crying, Peter. We're both grieving but in different ways. And I'm not as strong as you think. I was going to be a Mutter and you were going to be a

Papa. And now we're neither. Not in a real way, anyway." She hugged his arm. "Where do we go from here? I feel like we're standing at a crossroads. I'm hurting, but ... we can't let this destroy us."

Peter opened the trunk of the car and straightened the tarp, then laid the pail and shovel on top. "At work, I get sympathetic looks. People ask me how I'm doing. I don't know how to act, or what to say."

"We'll both get through this. You're a strong man, Peter. For now, you can escape behind your books and papers. That's why I mentioned Katarina's diaries. They may help you heal. Besides, I know you still want to find out what happened to your birth Papa, David. And your Mutter, Katarina. And so far, you've learned nothing about her son, Jacob — your stepbrother or cousin — whatever you call him. The 'not knowing' about him drives me crazy, too. You need to solve the mystery. Who is he? Where is he? Is he dead or alive?"

"Ja, he's like a ghost that hovers over unmarked graves. I don't know how to feel about him. I never have." Peter bit the corner of his mouth and opened the passenger door. "I've been thinking about something else, too."

"About?" Heidi slipped onto the seat and pulled her feet in.

"Reinhart said he talked to Max a few weeks ago." Peter kept his hand on the door. He couldn't believe he was telling her this.

"Max, who? The butcher Max?" Heidi tilted her chin and squinted at him.

"Ja. Apparently, Max is still willing to sell me his business if I want it."

"What? That's crazy. Do you ... want it?"

"I don't know." Peter closed her door, walked around the car, and crawled behind the wheel. "There's so much of my Papa in that place. So many memories. Good and bad."

"Could you do both?" Heidi adjusted the knitted blue shawl around her shoulders.

"Both? What?" Peter started the car and shifted into reverse.

"Work at the university and at the butcher shop at the same time? It would give you a chance to see if you liked it first ... without giving up your current job." Heidi bit her bottom lip and stared at the hood of the car.

Peter sighed. "Starting a business is expensive. I'm so tired of being poor. What if it fails? What if I mess up and destroy everything Max has built? Besides, it's really hard work."

"Everyone needs to eat. And Max's sausages are the best. If you follow his leadership, you won't fail." The corners of Heidi's pink mouth turned up in a half smile.

Peter reached over and squeezed her hand. "Will you do it with me?"

"Me? A *Metzger*? Wow, you give me far too much credit. I don't think I can operate those saws." Heidi's mouth wrinkled into a mischievous grin. "But on the other hand, you'll need bookkeeping help. And someone must manage the cash. I might be convinced."

"All right, then. I'll go talk to him." Peter started the car.

Heidi wiggled into the center seat and kissed his cheek. "Well, this has been quite the month. We have a child, then we bury a child, and now we're starting a business. We're turning a new leaf, Peter. Something good always comes out of the bad. It's going to be all right. We're going to be fine."

"But returning to the butcher shop will feel like I'm going back in time. Erasing the last fifteen years of my life and starting over." Peter exited the graveyard and waited for the bus to pass before turning onto Walther Strasse.

"Except you have more wisdom now, Peter. You're not a child anymore. You've become a man."

THE END.
(To be continued.)

TURN the page to learn the historical facts behind this story.

THANKS FOR READING. Please leave a kind review on Amazon at this link: https://bit.ly/3MZbPnH

KATARINA'S DARK SECRET
BOOK THREE: RUSSIAN MENNONITE CHRONICLES

An unexpected visitor from the family's past turns up at the butcher shop and Peter discovers the truth about baby Jacob. In 1918, during the German occupation of Ukraine, Katarina returns to teaching school and working at the newspaper office in Halbstadt.
But a contingent of the German army lodging on David and Anna's estate antagonizes the locals. When the German Lieutenant becomes infatuated with Katarina, she becomes a pawn for the rebels.
Love blooms.
But a new terror tests Katarina's faith and changes her future path. How will she handle the biggest challenge of her life?

To be notified about the next release date, follow the author on Amazon. https://amzn.to/3hPo6K3

Get free stories by signing up for the author's newsletter. Learn more about Ukraine's history, Russian Mennonite culture, the Russian civil war in Ukraine, and the Mennonite story in Ukraine. Stay updated on book sales. Sign up here: http://bit.ly/3nNyMkR

HISTORICAL NOTE

The Russian civil war raged from 1917-1922. In December 1917, the Ukraine territory declared independence from Russia. It officially became the Ukrainian People's Republic on January 22, 1918. But it was not to last. After much political turmoil *within* both Russia and Ukraine *and between* the two countries, Ukraine was absorbed into the newly created Soviet Union in 1922. Ukraine did not become independent again until 1991.

WWI amplified other challenges within Ukraine. Geographically pitted between Russia to the east, Poland to the north, Europe to the west, and the Black Sea to the south, it became a bloody battleground for armies crisscrossing the land. To make matters worse, Ukraine territory was viewed as "Little Russia," a child of Mother Russia — often symbolized as a defenseless cub needing protection from its mother bear.

Ukraine produced vital foodstuffs and other industries for Russia and provided easy access to international trading routes via the Black Sea. Despite declaring independence, Ukraine's sovereignty was not recognized by Russia, and the self-proclaimed parent continued to dictate the use of Ukraine's land and seaports.

To safeguard itself from utter destruction, a national identity with defendable borders was the only logical solution. But Slavic nationalism and religious loyalties divided communities. As outsiders with ethnic connections to the invading world, those with European ancestry — such as the Black Sea Germans, the Mennonites, and the Jews, who had colonized the southern steppes on the invitation of Catherine the Great — became targets of discrimination. Villages and fields were razed, farms and factories destroyed, and families murdered.

The political instability created lawlessness. Outlaws and renegade armies swarmed the steppes, attacking both wealthy and common folk.

In this book, *Katarina's Dark Journey,* I've referenced Marusya Nikiforova, a freedom fighter almost erased from the pages of history, but a pivotal player in southern Ukraine nonetheless. A one-woman commander of the infamous Black Guard detachment, the *Free Combat Druzhina*, she terrorized the southern steppes from 1917-19, aiding the notorious and infamous Ukrainian revolutionary Nestor Makhno.

Preaching insurrection and anarchy to destroy all capital and forms of government, Marusya committed every crime imaginable in her pursuit, even encouraging insurrection against the newly formed *Central Rada* — the governmental body of the Ukraine People's Republic. Fierce and intimidating, but charismatic to her followers, Marusya was a skilled orator who aided in weapon collection for Makhno's Black Army by disarming contingents through word and deed, even swaying the commander of the Soviet forces in Ukraine to finance her 'cavalry detachment' so she could purchase more arms. Her revolutionary activities came to an end on September 16, 1919, when she was captured by White forces in Crimea and executed for treason.

Nestor Makhno is known to most descendants of those Mennonites who lived in southern Ukraine and Russia during the early 1900s. A former farmhand for a wealthy Mennonite, Makhno was believed to have had a personal vendetta against the Mennonites. As the leader of the revolutionary Black Army, he conducted terror campaigns against wealthy landowners and Mennonite farmers from 1917-21, destroying property and murdering more than eight hundred Mennonites (known). In 1921, Makhno was declared an enemy of Russia and captured in Poland. He spent his final days in exile, writing his memoirs and supporting anarchist causes. He died from tuberculosis in Paris in 1934 at the age of 45. Today, a statue in his former hometown of Guliaipole heralds his Ukraine patriotism.

After witnessing the cold-blooded murder of their families and the rape of their women, some Mennonites abandoned their pacifist beliefs and took up arms against Makhno and the Bolsheviks.

After the threat of Makhno was eliminated, the Mennonites hoped for better days with Lenin, but it was not to be. Lenin's economic policies destroyed the Mennonites' agrarian lifestyle and banned religious privilege.

During the 1920s, more than one-third of the Mennonite population of southern Ukraine left Russia, seeking refuge in Germany, Holland, Poland, and other European ports. With financial support from those who previously emigrated during the 1870s and the Canadian Pacific Railroad, many Mennonites sailed to the free shores of North and South America.

Those who remained behind suffered further under Stalin's communist policies and in the Holodomor. During this time, the graveyards were razed to eliminate all memory of these peace-loving people.

The Land of the Mennonites in Ukraine no longer exists as it once did. Their descendants keep the memory of their ancestors alive by giving back through humanitarian relief efforts via the registered Canadian charity <u>Friends of Mennonites in Ukraine</u> (http://www.mennonitecentre.ca) The organization supports the registered charity in Ukraine, <u>The Mennonite Centre in Molochansk</u>, (formerly Halbstadt) in providing humanitarian aid to the less fortunate residing in the former Mennonite villages — a region devastated again by the 2022 war in Ukraine.

The author's ancestors and relatives from Russia and Ukraine include:

*1870s emigrants to Canada.
*1920s refugees sponsored by Canadian Mennonites
*Victims of Nestor Makhno and his anarchist army
*Victims of Stalin, the gulags, and the Holodomor
*Refugees from WW2 and Nazi Germany

FURTHER READING

Learn more about the Mennonite experience during the Russian Civil War in Ukraine:

History of Mennonites in Russia/Ukraine: https://gameo.org/index.php?
title=Ukraine

Mennonite Genealogy: https://mennonitegenealogy.com/1920s/

A Mennonite Story: https://gerhardsjourney.wordpress.com

The colonization of the Germans in Ukraine: https://sites.ualberta.ca/~ger
man/AlbertaHistory/Odessa.htm

The immigration story: http://mennoniteeducation.weebly.com/prussia-to-
russia.html

Videos: Memories of Migration: https://ctms.uwinnipeg.ca/projects/memo
ries-of-migration-russlaender-at-100

Anabaptist history: https://anabaptisthistorians.org/

Ukraine: http://www.encyclopediaofukraine.com/History

Russian Mennonites: https://en.wikipedia.org/wiki/Russian_Mennonite

ABOUT THE AUTHOR

Award-winning non-fiction Christian author, Miranda J. Chivers pens fiction as MJ Krause-Chivers. The author has a background in social work and tourism, and is a C-PTSD survivor. Her writings encompass themes of faith, mental health, and authentic living.

Russian Mennonite Chronicles is her first fictional series. Book One: *Katarina's Dark Shadow* was published in 2021.

This epic saga was inspired by the Mennonite story in Ukraine and is based on historical events. The patriarchal culture and faith elements in the series are based on the author's childhood and religious experiences.

As a second-generation descendant of Mennonite refugees from Russia and Ukraine, the author grew up surrounded by poverty and trauma. As a child, she yearned to record her grandparents' horrific emigrant journey from Lenin's and Stalin's Russia. Sadly, they passed before she could do so.

Later, she was inspired by other survivors' journals and historical notes about the Communist era. In 2014, she visited her ancestral lands in Poland and Ukraine.

Weeks before her visit, Russia annexed Crimea and war broke out in the Donbas. Consequently, she couldn't visit the former maternal lands in Bergthal located in the Zaporizhian Oblast near Melitopol, nor the former Mennonite colonies in Crimea (as of the date of this writing, these areas are still under Russian occupation).

While in Ukraine, she visited the former Mennonite colonies of Chortitza and Molotschna, and the national reserve — Khortytsia Island — where her ancestors gathered under the ancient, revered oak tree; and the village of Vitebsk where her paternal grandfather attended school (near the modern city of Dnipro). Sadly, many of the former Mennonite and Jewish villages, and the cemeteries were razed during the Stalinist years.

Somewhere — beneath the golden wheat fields growing there today — her great-grandparents lie in unmarked graves.

MJ Krause-Chivers lives amidst sprawling vineyards in the fruit belt of Niagara, Canada, and near the thundering waters of Niagara Falls. She enjoys historical books and movies, travel, nature walks, and ethnic food.

Find all of the author's works on Amazon:https://amzn.to/3hPo6K3

Contact: Via social media. Check for new links at: https://linktr.ee/mjkrausechivers

JOIN THE READER'S GROUP

RUSSIAN MENNONITE CHRONICLES follows Katarina and Anna — two wealthy Mennonite sisters from southern Ukraine — during the Russian Civil War. While safe inside their patriarchal traditions, the World War seems a distant threat until Russia implodes and Ukraine pushes to separate. Then, anarchy reigns.

When conventional structures fail and religious prescriptions no longer fit, the Mennonites find themselves in a frightening and unfamiliar world. Raised under the banner of non-resistance, sisters Katarina and Anna come face to face with life-and-death decisions. How will they survive the horrors to come? Can their faith endure?

As Peter tells the story based on the diary of his deceased mother, he struggles to understand the impact of trauma on Katarina's life and its effect on his childhood. At the same time, he struggles with his own emotional wounds.

This series tackles the eternal questions: Why do bad things happen to good people? And where is God in times of trouble?

Find free stories, recipes, and other fun giveaways. Get advance notice of upcoming releases.

Sign up here: http://bit.ly/3nNyMkR or follow the author on social media. Find updated links here: https://linktr.ee/mjkrausechivers

ACKNOWLEDGMENTS

*Special thanks to the dedicated work of https://www.mennon itecentre.ca/ Friends of the Mennonite Center in Ukraine Inc. and the Ukraine Headstone Project (through FOMCU) for your continued work in encouraging awareness about Russian Mennonite heritage and being the hands and feet of Christ to the impoverished communities in Ukraine. Your dedication encourages me.
*To the vast community of Mennonite cousins that I've discovered on the G.R.A.N.D.M.A. genealogical website and social media groups. Thank you for providing much-needed historical research and for inspiring me to learn more.

A big thanks to all those who supported me on Katarina's Dark Journey including:

•R.E. Vance and the wonderful authors' community at Self Publishing.com. Your encouragement keeps me writing.
•My editor Nicole Lamont
•My proofreading team: Author Daan Katz, Cathy Morgan, and TaniaRina Perry.
•My historical fiction beta team who prevented my historical mishaps: Authors P.C. James and Leonard Ebert.
•Cozy mystery author Kathryn Mykel who gets me out of bed every morning before 8 a.m. And our accountability writing buddies: Authors Violet Batejan, Jan Mau Hill, Virginia'dele Smith, E.V. Kerrigan, Jodie Taylor, and Marisa Moon.

•The Canadian Authors Association Niagara fiction critique group. Thanks for helping me clarify the first pages.

•To my fabulous new friends Astrid V.J. and the amazing authors of the anthology *Children of War* who demonstrated true teamwork during our joint venture.

•To my favorite critic and husband, Ron, who cleans my house, takes care of the yard, and disappears when I'm writing. I'm so glad you love golf.

•To my granddaughter, Artessa. I hope that one day you'll read these stories and desire to know your father's history. You are loved.

•To all my special friends, authors, and readers who applauded my author journey. Thank you for your support.

THANK YOU FOR READING MY BOOK!

I appreciate all feedback, and I love hearing what you have to say. I need your input to make the next version of this book and my future books better. Please leave an honest review on Amazon and GoodReads.

Don't forget to sign up for the reader's group and get a free story. Here's the link: https://bit.ly/3nNyMkR

or at: https://www.subscribepage.com/russianmennonitefiction

Thanks so much.

OTHER BOOKS BY THIS AUTHOR

All books are available on Amazon in Print and E-book. Other formats as noted.

FICTION: MJ KRAUSE-CHIVERS

Katarina's Dark Shadow: Ukraine 1915-1917 (Book One: Russian Mennonite Chronicles) (2021) *[2021 Global Book Awards: Bronze Medal Winner: Historical Fiction; 2022 Author Shout Reader Ready Awards: Top Pick]*

ISBN-10: 9781775189558

ANTHOLOGIES:

Astrid V. J. et al: Children of War: An Anthology to Support the Children of Ukraine (2022): MJ Krause-Chivers: Through Vira's Eyes.

ISBN-10: 9198799606 (Also available in Hard Copy)

CHRISTIAN NON-FICTION: MIRANDA J. CHIVERS

Unequally Yoked: Staying Committed to Jesus and Your Unbelieving Spouse: Study Guide with Journal (2023). ISBN-10: 978-1-775-1895-7-2

Unequally Yoked: Staying Committed to Jesus and Your Unbelieving Spouse (2018) [Awards: *2018 Readers' Favorite Silver Medal Winner — Christian Biblical Counseling; 2019 Author Academy Awards (Kary Oberbrunner), Top Ten — Advice; 2019 Top Shelf Magazine Finalist]*

ISBN-10: 9781775189503

(Print and Hardcopy available through Amazon and Barnes & Noble; and on Audio through Amazon Audible.)

CHRISTIAN COLLABORATIONS:

Hope When It Hurts: The Scars That Shape Us. (2020)

ISBN-10: 0999872540

Holy Resilience: Finding the Way Forward (2021)

ISBN-10: 195483800X

Peace in the Presence of God: Devotionals for Women with

Anxiety (2021)

ISBN-10: 1954838034

Worship In the Wilderness: Let Praise Lead the Way (2021)

ISBN-10: 1954838115

The Favor of Forgiveness: Find Yourself Again (2021)

ISBN-10: 1954838107

Christian Marriage: Devotionals from Both Perspectives (2023)

ISBN-10: 1954838123